ABOUT TH

Colin Tucker was born in Dar-es-Salaam, the setting for this novel, and came to England when he was ten. After his Diploma in Drama from Manchester University, he worked in the theatre, becoming interested in scriptwriting theory when reading plays for the Royal Court and National Theatre. He joined the BBC TV Drama Department as a script editor on Play For Today and worked with writers as diverse as Arnold Wesker, Trevor Griffiths, Jim Allen, Ted Whitehead and Jack Rosenthal. He began to see the serial form as the most appropriate for television and served as a producer on episodes of the original *Poldark*.

Colin produced over ninety hours of TV drama including multi-award-winners *Portrait Of A Marriage* and *Amongst Women*. He then ran workshops across Europe in writing for film, taught screenwriting at the Munich Film School and film in general at the London Film School.

He took an MA in Architecture at London Metropolitan University and an MA in Creative Writing at Royal Holloway College, during which he started this novel.

Colin is survived by Sarah his wife of 52 years, his three daughters, four granddaughters and four grandsons.

A LESSON FROM MR PUNCH

COLIN TUCKER

Copyright © Colin Tucker 2020

All rights reserved. No part of this publication may be reproduced, stored in or introduced into a retrieval system, or transmitted, in any form, or by any means (electronic, mechanical, photocopying, recording or otherwise) without the prior written permission of the author. Any person who does any unauthorised act in relation to this publication may be liable to criminal prosecution and civil claims for damages.

The right of Colin Tucker to be identified as the author of this work has been asserted by him in accordance with the Copyright, Designs and Patents Act 1988.

ISBN: 978-1-912892-89-1

Cover design by e-Digital Design

Typeset by Jill Sawyer Phypers

Printed and bound by CPI Group (UK) Ltd, Croydon, CR0 4YY.

For Sarah

Every empire tells itself and the world that it is unlike other empires, that its mission is not to plunder and control but to educate and liberate.

Edward Said, 'Blind Imperial Arrogance', *Los Angeles Times*, 20.7.2003

Women's lives – and bodies – have long been one of the key battlegrounds used by the west to stake out its claim to being a superior civilisation and at the same time cast those it wishes to subjugate as barbaric. 'White man rescuing brown women' was the thrill of empire, whereby desire for domination could be masked as virtuous duty.

Madeleine Bunting, *The Guardian Journal*, 22.1.2016

October 1932
Dar-es-Salaam
British Mandated Territory of Tanganyika

CHAPTER 1

'Oh, Walter!' she said, 'you do love a drama, don't you?' She ran a forefinger across the embossed letter heading. 'But calling it murder, that's a bit rich. Besides, they're taking you seriously: official Government House notepaper. Though "you are instructed to attend" doesn't sound very friendly. I don't care for "instructed".'

'Means nothing – mandarin prose, that's all.'

Winnie handed the letter back to him.

'Probably not,' she said after a pause. 'But just in case, you will be sensible, won't you? What's clear is that one way or another, they're going to bury the whole business, and if that means seeing the man hanged, they will. You're required to tick whichever box they choose, that's all. Witnesses aren't judges. So don't object, smile and nod and go along with whatever they want. You will, won't you?'

They'd arranged to meet in the Botanical Gardens. From somewhere in the direction of the sisal plantations Walter could hear a harsh, monotonous caw, one he'd come to know well – part croak, part retch, the absence of any musicality giving it a curious power, or so it seemed to him. He'd only ever mentioned it to Petrie, who'd not noticed it. Hearing the call now added to his unease. He shifted on the bench and looked up, away from Winnie, and into the branches of the towering iroko that shaded them. It had an appearance of strength but its roots were part exposed.

'Walter!' she said, concerned. 'You will be sensible, won't you?'

''Course I will. You know me, I'm always sensible.'

The bird cawed again.

'Are you, though? There are times, aren't there, times when you won't be told. This isn't one of them, I hope.'

Typical bloody Winnie. God, she can be annoying.

'This is all pointless,' he said. 'Speculation. Wellesley will know the truth when he hears it.'

He looked out across and beyond the oceans of bougainvillea surrounding them. He could see the tower of the Lutheran church rising clear of the palms that hid so much of the town. The glare of the low afternoon sun forced him first to squint and then to find better protection by looking down at the arid earth beneath them. His boots were scuffed and stained, and needed polishing. *Government House in dirty boots? Bad impression.*

He stuffed the letter into the back pocket of his shorts and kicked up more dust.

Her voice ran on. 'You worry me, Walter. The world is a nasty place and these people are where they are because they're nasty people. They know about things like murder and crime and how to deal with them and you don't. You're small fry; you don't understand the politics of it. You're not living in some fantasy, I hope – some dream of how things could be, not how they actually are?'

She was studying him, her sharp eyes scanning him as if for weak points she might exploit, catches she could prise open to discover the inner being, the self he needed to conceal and keep concealed. His head found the sanctuary of his hands, cutting out the intense light and muffling Winnie's insistent voice.

Nasty people? Jackman certainly, but Wellesley? Seen him in the Club: laughing, affable, courteous, a diplomat by nature – the Governor's right hand, didn't Charles call him that? Certainly not the type to collude in a gross perversion of justice. A decent bloke, one who saw the bigger picture, that was Wellesley.

'Are you? Fantasising? Living in some dream of noble deeds, determined to assert your version of events, ready to sacrifice yourself for the pleasure of feeling morally superior?'

He attempted a laugh and almost succeeded. 'Morally superior?' he said. 'Oh yes, that's me all right. But what I know isn't some arguable version of the truth – it *is* the truth.'

'Oh, Walter,' she said, her irritation plain, 'listen to me – listen! Your truth is beside the point. Promise me, promise me that whatever they want, you'll agree with it.'

He thought of Rosa, the rise and fall of her bracelets, the cascade of silver shards of light against her skin's rich dark olive glow, and how he'd treated her. He had to make amends somehow. *Anyway, they can't find him guilty – his is the British Empire and the Empire is the Law and the Law is the Empire. End of discussion.*

'All right, I promise.'

'Whatever they want? Really, truly?'

He had to force himself to look at her but the lie came easily. 'Really, truly.'

'Thank God for that,' she said, and clapping her hands, jumped to her feet. 'Come on, lovely boy, you need to smarten up.'

They walked in silence through the Gardens, astonishing in their freshness, bright emerald greens jostling with sparks of gold and opal, and it struck him that these few carefully tended acres were as out of place, as un-African, as he was.

They lingered at the gates, uncertain in each other's company, but reluctant to cut short their farewells. An elderly *shamba* boy was whistling in the azalea shrubbery behind them.

Seven months earlier
Oyster Bay
Dar-es-Salaam
British Mandated Territory of Tanganyika

CHAPTER 2

'Welcome to Dar,' Meg said. 'There are treasures to be found here.' A priestess in white cotton gloves, she removed a shell from the display cabinet and gave it to Walter. 'One of my favourites. A chiragra spider conch. This one's female – you can tell by the colour of the aperture; the males are much brighter. Also the male's shoulder fingers are the same length as its other ones, whereas in the female – look – they're quite obviously longer. Daggers rather than fingers.'

He tapped the point of the longest dagger. 'Ouch!' he said.

She laughed. 'Don't tease, they're sharp enough.'

The shell's outer carapace was rough and mottled. He turned it over to inspect the smooth inner surface. It glistened with pink and tea-rose and soft shades of tan, while a darker ribbing sprung away from either side of the elongated aperture. The porcelain delicacy of the inner lips captivated him. His thumb tested the texture, feeling the contrast between the rugged outer surface and the smooth folds of the lips. Raising the shell to his mouth, he blew into the narrow aperture but could get no note from it. She smiled and he grinned back.

'I thought conch shells could be used as trumpets,' he said.

'Yes,' she said, aware of the effect the shell was having. 'But not that one.' She watched him intently as he turned the shell over and over in his hands. 'I find the contrast so extraordinary,' she said. 'The six daggers – so aggressive, don't you think? And then the grace of the inner sanctum they protect.'

The inner sanctum, yes. He looked away. The view of the Indian Ocean from the steel-framed picture window was superb. A lawn stretched from the house towards the cliff edge, ending in a flourish of white trumpet flowers and yellow hibiscus. White horses leapt and foamed some hundred yards offshore, and a solitary dhow tacked away from them towards Msimbazi Bay. Only married men were entitled to houses like this, out here in Oyster Bay. He held out the conch.

'No, no,' Meg said. 'It's for you. Keep it, please.'

He didn't want it but knew he couldn't refuse. Keeping in with the boss's wife was too important. 'Thank you,' he said.

A tall servant in a spotless, neck to ankle white *kanzu* appeared. He was carrying a lace-trimmed cloth which he laid across a low table. Meg handed him her gloves.

'The seed cake, Juma, and the Darjeeling,' she said.

'About bloody time,' McLeod said.

The servant bowed his head, an oddly patrician gesture, not so much acceptance of an instruction as an agreement that Darjeeling and seed cake were indeed a good idea, and glided from the room.

'Can't stand the fellow,' McLeod said. 'Too silent. Don't know what's going on inside him. Insubordination, that's what it is. I should sack the bastard.'

'No, you won't,' Meg said. 'The house servants are my domain.'

McLeod snorted.

'So distinguished-looking. Somali, of course,' his wife said. She was in her early middle age, younger than McLeod, with a raw, flushed complexion and a thickening waist. Walter found her a comfortable presence.

'I pay him – I can sack him,' McLeod said.

'Then I'll re-hire him,' Meg said, 'and pay him myself.'

Walter crouched before the cabinet. 'What are the green shells?' he asked.

'And how, pray, will you do that?'

'They're lovely, aren't they? Such a wonderful depth of colour. *Turbo marmoratus*. I have seven of the beauties. Will you come shell-hunting one day, Walter? I can see you're interested. We'll find you a turbo, I promise. Now please, please, do sit.'

Walter lowered himself into a chintz-covered armchair, the conch on his lap. Meg closed the doors to the display cabinet and settled herself by her husband. He patted her thigh.

'Answer came there none,' McLeod said, and laughed.

'I'll find a way. He's the best houseboy we've ever had.'

'In your biased opinion.'

'Shut up, Johnny.'

McLeod grinned. 'Take my advice, Walter,' he said. 'Never marry.'

They sat in silence.

'How long have you been in Dar?' Walter asked. He directed the question at Meg but his boss answered.

'Ages. Dim mists of time. We were in Mombasa first, went right through the Great War there. Then after the Tanganyika mandate was granted, I was appointed Commissioner of Customs for the territory. So, ten years in Mombasa, then nine years here.

And ten more to retirement, eh, Meg? You'll miss your shells – no shells in Malvern.'

He patted her again, this time leaving his hand resting on her thigh. She removed it.

'Tell you what I won't miss. The smell. She boils them, you know. Gets a bloody great pan of water going and tips the creatures in. The stink! Juma doesn't care about the smell, do you, Juma? Do bloody anything for the mem, wouldn't you?'

Juma had returned with a tray and was settling the crockery on the table. He said nothing.

'Deaf, you might think,' McLeod added.

'Juma loves the shells,' Meg said. 'You should see the care he takes when he dusts them.'

Juma surveyed the table and made a few adjustments. The seed cake sat on a Royal Doulton plate covered by a paper doily and accompanied by a pearl-handled cake knife.

'Lovely, Juma, thank you,' Meg said. He inclined his head briefly and slipped away.

'Don't,' McLeod said. 'Just don't.'

'He's a human being.'

'He's black. And he's a servant. You don't thank servants for doing their job.'

She shrugged, turned to Walter and handed him a thick slice of cake. 'Boiling's the only way to extract the creature from the shell,' she said. 'Otherwise they're virtually impossible to get out. They clamp themselves in so tightly behind their doors, their operculums. I don't like boiling them but there's no alternative.'

'Just as there's no alternative to Paris Green for poisoning the ants.'

'All right, all right, I've accepted that. Despite what it's done to the lawn.'

'I'm delighted to hear it.'

'All I ask is that you are a little more discriminatory about where you put the stuff.'

'It goes where it's needed.'

'And you use too much.'

'I use exactly the right amount.'

'Oh yes? And if you're so precise, why then does it get everywhere?'

'It doesn't.'

They seemed to have forgotten Walter. He concentrated on the cake. It was too dry and the aniseed flavour of the caraway seeds too strong. He coughed and the McLeods fell briefly silent.

'Does Juma do the cooking?' he asked.

'God, no,' McLeod said, 'far too grand. As far as I can tell, he's only here to be decorative.'

'It's disgusting stuff,' Meg said. 'It says it is. It says it's poison – arsenic – it's written all over the tin. And you do use too much. You're poisoning the whole garden.'

'For heaven's sake,' McLeod said. 'Don't worry, Walter. We like a squabble every now and then. Keeps us fresh, eh, old girl?'

Meg looked away.

'Walter has a girl,' McLeod added. 'So I heard on the grapevine. A passionate creature, I imagine, if I read Walter correctly.'

Walter flushed.

'Stop teasing him, Johnny,' Meg said. 'You'll have to get used to it, Walter. Everyone here is subject to gossip – it's the essential currency of the territory. How many Europeans are there in Dar: four, five hundred? Result: everyone knows everyone's business. You're marked already.'

She had recovered her temper. 'But I do want to hear about her.'

Walter finished the cake and mimed a polite 'No, thank you', to an offer of more.

Meg waited, eager. 'Go on, do.'

'She's just a girl.'

'Oh no!' Meg cried. 'That won't do at all. Name for a start.'

'Winnie.'

'Winnie! And is she the love of your life?'

Walter reached for his teacup.

'Out with it,' McLeod said. 'She'll not let you rest. She'll want to know if you have *plans*.'

But Walter refused to be drawn further than the basic facts. How could he talk about plans? There were none.

'Shy,' Meg pronounced. 'Quite right, too. I like your new young man, Johnny.'

They left soon after tea. McLeod claimed he had business back in Dar but didn't elaborate.

'It's quite, quite dreadful,' Meg said, as they stood on the gravel drive beside the Singer. Patches of burnt grass disfigured the lawn and in places the bare earth was exposed.

'Can we get a move on, please?' McLeod called. He opened the car's passenger door.

'You will come out to the reef with us, won't you?' Meg said. 'We'll go to Kigamboni. I could do with an ally in the hunt.'

'I will,' Walter said.

'But I warn you, I'll expect to hear more about Winnie.'

He turned away, annoyed. Winnie, Winnie, Winnie. How to explain? That she was great but difficult? That he was on edge when with her, never fully relaxed, never as comfortable as he'd want to be? He knew that if he married her, if she accepted him, he might be able to claim a house like this, out here in prestigious Oyster Bay. But… there were so many buts with Winnie. He wanted her, of course he did, but did he love her? And what was love, anyway?

On the drive back, he turned the shell over and over, examining it, admiring the delicacy of its colour shifts, the palette of cream through to dark red-brown, stroking its crenellations and whorls.

They were almost halfway back to Dar before McLeod spoke.

'Barnes?'

'Sir?'

He felt a flutter of alarm.

'What d'you think of it? Dar, I mean. You've been here what, four weeks – drawn any conclusions yet? 'Course you have. Never been out of England before and already you're an old Africa hand, isn't that right? Ha!'

Walter said nothing. He'd disliked McLeod from the start but he was only a month into a three-year tour of duty and to cope with the man he'd settled on a simple strategy: never rise to the bait.

'Response came there none,' McLeod said. He sawed at the wheel to avoid a pothole, his knucklebones shining pale through his tan.

'Funny place, Dar,' he added. 'People get ideas. You've got ideas, haven't you?'

Ideas? What ideas? What's this about?

'People and their stupid ideas,' McLeod said, and then lapsed back into silence. They'd reached the Ocean Road Hospital before he spoke again. 'People think they're doing good by coming here. Damn fools. You don't, I hope.' He glanced across at Walter. 'Eh? Barnes? Here to do good, are you?'

What was he supposed to say? Wasn't doing good a basic tenet of the whole colonial enterprise? Walter had read *The Jungle Book* – no, more than read it, devoured it, the stories of Bagheera and Baloo, of Akela and Shere Khan, stories underpinned by the Law of the Jungle. They told him that the maintenance of human social order also depended on the wise application of law. Clear rules, scrupulously obeyed. Honourable behaviour. Doing good. He was a tiny part of the huge machine bringing civilisation to these barren lands, and at the same time advancing his own career.

He couldn't avoid saying something but still he hesitated, searching for the right, neutral words.

'I think, that is, I feel that…'

He got no further.

'You do – you think you're bloody doing good!' McLeod let go of the steering wheel and slapped his hands together. The Singer began to crab across the road and as it did so, a small handcart pushed by two local women emerged from the oceanside palm trees. McLeod grabbed the wheel and blasted his horn. The handcart lurched sideways and toppled over.

'Idiots!' McLeod shouted as they drove past. 'Go on,' he added, 'I love to hear newcomers' fantasies. As well as doing good, why else are you here?'

Adamson, his boss at Avonmouth, would never have been so personal. What was more, he'd trusted Walter's work, whereas McLeod was controlling, a nagger, constantly checking on him, doubting his competence. And now this intrusion.

'Well? Come on, come on, spit it out.'

Walter stared at the narrow tarmac strip ahead of them as it curved away from the ocean and towards the harbour.

'I suppose I'm here because—' he began, and then paused. *Because for one thing I'm a working-class lad from rural Wiltshire and it's the first proper chance I've ever had, and I'm going to take it.* '—it was an opportunity. Excitement, too – an adventure.'

McLeod snorted.

'Thought as much. You're out of luck then – dullest place south of Stornoway. I've had more excitement playing cribbage with my grandma.'

Walter didn't react. *I'm not like him, a sour old man waiting to retire. I've got everything in front of me – all the infinite possibilities of Africa. I'll be different. And maybe I won't do much good, but at least I'll try.*

'Go on,' McLeod said. 'More, please. I'm intrigued. For a start, how do you imagine that your arrival will benefit this magnificent country?'

He wasn't going to answer.

'Silence is golden,' McLeod said. 'You haven't a clue, have you?'

He pulled the Singer over at the start of the rutted lane to the bachelors' mess. Walter opened his door and stepped out. McLeod called him back.

'Forget doing good, Walter. Look beneath the skin and you'll see we're all savages – a few clever white savages and a mass of stupid black savages – but all savages through and through, all just out for number one. Remember that and you won't go far wrong.'

McLeod hauled the door shut and let in the clutch. The car jerked forward as he fought the gears, slowly gathering speed. Walter watched the Singer's erratic progress until it turned the corner into Acacia Avenue. He wondered where McLeod was headed. Dar held secrets, it seemed.

***

He checked on the gecko in his bedroom at the mess. Yes, there it was in its favoured spot, clinging to the distempered wall high above his chest of drawers. It had been in his room on and off ever since he arrived, and he appreciated the continuity. It was as if it accepted his presence in Dar, even approved of it.

'I'll do a good job here,' he told the gecko. 'I won't be a cynic like McLeod. I'll be a worthy servant of the Empire, that's what I'll be. That's my promise to you.'

He sat on the edge of his narrow cot, the mosquito net above him, knotted and looped out of the way until dusk when the houseboy Joseph would come and open it out. He examined the spider conch once more, stroking the cool surface and probing the entrance to what had once been the creature's home. It disturbed him and he was aware of a build-up of tension in his groin.

He caught sight of himself in the cheval glass, his thick mop of hair more unruly than ever, his armpits stained with sweat from the still relentless heat of the dying day, the unfamiliar sight of his legs in shorts and long socks. Who was he? A young man he didn't know; a young man in the process of becoming someone new. Dar-es-Salaam was the catalyst and despite McLeod's contemptuous dismissal of the idea, he felt certain that there were discoveries to be made here. That would be the real adventure, the one that underpinned the surface excitement, the sloughing off of the old Wiltshire skin and the emergence of the new, transformed Walter. He would discover himself.

'Who will I be then?' he asked the gecko.

He shared the mess with an older hand, Miller, and another first-timer, Petrie. He'd hit it off with Petrie straight away and they already had plans for what they might do on their first week of local leave. A trip to Zanzibar was top of the list. But tonight Petrie was working late. He was a legal clerk, one of a team involved in the drawing up of township regulations and had become involved in some tedious wrangle that apparently demanded his presence.

'They don't actually need me at all,' Petrie had said, 'but if the bosses have to work late, the minions have to suffer as well. Will you go to the Club?'

'I might,' he said.

He didn't want to.

* * *

The Dar-es-Salaam Club was a single-storey building that sprawled among jacaranda and eucalyptus and the inevitable bougainvillea at the northern end of the town near the Botanical Gardens. The decor aped that of a traditional London club, although humidity caused the striped wallpaper to hang loose and the leather armchairs to generate uncomfortable beads of sweat. McLeod had insisted that he join and he'd done so in his first week in Dar, the formalities overseen by the manager, Ferriggi – an elegantly youthful Italian whose cosmopolitan style seemed out of keeping with the pervasive heartiness.

Walter too felt out of place, unused to the overpowering public school atmosphere. He found it difficult to relax, unable to compete with the hearty guffaws, the confident assertiveness of the dominant accents. These were men with no doubts about their natural, deserved superiority. Though neither Walter nor Petrie admitted it, the place seemed to emphasise their social inferiority. Customs and Excise carried little cachet and a West Country burr, though better than Cockney or Brummagem, added a further penalty. Petrie did better. He came from Reading and had a naturally neutral accent but even so couldn't disguise the many more subtle indicators of his background, his use of the wrong word – *serviette, toilet* – his ignorance of the rules of rugby football. They were both accepted with apparent friendliness but Walter felt that at the same time they were condemned to remain as outsiders, cut off from both the gales of in-the-know laughter and the serious confabs that marked the men who mattered, the old boys exploiting their connections.

The Club was nevertheless the obvious choice for an evening's entertainment. He could go there and stand in the bar and smile and laugh when he heard his Wiltshire burr mimicked and exaggerated. *Ooo-arr ooo-arr*. It was all very amiable, open, said to his face and he loathed it. Worse still were the occasional kindly remarks he'd overheard, remarks he was sure were referencing him – *seems a decent chap, heart in the right place, ooo-arr ooo-arr*, and then more laughter.

Patronising shits.

No, he'd not tackle the Club, not tonight.

But what were the alternatives? He could always spend another evening here in the mess with Miller. Bugger that. Dusty, boring Miller from the Water Board, a Brummie, another outcast from the social hierarchy of the Club – Miller with his mud-brown eyes, his overhung belly, his battening on Walter as the ideal recipient for his tales of misery and misfortune. It was Miller who'd planted the notion in his head. The night before, trapped by a heavy and persistent downpour, they'd spent the evening in the common room, had both drunk too much Tusker, that was the trouble. They'd got talking, he'd said things, admitted things, got pulled into indulging the idea.

'Aren't brothels illegal?' he'd asked.

''Course they're bloody illegal,' Miller said, 'and no one takes a blind bit of notice. I quizzed one of our legal wallahs a while back. Instructions straight from the top. Policy is to allow them to operate – men got to have their oats. Provided they're discreet, of course. Used the Taj himself, he told me. Best knocking-shop in Dar, that's where you want to go. Asian women, none of your native whores. Still blackies, of course.'

'You've been?'

Miller grinned, said nothing.

'*On The City Wall*,' Walter said. He'd brought his anthology of Kipling's stories from Bristol.

'What's that?' Miller asked.

'Just a story. Kipling. About a high-class… I don't know how to describe her…' He searched for the word. 'A courtesan, I suppose.'

'Oh, a story.' Miller dismissed it.

He'd read the story several times. Lalun the courtesan, Lalun and her subtle ways, he could imagine himself with Lalun, could imagine their lovemaking, could revel in the fantasy. He was clear-sighted enough to know that a visit to the Taj, with its ridiculous name, could hardly offer the same experience. A knocking-shop! The conversation died but his curiosity had been aroused.

His fingers caressed the spider conch. Why not? One look and he'd be cured of any desire to return. One look was all it would take. The no doubt sordid reality would destroy any lingering fantasies.

He balanced the spider conch in his hands as though weighing it, then clambered to his feet and positioned it on the chest of drawers, centring it carefully, at first with the rough back uppermost and then, as if to confirm that a decision had been made, he turned it over so that the soft pink of its aperture caught the last glints of dying sunlight.

CHAPTER 3

He showered and changed into clean whites, but there was a looseness in his guts and he had to hurry to the jakes for his second visit of the day. As he cleaned himself with the hard, medicated and wholly inadequate paper, embossed with absurd pride 'Issue of H.M. Government', he could feel that the tension had still not left him. He quit the cubicle and went in search of Joseph. The houseboy was nowhere to be found, which was annoying although hardly a surprise. Joseph's presence could never be relied on, but the equipment cupboard yielded what Walter wanted: an acetylene carbide lamp.

He'd never ventured into downtown Dar at night. He headed into the Asian Zone, going south along Acacia Avenue and then turning right. He didn't need the lamp until halfway down Stanley where the feeble street lighting petered out. Its pure white beam guided him past the potholes and helped him avoid the scraps of rubbish that beckoned feebly in the soft night breeze. The early rains were now mostly over but a light cloud cover remained and obscured the moon. By nightlife standards, it was still early in the evening and the approach to the Asian Zone was quiet, although sounds of revelry could be heard from Kariakoo. *Pombe* sellers doing good business, no doubt. The temperature had cooled to an acceptable level, some figure in the high seventies perhaps.

The narrow tarmac strip down the centre of the street vanished. He'd thought to find himself in the heart of the Asian Zone, but if so the activity was hidden from him. He paused and peered into the darkness around him. He sensed that there was a vigorous life here but that it was not for outsiders to know it, that there were events of significance from which he was excluded.

He walked on, and now a few signs of activity appeared: a pair of slouching, turbaned teenagers, a huddle of older men gathered round a wind-up gramophone. They fell silent as he passed them but the *Chorus of the Hebrew Slaves* from Verdi's *Nabucco* pursued him for some distance before it faded and was replaced by a steady hum of voices that lifted and rose and declined again. He had no doubt he was being observed. The outlines of acacia trees appeared as strange life forms – spindly-legged and heavy-topped ghosts from the illustrations to a Grimm fairy tale. He came upon a vehicle lying on its side, its wicker superstructure warped by the pressure of the dirt beneath it. He could see the outline of the vehicle's owner as he attempted a rudimentary repair. A feeble torch flickered in his direction, then returned to its task.

The freshness of the salt breeze had long since died and the scents of the port had slid away with it. Any thoughts of his daily if not yet familiar life of duty removed itself with them. He was in a new reality, a place where he didn't belong, merely happened to be. The scents of this world were heavy and glutinous with notes of cooking spices, of turmeric, of coriander, above all of frying ghee. Walter slowed to a stop, impeded by the certainty of the odours and the murmuring voices, their claim on the territory indisputable. This was not an alien world, this was a home: valid, comfortable in its own sense of self. He was the alien.

A figure appeared before him, blinking in the blinding whiteness of the lamp's beam, his hands raised, his thin moustache warped by an unlikely smile.

'Sahib, sahib,' he cried, and gestured to his side, swinging both arms together, an athlete preparing to hurl a discus. 'Best curry house, best curry, sahib, sahib.' His flimsy shirt hung open to reveal thin ribs. Walter turned his beam in the direction indicated. An open doorway beckoned. Was this it?

'Sahib, sahib, everything the sahib wants – here, sahib.'

The man scampered towards the doorway. The lamp found him again. His parodic discus-throwing continued. Walter moved slowly forward and as he did so, the moustache responded with an upward curve. A light appeared in the building as though triggered by Walter's approach. The man scurried through the doorway ahead of him and as he disappeared inside, a small girl in a dirty blue and green sari emerged from the further recesses of the building clutching a floral tablecloth with which she fought to cover the one small table in the room. The waiter – as the discus-thrower had now become – reappeared, carrying a set of cutlery rolled in a printed cloth. He laid the table, lovingly caressing the cutlery's bamboo handles, making sure that Walter noticed their excellence, their value, their guarantee of the impeccable quality to be found throughout his establishment. More hand-waving gestured Walter towards a chair, upholstered in a ratty green, made of what appeared to be the same material as the girl's dress.

A scrawny woman brushed through the bead curtain at the back of the room. She attempted a smile. The waiter gesticulated more violently. Walter stood in the doorway, paralysed. His lamp stressed the high polish on his brown leather chukka boots.

'Sahib?' the waiter inquired. 'Curry?'

The question was enough. This was no brothel, this was not what he wanted. Walter turned and retreated back towards Stanley.

Bloody fool, Miller, bloody man. Why had he listened to him? Visiting a brothel? *Bloody fool yourself.*

He began to laugh, at the absurdity of his surroundings, but also at his own absurdity, his now exposed pretensions – the man he'd thought himself, the man superior to base desires now reduced to this, wanting a woman, any woman, subject to an indiscriminate urge to copulate. The uncontrollable shaking of his shoulders brought on a new vigour. Turning back? Without even seeing the place? Was he really that feeble? No, no, this was new territory and he wasn't giving up before he'd explored it.

The discus-thrower offered his pantomime once more. 'Sahib?'

Walter shook his head and smiled for the first time that week. 'Thank you,' he said, 'another day.'

'Best curry?'

Walter waved his lamp. The beam shone down the street, flickering across the cramped buildings, the corrugated iron roofs, the occasional discouraged mango tree clinging to life on a corner plot. He was conscious once more of Dar's night odours, but now there was a new one. It mingled with the cloying food smells, lay beneath them but with a sweeter tone all of its own. Sandalwood? He thought of Winnie, of burying his head in her neck, of the delicacy of her perfume as he inhaled it. But no, this scent was powerful; it lacked the subtlety of Winnie's perfume, was more reminiscent of incense, of the resin Father Maher would sprinkle on the glowing embers of charcoal in the thurible at Sunday evening benediction. He had been the altar boy, the thurifer, cassocked and cotta'd. A good boy now come to this, searching for a brothel. He laughed, a brief bark, an exhalation, hardly more. He waved a dismissal to the waiter and the memory of the altar boy and headed on deeper into the night.

The source of the incense pulled him forward. He stumbled once in his haste, and cursed as he pitched forward onto his knees, but didn't wait to dust himself down. The brave lamp hadn't flickered either: Lucas, a good reliable British make. Walter strode on and as he marched, a glow appeared to his right: starboard, hard to starboard my son.

And there it surely was. Single-storied, as were all the neighbouring buildings, a dim orange light in the window, a marker beacon for the traveller. He flicked his beam towards it. The words TAJ and MAHAL appeared, stencilled carefully on a board. The odour of sandalwood deepened. The door had a knocker on it, an iron torc. Walter took it in his hand and as he did so the door moved. Walter pushed, it eased open, and he moved cautiously forward. Keeping the door carefully ajar with his foot, he turned off the carbide lamp and as its brilliance faded his eyes began to adjust to the gloom. A dim oil lamp revealed an Asian woman sitting at a counter, draped in a light blue and gold sari and reading a book by the feeble glow of the lamp. She looked up and contemplated him. A silence followed.

'Yes?' she said, finally relenting. 'May I help you?'

She spoke in clear, barely accented English. There was nothing subservient in her tone, no formal address, no sahib. The room, he could now see, offered some attempts at decoration. The walls to the rear were unusual, timber, with a small hatch behind the woman's counter and, offset to the far side of it, a door painted in pinks and purples with an unlikely motif of oak leaves ringing it. A print hung next to the door: two country girls, rosily English, long-skirted, climbed a ladder to peer over a wall at some unseen activity. He edged forward the better to examine it. The girls had expressions of roguish amusement – whatever they were watching was not something they were supposed to see.

The woman came out from behind her counter, stood beside the print and tapped it with a scarlet fingernail. 'Is this what you want, young man? Girls?'

He cleared his throat. Was he serious? Surely not. But why else was he here? He couldn't go through with it. But still he didn't move.

The woman studied him for a moment. 'Sit,' she said. It was a command, accompanied by a gesture towards a bench pressed against the side wall, a small brass-inlaid table in front of it. Cushions, spangled with small mirrors, relieved its severity.

Walter hesitated, glanced back at the door. This was ridiculous, a stupidity. Five steps and he'd be out. He wiped sweat from his forehead – odd, sweat, it was so cool earlier, and now he was sweating. His gut mewed.

'A beer perhaps? A Tusker?'

The oddity of her elocution-school accent struck him for the first time. It was a charade, of course. The whole thing was phoney, an elaborate ritual, a necessary way to establish the roles that now had to be acted out. But he remained paralysed by indecision. The woman gestured again, this time towards a chair. He realised that she was younger than he'd thought at first, no more than a few years older than he was, and it came to him that she was handsome. He baulked at the word 'beautiful'. That only applied, could only apply, to pale skin but handsome, yes; he could think of her as handsome. The darker skin beneath her eyes was less a sign of age and more an indication of a life lived under pressure. A nose stud glittered in the oil lamp's feeble light. The painted inner door opened and a stout Asian man in a stained safari suit opened his mouth to address her, saw Walter and disappeared again.

'My accountant,' the woman said. 'I am very correct with my affairs of business.'

Accountant? Absurd. Walter glanced back towards the entrance. The door had shut itself, spring-loaded it seemed. An unlikely extravagance but perhaps of value to the establishment in some obscure way since it allowed an easy entrance and exit, the customer unpressured by stiffly turning handles or worse, keys. Yes, a good device, with only a push or a pull required, not an extravagance after all – the visitor has an illusion of control.

He didn't move but looked back at the woman. She caught his eye, dipped her head, pushed open the small hatchway behind her and spoke sharply. In Hindi? Urdu? Did it matter? A cascade of bracelets ran down and up her arm as she shut the hatch. The painted door slid softly open once more and a younger woman came in. She took a few paces towards Walter, then stopped, waited, turned, offered her profile, then her back, then turned once more to face him. She was perhaps twenty, her dress was more kimono than sari and in a nod towards modesty she wore a thin gauze headscarf, which she now removed, shaking loose her long black hair. She was dark-skinned, and he guessed that she was a Tamil. For a moment she looked Walter full in the face before lowering her eyes and standing before him, hands clasped below her waist, head bowed.

'This,' the woman said, 'is Emily.'

Walter looked away. The silence was broken by a distant screeching, a bird of the night, its call reminiscent of a carrion crow's harsh monosyllables. He slowly shook his head, repelled by the girl's willingness to submit. The woman spoke a word of dismissal, and the girl withdrew. The tension within him lessened, died, and was replaced by self-disgust. The image of the crow persisted, unlovely, ungainly, beak-heavy, head-heavy, and for a moment it had more presence than the room or the woman. It demanded to be acknowledged, demanded that he own up to his willingness to exploit the power he possessed, to his collusion in the reduction of sexuality to a monetary transaction.

He should leave. He turned on his lamp, the shining whiteness of its beam diminished now, or so it seemed to him. But he didn't move.

'A beer, perhaps?' the woman asked again.

Walter stared at her. He should leave, of course he should, but something held him back, a sense that to become worthy of the label, the adventure needed to be rounded off. If it wasn't, it would be nothing more than a nonsense. A beer? Why not? He nodded and sank down onto the chair. The lamp was removed from him, and turned off. He heard the snap of a bottle cap being removed, and a Tusker arrived in his hand, warm, some of its contents spilling as he took hold of it.

'Today I have no ice,' she said. 'And he hasn't washed the glasses.'

He? The accountant? Walter looked up. She had retreated to her counter and her book. A peal of female laughter came from behind the painted door. It bubbled up to a climax then subsided, a few small billows and peaks lingering on. Its effect was exorcism: the crow took flight. Walter shook his hand free of beer. The laughter surged again and it now struck him that it was directed at him, that he was the butt of the girls' amusement, his small-town parochialism, his prudery. What did he know of their lives that he should impose the morals of Pewsey village on them? He looked again at the ladder-climbing girls in the print. Their smiles were now innocent, directed at the antics of small children, perhaps, or a gardener chastising his underling. What he'd read as the sexuality of their gaze was no longer there. The bird cawed again from some distant rooftop. He wiped the top of the Tusker bottle and drank.

The woman turned a page. Her bracelets, thin silver bands, turned briefly golden as they caught the oil lamp's light. Among the murmurs from the room beyond, a man's baritone was now just detectable beneath the girls' lighter notes. Walter settled back on his chair, tilting it slightly as he did so. The bench with its cushions looked more comfortable and he rose and moved to it. The woman didn't look up.

From this new angle he could see her in profile, could see the slight inclination of her head as she concentrated, aware too of the formality of her hair, pulled back from her temples and held by silver combs. She turned a page and he imagined the sound of her fingers sliding down the paper. She had a dignity he had not expected to find in such a place. The situation was no longer tawdry. The girl's dismissal had eased him and he felt… He searched for the word. He felt… comfortable. Yes, that was it, comfortable. He liked it here, watching her, enjoying her calm presence and the embrace of the sandalwood scent. He took a long haul of the warm beer, relaxed and stretched. The crow was banished. *Walt, you're a marvel*, he told himself. *You're deeper than you knew.*

The accountant, if that was what he was, pushed open the painted door, acknowledged Walter with a raised hand, strolled to the counter and reached into an inner pocket of his safari jacket. Walter didn't want to watch the transaction. As he left, the man called out to him, 'The right place, dear sir – good choice, good choice.'

Walter ignored him. The accountant stepped out into the night. He should go too but he didn't want to. He didn't want Emily either, repelled by her submission, by the obvious nature of her motivation, her need. He wanted someone feisty, outgoing, an equal, a Winnie. He studied the woman at the bar. Hardly an equal but a fine-looking woman, nonetheless. Grave, serious. He liked that about her. Handsome.

'Another beer, please,' he said.

'You don't mind that it's warm?'

He shook his head.

'I don't know why there is no ice. He has forgotten, I think. Playing cards somewhere and forgotten the ice. But what can I do? Nothing. There is nothing I can do.'

She reached beneath the counter and produced a Tusker. As she rose from her stool to bring it to him, he too scrambled to his feet. She opened the bottle and handed it to him and as she passed it over, he brushed her hand with his. It was not an accident. He had wanted to touch her.

But the contact disturbed him and when he sat again he crouched forward, no longer so perfectly at ease. He put the bottle down on the table's brass inlay and looked up at her.

Her lips moved slightly in response. Was it a smile, he wondered? She picked up her book, glanced at it and put it down again.

'Young man, why are you here? You were curious, that is plain, but now you have seen, you have decided no, your curiosity is finished, is it not?'

It wasn't, and he didn't want to leave. He patted the cushions. 'It's comfortable here. I'd like to stay a little longer. If that's all right with you.'

She shrugged and returned to her book. He watched her, taking in the settling of her sari as she shifted slightly on the tall stool, the movement of her shoulders as she turned a page. The bird had returned. It screeched again and he sat up straighter.

'I wonder…' he began.

'Yes?' she said, not looking at him.

'Perhaps… Perhaps you could tell me about yourself?'

She closed the book and turned towards him. 'About myself? Why?'

He sensed that she was amused rather than puzzled by the request. 'You intrigue me. You're not what I expected.'

'And what does that mean? That you want me to explain myself, to tell you the story of my life?'

'Yes, the story of your life. I'd like to hear that, yes.'

'But why should I give it to you? It is worth more than two beers.'

'I'm sure it is. I'm sorry, I shouldn't have asked.'

'No. But instead you may tell me the story of your life. Will you? Of course not.'

'Why do you say that? I'll happily tell you but it's not very interesting. I come from Bristol – have you heard of Bristol?'

She raised a hand. 'Stop, say nothing more, it is not good that I know about you. To me you are a young man who drinks beer, that is all I should know.'

Her voice had a singing inflection, rising and falling with extended vowels and unexpected stresses. It was, he thought, a voice designed to calm and soothe, to send the listener to sleep at the end of a long day.

'Your voice,' he said. 'That's why I want to hear you talk, to hear your voice. I don't really mind what you talk about.'

And suddenly, as she contemplated him, she smiled. It was a small smile, a Gioconda smile, but unmistakable. He amused her, he realised. She slipped off the stool and came and sat by him on the bench. There was a brief moment of eye contact before, disturbed by her closeness, he looked down. She wore slippers, golden slippers, intricacies of gold thread and gold leaf, their fabric given spurious richness by the warm glow of the oil lamp.

'Look at me,' she ordered, but he couldn't. Rubies of glass adorned a band across the instep of each shoe.

'An innocent,' she said, and clasped his hands between hers. The scent of sandalwood intensified. It shared the vanilla note of Winnie's scent – what was it called? Shalimar! There was a song, an old song, *'Pale hands I loved beside the Shalimar'*. He looked down and saw that his were the pale hands, pale and freckled, while the woman's were lemon-brown; his fingers stubby, a workman's tools, hers longer, tapered to her carefully filed and painted nails. Two pairs of hands, motionless, touching, nothing more.

After a few seconds she released him. 'An innocent,' she said again and stroked his face once, twice, then again, the third time leaving her hand cradling his cheek.

In response, he took hold of her bracelets and pushed them up her arm. They fell back and he tried again. Again they tumbled back down her arm to come to rest on her wrists. *I'm an idiot*, he tried to tell himself, sitting here, *imagining what a fine creature she is. She's the madam of a brothel, that's all, and this is a business transaction. The accountant's a customer. As I am. For beer, anyway.* He took a single bracelet and this time it held for a few seconds, trapped by the plumpness of her upper arm before she pulled away from him and stood. He was beached in strange territory, not quite on firm ground, not quite at sea.

'Finish your beer,' she said, 'and then you must go.'

'Must I? Why?'

'Because I say so, because this is not the place for you.'

She was right, intrigued by her and wanting to stay though he was, she was right. This was not the place for him. He drained the bottle and stood.

'The beer is fifty cents; the girl, if you change your mind, ten shillings.'

He searched for the cash, and put a single coin on the counter. She ignored it.

'Your English is very good.'

'Nuns taught me, Loreto nuns. In Kohlapur. I loved Mother Louis, she was so kind. I worked hard for Mother Louis.'

Now he looked at her. She smiled again, a proper smile, broad and open. It was, it seemed to him, an invitation, a hint that their closeness had been motivated at least in part by a genuine warmth. He extended a hand but she did not take it.

'Go,' she said.

She turned away, her face obliterated by the darkness beyond the oil lamp's spread of light. At first he hesitated, reluctant to leave, but then realised that her withdrawal into the darkness was a clear signal that their encounter was over. He collected his carbide lamp, pushed open the door, and stepped out into the now cool night. The bird screeched again.

As he retreated back up Stanley Street, a torch approached and its beam flickered briefly across his face. The cloud cover had lifted and a patch of moonlight allowed him a glimpse of the torch's holder. Walter recognised him: Spencer, a cadaverous ex-military type, a regular at the Dar-es-Salaam Club, possessed of a bristly personality to match his bristly moustache and his reputation for not suffering fools. He glanced at Walter, a complicit acknowledgment from a man on an errand, acknowledging one who'd completed the same task.

Walter continued towards the junction with Market Street. Seeing Spencer had lightened his mood further; the look he'd received had been almost congratulatory. He passed the dingy curry house, slowed to see if he might be accosted once more, and felt a slight disappointment when the discus-thrower failed to emerge. The bicycle cart had gone. He increased his pace and a jauntiness entered into his stride. A pair of locals pushing a barrow came towards him, muttering *salaams*. The contents of the barrow were shielded from sight by coconut palm leaves. He couldn't be bothered to demand their passes. They were almost certainly up to something, natives out late in the Asian Zone. But then everybody in Dar was up to something. Hadn't he been up to something?

He wouldn't bother going there again.

CHAPTER 4

He spent the next evening writing a careful letter to Winnie. He stressed the attractions of Dar-es-Salaam, described its history, the German legacy the British had inherited after the Great War, the botany, the villas for married men overlooking the sea at Oyster Bay, the exotic attractions of the dock area.

'As for the town itself,' he wrote, 'its name means Haven of Peace and everyone jokes about how appropriate that is. Nothing ever happens here. It's both small and yet quite spacious, at least the European Zone is. The Commercial Zone is where the Indians live, so it's sometimes called the Asian Zone and is much more crowded. All our clerking staff are Indian, mainly Goanese, I don't know why. The locals aren't up to it. They have to keep to the Native Zone unless they have work outside it. They're supposed to carry passes but hardly ever do.

'My tasks are mostly the usual excise work, rummages, collection of duties, the occasional seizure. The huge amount of dhow traffic means non-stop petty smuggling and the tricks these skippers get up to would amaze you. My promotion has however brought a lot more paperwork. For example, right now I'm working on a proposal for an East African Customs Union. The Governor's Office, no less, has ordered it, so it's a chance to make my mark as someone with ideas.'

He wrote several pages. *Useful job*, he thought. *She's primed now*. But he held back from any hint of commitment.

* * *

They'd last made love the afternoon of the Saturday before he sailed. He'd wanted to make an occasion of it but she'd refused.

'Why should I celebrate your leaving?' she said. 'Three years you'll be gone! No, we'll just do what we always do, and then I won't feel obligated. I'll be able to forget all about you with an easy conscience.'

She laughed and patted his cheek.

His irritation took time to subside and he didn't enjoy the picture, *West Of Zanzibar,* starring Lon Chaney. She thought it fun but he found the melodramatics tedious and her presence distracted him.

They didn't bother with the B feature but went to Carwardine's where they ate scrambled eggs on toast, at first saying little, intimidated by the unasked question. Walter laid down his cutlery. It had to be addressed.

'Africa's not like that picture makes out,' he said, 'all naked savages. It's becoming civilised.'

She was watching him, head slightly cocked, expectant.

'But then this place, Dar-es-Salaam, who's ever heard of it? I looked it up and it only has a handful of Europeans living there. Are there any women? I don't know, it's not India. I would have preferred India – everyone hopes for India…'

His voice trailed off, defeated.

She was as direct as he'd known she would be. 'You need to see if the natives are friendly. Are they cannibals perhaps? Or is it the white slave trade that's the problem? What would I fetch, I wonder? A good price, I'd hope. My lover, thinking of what's best for me…'

The sarcasm bit.

'The Colonial Service is my big chance, you do see that, don't you? Straight in at Inspector-in-Charge level, that's already something. And suppose I'd stayed in Bristol, stayed at Avonmouth docks, earning a pittance, waiting ten, twenty years for promotion – you wouldn't have married me, would you?'

'You never tried to find out,' she said.

He shook his head. 'But suppose I had asked you. Would you?'

Her lips contracted. He looked away.

'You don't really expect an answer, do you? Well, I'll give you one anyway. I might have. I'd have needed to think about it, though – think hard. I'm not very taken with you right now.'

Her cheeks were flushed, the powder unable to conceal the rush of blood through the capillaries to the revealing surface. The next words came in a rush. 'Would I have married you? Not will I, but would I! And not even on your bloody knees! Go away then – go to rotten Africa. Go and tell me what it's like. Write me a nice long letter.'

They sat in silence, neither looking at the other.

'Bugger bugger bugger,' she added, and laughed at Walter's expression. 'Women – correction, ladies – shouldn't swear, should they? Am I a lady, though? There's a question. Ladies have money and motorcars and go to Paris. I'm a typist and I travel on the bus like any common Jane, and all I can look forward to is a trip to the pictures, a knickerbocker glory and the church hall ceilidh. Men have it all; women have nothing. Go, go – you're right to leave. Go to Africa.'

They fell silent. The café's glass doors swung open and shut and caught their reflections with every movement. *We make a handsome pair*, Walter thought, *and an observer might think at ease with each other*.

'What now?' he asked.

'It's a beast, isn't it?' she said, and her eyes widened. 'Poor little lambs who've lost our way.'

Her fingers, nails filed short where she bit them, tapped the tablecloth.

'What a stupid life this is,' she said, and a crooked smile lifted the corner of her mouth. 'Scrambled eggs, for heaven's sake. I'm easily satisfied, it seems. Or so you think.'

Her eyes were hazel and he could see the green rim that circled the iris. The edge of anger in her voice unnerved him. He didn't think her easy to satisfy. Anything but.

'You're a witch,' he said in an attempt to lighten her mood, and spread his hands as though they held some occult power. His fingers flickered a silent spell at her. 'A magic creature.'

She didn't laugh. Instead she stared at him and her lips tightened. 'Why do you say that?' she said. 'It's stupid. Would I be here if I was a witch? I'd be far away, I tell you. Over the hills and far away. Not in rotten Africa, though. I'd be in Paris or Berlin or Stamboul, maybe.'

Walter scraped a piece of toast around his plate. Their silence dominated the conversations that surrounded them. Then Winnie stood up, rocking the table as she did so, and marched off. A fork clattered to the floor behind her. She pushed through the doors against a trio of older women and leaned back against the glass frontage of the café, opened her handbag and produced a compact. A waitress slapped a chitty in front of him.

'There's customers queueing for a table, so if you're done...'

It wasn't a question. He sorted carefully through the coins in his jacket, found the exact amount and scattered it on the table. *No tip for you, my girl.*

As he left the café, Winnie turned and headed off, compact still in hand. Walter caught up with her at the bus stop but she ignored him and concentrated instead on her lipstick. He stood beside her, uncertain, as she finished her lips, made a moue and then spread her mouth wide before settling it again. She tightened the lipstick, carefully screwed the cap in place and put it back in her bag. Very slowly, she then raised the compact to eye level and angled it to catch Walter's image. He flared his nostrils and crossed his eyes. The compact snapped shut. They stood silent. Winnie began to laugh.

'Oh God! What a miserable cow I am, and you trying so hard. Here's the forty-two – about bloody time.'

She skipped onto the platform at the back of the bus. He didn't move until she extended a hand.

'Well,' she said, 'are you coming?'

As always, the clutter in her rooms surprised him. Stockings lay draped over the back of a faded green plush armchair. A rattan sewing basket sat on the floor with its lid open, alongside a torn petticoat. The gas fire had edged adrift from the wall, taking a strip of floral wallpaper with it.

'When did that happen?' he asked.

'Oh, sometime last week. Open a window, darling,' Winnie said.

He wrestled briefly with the misaligned sash before managing to force it upwards a fraction. He stayed looking out at the dull red brick of the houses opposite. Winnie came up behind him, put her arms around his waist and laid her head against his spine. They stood, unmoving. Eventually Winnie released him, settled herself in the chair and kicked her shoes off.

'Look at me, then,' she commanded.

Walter turned from the window.

She contemplated him. 'My lover,' she said, and smiled.

Walter moved away from the window, crouched by the fire and tried to settle it into its correct position. It resisted him. Every time he released it, it sagged away from the wall once more and returned to its comfortable crookedness.

'You must get this seen to,' he said. 'Have you told the landlord? It could be dangerous. A small crack in the piping and the whole place could go up. He could be prosecuted, too, letting out rooms in this condition.'

Winnie ignored him. She stood and padded on shoeless feet into the room beyond. He waited a full minute and then pushed open the door to find her stretched out on one of the twin beds. She sat up as he came in, and held out her arms. He pulled her to her feet, clasped her full hips, buried his face in her neck and inhaled her scent.

They took their time undressing. Each watched the other as the garments fell away. Her long skirt with its below-the-knee flare slid down onto the thin rug and she kicked it aside. He shrugged off his jacket, stepped out of his trousers and, with care, arranged both over the second bed. She undid the mock pearl buttons of her cream blouse in careful sequence from the bottom up, and in a conscious decision he matched her, starting with the lowest button of his shirt. This too he folded and placed decorously on top of his jacket, the black and gold epaulettes of the Customs and Excise service uppermost. Throughout this, their eyes never left each other. She crossed her arms to pull the thin silk petticoat over her head, and that too fell to the floor and lay there in a crumpled heap. She turned her back, offering her brassiere for him to unfasten. He managed the hooks easily, and as he did so she cupped her hands around her breasts, and faced him once more. Then her arms fell to the side and the brassiere too slipped to the floor. Her breasts were small and firm; the nipples dark and erect. He fell to his knees and kissed her navel, feeling the softness of her belly. In response she tugged at her knickers, clasped his head and forced him down to where she wanted him.

There was a slow, rich, fleshy sensuality to their lovemaking. He arched himself away from her the better to see her face, her head pressed against the pillow, her lips apart, her eyes at first searching his, and then losing focus and closing over. Then he too came and she kept him inside her, holding him there until he'd finished and for several seconds afterwards, until his erection subsided and he slipped out of her and out of the sheath, too.

'Damn,' they said in unison.

'Not again!' Winnie said. 'Do you think anything leaked?'

He shrugged. 'Probably not.'

'That's hardly encouraging,' she said. 'Oh well, just in case.'

She sat up and swung her legs over the side of the bed. She sat there for a moment, legs dangling, then crossed over to the basin in the corner of the room. Walter watched as she ran the water, cursing the feeble flow, then took a flannel, wet it, shivered, spread her legs and began to wash herself, grimacing as she did so.

'So bloody cold,' she muttered. 'Go on, look away.'

He didn't, but instead propped himself on an elbow in order to get a better view.

'It's always the women,' she said. 'Whatever the mess, we're the ones left to clear it up. Or be lumbered with it.'

Walter said nothing.

She ran in more water and repeated the process. Water splashed onto the already sodden mat beneath the basin.

'Worth doing for other reasons anyway,' she said. 'And I told you to look away.'

This time he did so, turning over to lie face down. He could hear her grunts and muttered curses and after listening to them for a few seconds took a pillow and pulled it over his head. A little later he felt the bed move as Winnie sat beside him. She pulled the pillow away. Walter turned over onto his back and she ran a hand through the hairs of his chest.

'Darling,' she said. 'Lovely Walter. I liked that.'

Her smile was broad, given extra charm by a smudge of lipstick that remained in the corner of her upper lip.

This was the moment.

Put the question. Just do it. That's what she wants. But isn't this where love should play its part, become the deciding factor? With love the question would be easy. No more would *you marry me, but* will *you marry me? Not a hypothetical question, but for real, serious, meant. Marry me and come with me to Africa.*

He couldn't say it.

He desired her and felt proud that this girl, so smart, so witty, was *his* girl but still, still…

He was afraid of rejection but even more afraid of acceptance.

'What are you thinking?' she asked. 'You're thinking something.'

'No, nothing,' he said and turned away onto his side, closing his eyes.

'All right, be like that,' she said. 'It's your fault, you know. You need to buy a better make of johnny. Now snap out of it and let's go and find a pub.'

CHAPTER 5

The wait for her response was frustrating but hardly surprising. Sea mail meant the Union-Castle mailboats: the *Llandovery Castle*, *Llandaff Castle*, *Llangibby Castle* and several other Castles. They sailed from Southampton to Lisbon, then either Genoa or Naples, on past Stromboli, through the Straits of Messina, Scylla and Charybdis, on to the Canal, the Red Sea, Aden, past Socotra, and onwards to Mombasa, Zanzibar and at last Dar. Average time sixteen days.

There was an alternative: airmail. From his office he could see the newly erected sign advertising the Imperial Airways flying boat service, London to Cape Town in four days. A flying boat leg followed the course of the Nile and then continued on to Mwanza on Lake Victoria from where the railway ran to Dar via Tabora. The cost, even for a single flimsy letter, was uncomfortably high. Nevertheless, if it saved this waiting time it could be a worthwhile trade-off. He'd have to think about it.

At last the letter arrived.

137b Woodbridge Road
Knowle
Bristol

Saturday 9th April 1932

Dear Walter Barnes
Have we met? I presume we must have done. How kind of you to write to me all the way from Africa with such lovely descriptions. I was fascinated to learn that frangipani trees have milky sap. As for the proposal for an East African Customs Union, well, I have rarely read anything so utterly gripping, better than anything by Dornford Yates or Michael Arlen.

I was pleased to note that you say you miss me and have fond memories. I too have many fond memories – of my Aunt Esmeralda, for example, who knitted silk shawls to be worn at funerals, and of my cat Crosby with his sleepy eye. My, my, such reminiscences!

Do write again.
Yours truly,
Winifred Docherty

Fair enough and funny – have to admit it. She has a wit. What now? Another letter, must be. And definitely airmail, whatever the cost.

P.O. Box 453
Dar-es-Salaam
British Mandated Territory of Tanganyika
Thursday April 28th 1932

Dear Winnie
That made me laugh. Sorry for being such a prig but you know I have difficulty opening up. I'll try a bit harder in future. And I did mean it when I said I miss you. It would be so good to share the business of discovering this place with someone. I'll admit it, I wasn't sure about it at first, but the more I get to know it the more I like it. I'm managing to have a few laughs with the bloke I came out with, Petrie. He's with me here in the bachelors' mess and tho' my boss is difficult, his wife is a lot nicer.

So there are good things here. Having servants is a bit strange. I find it difficult to get used to them but otherwise you hardly notice the blacks, they're just this mass of faces you give orders to. The Asians are different. I work with them, of course, and am being pestered by the typing pool supervisor, Miss Fernandes. She's Goanese and Catholic and I see her at Mass, all fluttering eyelashes. Don't know what she expects from me. Well, perhaps I know what she's hoping for, but no thank you, ta very much, I'm not an admirer of the fatter figure. Besides, she's Asian.

Dear Winnie, I'm scribbling this off at speed to catch the airmail service. Hope you can read my writing – it's getting worse by the word, isn't it? I just wanted to say I'm not always the stuffy creature who wrote that first letter to you, and I do miss you, and please write a lovely long letter with lots of news.
Your true friend,
Walter

Wednesday May 4th 1932

Dear Walter
That's better. I like it when you stir those hidden depths. But are you still hiding things from me? What I wonder do you do for ooh-la-la? This Miss Fernandes now, she does so intrigue me! I suspect you of having a torrid affair with her – admit it, you beast. Her first name is probably Lulubelle and she wears the most glamorous corsets, like a cabaret star, all stripy, and you have to spend hours prising her out of them. Or is there another dark, dark lady in a grass skirt you're not telling me about? Poor Winnie: you'll soon have forgotten all about me. I'll just go into a corner and snivel. Boohoo!

More news, please, from this strange place you've found yourself in. I envy you, you know – you're in Africa and I'm in boring Bristol. There was a moment when I thought I really mattered to you. But, but, but, there are always buts, aren't there? You were never quite sure, were you? And I needed you to be sure. Oh dear, it's difficult being serious when putting words in ink on paper, so I'll stop now and you'll just have to accept me as the frivolous trollop I seem to be.
Lots of kisses,
Winnie

He was never quite sure. She'd known it all along.

That night as he lay in bed the thought possessed him. He was never quite sure. But that was when he was in Bristol and now he was in Dar. Seen from here she'd begun to mutate, becoming a different Winnie, magnified by distance – rare, strong, desirable in ways beyond the sexual. He could see that Dar for an outsider, a man on his own, could become a bad place to be.

With no one to turn to, no partner to rely on, he was vulnerable. The woman at the Taj had revealed one potential weakness, his need for human contact at the simplest level. With Winnie at his side things would change. He'd be in a new social world, that of the married couples, the strong, the secure, the prosperous. He ran a hand down the mosquito netting, tugging at it as though it were a bell rope, as though it would chime a carillon of positive answers, *yes, yes, yes,* to all his questions and thereby allay all his doubts.

Sleep resisted him. He lay still for some long time, his only movement an occasional idle scratch.

That woman at the Taj now, she has a quality, something I can't put my finger on, and sensible, attractive too. Educated by nuns, eh? Wonder what they'd think of her now. Wonder what I think of her. No, no, mustn't think of her at all. Think of Winnie, what she's really saying in this letter. Ask me, *isn't that what she's saying?*

He looked at his watch with its luminous dial. Three ten.

He wondered what to write.

No, he thought, *forget writing. Jump! Go on, isn't that what she's saying? Propose. Take a bloody risk! Do what you never do, take a risk.*

But the doubts were still there. Could he ever be sure of her? Wasn't she Kipling's Cat That Walks By Himself? And then, hidden away in the back of his skull, the word that worried him most, the word he shied away from, uncertain what it meant, indeed if it meant anything at all.

Love.

He needed her but did he love her? And if he did or if he didn't, did it matter? What was love, anyway? He needed her.

A pair of mosquitoes whined their mocking song. He needed paper, didn't care about bites, and there was no malaria at the coast. He pushed back the netting and slipped out of bed to scrabble in the pockets of his shorts where he found a crumpled sheet, a discarded Shelter Deck Certificate. He located a pencil and retreated back to bed.

A hideous clarity gripped him: the objectivity that comes at 3 a.m. If he married Winnie it would be because he needed her, yes, but there was also another reason, one he had tried to avoid acknowledging, a shameful reason. Ambition. Dar could open doors to greater career and social progress than he'd ever previously imagined, but he lacked the key with which to unlock the treasure chest. And even as night and tiredness began to fog his brain he knew that Winnie could provide it.

Although not an out-and-out beauty, she possessed much more important qualities. She was outgoing, vivacious, popular with everyone everywhere, but sharp-witted too, strong-minded – a woman who would accord kudos to the man who possessed her, kudos and admiration from the types at the Club, the public school men, the men who mattered. And of course marriage would provide a house. Even now new villas were being built for the ever-increasing number of administrators of Empire, some of them out at the prime location, Oyster Bay, houses like the McLeod's, perched on the cliffs, the empty beach below and rollers breaking on the reef beyond. And once married they'd host sundowners, accept return invitations, enter the social scene.

As for love, it would come, wouldn't it? Given time?

He began to write. His head drooped. The pencil slipped from his fingers and found a resting place in a pocket of the net.

He woke several hours later, yawned and stretched. An arm made contact with something – a pencil. Oh God, yes. He'd written something, but what? He located the scrap, now a scrunched ball trapped between net and mattress. He tried to smooth it out, running the flat of his hand backwards and forwards across it, but soon gave up. It was legible enough. After all the crossings-out and emendations and elaborations the final, bald summary was squeezed into the last available corner. A telegram.

> You'd love it here. Stop. Marry me. Stop. I mean it. Stop. I love you. Stop. Walter.

Dear God, what was he thinking? He recalled the cold logic of the night, and it appalled him. He wasn't like that, was he? So nakedly ambitious? Or had his Bristol self merely buried his ambition, knowing that in a Britain gripped by depression, but more profoundly locked into the fixed tramlines of class, such dreams were futile? Whereas now, here, in this place, his ambition had become virulent, erupting as both a canker and a liberation. The scrap of paper became a tight ball once more, squeezed and crushed until he could compress it no further.

CHAPTER 6

'Walter?'

Petrie stood in the doorway, his small frame exaggerated by a combination of baggy shorts and tight shirt. He was adjusting his spectacles, fiddling with the spring of coiled wire that curled itself behind each ear. The round lenses gave his pale blue eyes a washed-out, hazy quality, as though not only they but also the man himself were not in focus. He patted his hair, slicked down with brilliantine, flat across his scalp.

'Thought I'd better check on you. It's late. The Empire calls.'

Walter dressed at speed and grabbed a hasty breakfast – a pawpaw and a banana. In the jakes he took out the ball of paper, smoothed it flat, and studied it a second time.

Marry me.

Well, why not? A wife would make this a good life, no, better than that, a near-perfect life. And as they got more comfortable in each other's presence love would surely come. Wasn't it obvious?

Time would do the trick. Besides, love on its own was a dodgy commodity, unwise to put too much trust in it. What was it, anyway? He washed his hands in the thin trickle of water, faintly coloured as always by a reddish iron oxide stain. Winnie wasn't going to like that. His complaints to Miller had run into the usual stonewalling.

'You're lucky to have running water at all,' Miller said. 'You've no idea what a bloody difficult job it is, supplying water.'

He studied his reflection in the cracked mirror.

He'd send the telegram. Today.

No, not today. He needed to be sure, absolutely sure.

Tomorrow – he'd send the telegram tomorrow.

* * *

Petrie was waiting for him, leaning against the flaking ochre plaster of the building's frontage and watching two chickens as they attacked the dirt at the base of the veranda. Together they trudged up the dusty unmade track towards the sports ground, Acacia Avenue and their offices beyond. The Customs and Excise buildings were by the harbour with its acrid smells of poorly maintained petrol engines and misfiring generators, but here the early morning scents retained some freshness.

Joseph was in his *shamba*, hacking with a *panga* at tangles of brush. When he saw them he ducked out of sight.

Up to something. A veg patch, perhaps, on ground that wasn't his? Walter found dealing with servants difficult and he'd said so to McLeod. 'You'll learn,' was the reply. It was what McLeod said about everything.

'Pass,' Petrie shouted, and kicked a pebble. 'Pass, Walter!' For the next few minutes they played football until the ruts defeated them and the pebbles were abandoned. Petrie began to talk about his current work.

'All a matter of wording – got to get the wording right,' he repeated at intervals. He had ambitions to qualify as a solicitor, and felt that his experience in Dar would get him well-paid work back home.

'That's if I don't stay on after my tour. And why not? This country is going to boom. I heard a rumour that there's been another gold strike, this time near Moshi. If it's a big one, ho, ho, can't you see it? My God, this place could change. We could make our fortunes.'

'You'll turn prospector?'

'Me? Think I'm an idiot? Let others dig, say I, and then see what happens.'

'And what will happen?'

Petrie rattled on. 'Claims, old son, claims! And claims need regulation, adjudication, intelligent coves who know the score. Even if I haven't finished my articles I can set up an advice shop. Plenty of moolah to be made, eh? This is the place to be, I tell you.' As though to convince himself he raised both hands in a boxer's salute.

'And if there is no gold?' Walter said.

'There'll be something else. Africa has such potential, Walt. Africa! God, I love it. Blighty has nothing on it – our futures will be made here. Seize the day, eh – isn't that the thing? Just need a girl for perfection, a girl like your girl. She sounds great.'

Walter didn't answer. He'd told Petrie too much about Winnie, some of it true.

They reached the corner of the sports field. Petrie put out his hand and pointed to a stunted blackwood tree under which two natives lay.

'Gawd help us,' he said. 'What are they doing here? Can we ignore them?'

'They're hardly a problem for the Customs Service.'

'No, but they are for me. What are they doing in this zone? Do they have passes? If they don't, if they're in violation of township regulations and that makes them my business. It's exactly what my brief is all about.' He hesitated. 'Shall we ignore them? Oh dear, what to do? Suppose I'd better do my job.'

Petrie headed across the stunted grass towards the men. Walter trailed after him, then stopped and watched from a distance. The two men struggled to their feet, their lean, shabby silhouettes and dirt-stained vests contrasting with Petrie's pressed linens, their unkempt hair pointing up the neatness of his short back and sides.

'Papers,' Petrie demanded, a hand stretched out towards the men. 'Passes.'

There was a brief pantomime as the men patted non-existent pockets. They then abandoned the pretence and stood towering over the little man, heads bowed. Petrie seemed at a loss as to what to do next. Walter wandered over. Petrie flapped his hands at the sky.

'What can I do? Layabouts, *wahuni*, in Zone 1 without permits. Typical – they know perfectly well they're not allowed here, but what can I do?'

Walter sniffed the air. 'I smell *pombe*,' he said. 'Spent the night getting tight on it, I'd guess. You need an *askari*.'

'I know I do. Summon a bobby and get them packed back to wherever they come from. Upcountry somewhere, no doubt – shouldn't be in Dar at all. But is there an *askari* in sight? Is there ever? Not on your nelly. Like policemen everywhere.'

The men waited patiently. Petrie tapped his foot, groaned with exasperation and pointed in the direction of the Native Zone. 'Go on then. Get back to Kariakoo.'

Neither man reacted. The taller one began to scratch an arm. His long earring, beads threaded on wire, shook.

'Kariakoo, savvy? Kariakoo! Native Zone! *Imshi, imshi!* buggeroffski!'

The shorter man began to edge away from Petrie but kept watching him as if to check that this was the correct response. His friend followed, still scratching. They avoided Walter and started to walk slowly towards Acacia Avenue, looking back frequently. When Petrie made no attempt to follow them, they began to walk faster, then broke into a long-legged trot.

'Good,' Petrie said. 'Got the message.'

As he spoke the two natives made an abrupt right turn into Smuts Street, began to run and in seconds were out of sight, vanished behind a mass of bougainvillea.

'Look at that!' Petrie said. 'Where in hell are they going now? That won't get 'em to Kariakoo.' He clenched his fists. 'Can't trust 'em an inch. Control orders, useless! This place needs taking in hand.'

They set off again, in silence for a time.

'I despair sometimes,' Petrie said. 'It does annoy me, at times it makes me want to weep – all our bloody work, approved policy, all of it, and they persist in ignoring it. It's simple enough: natives are not allowed in the European Zone without passes. They're not allowed in Dar at all if they haven't got a job. We can't have every upcountry hick coming to Dar, can we? The place would be overrun. Same with zoning. Can you imagine our zone open to that crowd? What a nightmare that would be. Why can't they understand: it's the law, it's clear enough, now bloody obey it. And yet they continue to do as they please. Why?'

Walter laughed. 'Because they can get away with it.'

'Yes. And that's our problem. We create the policy, zoning is approved, boundaries specified, separation of the races duly ordained, but what then? There's not enough follow-through, not enough enforcement. The Boers down in South Africa manage it better. We're too soft.' Petrie punched the air in front of him.

Walter slapped him on the back. 'You did what you could; you're not the police.'

Petrie shook his head. 'I sometimes wonder though. Are they villains, *wahuni*, thugs, what have you, or no more than idle chancers? Mind you, either way they should be in a paddy wagon out of here.'

'I think they're just blokes,' Walter said. 'Anyway, ours is not to reason why.'

'Maybe not, but we know how that lot ended up.'

They walked on. Petrie's grumbles continued.

'We can't run the country if every blasted native thinks he can do what he wants, can we?'

'Don't get worked up,' Walter said.

'I try not to. It's just that sometimes it strikes me as a bit unfair on them. It's circular: without a permit they can't get a job; without a job they can't get a permit.'

They parted at the *askari* monument.

'Politics – steer clear of politics,' that's what Dad had always said. 'Stick to the rules, you won't go far wrong. Whatever your betters say, agree, smile and agree. No sticking your head above the parapet.' Walter agreed wholeheartedly. No involvement in politics for him.

He rubbed his hands together and stepped up his pace. An idiotic song came to him and he was still singing it as he entered the general office. *Give 'em a treat*, he thought, and upped the volume:

*'I scream, you scream, we all scream for ice cream,
Rah! Rah! Rah!
Tuesdays, Mondays, we all scream for sundaes,
Sis-boom-bah!'*

The typing pool stared at him. He needed a finale so gave them a brief buck-and-wing, the only tap step he knew. Miss Fernandes giggled and a round of applause broke out. He bowed and then took up a Charles Atlas pose, right leg bent, right elbow resting on the knee, right fist to his forehead. A second burst of applause erupted then rapidly died.

McLeod stood in his doorway. 'A word.'

McLeod lowered himself into his leather-trimmed office chair. Walter stood by the window, pushed up the slatted blind and stared at the activity on the dock outside. A small freighter was positioning itself in the harbour, the *Maria Elena* out of Mozambique. Its presence cheered him; boarding it would offer an escape from the office, from McLeod's glowering presence.

'An explanation, if you'd be so kind,' his boss said.

Walter let the blinds settle. 'Explanation?'

'Just now, in the outer office.'

'Oh. Having a laugh with the troops. Not a problem, is it?'

'You don't get it, do you? Have to spell it out, do I? Right.'

Ah. Naughty schoolboy time.

An index finger extended towards him. 'You're officer class here, whatever you were back in – where was it – Avonmouth. Here you're officer class and the officer class does *not*, repeat, does *not*, fraternise with the troops.'

'Surely a joke or two now and then, that's okay, isn't it?'

McLeod slammed a hand onto his desk. 'No, it is not. We are white: we do not fraternise with the blacks. Get that into your skull, will you, and you'll find life in Dar a lot easier.'

'They're not black, they're Asian.'

'You being funny?'

'No.'

'Right.'

The index finger again. 'So here's an instruction for you. You do not repeat the scene I have just witnessed, never, ever. Nor do you chat to Catarina Fernandes – yes, I've seen you talking. Perfectly decent woman, runs the typing pool well enough, but you *do not* fraternise with her. Nor with Da Silva, good office manager he may be – even so, arm's length, if you please. Nor with any of them, whatever they are, Asian, Goan, local, that's irrelevant: they're all black. Black. Got that? And if I find you getting familiar with any of them beyond the normal levels of courtesy, I will have you on the carpet lickety-split and likely heading straight back to Blighty where you can behave however you bloody well like. Yes? *Comprenez?*'

Walter said nothing.

McLeod spread his hands wide, waiting for an answer, then threw them upwards and stood. 'All right, I'm exaggerating, kicking the point home. I just don't want to see you go down the wrong route, Walter. I'm sure you're a good lad but there are codes here and transgressing them causes trouble. You do get that, don't you?'

'I take the point.'

'Good, that's the attitude.'

McLeod laughed, a short bark. 'Time to get on, eh? I see the *Maria Elena*'s in port. Watch it when you board – master's a thoroughgoing rogue: Luis Veiga, typical Portuguese, full of tricks. Has a black wife and a tribe of piccaninnies. Actually married the mother if you can credit it.'

'I'll watch it.'

Walter had just opened the connecting door between their offices when McLeod spoke again.

'Think I've been a bit hard on you? Perhaps I have. Not a natural transgressor, are you? No, a rather conventional type, I think. But then I approve of conventional types – men who do what they should do, what's expected, above all what they're told to do. Don't want trouble, do we?'

'No.'

'No. Let that message sink in and you'll fit in very well.'

Walter waited for further character analysis but McLeod waved a dismissal and Walter continued on into his own office, closing the door carefully as he did so, making sure that the barrier was in place. He stared at the naval chart pinned to the wall, a relic of his predecessor, Shanklin, who'd curtailed his tour supposedly for reasons of ill health. A few days ago he'd asked Catarina about the nature of Shanklin's illness and she'd shaken her head and put a finger to her lips. It was evident from her coy reaction that whatever had caused the man's departure had not been sickness but something murkier, presumably of a sexual nature. He'd hoped to hear more from her but McLeod had now put the kibosh on that. A sudden surge of anger gripped him. It was ridiculous. The occasional friendly chat, a bit of gossip, why ever not? Did the Empire depend on segregation? Apparently it did.

And although he didn't much care for being called conventional, he knew there was truth in the charge. He'd always been the boy who did as he was told.

He pictured Dad's wagging finger. 'Never get uppity, boy.'

Dad was always right. He wouldn't be getting uppity.

* * *

He worked on past five o'clock, made sure that his boss was aware of his dedication and then as soon as McLeod had left, he did too. Petrie was waiting for him at the mess, standing in the doorway, towel in hand.

'What say?' he shouted, and waved the towel. 'Not too late, is it?'

'I say aye,' he called back. 'You're a mind reader.'

Night was already closing in but they knew the path well. It wound its erratic way through groves of untended scrub until it reached the coconut palms that fringed the shore. They stood there for a while in contemplation of the developing darkness, hypnotised by the soft whispers of the dying wavelets. There was scarcely any wind and the little there was sided with the incoming tide. On calm nights like this the ocean pulsed to a heartbeat of astonishing delicacy, unlike anything Walter had heard on his rare trips to the Bristol Channel at Portishead or Clevedon.

'We're so lucky,' Petrie said. 'Admit it, Walter, aren't we just? And all annoying bosses can off-gebugger.'

Walter laughed. 'We are lucky,' he said, 'we are.'

They undressed at speed, flinging off shirts and shorts and cursing the delay caused by tightly knotted bootlaces. Underwear, too, was thrown aside with no pretence of modesty. Once free of clothing, they charged across the cooling sand and hurled themselves into the still warm sea.

They lay floating on their backs, buoyed up by the salt water, staring up at the infinity above them. The stars were a courtship dance of celestial fireflies. The waves whispered to them and in the spaces left between the ocean's messages the distant shouts of children could be heard, a descent to the rumbling bass of the surf.

'A girl now – a girl here, now – wouldn't that be the bee's knees?' Petrie said. 'Imagine your girl here, now. Perfection.'

Walter said nothing.

No one's perfection.

Petrie began a slow backstroke paddle and Walter followed him. Prone on his back, he searched the stars, their positions still so unfamiliar when viewed from here, from south of the Equator, but they had no message that he could discover, no advice to offer. Marriage to Winnie? Why not? But first she had to say yes. No, first he had to send the telegram. Tomorrow, he promised himself, he'd send it tomorrow.

CHAPTER 7

By mid-morning the next day the wind had strengthened considerably and changed direction. It was now offshore and its battle with the incoming tide created erratic surges of water. The smaller boats hadn't put to sea and the Customs launch needed three attempts to secure itself before Walter could finally scramble up the rope ladder onto the *Maria Elena*'s cargo deck. She was based in Beira, a coastal tramp with a regular beat from Durban north to Aden and the Red Sea ports. There was a sense of excitement among the crew, shouting and argument. The cause was obvious: a car was roped to the starboard deck, an elegant four-seater with a folding roof. Several broad canvas straps sat coiled on the deck and the hook of a lighter crane hovered above, while an anxious crane driver watched and shook his head.

A pair of legs in yellow drill trousers protruded from beneath the car. Walter approached them.

'Senhor Veiga?' Walter asked.

A grunt of what he took to be assent came from beneath the car.

'Customs and Excise.'

An eddying wave hit the coaster side-on. It lurched, causing the yellow trousers to jerk upwards and collide with the chassis. A secondary wave caused a further twitch and another, duller, thud.

'*Filho da puta!*,' came a muffled bellow.

Walter crouched to peer under the car. The day had turned colder and for once he wore his uniform jacket.

'Senhor Veiga?' he said again. The yellow trousers lay still.

'Walter Barnes, Customs and Excise.'

A foot twitched. There were traces of oil on the deck and Walter straightened up, conscious of his jacket and his dignity. He rapped on the car door.

'Senhor Veiga, did you hear me? Senhor Veiga?'

The legs lay still for a moment longer, but then there was a grunt of acknowledgment and Veiga shuffled out from underneath the vehicle. He lay on his back, stretched out across the deck with his feet in the shallow gutter alongside the railings and offered Walter a smile as broad as it was patently false.

'Senhor Barnes, moment,' he said, and raised a finger.

'Are you sure you know what you're doing?' Walter asked. 'Have you carried vehicles before?'

Veiga rubbed his forehead, where a dull red bruise was beginning to emerge. He snapped his fingers at a seaman. '*Documentos, prontamente.*'

The man scurried off. Veiga raised himself on an elbow to watch him go. Walter offered a hand to pull him to his feet.

'Moment,' Veiga repeated. He ignored the hand and instead seized the tail of a canvas strap, yawned, lay down and worked his way back beneath the car.

The crane driver came to stand by Walter. He was barefoot

but carried a pair of canvas shoes which he waved vigorously at the car. The gesture demonstrated his status as a skilled man, a trained man, not a mere labourer like the others who had gathered to watch.

'*Bwana*, Customs, *jambo*!' the crane driver said. '*Matata, mingi matata*, bad, bad.'

He shook his head and waited for a response. Walter ignored him. The problems were obvious and didn't need pointing out.

The crane driver accepted the snub. '*Mingi matata*,' he said again.

'Indeed,' Walter said, relenting. 'Your skills will be tested.'

The crane driver nodded. He had understood the tone of Walter's remark if not its literal substance, and now he retreated a few paces, at the same time looking around, checking that their exchange had been observed and his position in the pecking order reaffirmed.

The seaman returned and handed Walter a clipboard with some cyclostyled sheets pinned to it, covered in a handwritten scrawl. Walter flicked through them, exasperation mounting.

'Is this the manifest? The full manifest? Is there nothing else? No other paperwork?'

The seaman shrugged. The pages rustled in the vigorous wind.

'You don't speak a word of English, do you?'

The seaman looked concerned, and leaned his head to one side as though waiting for further enlightenment.

Walter gave up on him and bent down again. 'Senhor Veiga, I need to talk to you. Where is the paperwork?'

'Moment!' came another muffled shout. Veiga's legs disappeared completely and a few seconds later the man himself scrambled out on the far side of the car, clutching the further end of the canvas strap. He then transferred the end to his teeth and used his hands first to massage his head and then to adjust his underwear, hauling at the waistband of a pair of pristine white underpants and pulling them up so that they showed an inch above his yellow trousers. He adjusted his crotch, handed the strap to a crew member and shouted a few impressively stern orders in Portuguese. No one moved in response. Veiga turned his attention to Walter.

'Senhor Barnes!' he called. 'I hear all about the good Senhor Barnes, everyone tells me, all skippers tell me, Senhor Barnes, good man, and now we meet, that is very good. Time for a beer, yes?'

'Senhor Veiga, the manifest! And furthermore we need to discuss whether or not this vessel is properly equipped for the transfer of complicated machinery such as this vehicle. Do you have the necessary safeguards in place?'

'Yes, yes, no problem. We lift many things, crate, car, all same, no problem.' He headed towards the bridge.

Walter strode briskly after him, the clipboard with the scruffy notes brandished in his right hand. 'Which shipping agent arranged the car's passage with you? Senhor Veiga, I am unhappy with so many things here.'

'Yes, yes, beer make happy, please come with me, Senhor Barnes. I have present for you.'

'Senhor Veiga, you know I cannot accept presents.'

Veiga raised his hands in submission. 'Okay, no present. But beer, Senhor Barnes, from Durban. Castle Lager, you like, promise.'

'I can accept a beer though,' Walter said. 'And we will go through the manifest.'

To his surprise the *Maria Elena*'s bridge was well kept and gave an impression at least of efficiency. The telegraph and other instruments were as polished as those on any liner and the chart table was free of clutter. There was both pride and practicality on view.

A tall black woman, elegant in a cotton *kitenge* knotted over her left shoulder, presided at the icebox.

'My wife,' Veiga said, 'Paola.'

'Senhora,' Walter said.

'Speak only Portuguese. *Meu amigo*, Senhor Barnes.'

The woman handed Walter a bottle. 'Senhor,' she said. Veiga kissed her cheek, she smiled at Walter and then disappeared down the companionway. It struck him that her gestures and movements were almost balletic in their grace and precision.

'A very beautiful woman,' he said, and meant it. Veiga studied him.

'You are good man, Senhor Barnes.'

Two hours and three beers later, the manifest had been assessed, reassessed, revised and at last approved, Walter had completed the rummages and all details had been entered in the Ship's Blue Book. The Customs launch was on its way to collect him. The car, now swathed in half-a-dozen canvas bandages, had been lifted onto the lighter to begin its slow journey through the still choppy sea towards the lighterage quay. The crane driver had demonstrated considerable skill in hoisting it clear of obstacles and keeping it steady in the brisk wind and now posed alongside it, hand on bonnet, his job well done and seen to be well done.

Walter and Veiga leaned on the *Maria Elena*'s railings and watched the harbour's activities. The shore seine fishermen were active out towards Magagoni, and two outriggers were trying their luck further upstream past Ras Malabe.

'Zanzibar next?'

'No Zanzibar, Tanga.' Veiga scratched his stubble.

'Give my regards to Fairweather,' Walter said. Fairweather was the Customs and Excise officer in Tanga, a small port further north near the Kenyan border. He was widely regarded as an oddball who, it seemed, preferred a life of isolation, seeing no Europeans apart from a few sisal farmers and the occasional missionary.

'Ah, Senhor Fairweather, good man.'

'Keeps you on your toes, I'll bet.'

Veiga laughed and slapped Walter on the back, resting his hand there for a moment. 'Like you do, Mister Barnes.'

'I hope I do,' Walter said.

The slap intrigued him. He detected warmth in it and approval. How odd. And odder still was the realisation that he reciprocated the feeling. He had begun to like Veiga. The man was decent, and for all his casual attitude towards paperwork Walter couldn't see him as the rogue described by McLeod. Yes, he liked him. Strange. How had that come about? Was it that Veiga loved Africa, loved his African wife, belonged here? Wanted him to love it too? And see it through his eyes? He didn't think he'd be marrying an African woman though. Now that would really be a scandal. Or marrying a Goan, Catarina say. Or what about the woman in the Taj? She was undoubtedly attractive, but even so. He grinned at the thought, at the sheer absurdity of the idea.

The fresh breeze tempered the heat. The dense aromas, dominated by copra, had a sweetness to them. The harbour was going about its apparently chaotic but secretly ordered business, and the thought that had just arrived – no, no, the thought that had been there for some time, waiting to be released, waiting for that slap on the back – the thought was such a simple one: *Africa is the place for me, and I'm going to do a good job here.*

And if underneath the scent of copra lay the acrid fumes of the harbour, they too had their place; they spoke of necessary work, of things to do and things being done, of activity, of the essential business of a port.

'Do you know,' Walter said. 'I like this town and I like the people and I like the work.'

And wouldn't Winnie like it too?

Veiga inspected him.

'You are good man, Senhor Barnes,' he said for the second time.

'And you, Senhor Veiga. Except in the matter of…'

He didn't continue, but Veiga threw his hands wide.

'*Documentos!*' he cried. 'Paper, paper, paper. I don't change, Mister Barnes – I need you help me with my paper, my *documentos*.'

The Customs launch hovered below them. They shook hands and Walter scrambled down the jolting rope ladder and settled back on the leather bench reserved for the officers. On the brief trip back his mood lightened further. In the patchy sunlight that highlighted the town the buildings were no longer merely utilitarian. Seen from this distance, the shabbiness was hidden and he could see them as simple, functional, with a formal beauty that didn't boast but moulded them quietly, appropriately, into the palm groves and oleander thickets. He liked Dar but more than that he sensed again that it was changing him. He had status here and that brought respect with it and, at least potentially, power. This place held his future.

They approached the jetty. A European male stood there, leaning back on a shooting stick, his hands in the jacket pockets of his pale linen suit, his golden hair ruffled by the breeze, a stray lock flopping across his forehead. Walter recognised him from the Dar-es-Salaam Club; Charles Mallinson, one of the Governor's young men. Walter raised a hand in token greeting, but the man's hands stayed buried.

'Snobs like that, best to ignore 'em,' Dusty Miller had said. 'That's what I do.'

Walter had no intention of ignoring Mallinson and his kind. Despite his first experiences at the Club, perhaps because of his first experiences at the Club, he wanted to get them to know him properly, to forget his accent and instead to acknowledge his qualities and to accord him respect without patronage. He was an individual and wanted to be known as such and not as some comic peasant from darkest Mummerset. They were a challenge he wasn't going to duck and here was an opportunity, one not to be missed and one he'd prepared for.

The Club's games room had a green baize noticeboard. Sport occupied most of the postings and tennis was the favoured game. Walter had never played it. But he had played billiards and there was a billiards ladder pinned up on the board together with a call for more players. Walter had first played the game at the age of ten, learning it in the sergeant's mess in Devizes Barracks where Dad, long pensioned off from the regiment, earned pin money as a caretaker. By the age of sixteen, when Dad finally gave in to his numerous ailments and the visits to the Barracks ceased, Walter was established as a local champion. Why not here? He felt sure he could beat most of his likely opponents. And even if he didn't make it to the top of the ladder that wasn't the point. Each game could provide an opportunity to engage with one of the opinion-formers, a chance to talk as equals, to impress them with his intelligence, his solid virtues. The public schoolboys' competitive urges meant that they'd want to play him, indeed would welcome the chance to thump someone from the lower orders. The Gentlemen vs. Players game at Lords, always popular.

He'd added his name to the ladder and had played and won two games so far but the strategy hadn't yet delivered. His opponents evidently resented the ease with which he beat them and as a result any attempted conversation died. He should have made a few mistakes, kept them thinking they were in with a chance, even let them win.

And now the name immediately above his was Mallinson's.

He scrambled up onto the jetty.

'Been checking on my car, have you?' Mallinson said. 'Elegant, isn't she? Bought her from a chap in Durban. Humber 16/50, open tourer – could be ideal for round here.'

'She's yours, is she? You took a risk, you know, booking her on the *Maria Elena*.'

'Oh, don't tell me, I know, I know. Thoroughly dim. I rashly agreed the cheapest shipping deal, and from the look of that vessel rather wish I hadn't. But all's well, as the bard has it.'

'There's still paperwork to do. You can't have the car straight away.'

'Didn't expect to. Just here to welcome the darling, see she arrives safely. And isn't she a beauty? I think I'm half in love already. You do your stuff, eh – paperwork has to be attended to, 'course it does, wouldn't suggest otherwise. Then when d'you reckon I can collect?'

'Later this afternoon, perhaps fourish.'

'I'll pop along. Don't let me keep you.' He snapped the shooting stick shut. 'Are you Barnes by any chance?'

'Yes.'

'We have an appointment, I believe. For a game. I hear you're good?'

'Don't know about that. Not bad, anyway. Shall we fix something?'

'Yes, we must, yes,' Mallinson drawled. 'Unfortunately not just now, fearfully busy I'm afraid, chocker. I'll have to let you know. Billiards not quite top of the priority list as of the here and now.'

Damn. But the topic had been opened and in time would bear fruit.

Paperwork completed, the Humber was released to Mallinson by mid-afternoon. He collected it from the inward goods warehouse and Walter watched from his office as the car, hood down to reveal its cream leather seats, idled down Main Avenue in the direction of Government House and the other admin buildings. Mallinson drove slowly, holding the wheel with one gloved hand, and with the other giving a tap on the horn as he passed the Customs and Excise buildings. Walter raised a hand. Mallinson tapped the horn a second time.

CHAPTER 8

The post and telegraph office building was single-storied and took no pride in its appearance. Cream paint clung feebly to its concrete walls and a loose board groaned beneath him as he leapt up the three steps onto the veranda. It was late in the day by now and the blinds were lowered and the shutters folded and barred. Walter wasn't surprised; it was nearly sundown after all and Dar offices tended to cease functioning with the fading light, whatever the official hours proclaimed. Still, the post office was supposed to stay open later than most.

The tin roof creaked in the wind as he rapped on the frame of a blind window and called for Mohinder Singh. No answer. Damn. He'd made the decision, for right or wrong, and he didn't want it subverted by something as stupidly accidental as the postmaster closing up ahead of time.

He walked around to the row of small sheds at the back of the building and called again. The only reaction came from a skinny pi-dog which backed away into a gap beneath one of the sheds from where it eyed him, neither hostile nor welcoming, just cautious. He liked dogs but in Dar the creature's caution was understandable. *Wait and see*, it was no doubt thinking. *Don't be hasty, there might be a scrap of food on offer*, but a flung stone was much more likely.

He returned to the veranda and rapped again on the window. The dog reappeared and watched him from the corner of the building as he prowled up and down, his exasperation turning to a dull anger. He tried one last shout for Mohinder Singh. The dog twitched at the rasp of his raised voice. A low rumble from inland warned of the imminent arrival of rain. The dog edged forward and the movement caught his eye. He stepped off the veranda and crouched down a few yards from the animal. It backed away, but maintained eye contact.

'Here, dog,' he said, and held out a hand. Having done so, he realised that this was a gesture unknown to the animal. Squatting on his haunches, he moved a foot closer to it and was delighted when it stood its ground. The wiry waywardness of its scant hair shared something of his father's much-loved Bella, an approximate version of a fox terrier, scruffy but full of character.

'Here, Bella,' he said.

'Dog is diseased, Mr Barnes, sir,' Mohinder Singh called. 'We don't want it here. Wrong type altogether.'

Bella slid away into the twilight.

The postmaster stood in the now open doorway to the post office carrying a tea cloth with which he wiped his hands, finger by finger, as if to emphasise that he had been interrupted in the course of some important task. 'Yes, Mr Barnes?'

No turning back now.

'I need to send a telegram. You're not supposed to be shut, not yet anyway.'

'I am not shut, Mr Barnes, as you see. Here I am.'

There was no point in making a fuss. Dar had its downsides and he had to live with them.

They went inside.

The tea cloth was folded and placed on the counter. Walter undid the buckles on his satchel and pulled out the draft he'd prepared, printing everything in block capitals. No misspellings, please. He was tempted to take one more look, but resisted. Too late to rethink. He handed it to Singh, who studied it for several seconds, then laid it down beside the cloth.

'A very important message, Mr Barnes. You may of course rely on my discretion in all personal matters.'

'Thank you,' Walter said.

'And I trust that very soon I will be able to congratulate you.'

'Yes. Do you need me to wait while you send it?'

'No, sir, no. It will go immediately.' He was counting the words as he spoke. 'Twelve words only, sir, very much to the point. As an observer, I would say that a decisive note is struck. The ladies admire that.'

They said nothing more. Walter handed over a ten-shilling note, collected his change, walked back down the veranda steps and trudged off. His future was out of his hands. She would get the telegram tomorrow morning, maybe even this evening. In a few minutes it would become a live thing, would pass from telegraph station to telegraph station, would travel up the length of Africa and across the Mediterranean, would leap over France and would finally land, breathless, in Bristol.

Astonishing.

The dog had appeared again. He raised a hand, the preliminary to a wave, and it began to back away from him, wary, uncertain.

Yes, astonishing. And then? The telegram in her hands. Would she dismiss it? Or embrace it? She was as unpredictable to him as he was to the dog.

'You can trust me, Bella,' he said, unaware that he'd spoken out loud.

***

The next day was damp, the rains having made their brief return in the form of a light drizzle which transformed Dar into a grey town. Walter generated his own damp too, patches of salty sweat appearing under his arms, in his groin and down his spine where he leaned against the upright back of his office chair. It was a carver with a padded and embroidered seat and back and it displayed signs of earlier sweats, faint white contours on the raised padding. When the postboy arrived, he was attempting to write a codicil to the third chapter of his draft report on the proposal for an East African Customs Union. This had now been raised by Admin to the status of an Interim Report, which in turn meant a thorough elaboration of the entire document.

'No loopholes now,' McLeod instructed him. 'I'll deal with the sections on mineral deposits, that's the tricky area, that's the one that excites them, but I'd like you to review the rest of it. I should ask Thornton to do it, but I thought I'd give you a chance to show off your mighty analytical brain.'

He laughed, a short *ha!* that contrived to underline the potential for insult in the remark. Thornton was his Deputy, a pale presence who kept himself to himself. He worked from an office further down the front alongside the lighterage quay and was noted for his obsessive pursuit of correct procedures and for being the butt of much of McLeod's humour.

'We need more detail on the likely effects of a unitary duty – you know the sort of stuff, positives and negatives, a balanced view. Start with the luxury goods category.'

'I'll give it a shot.'

'You'd better do more than that.'

Walter found the category hard to define: what was luxury? A bathroom suite? Or just a particularly expensive bathroom suite? A groan escaped him. This was going to be a slog.

The postboy was waiting. He pushed the document aside and held out a hand.

The lad, a Sikh, turbanless but with his hair in a topknot, handed him a small brown envelope and hovered, dripping muddy water, waiting for a tip. Walter searched for change but could find nothing smaller than a shilling. It was excessive but would have to do. The boy accepted the coin with apparent indifference.

When he'd gone, Walter turned the envelope over and over in his hands without opening it. New sources of damp appeared. Pinpricks of sweat erupted on his forehead and he needed to wipe his palms on his shirt. He was also aware that the outer office was remarkably quiet, the clacking of typewriters silent. Mohinder Singh had no doubt spread the word of his proposal, but had he also contrived to inform the staff of Winnie's response? Yes or no, the staff's interest now lay in observing Walter's reaction.

He breathed in, held his breath and then in one powerful movement ripped open the envelope and pulled out the telegram. As he did so, there was a rapping on his door. He hesitated, glanced at the telegram without reading it, then flung the door open.

Catarina stood there, her eyes behind her heavy black horn-rimmed spectacles glinting with curiosity. She held out a letter form. The postboy stood behind her.

'Could you sign this, sir? I thought the boy could take it back with him.'

Catarina beamed, innocent. Walter grabbed the letter and dropped the telegram as he did so. She crouched to pick it up.

'Leave it!' he snapped. Catarina stood, levering her awkward bulk upwards with the aid of a hand on the corner of his desk. She smiled, humourless. He realised that his abrupt reaction would be interpreted. The story would circulate instantly: he's in a bad temper; she's refused him. He attempted a countering smile. They beamed at each other. He signed the letter, one of a batch to be sent to cotton growers attempting to expand the industry in the countryside north of Bagamoyo. There was nothing urgent in it. Miss Fernandes left, still smiling fixedly.

He picked up the telegram and sat back at his desk. His hands were still damp but he didn't bother to wipe them.

Lovely Walter. Stop. Two proposals in one week. Stop. What's a girl to do. Stop. Thinking. Stop. Letter follows. Stop. Winnie.

He laughed, a silent chuckle. What a fool. As though life were ever simple. He'd have to wait, she was right, of course she was, she needed thinking time – one up to Winnie. And it seemed he had a rival, a new man courting her. But who? He couldn't think of anyone. The letter would no doubt explain everything.

The waiting would be intolerable.

And with that thought came another, an electric stab of truth: he not only wanted Winnie, he did indeed want to marry her. And not for solely unworthy reasons, no. The idea had begun to take hold and as it did so, he began to appreciate her virtues, her practicality, her common sense and above all her vivacity. He felt he was on the verge of loving her.

He reread the telegram and his spirits lifted. She hadn't shut the door on him. There was hope. He chuckled again, louder this time, and opened his office door.

'Miss Fernandes!' he called. 'Dictation, please.'

His good humour would confuse the gossips. Well, they'd have to live with that. He rubbed his hands together. His palms were dry.

CHAPTER 9

It had been a frustrating morning. McLeod had packed him off to the dhow harbour to talk to Abu Saleh. Quantities of ivory and rhino horn were going out from somewhere, export duty unpaid. In all probability the trade was being conducted out of one of the creeks to the north of the town and Abu Saleh was reputed not merely to know all the dhow movements but to control many of them. He was a large, affable Omani with a neat black goatee beard. *Dyes it*, Walter decided.

They sat on low couches in Abu Saleh's cluttered office and business was delayed until mint tea had been prepared and served. Only then was Walter permitted to explain his mission. Abu Saleh listened, nodded time and again with the utmost gravity, spread his hands wide and frowned and exclaimed and agreed that it was an utter disgrace. Duty should be paid, as should all taxes, gratefully, in acknowledgement of all the excellent things the British had achieved, were achieving, and were going to achieve in Tanganyika. He, and he could speak for all the other Omani merchants, was fully behind the Government in every aspect of its policy. With particular reference to the admirable activities of the Customs and Excise Department, without whom who knew what chaos would prevail?

But alas! He knew nothing. These dhow skippers were such cunning rascals! They had a thousand tricks up their sleeves! They were such accomplished liars! He beamed at Walter. 'More tea, Mr Barnes, I insist, and halva! Halva! Why have we not had halva?' He clicked his fingers and his serving boy, a youth of perhaps ten, bowed and exited. Walter attempted to leave but Abu Saleh stayed seated, and Walter knew that to go would be insulting, and would deepen the split between them. To gain any information at all he would have to stay. He did, and listened while his host discussed the intricacies of Persian carpet design, the subtleties of Sufi poetry, and the inestimable advantages of trading under the control of the British. He gained no information but the halva was sweet and the tea refreshing. As he left, Abu Saleh clasped a hand in both of his.

'My good friend, we work together, yes?'

Walter didn't answer. It was hard not to admire the man, not to applaud the finesse with which he'd been so outmanoeuvred.

He reported back to McLeod.

'Didn't handle him right, did you?' his boss said. 'You need to treat these types firmly. We're in charge here and they damn well know it. Toughen up, Walter, if you're to be of any use to me.'

He was dismissed with the flip of a hand.

Thanks, Johnny, really helpful.

* * *

What now? It was Saturday and he had the afternoon free. For what? For a chance to watch Rovers, then a relaxing seat in a pub and a decent pint of Ushers, above all a laugh with Reg and the other lads. Or a picnic with the Brennan sisters, Kitty and Deirdre, a trip out to Iron Acton, say.

But that was Bristol. Bristol offered diversion; Bristol offered entertainment. Saturday afternoon here and there was nothing on offer other than the Club.

Had Petrie been around, they might have gone to the beach behind the mess but Petrie was away, sent on a tour of upcountry centres of population: Dodoma, Tabora, Kigoma, Mwanza, Arusha and finally Tanga, with instructions to examine the efficacy of the measures aimed at stemming migration from the countryside to Dar.

'I appreciate the policy,' he'd told Walter as they walked along Acacia Avenue towards the train station. 'Contamination of indigenous culture by exposure to Western ways to be prevented, fine. Native traditions to be protected, fine. But we all know it doesn't bloody work!'

He waved a hand at the tree-lined street, at the castellated frontage of Barclay's Bank, at a row of three parked cars, at the bold enamelled shop signs.

'Why stick with life in a mud hut when there's this to be seen? It's too big a lure, it's irresistible. Seize the nettle, I say, let 'em come, and then educate 'em. Don't leave the poor buggers fossilised in some remote backwater.'

The train had a single first-class carriage. With elaborate and, in Walter's opinion, unnecessary formality a white-gloved attendant showed them to the reserved compartment where Petrie's bags were waiting.

'It's pointless,' Petrie said, slumping into a corner seat.

'No, no.'

'I know what I'll find. Everyone knows what I'll find. I might as well not go.'

'You'll have a fine time. I wish I was in your shoes. Be selfish, enjoy yourself, see the country.'

Petrie's gloom deepened.

'You're a pal, Walter.'

A guard clutching a green flag rapped on the window. They shook hands. Walter waited to see the train leave.

No, not the Club. He couldn't face the Club. What would he do when he got there? Mallinson still hadn't made an effort to set up a game. Walter had left him one reminder note but sensed that that was the limit. Anything more and he'd be categorised as a bore. The Club was out.

He wandered aimless along the harbour front.

'*Salaam, Bwana.*'

A dock worker saluted him, and another and then another, ducking their heads as they did so. He liked seeing this. It reinforced the growing sense of himself as a person of significance, a man with position. Power had an addictive quality; it gave a satisfying edge to encounters like these.

He wandered past the one-storey go-downs, each with its characteristic odour, the leather warehouse with its stacks of skins new from the tannery at Bagamoyo out-stinking the rest. The glare was unpleasant, aggressive light striking off windows and roofs, and Walter had to narrow his eyes to cope with it. His armpits were damp and patches were already forming on his shirt. A truck bumped past, laden with *askaris* perched in a double row on the open back. They too lifted his spirits, their red fezzes and gleaming Sam Browne belts a sign of coming order and progress. The Law was here. Empire was delivering its promises: the clear rules that Kipling endorsed. The Law of the Jungle which relied on obedience, on an understanding of one's place in the wider social sphere, was here and in time would come to be accepted by all ranks, including the natives.

He stepped up his pace and marched on past St Joseph's cathedral and the prison before striking inland to the commercial sector. The pedestrian hubbub closed in around him. A nearby bar offered beer. A beer. Yes, a Tusker was better than nothing. Walter headed towards the bar, then stopped.

The turn into Stanley Street was perhaps a hundred yards ahead.

It was an easy decision.

He could talk to her, couldn't he, just talk? And a Tusker was a good excuse and a genuine one. He needed a Tusker.

The day had acquired a purpose.

***

He set off again, but slowly now, deliberately delaying the moment. *Look casual*, he told himself, *the curious sightseer, the engaged social observer*. He began to enjoy himself, to enjoy the play-acting, the appearance of innocence. At the intersection with Stanley he paused, glanced in all directions and, as though accidentally, made the apparently arbitrary choice.

His pace slowed further. Ebony sculptures diverted him, small wooden figurines, spindly and heavily abstracted, offered by a local squatting on a sisal mat. A crude sign read MAKONDE. Walter didn't know what to make of the work. He was more impressed by the fortitude of the carver, who ignored him completely and made no attempt to sell. He simply squatted, staring ahead, chewing steadily on a sugarcane stem. Walter moved on.

Stanley Street by day seemed unrelated to its night-time avatar. The friendly discus-thrower failed to appear, his establishment shuttered and quiet. Walter received a few curious glances but nothing threatened, no one winked or grinned, there was no one complicit with his intentions. The ghostly acacias of the night were now smaller and rooted. In daylight his presence was accepted. A cassocked White Father hurried towards and past him with only the slightest sideways look. He congratulated himself on his perfect disguise and as he did so realised that he was wearing his uniform shirt with its distinctive epaulettes. A small worry surfaced but he brushed it aside. Why would knowing his position give anyone a hold on him?

And then he was there.

The Taj too was transformed by daylight. The shutters on the only window had been folded back and pinned. Gauze hung in their place, equally effective at disguising the interior. Only the red and gold paintwork on the window frames hinted at the underlying function of the establishment.

The door swung open and a shaft of stark white light stabbed the room. Walter paused in the entrance. The room itself was quiet, but he was aware of others being present. He waited for his eyes to adjust. Two Asian men sat on stools at the bar, and swung themselves round to inspect him. He cleared his throat, his earlier confidence now dissolving, the charade of the casual, curious social explorer gone. He summoned courage from somewhere.

'Is the bar open?' he enquired.

One of the men slipped from his stool and scurried through the back door. Walter waited. A chatter of animated voices drifted towards him from somewhere beyond.

'Sahib?' the second man offered.

'I was looking for a bar, a beer, that's all.'

'Very good beer, Younger's Scotch Ale.'

Walter stared at him. *Surely not. Younger's? Here?*

'Double Diamond, Ind Coope, India Pale Ale, all good beer, Worthington.' Then, as a triumphant conclusion, delivered with a raised forefinger, 'Bass.'

'You sell Bass here?'

'Very good beer. Bass. Very good.'

The finger raised again. 'Best beer: Double Diamond, Younger's Scotch Ale.'

'Yes, but here, *here*, in this bar?'

'Best bar, Dar-es-Salaam. India Pale Ale, best beer.'

'I do agree. But perhaps…'

The back door opened.

'Are you coming in?' she said.

Her tone was even, the question uninflected, a polite inquiry, no more, but it had the effect of a summons. Walter stepped forward and the door eased shut behind him.

She gestured towards the bench. 'Please.'

Walter hesitated. 'I didn't think I'd see you again.'

Another pure statement, or so it seemed to Walter, a statement unfreighted by hidden codes. He stumbled his way towards the bench and sat. The voices peaked and troughed in the room beyond, with occasional surges of subdued laughter. She took her seat behind the bar. An open book lay face down in front of her.

'I was passing.'

'I see.'

'Might have a beer, I thought.'

'Yes.'

'This gentleman has a fine knowledge of beers, but you have…?'

'Tusker. Only Tusker.'

'Thought so. I'll have one.'

His eyes had adjusted fully by now and he could see her properly. She wore a different sari, squares of red and gold, with narrow bands of deep blue intersecting the base pattern. She gestured towards a shelf of bottles and he could hear the music created by the bangles on her forearms as they crossed and intercrossed, chips of delicate sound, their resonance damped by the contact with her flesh.

'I have whisky soda if you prefer.'

Walter shook his head. Whisky was the drink of choice at the Club, either that or pink gin. Snobs' drinks.

'Tusker, please.'

She reached below the counter, produced a small icebox and sat it on the bar. As she did so she spoke commandingly but not harshly in Hindi. The man at the bar protested, but when she spoke again there was an edge to her voice, and he spread his arms wide in a gesture of reluctance before obeying. He moved awkwardly and Walter now saw that his left leg was trapped in a set of crude iron callipers. His left foot turned inwards and dragged helplessly as he stumbled towards the door.

'I hope he isn't leaving because I'm here,' he said.

'He has business to attend to,' she replied crisply. She collected a glass from the recesses of the counter, picked up the bottle, and brought them over to Walter. She didn't hand them to him at once but stood beside and above him, her sari still flickering slightly from the journey across the room.

'Will you be staying?' she asked.

'I just want a beer, thank you.'

'Of course. Today we have cold beer. And the glasses are clean.'

She handed him the Tusker and the glass and returned to her station. Walter poured his beer, settled the half-empty bottle on the brass-inlaid table and sank into the cushioned back of the bench. He raised the glass and inclined it towards her. A smile escaped him as he did so. Then he drank, aware that she was watching him.

'I mean it. I haven't come for a girl,' he said.

'Why come then?' she asked.

'I told you, for a beer.'

'And this is the only place in Dar-es-Salaam where you can buy a Tusker.'

He laughed. 'I admit it, there are other reasons.'

'To hear me talk, yes?'

'Yes.'

'Yes. Then perhaps I should charge you for this service. What would you think fair? A shilling a minute?'

'That seems rather steep.'

'But the service is unique. Where else in Dar is it available, a conversation with a brothel-keeper?'

'I don't care for that word. Please don't call yourself that.'

'But it is what I am.'

They looked at each other, serious now. She picked up her book. He felt absurdly self-conscious. She was right. This wasn't an adventure, this was more the act of a bored teenager, something to snigger about later in the day, *he-he-he*, a brothel! Talking to the madame! He should finish his beer, leave.

He didn't move. She had shifted slightly on her stool and was now in three-quarters profile. The furrow in her upper lip, narrow and sharply outlined, caught his eye. He ran a thumbnail across his own upper lip, as though to test it, to compare it, and as he did so he knew that what he wanted, as of this instant, undeniably, was to kiss her. A momentary panic seized him and he stood up, rocking the table as he did so. She turned and faced him, expressionless, still. He ducked his head, looked away.

'Goodbye,' she said.

The word struck him as a challenge and the panic subsided. He wasn't an adolescent kid. He was adult, successful, in command of his life. He was here because he wanted to be here, no further excuse was needed. Not to kiss her, no. That was nothing more than a passing lunacy to be dismissed without a further thought. He was here, he decided, to explore. The situation was odd and it was one he'd put himself into. That was what he wanted to explore: himself.

He sat again. She was still watching him, curious, aware of his uncertainty. And now it occurred to him that her gravity lay on top of something else, a restlessness, a dissatisfaction, even a vulnerability that he hadn't seen before. She wasn't Lalun the sophisticated courtesan, no. She was a being from a different story, less confident than he had at first supposed, and more intriguing. His thumbnail ran across his upper lip a second time. She turned back to her book.

He searched for a new subject to sustain the conversation. 'You don't have a caste mark,' he offered.

She frowned, and he tapped his forehead.

'Those are not caste marks,' she said, and picked up her book. 'That is a common mistake and an irritating one.'

Walter drank again, deeper this time. There was a burst of laughter from the rooms beyond, as if to mock his error.

'I have a lot to learn.'

'Yes, you have. Besides, it is you, not me, who has the caste mark.'

'I do? Where?'

She didn't answer.

'No, tell me, please.'

She laid down her book and shook her head. Amusement lines returned to break the severity of her face, and he felt a stir of achievement.

'Tell me,' he said again.

'What an innocent you are,' she said. 'Do you really not understand?'

He waited for her to continue. She brought her hands together to form a funnel about her lips as if to convey a message of great importance, one that could only be whispered, and in private.

Her eyes widened to stress the significance of what she was about to say.

'Your skin.'

He laughed again, delighted, and she lowered her hands.

'Of course,' he said. 'My skin is my caste mark. And what does it signify?'

'Signify? Why, the obvious, that you are one of the masters of this country.'

He raised a hand in protest. 'No, heavens no, I'm no master. I'm a servant of the Crown, just another small cog in the machinery of government and law. I help to deliver the Law.'

She stared at him, then picked up her book and brandished it at him as though it were a weapon, a club perhaps. When she spoke, anger fuelled her speech. The musicality was still there, but the notes were deeper and darker now.

'Law? Is that what you tell yourself? Law says this place should be closed – it is unfit, immoral, but Law does nothing. Law says but does not do. There are countless ways, here in Dar, where Law does nothing, yes, nothing. Law does not apply to us or to the blacks. Law is a privilege reserved for you, the lucky whites. You have Law, and pretend that it is shared with all of us. It is not.' She hurled the last words at him. 'It is not.'

Her calm reserve had been ripped from her by this eruption of emotion, coming out of nowhere, or so it seemed to him. Faced by it he felt lost, unschooled, incapable of any response other than a feeble attempt at rational debate. 'No, no, I'm sure you're right in many ways, but in theory, in theory the Law is there, it's just human failings that let it down.'

She turned away from him and he felt as though he had failed some obscure test of character, the questions written in a language he'd never before encountered. He plucked at the sweat staining his shirt and wiped his palms on his handkerchief.

'I know very little about these things. I'm just an ordinary bloke,' he said, and as if to prove it, drained the rest of his glass in one long swallow. 'Another Tusker, please.'

At first she ignored him. He waited. It was all he could think of doing. Then, with a shrug of her shoulders she reached into the icebox. The bracelets slid up and then back again.

'Don't they irritate you?'

She paused and looked at him, puzzled.

'The bangles.' He pointed at them.

She placed the unopened Tusker on the bar counter and slowly raised both arms. Her hands arched backwards, then flipped forwards and spun around, and the bracelets began to dance again. Their gentle silvery notes were now, it seemed to him, birdsong, perhaps that of a blackcap warbler newly arrived at its chosen summer habitat, its long migration over, and greeting the world with the sheer pleasure of achievement. She increased the tempo and the facets of silver and glass sparkled in whatever light they could catch. Walter watched, captivated, and began to clap. Immediately, as abruptly as she'd begun, she stopped, picked up the bottle and snapped it open. Her sari billowed as she made her way towards him.

'I liked that,' he said. 'And watching you I thought, I don't even know your name.'

'You don't need to know my name,' she said, and handed him the Tusker. Her voice was still raw from the after-effects of her outburst.

'But I'd like to.'

'I am Madame Rosa.'

'That's not your name.'

'It will do.'

She settled again on her stool and picked up her book.

'I don't want to call you Madame anything. Perhaps we could

trade – I tell you my name and you tell me yours. When I was a kid we called it swapsies; we could do swapsies.'

She ignored him. He pressed the cold bottle against his forehead. The harsh afternoon light that outlined her was softened by the nets at the window and as she read he remembered a painting he'd seen in some book, a woman in profile, grave, concentrated, calm. He watched her for some time, intrigued. He wanted her to look up, to look at him. He wanted to hear her voice as he'd first become aware of it, with its warm musicality and its scent-like notes of blossom, of winter jasmine and honeysuckle.

He began to pour his beer, stopping only when it lapped the top of the glass, then wiped the mouth of the Tusker bottle and drank the remainder from it, finishing in one long swig. The room's floor, he now saw, was no more than compacted mud disguised by two thin strips of carpet. He placed the bottle by the glass, and waited for her to look up.

She continued to ignore him.

'What are you reading?' he asked.

She turned the book over to inspect its spine.

'*The Solitary Summer.*'

'Is it good?'

'It's about gardening. I don't have a garden.' She placed a finger on the page in front of her as though concentrating on some important observation.

'Tell me more. About you, about your life.'

She turned another page.

'Please.'

At last she looked at him. 'Why should I?'

'There's no reason. Just that I'd like to know about you. I feel sure you have stories to tell of your life in India, in… Where was it?'

'Kohlapur.'

Her forehead was creased by frown lines but she was calmer now.

He spread his hands wide. *I'm an innocent*, the gesture said. *You can trust me.*

She studied him, then laid her book on the bar, slipped off her stool and came and sat by him on the bench. She took a hand in one of hers. 'Yes,' she said, 'you are curious. That is good – so many of you are not. We are not of interest any more than cockroaches are. We are a nuisance that must be borne.'

He barely heard her, his attention fixed on his hand clasped in hers, locked there it seemed to him by some external force, one too powerful to resist.

'What shall I tell you?' she said.

'How you came to Dar, perhaps?'

'If that interests you?'

'Very much.'

She settled herself further back into the cushions. 'I came to Dar-es-Salaam sixteen years ago. I was fifteen, a child, and I came with my husband.'

She paused and began to run the fingers of her free hand across the back of his trapped one.

'My husband, yes, he worked for the Germans when they were the masters. He was a tax gatherer, a rent collector. And when the Germans left the British found him useful, too. But he was a gambler, a good man in some ways, but a gambler. He died and I found I had nothing. A high-class lady from Kohlapur, become nothing in Dar-es-Salaam, nothing. Can you understand what that means, to be nothing, to have nothing? I could not go forward, I could not go back. What could I do?'

She released his hand. When she spoke again, the flower notes were replaced, not by the harsh rawness of the initial outburst but by an acidity, a bitterness.

'How can you understand this – you with your easy life. What could I do? To survive, that is all I wanted, to live, no more than that and I did what I had to do. I took on a trade, this trade. In my culture it is not always seen as dishonourable, it is recognised as practical. I tell myself there is no shame in it, in these couplings, anymore than there is for the pi-dogs in the street. I tell myself it is you poor Christians who think it shameful, or so you pretend. But you are the masters, and I am not in Kohlapur, I am in Dar-es-Salaam and if you say it is shameful then it is. That is how a high-class lady became an untouchable, a brothel-keeper. And here in this stupid town my culture has become your culture, and I have been spat at in the streets.'

She was about to say more but stopped as the door to the street pushed open and the sounds of day followed it inside, raucous and practical. The lame man stepped a pace into the room and leaned against the spring-loaded door. She glanced at him and then as if there existed some private signal between them, she stood up and pointed Walter to the open door.

'Go away now, shoo, shoo, you have no business here. I waste my time with you.'

She gathered up her sari and returned to her seat at the counter, again glancing at the lame man as she did so.

'Shoo, shoo,' she said again, and waved him away.

He didn't move. Her story both troubled and intrigued him. Spat at?

'Shoo, shoo.'

His glass was still half full. He sipped at it. 'I'll want another Tusker,' he said. 'When I finish this.'

She looked across at the man in the doorway a second time, almost as though for approval. He turned, impassive, and hobbled out, the door closing behind him.

He didn't want another Tusker. He wanted to stay with her.

He wanted his hand clasped between hers. He wanted the heat of her body next to him, wanted to inhale her scent, the sensuality of the harmonies lying beneath the pervasive sandalwood. He wanted to recapture the amused affection of their earlier exchanges.

She stood in front of him. 'Your beer, sahib.'

He took the bottle and put it on the brass-topped table by his side. 'Please don't call me that.'

'Why not? I say to you go and you refuse. Sahib's rights, is that not so?'

He could think of nothing sensible to say.

She leaned forward and placed a hand on his cheek.

'My shame,' she whispered, 'is your shame.'

He didn't care about shame, that ugly word. It had no place in what was happening to him, defeated by the simple contact of her hand. He closed his eyes and the sounds of the street faded, as did the voices from the back room. The objective world dissolved and with its disappearance his senses became focussed entirely on the woman, his actions running ahead of his thoughts. He reached up, took both her hands and tried to pull her down to him, to bring her into an embrace, to kiss her, but she shook herself free, gathered her sari about her and retreated towards the counter. He clambered to his feet to follow her, but stopped, aware of her simmering anger.

'Enough,' she said. 'This is stupidity.'

'I thought…' he began, but trailed off. He had no idea what he thought. His body wanted her but his sense of himself would not permit it.

She clapped her hands, a series of three firm and resonant smacks punctuating her speech. 'No, no, and no. No thinking, no explaining. You come here and drink beer and refuse my girls. You stay and stay and refuse to go. You think I want you here? I do not.'

He sank back onto the bench.

'And you are foolish too. In your world to come here for a girl, that is understood. To come here for chit-chat, and in the daytime, that will not be understood. They will say "He's gone native." And once that has been said, it is the end for you. I know about reputation. I have none.' She waved a hand as though brushing away an insect. The bracelets flashed and chinked together. 'Go, and don't come here any more.'

A quarrel had erupted in the street outside and he became aware of several male voices raised in anger. Other sounds returned too, a creaking trolley wheeling past, a distant hawker offering his bargains, a yelp from a chastised animal, the low murmur of busy lives.

In the back room the filigree lightness of the girls' voices was counterpointed by a bass rumble.

'Can I finish my beer?' he asked. 'Please?'

'Finish it and go.'

He took the bottle and the glass and started to pour but his hand shook and drips spattered his shorts. It struck him that he was obeying an order, and the irresponsibility was a relief.

'You are right,' he said. 'I told myself that I came here for a beer, but that was an excuse. I know now that I came to see you, to talk to you. I like talking to you, hearing you talk. There is no one in Dar-es-Salaam I would rather be with than you. To spend time with you, that's what I came for.'

She was no longer looking at him. In the silence she lowered her book and stood for a moment, irresolute.

'You want something I cannot give you,' she said, her voice so soft he had to strain to hear her. There was a further pause. 'Come.'

She held open the door to the back room. Another order! He took a last draught of Tusker, stood up and walked past her and into the inner space.

Two girls sat on a settee which groaned as they stood up. The Asian man he had seen earlier was sprawled across a second sofa, a third girl by his side. He recognised Emily but she appeared not to know him, or if she did was not prepared to react to his arrival. A plate of sweetmeats on a side table explained the crumbs of sugar adorning the man's moustache. The room repelled him. It was festooned with draped fabrics, swags of bunched and ruffled and concertina'd cotton and muslin. A brass chandelier with electric lights hung slightly off-centre, and a second icebox stood isolated and unadorned in a corner. An alarm clock on stumpy legs ticked violently. A window opened onto a courtyard with a flowering mimosa whose yellow flowerheads picked up the sunlight and played with it.

The door closed behind Walter. He spun round, but she had not abandoned him.

'You have seen Emily,' she said, 'and this is Margaret and Beatrice. They are very willing, very good at pleasing a man. Choose, enjoy, go.'

The girls bobbed. Their pretty, demure faces broke into smiles. They looked utterly charming. Walter turned and left the room. She followed him.

He turned on her, furious, trembling with violence. He slammed his hand on the bar.

'Why do you do this?' he shouted. 'I thought you understood the sort of man I am, but you don't, do you? You just want my money, is that it – you want cash? Here, here…'

He shoved a hand into his shorts pocket, seized a fistful of change and flung it at her. She didn't move. He raised a hand as if to strike her. She didn't flinch. Why was he so angry? He couldn't understand it, couldn't understand himself. He was never angry, always in control. But not it seemed in Dar. In Dar, in the Haven of Peace, here in this illicit building, he understood for the first time that the supposedly calm order imposed by the authorities had an uncertain foundation.

And then: *That's the way to do it!*

The voice reverberated in his skull. He recognised it immediately. As always, the same hideous image accompanied it: papier mâché varnished to a sweaty sheen, the face mottled with reds and creams, the clawed hands gripping their heavy club and urging the world to violence. And now, for the first time ever, the voice wasn't offering a general instruction but had a specific aim: *Now's the time to do it! Go on, show her who's boss!*

He could feel the urge to do as the voice told him, to demonstrate his superiority, to strike her. Mr Punch, the nightmare figure of his boyhood dreams, refusing to let go of him, insisting on his legitimate position in Walter's psyche, the horror-puppet he'd long thought buried, safely exorcised, now risen vampire-like from its tomb to claim a place in his waking life.

He'd first seen the traditional puppet show of Punch and Judy in its portable theatre on Bristol Downs the summer before the outbreak of the war with Germany. All the traditional scenes had been included, Mr Punch hammering the baby's head on the sill of the theatre, Mr Punch slamming his baton into Judy's belly, Mr Punch hanging the hangman, law and order powerless before his violent anarchy, his brutish mayhem triumphant, yelling his gleeful instructions to his audience: *That's the way to do it! That's the way to do it!*

This is me, Mr Punch tells the open-mouthed children, avid with fear and excitement, *and this is you, too. I'm your dirty secret. I'm the shit you produce daily. I'm part of you. I'm the violence that sits inside you. You can't deny me, I'm there, I'm always there. Just give me a chance and I'll show you what you're capable of. This is my lesson – this is the way the world wags.*

At the age of six he'd been terrified but fascinated too. He'd pleaded with his mother to take him home before it was over, only to ask the very next day to be taken back to the Downs to hear Mr Punch's lesson all over again.

Years had passed and Mr Punch had faded, drifting away from his memory, muted by the necessities of adult life, the practicalities of daily living, only now to return here, in Africa, summoned up from some deep corner of his consciousness and targeted at him. Why? Was Mr Punch now offering not a lesson but rather a warning? That violence was present in this sleepy seaport, this Haven of Peace, and he could be infected by it? Or already was? He shook his head and as he did so he knew that his anger had left him.

'Good, now you understand,' she said. 'This is what we do here. We do not do chit-chat. We do not sell beer. We sell ourselves. That is all we do. We do not offer more. Now go.'

She remained calm, still, statuesque. Her dignity was magnificent. He began to collect the coins, kneeling on the mud floor, searching for them where they'd rolled under a table, below the bench, into a soakaway.

'I'm sorry,' he mumbled into the mud, 'sorry, sorry.'

She watched him but said nothing until he paused and looked up at her. 'The girls here, they know what they are doing, and why. It is to make money to send to their families. They are sensible, coming to Dar. Who will know? Their families – yes, they know. No one else need to. Then they return home with money for a dowry, and life begins for them. And they are happy with the British: the British pay well. Except you – you are of no value to them. And of no use to me.'

He inclined his head. He couldn't meet her gaze. What had she said? *We sell ourselves?* The last coin, a five-cent piece, had lodged itself against the back wall. *We sell ourselves.* He reached for the coin and then, very slowly, stood up. 'Should cover the beer,' he said, piling the coins in a column on the counter, neatly, in the order of their value. He centred them carefully and then reached out to take her hand. She jerked it away, burying it behind her back.

'Go,' she said again.

But he had to know. 'You said we sell ourselves. We. Ourselves. What do you mean? That's a lie.' He was pleading with her to agree: *Yes, it's a lie*.

She shook her head. When she spoke it was with a matter-of-fact brutality. 'You think I do not do what my girls do? You are wrong. I am the same as them. There are men who admire me and pay for me. I take their cash.'

This was unthinkable. He shook his head. 'No.'

'But yes. It doesn't bother me, why should it bother you?'

'Because…'

He didn't know why, he just knew it did. An image of her, on her back, exposed, hovered at the back of his skull. *Of course she does, why be surprised? That is what she is. The rest is imagined, the rest is fantasy.*

'I have told you before. This is not a place for you, a raw young man like you. Don't come here again, unless you come to buy a girl. Or me. You can buy me but I am more expensive. Would you like to buy me?'

He pulled at the door handle and a shard of light pierced the room. The quarrel outside had run its course but even so the light brought with it a sense that this place, Dar, had revealed a truth about itself, that whatever else it was, Mr Punch also found himself at home there. He released the handle and the door swung shut. He stood with his back to her.

'Would you?'

It was a challenge. He understood with sudden clarity that to respond to it, honesty was required of him. Without honesty he would be allying himself with Mr Punch.

'Yes,' he said slowly, with deliberation. 'I would like to buy you. But not here, not in this place. This place contaminates you.'

'Not here? You want me but I must come to you? Where shall I meet you? Or shall we go somewhere together? Will you take my arm and walk with me through Dar-es-Salaam to the New Africa Hotel? Yes? No? Why not? Come!'

She moved slowly and deliberately to the door, picking up her sari as she did so and holding up her left arm for him to take. 'No?'

He stared at the dirt floor.

She snapped out of the pose and retreated to the bar. He looked up.

'You see?' she said. 'Shame. You know it. Touch me and my shame becomes your shame. Now go and stay away from me.' She waved a dismissive hand.

He had found the door handle again. 'Is there nowhere else? Some other place where we could meet?'

'Meet? No, we will not meet. Except here, in this place. This is the place where I work.'

She picked up her book and spoke without looking at him. 'There is no other place. Here is where I am, every afternoon, every evening. In the mornings I shop, and visit the temple. That is all I do, that is my life. Yes, it is a bad life, but it is a life.' She turned a page. 'To see me, you come here. To see me, next time, you pay. For chit-chat too, you pay.'

* * *

The still furious heat of the late afternoon hit him as he stepped out into the busy street. He didn't look back but started walking rapidly, with apparent purpose, until his military stride failed him and he stopped. He heard a familiar, harsh, unwanted screech but as always the bird itself remained invisible. A flock of pigeons lifted from the roof of a single-storey shack. The bird screeched again and now he heard it as an emissary of the horror-puppet, the screech a translation: *That's the way to do it!*

He needed diversion, needed to be rid of the vile homunculus and its urgings. *Work, that's the thing.* He had the keys to the office and there was yet another document he needed to get to grips with: Tariff Regulations for the Trans-shipment of Goods between Crown Colonies and the United Kingdom. McLeod was nagging him about it, asking questions, testing his knowledge. Work was the answer.

'Ultimate antidote.'

A boy tugged at his shorts and he realised he'd spoken aloud. *Going mad now.* The boy held out a hand but he had no change left. He ignored the child and walked on. He needed to kill her off, destroy all thoughts of her. He started to count how many paces it was to the office. Eight hundred was his estimate but having counted out two hundred he realised it would be many more. He started a fresh count but soon lost control of it. Thoughts of the woman possessed him. He'd got carried away, he told himself, he'd been hypnotised by her. He recalled the conjuror he'd seen perform at the Prince's Theatre, who'd borrowed Reg's silver watch, smashed it in a handkerchief, and then pulled the watch, intact, out of Reg's jacket pocket. Marvellous. How did he do that? The bracelets slid down the woman's arms, down the warm dark lemon-olive smoothness of her arms.

Stop this, he wanted to shout, *stop this stupidity. I'm going to marry Winnie. She'll say yes, of course she will. She loves me, I'm sure she does, and I love her, don't I? We love each other. We'll have a great future together, here in Dar. Yes, we will. We will.*

He stepped up his walking speed and as he marched he began to count his paces again. This time the silent metronomic chant worked. *Ninety-two ninety-four ninety-six ninety-eight one hundred!* He wouldn't see her again.

Once in the office he took down the relevant file and settled at his desk. Tanganyika was not strictly speaking a Crown Colony, and the document would have to be adapted to fit the Territory's peculiar mandate from the League of Nations. He turned a page but the writing blurred. He buried his head in his hands.

Oh God, he pleaded, *help me. I need a woman in my life. Please, God; please, Mother Mary – intercede for me. Get Winnie to say yes.*

CHAPTER 10

The same small boy was ushered into his office by Miss Fernandes. Walter placed the envelope carefully on his desk alongside his current paperwork and handed the boy the smallest coin he could find. *Teach him not to expect a shilling every time.* The lad left, but Miss Fernandes hovered. Walter ignored her and after a few seconds she took the hint. He settled back in his carver, took out an ivory-handled paperknife and with care and concentration slit the envelope open. The letter was two pages long, written in blue-black ink on pale blue paper.

Tuesday 1st June 1932

Darling Walter,
I'm going to surprise you, but then you know me so perhaps you won't be surprised after all. The answer to your question is – and I've tried to write this several times, it's sooo difficult

– is maybe. Oh, now you're sad! But I have a suggestion, so keep reading. I said no to my other suitor, by the way. That was easy. Did you think it was a new lover? Well, it wasn't. I just wanted to tease you with the thought. It was my boss – the Toad we call him. His wife died last year and he thought I'd do as a replacement. I had to be ever so grateful and flattered and eyelash-fluttering, but then said I was saving myself! For perfect love! Actually, I think he was quite relieved. It was one of those mad moments that even toads are given to. So that was that, and now he's very nice to me, thanks to me turning him down.

So then there's lovely Walter to think about. And I'm oh so unsure, and oh so tempted. Mind you, if you'd asked me properly in Bristol, and I didn't know about your going to Africa, I'd have said no. I wouldn't have wanted to be the wife of a bloke who works in the Customs at Avonmouth Docks. Boring! Sorry, my dear, but as you know, Winnie wants more.

Africa, though – Africa makes things different. I like the thought of Africa. It changes things. But has it changed you? You can be a little stuffy, you know. Not always, of course. I've seen you larking about with Reg. He's missing you, poor lamb: no one to booze with in the Prince Consort. But you need to lark about a bit more with me. We've had some laughs, so you can do it. And I know you're a good man and would be a good husband, so all you have to do is relax more, have fun.

I won't go on. Which maybe means: while I'm here and you're there, the answer has to be 'no'. But if I was there with you, it could be different. You say now that you love me and I wonder, do you love me enough to send for me? Could you afford it? So that I could come out to this strange place you're in, no strings attached, and see how things are with us? And then, maybe. It's a bit of a cheek, I know, cos I might say no after all. But my dear lovely Walter, if I don't come that no is definite.

I'm not very happy with this suggestion, but there you are, darling boy, it's the best I can do. Shilly-shallying isn't really me, is it?

Lots of kisses,
Winnie

Walter read the letter twice, the first time no more than a quick scan to collect the basic message, the essential maybe. Shilly-shallying! Yes, untypical of her, but the door remained open. What's more, there was an honesty to the letter, and it reinforced his willed conviction that Winnie was the woman for him. He need have no qualms about marrying her. She was the woman for him, the only woman.

Miss Fernandes knocked.

'Yes!' he shouted and beamed at her as she came in. A few minutes of dictation followed, and then he sent her back to the typing pool to spread the news: *Mr Barnes was smiling. We know what that must mean.*

He read the letter a third time, with practicalities in mind. Could he afford to pay for her passage out of his salary? Not a chance in hell.

He rolled the problem around in his mind. Unless. Unless what? Unless he could raise a loan. But who from? There was only McLeod. Might he not? For a girlfriend, no, but for a fiancée? Wouldn't it reinforce the notion of the conventional Walter? At work during the last few days he'd set out to bolster the image of himself as a thoroughly reliable public official, had diligently followed all instructions, made suggestions and been rewarded by a thaw in McLeod's attitude towards him, even by the occasional guarded word of praise. Marriage would complete the picture and there'd be reinforcement from Meg, who'd no doubt go into romantic raptures.

Winnie though, Winnie would have to acknowledge that they were engaged. There'd need to be a ring and she'd have to wear it. He got up from his desk and began to pace about the small office. If it all went wrong and she returned to Bristol, he could easily explain away the failure: Africa wasn't for her, etc., etc.

He joined McLeod for a sandwich lunch and afterwards, as they sat with cups of tea in McLeod's office, he broached the idea of a loan by first asking for advice. His boss reacted instantly, making it clear that much though he sympathised with Walter's desire to be with his fiancée, he himself was not in the money-lending business and Walter shouldn't pin any hopes on him as a source of cash, however favourable the interest. A bank loan was the only option but surety would be required. Banks didn't just give money away. The best McLeod could do was to write a letter to the manager assuring him that Walter was a diligent and trusted civil servant on a three-year tour of duty, who would be able to repay the loan over a twelve-month period. That might do the trick.

'I doubt they'll give you longer than a year,' he added. 'And you'll be left short. You won't be able to splash out on the girl. Where's she going to stay?'

'I hadn't thought. I've only just got her letter.'

McLeod softened. 'I'll speak to Meg. She likes you. We could probably put her up for a little.'

'That would be very kind of you, Johnny.'

'Depends on the mem, mark you. Is a marriage out here the idea?'

'I hope so.'

'Meg will like that. Very correct when it comes to that sort of thing.'

'I'm sure.'

'Church job, I imagine, you being R.C.'

'Definitely.'

'You'll need someone to give her away. And who knows, you might be able to twist my arm.'

'What a great idea.'

'Tell you what, let's have a snifter.' McLeod produced a key from the rear pocket of his khaki drill shorts. It was attached to a chain hooked onto his belt. He unlocked a filing cabinet and from under a pile of yellowing official papers produced a bottle of malt whisky.

'Never say bumf isn't useful,' he said. 'Nobody ever looks any further.' He poured a generous slug into their teacups. 'Bottoms up.'

It was all getting out of control. Walter needed to apply the brakes. 'She wants to see the place first though.'

'Sensible girl.'

'Could be she doesn't care for Africa, the climate, whatever.'

'Of course, always possible.'

'I mustn't presume.'

'No, no. Drink up. There's time for another.'

Walter held out his teacup. 'If we were to marry, though…'

'Yes?'

'We'd get accommodation?'

'Yes, but depends what's available. Don't count on Oyster Bay – could be in town. Admin has houses in Speke Street.'

'A house, though?'

'I should think so.'

They sat in silence, trying to ignore the hubbub of the docks. Life was good, Walter told himself, and would be better.

'You're with Barclay's?'

'Yes.'

'I know the manager, Henry Horton. We've had dinner a couple of times. Bit of an old stick, but solid, reliable. I'll give you a note to take round.'

'Thank you.'

The noise outside was increasing. McLeod stood up and crossed from his desk to the window. His office was large and he kept the slats of the Venetian blinds open just enough to admit light but prevent the curious from looking in. It was on the first floor, and it was possible to see straight into it from the derricks on the lighterage quay some fifty yards away. Now he widened a gap in the slats with his fingers and peered out at the harbour view.

'Gawd,' he said. 'What's all this?'

He beckoned Walter over. The activity on the quay appeared as disorganised as ever. Men ran, men shuffled, men congregated, men squatted, men heaved sacks, men wheeled trolleys, men loafed, men marched. This apparent chaos was usually quite purposeful, although its underlying shape was often hard to locate. A new element had been added, however. A truck lay on its side, skewed sideways across the roadway to the quay, blocking it. A second truck waited to get past, the driver leaning against the door to the cab. From time to time he reached into the cab to give a toot on the horn. No one responded. The large crowd offered vocal advice, but there appeared to be no practical measures in hand.

'What a shower,' McLeod said. 'Hopeless, aren't they? What goes on in their heads? We'll never know. Does anything at all? Our fault, the reds say. We should do more, educate, build up a local bureaucracy. But would it work? 'Course not, unless we're prepared to wait a few hundred years.'

They squinted through the narrow opening.

'I'd better go and sort it,' McLeod said and let the slats snap back into place. He ran a hand over his smooth bald pate and sat down again. 'Utterly feckless, utterly feckless. Maybe the Bible's got it right for once – hewers of wood and drawers of water. If so, round pegs in round holes, recipe for happiness, so leave 'em be. Eh? What say you?'

'That's the policy, I believe,' Walter said.

'Cautious bugger, aren't you?'

'My dad was a soldier, a sergeant. He used to say if it's officers business, stay well clear.'

'Sound advice.'

McLeod yawned. 'You'd better get out there, go on. Sort it if it's sortable. Can you imagine that crowd in this office, eh? Have they any idea what we do? Marks on paper, that's all it is to them. So we import the boorjoisie, mail order care of British Consul Goa – there's a crowd won't ever cause trouble. Just want to make their cash and sod off home: ideal solution.'

McLeod rubbed his hands.

'Tell you what, we'll leave them to it. See how long it takes. What say we have another, yes?'

Tuesday 21st June 1932

Dear Winnie

I'd love it if you came to Dar-es-Salaam. I think you'll see what a wonderful life we could have together here. There'll be a house most probably and servants to do all the housework, cooking, laundry, etc. You'll be the most popular girl in town, I promise you. I'll have to take out a loan to pay for your Union-Castle ticket, and here's the tricky bit. My boss is prepared to stand surety with the bank, but he's presumed that you are properly my fiancée and that we will be getting married sometime. We'd have to get you an engagement ring. You'd have to say that we're getting married. How do you feel about that? If it doesn't work for you, we can just say that Africa didn't appeal to you or some such.

I'm so excited, I can hardly believe it. You must come, Winnie. I love you and we will be so happy together, I know it.

All my love,
Your own Walter

Agreed. Stop. Arrange ticket soonest. Stop. Darling Walter. Stop. Love Winnie. Stop.

Ticket sent. Stop. Can't wait to see you. Stop. Love Walter. Stop.

Ticket arrived. Stop. Packing. Stop. What a lark. Stop. Love Winnie. Stop.

He arranged Winnie's passage through the Smith, Mackenzie shipping agency. She'd travel on the *Llanstephan Castle* and it would be four weeks before she arrived. The Imperial Airways passenger service was operating but he couldn't possibly afford it. *Four weeks will pass quickly enough*, he told himself. *Four weeks and I can start getting my life back into balance. I'll bury myself in work and avoid Stanley Street.*

He opened his wallet, took out the snapshot of her leaning against the wall of the Prince Consort pub and took it to Choitram's to find a frame for it. Choitram, if the paunchy Asian who sat at the end of the counter guarding the cash register was indeed Choitram, had cornered the market in Dar for the off-beat. Other stores specialised, but Choitram's was the place to go for the less usual request. It had a limited range of goods on show, but a warehouse apparently chock-a-block full of other items was somewhere at the back, out of sight. Assistants would discuss a request with the customer, and then disappear for several minutes before returning with what they would insist was the one and only possible object.

Walter was privileged. No fewer than three frames were presented to him and he selected a plain ebony one. The photo didn't quite fit, and he had to wait while the assistant disappeared with both photo and frame to prepare an inset mount.

He handed it to Walter, who examined the result carefully, holding the newly framed snap as though it were a fragile jewel or perhaps a grenade, and not for the first time Winnie's smile struck him as having an edge of calculation to it. He studied the wide eyes, remembered their flecked hazel depths and as he did so, he knew he ought to reject the thought. It was unworthy: Winnie was anything but sly. The thought was his alone.

But still, it was irritating that she hadn't written, hadn't expressed a view on the tricky business of the engagement. And what did she mean by *what a lark*? Marriage was a serious matter.

He put the picture on his desk so that it could be inspected. Catarina led the way with chirruping cries of admiration and a request that the rest of the general office be allowed the privilege of viewing Walter's fiancée. Nevertheless he was aware that following the news of his engagement her attitude towards him had cooled.

CHAPTER 11

The mess had been invaded by cockroaches. They'd found safe havens in the splits and cracks of the poorly applied plaster where walls met floor. He woke in the small hours and, seeing several scuttling across the floor, pushed aside his netting and spent a futile ten minutes attempting to stamp them out. In the morning light he realised his folly: mosquitoes had seized their chance and attacked, showing particular interest in his forearms. He slapped on calamine lotion which had some effect but the bites continued to irritate throughout the morning.

There was paperwork to be done. He prepared a batch of letters to shipping agents alerting them to a recent duty change affecting the import of motorcycles and gave it to a sour-faced Catarina to distribute to the typing pool. There was a backlog of other letters, she told him, and these ones wouldn't be ready for signature until the following morning. He expressed an entirely spurious concern, which seemed to satisfy her. He then finished the last paragraphs of his work on the Interim Report and handed them to his boss for approval. McLeod hadn't completed his section. The tricky area of mineral exploitation had proved even more awkward than anticipated. The Kenyans, for example, saw no reason to share their profits from the export of soda but at the same time felt that their senior position entitled them to claim a share of export duties relating to potential, if as yet undiscovered, Tanganyikan mineral deposits. There was money to be made in minerals.

'There'll be one humdinger of a row,' McLeod said. 'I'm going to have to fudge. Our masters can take the hatchets to one another, and in the meantime I'll slip round the corner for a nap.'

Idleness allowed the bites to return to their full virulence. He applied more calamine, which decorated his arms with white patches as it dried. But the itch remained and diversion was needed. He could always justify getting out of the office. His title, Inspector-in-Charge, pointed up the policing element in his role; he could imagine himself a bobby on the beat. And now he had a bike.

He'd been back to Choitram's and bought the only model they had on offer. Black, sit-up-and-beg, no style at all. Reg would laugh. It didn't even have a three-speed gear and was altogether middle-aged. He'd become sensitised to questions of status and worried that the bike robbed him of dignity, creating a figure of fun rather than one of authority. At least it made getting around easier. He'd made several journeys into the countryside and found that these small expeditions helped to divert him from thoughts of Winnie, from his examination and re-examination of the pluses and minuses of his potential future with her. He couldn't deny it – there would be times when he'd find himself on edge with her, looking out for the traps she set, for her sudden, unexpected bursts of scathing sarcasm, her summary dismissal of some casual remark he'd made.

He rode south towards the repairs dock and the physicality of the act soothed the itching. But the journey lacked point, lacked a destination, and this absence of a reason irritated him. He rode slowly, looking for something to catch his attention and eventually stopped at the open-air carpenters' workshop. A grizzled chippy crouched on a raised platform alongside a beached dhow. It had been stripped of its starboard timbers and reduced to a whale's skeleton: the victim, Walter presumed, of either accident or age.

'*Bwana*?' the carpenter asked.

Walter waved, the gesture led by the back of his hand, the universal instruction to carry on. The carpenter returned to his task, running his fingers along the edge of the plank he was working on, a craftsman sensing the wood's potential, and then taking up his plane. His devotion to his craft was almost religious in its intensity and as he watched Walter realised that there was after all a place to visit, a curiosity to be satisfied. He swung the bike round to head west, and began a circular journey around the outskirts of the town as far as Bagamoyo Street. From there he cut inland towards the Kariakoo market and the Asian Zone, where he had to force his way through the narrow and crowded streets of the bazaar, ringing his bell constantly, uncertain of exactly where he was but trusting to luck. And then there it was, unmistakable, signalling its presence with a violent clash of colours, yellows and greens and reds, even more exotic than he'd imagined. He dismounted, looked for something to prop the bike against but then decided that holding on to it was the wiser option, and stepped back to contemplate the building.

Chaos! She'd accused him of being rational and faced with this architectural madness he had to agree. He felt that a temple should be a place of harmony, peace, restraint. This building was fun in its way but he found it infantile. The many-armed goddess dancing in rainbow colours over its entrance was typical of the overwrought statuary that adorned the place. It was all quite laughable, an absurdity. *Well, well*, he thought, *that's a mild curiosity satisfied and a mission accomplished.* The temple was interesting in its own way but he felt no need to linger. It wasn't as though he were looking for her, he assured himself.

He remounted and cycled off, weaving through the thronged streets.

And then, several wrong turnings later, it happened.

In Bristol punctures were easy to repair. Even the cobbled streets that occupied the more derelict parts of the city caused few problems. But this wasn't a puncture, this was a gash, acquired thanks to a thin strip of metal he'd ridden over. It had reared up as he hit it, and its razor-sharp edge had bitten through the tyre and into the inner tube. He'd bought the bike without bothering to inspect the small box containing the John Bull puncture repair outfit that came with it, and examining it now it was obvious that it wasn't up to the task. It contained a lever tool for stripping the inner tube out of its casing, a dozen small oval and round patches, a thin rubber binding strip, a tube of adhesive and a piece of white school chalk. It might have dealt with a small hole left by a nail but Walter was faced with a two-inch tear. The box was useless.

He up-ended the bike to inspect the damage more closely, carefully balancing it on its saddle and handlebars. It waved its wheels in the air, a giant bug pleading for mercy. The inner tube hung down, flaccid, a surrendered captive. He could remove it, but why bother? What would he do then?

He inspected his surroundings more closely. He was in an area where stalls had given way to shabby concrete bungalows with tin roofs. A few had scrawny plots, but little grew in them. A net curtain twitched in a nearby window and was then pushed upwards, briefly framing an elderly Asian woman with wire-rimmed spectacles. Walter gave her a defiant stare and the curtain fell back into place.

He returned to his contemplation of the repair outfit.

Bloody Dar. Bloody, bloody Dar.

He gave in to his anger and began to tear at the gash in the inner tube, attempting to rip it wider. The pink rubber snake resisted, stretching but not tearing. He gave up and instead kicked the bike. It fell over. He stood over it, trying to come to some sort of sensible decision. Instead, a lethargy overtook him. He was a small sea-based organism clamped to a rock, waiting for sustenance to drift by and offer itself to him.

The elderly Asian had moved to her doorway for a better view of the entertainment. Her interest was shared by three native youths who'd wandered along from the direction of the bazaar. They stopped some ten yards distant and he felt a prickle of alarm. *Wahuni*, perhaps, notorious boosters of the petty crime statistics, opportunists, robbers. It was time to go. Walter hoisted the bicycle to its upright position, lifted the failed front wheel and, his back straight, his left hand casually empty, his right hand gripping the pivot point of the handlebars, he headed towards what he hoped would be a part of the town he recognised.

'*Bwana*,' said a voice behind him. Walter glanced back. One of the trio, hardly more than a boy, smiled broadly at him. His eyebrows lifted inquiringly and he pushed out a hand, palm upwards.

'*Bwana, nikusaidie?*'

From its intonation it was evidently a question. Walter didn't reply but kept on walking. He could hear the boy's footsteps behind him, the bare feet slapping on the mud roadway. He drew level with Walter, seized hold of the saddle and began to tug the bike away from him. His two companions watched. Walter resisted.

'*Nikusaidie?*' the youth repeated and then shifted his position to get a grip on the upright bar the saddle sat on. Thin though he was, he had surprising strength. Walter gripped the handlebars with both hands. His jaw set. The sheer brazen nerve of it! The urge to action was uncontrollable. He pulled hard on the handlebars and then, as he felt the strength of the young man's opposing power, reversed direction and pushed instead. The bike jerked forwards and slammed into the young man's belly. The boy grunted, released the saddle and fell backwards.

Walter's right hand abandoned its hold on the handlebars and curled itself into a fist. The victory was too easy, over too soon. Unsatisfied adrenalin surged through him. More was needed, one sharp punch to the jaw to complete the action.

That's the way to do it!

But the youth lay still, his hands extended in submission and the gesture could not be ignored. Walter scowled, dissatisfied. The simple pleasure of violence had been indulged in, and much though he wanted to, to take it further was beneath his dignity. The young man lurched to his feet and, bent over and clutching his belly, made off through a grove of stunted bananas, flanked by his two companions.

Mr Punch's recipe had succeeded but the nature of his victory worried Walter. He needed to devote more time to his efforts to learn Swahili. Was it just possible that the youth was trying to help? Whether disinterestedly or in hope of a tip, did it matter? Even the maligned *wahuni* – if that was what they were – might do an honest job in return for a shilling or two. The elderly Asian woman had watched the incident without showing signs of alarm. Well, whatever it was, a threat or an offer of help, it was over. And he couldn't prevent a small twitch of satisfaction tugging at the corner of his mouth. Pity, mind you. One clean blow, he'd have liked that, would have liked to test his power.

He adjusted his grip on the bike and moved off, not hurrying, trying to appear in control but cursing the awkwardness of the machine as it swivelled in his grip. The dual pose required concentration and he almost didn't see her standing by a fruit stall that offered plantains and discoloured mangos. She raised her hand and pushed her scarf back off her forehead and it was this small action that made him glance sideways. *Ignore her*, his inner voice counselled. *Walk straight on. She has no part in your life.* But he didn't. He stopped a few yards away, uncertain, not looking at her, waiting for her to say something, to take the initiative.

She assessed him, assessed the bike.

'Come,' she said. It was both invitation and command. 'But walk behind me.'

She walked away from him, rearranging her headscarf, not looking back. He hesitated, aware of the potential significance of the moment. To follow her was both bold and cowardly. To ignore her was no different. He had no reason to choose either option. She walked away down the dusty street. *I should let her go, that's what I should do.* And as that thought arrived he knew he couldn't.

He trailed after her. They passed the site of the fracas. Walter imagined the net curtain twitching, all the net curtains twitching, observers everywhere watching his passage as he followed the woman. He was far enough back for them not to appear connected, wasn't he? Did it matter? White man trails brothel-keeper. Why? The bike twisted in his grip and crashed to the roadway. He picked it up, resigned to its awkwardness. Where were they going? He should turn around. Beads of sweat coalesced under his shirt.

She approached a row of cheap, shoddily built bungalows, pushed open an unpainted plywood door and disappeared inside. Walter paused, reluctant to go further. He looked back in the direction they'd come and turned the bike round. He was leaving and he meant it, but had taken no more than three steps when the door opened again and the man with the gammy leg emerged, the woman behind him, issuing instructions in what he now recognised as Hindi. There was an aggression in her. She propelled the man forward with a push in the back. He limped across to Walter and, crouching as best he could given the iron frame clamped to his leg, produced a tape measure.

'Come,' the woman said again to Walter. 'Leave him. He knows what to do.'

The man had begun to measure the diameter of the bike wheels. The woman pointed Walter towards the bungalow but he didn't move. She went inside. He still hesitated, aware of his visibility to any passer-by. She appeared in the open doorway and waited, calm, unmoving. She offered no invitation more than the open door. The street seemed empty enough. He stepped forward.

The room was small, crammed with her possessions. A treadle-operated sewing machine dominated the only table. A low couch in one corner was freighted with swags of material and more swathes of cloth were draped over the back of a collapsing armchair. Heavier cloths hung from the walls, cloths with complicated patterns, the glitter of small inset mirrors alleviating the dominance of the designs. There was a curtained alcove to his right beside which was a full-length mirror, its silvering decayed, propped at an angle. He caught a glimpse of himself and hastily looked away.

'That man,' he asked, 'who is he?'

'He does things for me. He is of no consequence. He will repair your machine.'

'It can't be repaired. It needs a new inner tube.'

'Then he will get one. Sit, please.'

There was only one free chair, a metal upright. Walter perched on it, determined not to relax, determined to stay on guard.

She smiled for the first time. 'You choose to be uncomfortable.

It's your way of telling me things. Good. There are times and places where men should be uncomfortable. Perhaps this is such a time and place.'

Walter stood. 'You want me to leave?'

'And if you left where would you go?' she said. 'Your machine is broken. I will make tea while we wait for him to mend it. Sit here.'

She hauled a swag of material up onto the table. An armchair was revealed, button-backed in gold plush, its wings broken and trailing.

'Not much better, but a little. Sit.'

Her territory, mustn't relax. He stayed standing.

She contemplated him and watched his hands as, driven by uncertainty, they twined and intertwined. Then she pushed aside a cloth in the back wall to reveal a door.

'Very well. If you will not, you will not,' she said, and left him. He went to the front door and opened it. His bike stood upended and propped against the unpainted concrete wall. There was no sign of the cripple. He stepped out into the vicious heat and was about to take hold of a wheel when he heard a car horn give three blasts. He looked up and saw the vehicle in the distance, fighting its way through the mass of pedestrian traffic. The horn sounded again, a sonorous boom indicating an impressive vehicle. Whoever the driver was, he was a high-ranker. And a white man in a neatly pressed colonial uniform seen stepping out of a dirty bungalow in the Asian Zone would undoubtedly lead to questions. He ducked back inside and went through to the second room.

She had turned on a small cooking ring, one of two powered by gas from a metal cylinder located beneath it. A tin kettle perched awkwardly on the ring. A mesh-fronted food cupboard stood by the cooker. A narrow divan claimed space alongside a wall. There was no sink, and the room was otherwise bare. The back door was propped open and he could see a small patch of well-tended vegetables with, at the far end, a wooden shack. A privy, Walter presumed. She was outside, rinsing a couple of mugs in the stream of water from a standing tap.

'You see, I am a wealthy woman,' she said, shaking the mugs. 'I have running water.'

He'd never wondered how she lived, how any of these people lived, had never before imagined the reality of poverty.

'I thought the natives lived like this, but not...' He couldn't find a way to end the sentence.

'Oh no, there are plenty of poor Asians. And careful ones too, the savers, as well as the ones like me who would not be welcome elsewhere. But you mean, it's all right for the blacks?'

'Perhaps they don't expect much more.'

'If you think so. After all, what have they done to deserve running water? They are only blacks, isn't that so?'

She pushed past him into the back room and set about making the tea. He watched, awkward. Sensing this, she pointed towards the front room. 'Go, wait.'

He did as he was told. Ignoring the button-back he perched again on the metal chair. An elderly alarm clock, a sibling of the one in the Taj, hung from a hook by the one small window. Like its drunken brother it made its presence known by an aggressive and erratic ticking. The low couch in the corner must be, he realised, her bed. And the curtained alcove presumably hid clothes. Lalun's rooms would not have been like this. Had Kipling imagined them; had he romanticised them, perhaps romanticised Lalun herself? No, Kipling told it straight. Kipling could be trusted. Dar was not India.

'Do you try to save then?' he asked, as the woman came through with the mugs and a teapot on a metal tray. She set this on the floor and took up position in the armchair.

'In two, three years I will return to India. I will go to a town where I am not known and I will open a fabric and fashion shop. But I need to be sure of my capital.'

'That's admirable.'

'It is practical. So. Welcome to my home. Were you looking for me?'

'No, no, you'd mentioned the temple. I had some free time, so…'

She examined him, a headmistress contemplating an errant child and its feeble excuse.

'Of course,' she said. 'The temple. And what did you think of it?'

'It's very different. Those strange gods – the one with an elephant's head and that woman with the arms everywhere.'

'You find them ridiculous, yes?'

'No, no.'

'But they are. To a white man they are ridiculous. And crude – the whole temple is so crude. Admit it: that is what you think.'

'No, no, it's different, rather.'

'It is crude. But also it is proud of itself. Isn't that good?'

'Very good. I'm glad I saw it.'

'Such a polite man,' she said. 'So English. You are all so polite.'

There it was again, the bitter edge to her voice. He didn't want to talk about the temple.

'But then I had the puncture.'

She studied him. Her gaze probed the way he was dressed, the ever-present sweat stains, the already darkening jowl, the rich wiry hair. Then she looked away and as she did so she spoke as if to herself, so softly that Walter strained to hear her.

'What do you want with me?'

He wasn't sure enough of what she'd said to be able to reply. They sat in silence for perhaps a minute. He wasn't sure of anything, he realised.

'I want to know your name,' he said at last.

'I told you. Rosa. You need not believe me, but it is true, for now, in Dar-es-Salaam. In this place, it is true.'

'"What is truth?" said jesting Pilate…' He could hear Dad's voice, that rolling Wiltshire burr. It was a legacy he was proud of. How did the quote go on – '…and would not stay for an answer.' There were, he knew, big truths and little truths, and the little ones could matter just as much as the big ones.

He tested the name to see if it rang right. 'Rosa.'

As he spoke he extended the vowels and the name grew. It abandoned its mock-Englishness and mutated, becoming a tea rose, heavy with sandalwood, and then elongating itself once more, enveloping him in the clotted embrace of a rambler.

'Rosa,' he said again. 'I'm Walter.'

She reached for a tin spoon and stirred the tea.

'Walter. Shall I be mother, Walter? Isn't that what I should say? The nuns all said that, I thought it so sweet. So, Walter, shall I be mother!' She poured the tea, a creamy brown mixture, and handed him the mug. 'Chai, Indian-style. Very sweet, with condensed milk. I warn you, it is discourteous to reject hospitality. You must tell me you like it. There is no other option.'

Walter drank, and his teeth reacted to the sweetness of the liquid. He shook his head and looked for somewhere to put down the mug. She nudged the tray towards him.

'It's good,' he lied, placing the mug beside the pot. She laughed and he was once more conscious of her bracelets as they shook and chimed against each other.

'Thank you,' she said, 'you need say no more. That will be sufficient.'

His mother disapproved of jewellery, often remarking on other women's earrings or necklaces. 'Unnecessary,' she said. 'No, worse, signs of vanity.' Beauty was natural or it was nothing. Now, on this woman, he saw the bracelets as something more than simple decoration. They proclaimed her, asserted her, spoke of inner music.

'We have plenty of time.' She spoke gently, aware of his uncertainty. 'He is quite good with his hands, but not very good. It will take him time to do the repair and he will knock when it is done.'

She sipped her tea. As she raised the mug to her lips the bracelets slid down her arms.

'You've been careless,' she said.

She saw his puzzlement. 'The bites.'

Traces of calamine, blotches of dry white powder, still clung to his arms.

'Did your mother not teach you to look after yourself?'

He brushed the powder off. No, not after Dad died and she became free to lay her expectations on him. 'My mother and I didn't get on. She wanted me to become a priest – can you imagine that, taking a vow of celibacy? She's very devout and I'm her eldest son and there's not quite a tradition but a sort of anticipation in some Catholic families that the eldest son will take holy orders. I might have except for the celibacy, but no, never to make love, no, quite impossible. So I refused and from then on…' He shrugged. 'Rows, rows, rows.'

She shook her head.

'Celibacy. And you think our gods are strange?'

He sipped the tea, struggling with its richness. He was aware of her closeness, of her seductive ability to combine the maternal and the sensual. Winnie was sensual but hardly maternal. If by some miracle she could learn from Rosa then loving her would be no problem.

'My girl's coming,' he blurted out. 'The girl I'm going to marry. She'll be here a few days from now.'

Her eyebrows lifted in mocking surprise. 'That is very good. I'd like to meet her. Will you arrange it?'

He laughed and drank a little more of the chai but it was already cooling and he didn't finish it.

The itches were still active and he began to scratch at an arm. She put out a hand to restrain him. 'No,' she said. 'You will harm yourself.'

She stood and went into the back room, returning with a half-full bottle of calamine lotion.

'Here,' she said, pointing at the armchair. He did as he was told, settling himself into it and then pulling up the sleeves of his shirt. She picked a scrap of printed cloth from beside the sewing machine and used it to apply the lotion, dabbing at his skin while he sat mute. He watched her hands as they worked, efficient and thorough. She wore no rings, but the bracelets seemed to him a better choice, more alive, their colour shifting as they spun and slid over her wrists. Her forehead puckered as she concentrated.

'You seem different here,' he said.

'Different? How?'

He had to think. 'Lighter, easier, and I sense…'

'What do you sense?'

'That in that other place you are… presenting yourself, a façade for the world, a mask. I don't sense that here.'

'That is possible. In that other place I am working: I have to maintain a tone, I have to look responsible. I cannot seem weak: people take advantage. That was one thing the orphanage taught me.'

'Orphanage?' he asked, puzzled.

'It was a hard place.'

'What orphanage?'

'Did I not tell you? Yes, my mother died when I was seven and I had no father. A typical slum kid. A neighbour, Auntie Lal, took me to the nuns and persuaded them to take me.'

'I thought you were, I thought you said, a high-class lady?'

She laughed. 'Oh, I say that sometimes. It is more dramatic, do you see? More dramatic than being another slum orphan – that is so commonplace, so dull, don't you think? It is a good story to tell my Asian customers. It matters to them.'

'They don't realise it's a lie?'

'Why should they? It doesn't matter. Everyone tells lies.'

'I don't.'

'No? You are a very special person then.'

'At least I try not to.' He thought for a moment. He'd always understood that lies had a sting to them and although he recognised her vulnerability he couldn't understand her need to fabricate stories about herself. But then what did he know about the effects of orphanage life? Would such places not generate fantasies? 'You remember your mother, though?'

'Very little.'

'That surprises me. If you were seven…'

'Or maybe six, or even five. I never knew my birth date. The nuns gave me one – they said it was as good as the real thing. So you see, nuns tell lies, too.'

'But still, I'd have thought, six or five, you'd remember quite well.'

'Perhaps I don't want to remember. Perhaps what I do remember are the beatings and the work and the bare feet and the stench of life in the gutter. Things to forget.'

'Do you mean that?'

'Oh yes, this is not a story. This is how it was. My mother didn't want me. I was a burden to her, a useless weight. So when she died and Auntie Lal took me to the orphanage, *oh! oh! oh!* Just imagine, a bed of my own, a clean bed, and food not from time to time but every day – every day! I thought I was in paradise.'

'But you left the orphanage?'

'I was told *Go, go, go and marry*. I was fourteen and I had to marry. Fourteen! And he was an old man, fifty-three. I was told I was lucky – I could have been married much younger, even before my monthlies began. I was asked for many times but Mother Louis always refused, so she told me. "Lucky girl," she said, "you will always be a lucky girl." So she married me off to a gambler. He was not a bad man, but he had a madness in him and he ruined himself and left me here, a whore in Dar-es-Salaam. Isn't that lucky?'

The melody of her voice had flattened out into a near monotone.

'Don't use that word.'

'Why not? It is the truth. I am a whore.'

'It's not the truth. You are more than that, so much more. I knew when I first saw you, I knew that you were, I knew…'

He fought for the words but they would not come. She pressed a finger to his lips, then took it away and returned to her task, pushing a sleeve up towards a shoulder in order to reach a particularly virulent patch of bites. As she did so their eyes met. He reached across with his free hand and covered hers. She looked away, back towards the door, and he thought of the street outside and the man crouched by the bike and their irrelevance.

When she looked back she did not meet his eyes but instead slid her hand down his arm, took the bottle of lotion and upended it to drain the last drops of calamine before concentrating once more on the final patch of inflamed skin. Finished, she screwed the cap back onto the bottle and put it on the table.

She still didn't look at him. 'Yes,' she said.

Then she did look at him, took his head in her hands and kissed him on the lips. The kiss was sensual, demanding. Their tongues met and explored each other, and then it became inevitable or so it seemed to him. He reached out for her and she responded, slipping underneath him, naked under the layers of sari. The armchair groaned beneath them. The lovemaking began gently but an urgency soon possessed him, a heedless speed, encouraged by her matching desire. She moved to his timing, as though encouraging him and he came quickly, accompanied by a series of short gasps and then, shortly afterwards, a long exhalation.

He slid down the chair and knelt with his head on her belly, listening to the sounds of her body, listening also to the clock ticking, its beat erratic but persistent. One of her silver combs had come loose. She freed it completely and, delicately at first but then more forcefully, began to push it through his tangled hair.

'When I was a child,' she said, 'when the nuns took me in, I thought that fate had smiled on me. I was Mother Louis's favourite. I thought she would protect me always. But no, no, she did not. I loved her, but that was not enough. Love on its own is never enough.'

She fell silent but her comb continued on its challenging task. The clock's irregular pulse dominated the room.

His mind began to race. What had possessed him? With Winnie's arrival imminent? And why was she talking about love? Loving her was not to be contemplated. He knew that and surely she did too? He jerked his head away and the sudden movement ripped the comb from her hands but left it trapped in his hair. He tore it free, staggering to his feet as he did so, and tossed it into her lap.

'What we've just done,' he said, 'that wasn't love. That was desire.'

'I know,' she said. 'I know.'

She began to gather up loose strands of her own hair and pin them back in place.

'You needn't be worried,' she said. 'I don't believe in love, not that sort of love. That is only for fairy tales to send children to sleep. But desire is a part of love, is it not? A small part perhaps, but still a signpost to tell you that this is where you may be going. And now, here, in this room, are we not lovers?'

'Lovers?' he said, alarmed.

She laughed. 'Oh yes, lovers. I expect much from you now: gifts, flowers… Roses are good, but I prefer lilies – white lilies, please, with a ten-shilling note tucked into them, of course.'

He knew she was teasing him but there was bitterness in the humour.

'Oh yes,' she added, 'I am truly a whore and money is what I most desire. With enough money, my wishes could come true, just like in a fairy story. I wish for…' She trailed off, concentrating on pushing a final comb into position. 'Don't you want to know what I wish for?'

He didn't but couldn't avoid asking. 'What do you wish for?'

'Oh! For many things. But perhaps most of all to be in charge of my own life. To be able to do what I like to do and when and who with. Simple things: to be released from that place for just a day, to walk to the shore and swim and not care about anything. That is what I wish for.'

He said nothing.

Without looking at him she went into the back room.

He clambered to his feet and fumbled at the buttons on his fly. As he did so a shockwave of disgust erupted and engulfed him. His anger started with himself but then transferred to her, so that she became its focus. He wanted nothing more than to leave, to get his bike and get out of this place, to obliterate his folly, never see her again. He pressed his forehead against the wall and leaned there, breathing deeply, steadily, trying to calm himself. He must leave, walk out. Just go.

His hand was on the door latch when she returned.

'Are you leaving? Has he finished already?'

'I was about to find out.'

'That is not necessary. He will tell us when it's done. Sit, please.'

He came back into the room but stayed standing, his hands on the armchair's backrest. She settled herself on the upright chair and smiled.

'Yes,' she said. 'A man who likes to be uncomfortable. You have heard my story, and now it is your turn to tell yours. This place now, Bristol – tell me about Bristol.'

He turned away from her.

'I would like to see Bristol,' she said. 'If I could change my life I would go to England. I would say, what would I say? Perhaps that I am an Arabian princess. Yes, from those stories I have read, the Arabian Nights. I would be admired, would I not? An Arabian princess. Tell me I would be admired.'

He remained standing with his back to her and said nothing.

When she spoke again something had changed. There was now an intensity to her. 'Look at me,' she ordered. 'Look at me and tell me I would be admired. In England. In Bristol.'

He half-turned, offering her his profile and then, reluctantly, gave in to her demand.

'Yes,' he said. 'You would be admired.'

'Thank you. But however much I wish it, I am not in charge of my life, am I? I do not have that possibility. That is another fairy tale, a stupid dream. How could I get to England? I am not one of the masters, I am not like you. I cannot go to England, no, unless I am taken. Perhaps you will take me? Will you?'

He looked down.

What an absurd idea. He'd do no such thing.

She stood up, came over to him, put her arms around him and rested her head on his shoulder. 'Of course not,' she said.

'In a better world…' he began.

'Oh,' she said, 'oh yes, in a better world. Let's pretend, let's play games. I like these games – I have played them before with other young men. I have had promises made. Will you be like them: will you make me promises?'

The post-coital nausea began to reassert itself. His gullet tasted bile.

'Of course not,' she said again. 'Poor man, what trouble you're in. Involved with a woman like me.'

He could no longer tell if she was teasing.

'Stop that,' he said, pushing her away so that she stumbled and had to put a hand on the sewing machine to steady herself. Her feet were bare and he saw that she had scuffed up some dirt from the mud floor. A trickle of sweat ran down his back. He thought, *What fantasy might she be indulging in? More to the point, what fantasy was I indulging in? Was it about Winnie? Testing my feelings for her? Comparing her?*

She was watching him.

'I'm not involved with you,' he said, 'so please don't joke that I am. We shouldn't have done that. But we did and now I must pay you.'

'Yes,' she said, 'pay me. Show me what I am – a thing for sale, a whore. But I know what is real and what is not.'

'Do you though?' he said, spitting the words at her. 'You tell lies.'

'Oh, you're so serious! And why should it matter to you if I make up stories? Stories to amuse foolish men, stories they like to hear. Stories you like to hear. But I do not make promises I cannot keep.'

'I've made no promises to you. How much?'

'No, you have made no promises and we are not involved but still I will not take your money,' she said. 'It was my choice, was it not? A foolish choice, unimportant and foolish. Wait there.'

She went into the back room. The drunken alarm clock by the window ticked on, relentless in the silence.

She returned, carrying an unopened bottle of calamine. 'How are your bites?'

He inspected the patches of dried calamine, white and powdery. 'I need my bike,' he said. 'I need to go.'

'Let me see them.' She reached out to touch him but he jerked backwards, rocking on his heels, a boxer evading a punch.

'Yes,' she said. 'I see.' She attempted a smile. 'It was my mistake. And don't worry, I was only teasing.'

He couldn't look at her.

'Sahib,' she said. 'Sahib enjoyed himself, that is what matters. She is grateful to Sahib for this great honour.'

She curtseyed and as she did so there was a rapping on the front door. He backed against a wall, not wanting to be seen. She strode across and flung the door open.

The man in the iron leg brace stood outside. She beckoned him into the room and there was a brief conversation. The man seemed oddly agitated.

'He has bought a new tube,' she said, 'and fitted it. You should pay him four shillings for the tube and whatever you like for his services.'

Walter stood and felt in his pockets. He found five shillings and a few coppers. 'That's all the change I have,' he said, showing her.

'It is good.' She waved her hand in the general direction of the town. 'You can go now.'

He began to turn towards the man to hand him the cash. As he did so a tremor, violent and out of control, ran through his entire body, down through his torso and into his legs. He felt as though he could barely stand. The lame man waited, patient. The tremor left him and he handed over the coins. The man brought his hands together as if in prayer, bowed and murmured a few words.

'He is saying thank you.'

Walter wanted to say something but his mouth was too dry. He managed a nod instead. The man bowed again. This time the bow was deeper, but too deep and too prolonged, and it occurred to Walter that it was false, that it mocked him, mocked his ludicrous pretence of superiority. Then, as he straightened up, the man raised an imaginary glass to his lips.

'Double Diamond,' he said. 'Best beer.'

She reacted instantly, speaking sharply in Hindi. The man replied, soft-voiced, apologetic, and left.

'It is time for him to open up,' she said. 'The other place. As I told you, he is a useful man. And how else will he earn a living? An imperfection like that, it is seen as an insight into his soul. Such stupidity.'

Her tone had changed. 'What a good, caring person I am, don't you think?'

The bitterness had returned.

'Women see so clearly. You men, the lords of creation, the rulers, you are so trapped. How others see you, that is what matters to you – how you seem to others. All these things you claim – dignity, morality, nobility, Doing the Right Thing! What stupidity! And what is the reality? Power! Power, power, power, that is what you truly wish for. You do not possess a woman for love. No, you possess her for the power you have over her. That is the true attraction, that is what satisfies you – the sex is only a demonstration of power.'

Her arms waved in broad circles. The bracelets clattered. Her voice was hoarse. It echoed her outburst about the Law, powerful and passionate, the musicality absent.

He tried to tell himself that he was a scientist, detached and observant, the subject of his scrutiny some distant, alien behaviour. As a scientist, what would he see? A foolish man and the cause of his folly.

He took hold of her wrists and held her arms still. The bracelets slid down. He thought of handcuffs. He pushed her arms behind her back and leaned forward, his head on her shoulder. She made no attempt to shake him off. He no longer mistrusted her but instead could sense a desperation in her, a need for something beyond his ability to provide. She was limp in his arms, unresponsive, a rag doll. He felt an urge to shake her and shake her until her vitality, her humanity returned. *Suppose I snapped off a limb, what would spill out? Sawdust, perhaps, or kapok?* He let go of the doll, half expecting it to concertina down onto the floor in folds. Instead, she straightened up and once more stroked his face. He turned away from her and lowered his head.

'I'm a good man,' he said, 'but there are things I can't cope with.'

'I know,' she said. 'I know. But it was real, for a moment it was real. Deny it if you wish. Marry your girl and stay away from me. Sahib.'

'Don't use that word.'

He stared down at the mud floor, struck afresh by the poverty it revealed. Poverty and powerlessness, he thought, in the Harbour of Peace. Am I really the one with power? When I feel so weak, when in my world I do nothing but accept, obey the rules, the social mores?

He heard her as she collected the tray and its contents and went through into the back room. He heard the water tap running. He heard the mugs as they clattered into the bowl. He looked up and saw that the man had returned and was watching him.

'Sahib,' the man said, and Walter wondered again if there was a note of mockery in the salutation. If so, fair enough. The man opened the door. It was well past noon. The heat was savage and the streets were deserted. He tested the bike tyres. Both were firm. A good job had been done and he rode away not looking back.

CHAPTER 12

Petrie had returned.

An agitated Joseph intercepted Walter at the end of the track. '*Bwana* Barnes, *Bwana* Petrie *gonjwa sana*, sick, very sick.'

Petrie lay on his bed. His hair, freed from the control of brilliantine, stuck up at wild angles and one of his spectacle lenses had a crack in it. At first Walter thought he'd been the victim of a robbery.

'No, 'fraid not, nothing so glamorous. Truck I was in hit a pothole at full speed, the whole wretched vehicle rose three feet into the air or so it seemed, and my old napper took one hell of a thump from the dashboard. Had a very fine lump for a few days and my specs flew off as well, hence the crack. Could have been worse, I suppose. As it was, we were stuck with wildlife for company for a day and a half until a competent mechanic turned up from Arusha. We had to sleep in the truck – a wise move as it turned out, 'cause in the morning there were pug marks in the sand within a few yards of us. Quite an adventure, eh? How do I look?'

'Look? Bad. Terrible. Horrible. The ugliest bloke I know, in fact.'

'Oh God, it's so good to be back in Dar. Haven't had a laugh for a month.'

'Good to have you back. Is it malaria?'

'Yup, 'fraid so.'

'Didn't you take your stuff?'

''Course I did. Didn't do much good. The quack in Arusha looked me over and upped the dose. Seemed convinced it'll do the trick. Could you do the honours?'

He waved a hand towards a small brown bottle that stood on the tiled floor beside the bed. Walter examined the label: Ammoniated Tincture of Quinine. Adult dosage, one teaspoonful in a wine glass of water twice daily.

'I like the wine glass bit. D'you think Joseph has one?'

'Surely. Often told me how he likes a decent claret with his supper.'

Walter put his hand on Petrie's forehead. 'That's quite a fever.'

'Seems so. Not to worry.'

'I'll find a glass.'

When he returned with a tumbler, a teaspoon and a water jug, Petrie had struggled to a sitting position. Beads of sweat had broken out on his forehead and he had begun to scratch at a patch of broken skin on his left arm. 'Africa, eh?' he said. 'I still think it's an improvement on dear old Blighty. Mustn't be downhearted, must we?'

Walter measured out the quinine. Petrie's arm shook as he reached for the tumbler. The liquid slopped about and he used both hands to control it.

Walter sat on the end of the bed. 'Did you find out anything? Your mission, I mean.'

'What you'd expect. The word's got out that Dar's the place to be. I think our coming here, the Empire, well, it's like letting the djinn out of the bottle and the bugger won't go back in. The world outside has arrived in Tanganyika and young lads want a part of it. Traditional culture, forget it. They want to see cars and ships and trains and aeroplanes. They want to learn stuff too – it's an adventure for them, just like it is for us. *How ya gonna keep 'em down on the farm, after they've seen Paree?*'

He handed the tumbler back to Walter and lay down again. 'It's not the fever that gets me, it's this bloody steamhammer of a headache.'

'I'll leave you in peace.'

'No, no, don't. It's so good to see you, Walter, so very good. Oh blast and damnation. I'm sorry, can't help it – just seeing you.'

Petrie was crying. Small tears moistened his eyes and escaped down his cheeks. He mopped at them with the corner of a sheet. 'I'll be all right,' he added. 'They won't care for my report though.'

'Don't write it, then.'

'I thought of that. Soften it, anyway. Two-track approach: preserve traditions, introduce the new, hand-in-hand.'

'Might work.'

'Not a snowball's chance in hell. Pure bloody fantasy. Just the thought of trying gives me heartburn.' He began to cough, a dry rasping bark with no fluid to soften it.

Walter waited until the fit had passed. 'You should sleep.'

'We're playing ostriches, heads buried in the sand.'

'Stop thinking about it.'

'I know, I know. Can't seem to. I'm not a rebel, Walt, you know that. I want to tell 'em what they want to hear. But how can I? What to do, what to do?'

Walter stood. 'I'm going to get you to the hospital.'

Petrie shook his head. 'I'm fine here.'

'And you can forget that nonsense. I can't leave you to Joseph's care and it'll give you breathing space. Can't write a report while you're hospitalised.'

Petrie settled back, turning his face onto his pillow and scratching at his arm again. Walter rested a hand on his shoulder, then took his wrist and held it to feel the pulse. It was fast, but Walter was more struck by the ease with which his fingers were able to encircle Petrie's wrist.

'I have some news for you,' he said. 'Winnie's coming to Dar.'

Petrie rolled over onto his back. 'My dear chap, how wonderful. That'll be something to put in the letter home. That'll please the sisters when I write next – they love the human angle. When?'

'On the next Union-Castle. McLeod's Meg's putting her up – decent of her.'

'That's so good. And I'll be back on my feet in no time. Can't wait to meet her. What a tonic!'

* * *

There was no telephone in the mess and Walter had to cycle to the Club to summon one of Dar's handful of doctors. Mallinson was in the hall, a glass of whisky in his hand, chatting to Dominic Wellesley, the Governor's senior secretary. Both wore dinner jackets, Wellesley's corpulence exaggerated by the cummerbund that attempted to rein in his belly. He occupied the centre of the passageway and made no attempt to move as Walter approached.

'Barnes!' Mallinson called. 'Good. When d'you want to leap me on the ladder? Got your diary?'

'Sorry, in a bit of a rush, illness, need the phone.'

'Illness?'

'Petrie's back from his tour – malaria, bad dose.'

'Petrie?' He turned to Wellesley. 'Do we know Petrie?'

'In Regulations, I think. He's a legal of sorts,' Wellesley said. 'Doing a survey for us. Malaria, eh? Poor devil – can't have taken proper precautions.'

'Sorry, I really do need the phone,' Walter said. 'He can't stay in our quarters, there's only the houseboy. He needs a few nights in hospital, get the fever down. Excuse me.'

He started to edge past the two men but Mallinson moved ahead of him, striding down the hall to the manager's office. He reached past Ferriggi and without waiting for permission picked up the phone's bakelite handpiece, rattled the hook and demanded to speak to the Ocean Road Hospital. An hour later Petrie was in a bed there, attached to a saline drip.

'Useful diversion,' Mallinson said as they walked back through the cool hospital concourse to the waiting taxi. 'I'll miss one dull speech and the first course – mulligatawny soup I'll lay, or some other such culinary joy.'

The Sikh driver held the taxi's back door open.

'Government House,' Mallinson said. 'Club for you?'

Walter felt helpless, overwhelmed by the easy certainty with which authority flowed from Mallinson. Once seated he forced himself to look away from the man, turning towards the seaward side of the road as they skirted the ocean. A few distant dim lanterns from the night-time fishing boats were visible but otherwise the world was obliterated.

'Formal dinners never get to the point until the port arrives,' Mallinson continued. 'That's where the real business is done, the rest is pure tedium. As for this billiards game, shall I just give it to you? I've heard how good you are.'

One of the lights out at sea vanished then reappeared. Walter forced himself to turn back to Mallinson. He was looking straight ahead, hands clasped in front of his mouth, a forefinger resting on his lips. He might almost have been smiling.

'No, no, I've just had a lucky run.'

The hands detached themselves by an inch or so. 'If you say so. Trouble is, I'm fearfully busy. God knows when I can find the time.'

Mallinson was slippery but this was an opportunity and he didn't want to let it go.

'Perhaps we could pencil something in? We could make it a single frame if you like. If there's a problem you can always get Ferriggi to leave a note.'

'Fair enough. How would Monday week at seven do?'

The taxi swerved to avoid the first oncoming vehicle they'd encountered, hit a pothole, ran off the road and stopped.

'Did you see that, sir?' The driver pushed back the sliding glass window that separated him from his passengers. 'Only one light showing, damn idiot driving. Now bloody engine stalled.'

He banged the partition shut. The taxi's starter motor groaned and whined but the engine refused to turn over. The driver bent down out of sight of his passengers only to reappear a few seconds later clutching his starting handle. He clambered out of his compartment and came round to Mallinson's window brandishing it. Mallinson ignored him.

'Was that McLeod?' Mallinson asked.

'I don't think so.'

'Thought I recognised the car. Man's a maniac behind the wheel.'

'It was too dark for me to see anything.'

But it was McLeod. He knew the Singer well by now, could identify its particular engine note, higher in pitch than most of the other vehicles in Dar. He looked away, peering out into the murky night. A heavily laden mule laboured past them, its rider perched on top of bulging sacks.

'I gather you've a fiancée coming out?'

Walter stared at him.

'Petrie said something to that effect. Wedding bells in the offing, eh?'

'No, no. No, not for sure. She's coming out to see what she thinks of life here. She may hate it, may not want to stay. Nothing's definite.'

'Sounds a sensible girl. She'll be a rarity.'

The taxi swayed as the driver took a swing with the starting handle. The engine coughed and burst into life. The driver returned to Mallinson's window and raised the handle in triumph.

'Oh, get on with it,' Mallinson muttered. 'I've got a dinner to get to.'

The car ground back up onto the roadway. Mallinson stretched his legs.

'So what's her name, this fiancée?'

'Winifred… Winnie.'

'Ah, Old English. I do approve. You'll have to introduce me to her.'

'Of course.'

Walter felt a warm glow of satisfaction. It was as he'd forecast. Winnie was the key to a move, perhaps several moves, up the social ladder.

The Club's lights beckoned in the darkness. As the taxi slowed Walter opened the door.

'Thanks for sorting Petrie.'

'No thanks needed. Stick together, eh?'

The taxi was still moving as Walter jumped from it. He watched as it pulled away across the gravel.

'Playing your cards well, I see.'

Miller stood on the veranda, alone, risking the night's insect attack. He raised a beer glass. 'Who'd have thought it?'

CHAPTER 13

On Sunday McLeod drove the three of them out to Magagoni to watch the *Llanstephan Castle* as she negotiated the point and made her cautious way into the safety of the harbour, shepherded by the pilot launch. She was one of the smaller Union-Castle liners and Walter thought there might be a chance to catch a glimpse of Winnie. He made several passes with McLeod's binoculars along both main decks. Passengers leaned across the rails, pointing out sights to each other, but he could see no sign of her.

'She must be larboard side,' Meg said.

Or she's changed her mind, Walter thought. Was that possible? No, an unworthy notion. *Winnie deals straight, she'd have telegrammed any change of intention.* She was somewhere on board and would appear soon enough. The binoculars were unwieldy and he kept losing focus.

'Describe her,' Meg commanded, taking the glasses and peering through them. 'Hair colour?'

'Dark.'

'Oh, very helpful. Come on, Walter, do better.'

'Curly, short. She's quite short, too: five foot two, I think.'

'Everyone's wearing a topi. Oh, it's hopeless, far too far away. What are we doing here?'

She handed the binoculars back to Walter and marched off towards the car. The *Llanstephan* was now into the harbour and the ferry from Magagoni could begin its southward journey. They climbed into the Singer and McLeod drove round Azania Front to the Customs jetty. A crowd had gathered to welcome the liner, and skiffs and dugouts were heading off towards it in the hope of securing some small business. Both passenger transfer launches had already begun shadowing the liner, waiting for the accommodation ladder to be swung out, together with the rope painters that would secure the launches to the platform. Cargo tenders headed for the stern of the liner to collect the trunks and other baggage belonging to the long-term arrivals. The harbour was its customary calm anchorage and transfer accidents were rare.

McLeod parked in his space alongside the main Customs shed. He received salutes from the squad of *askaris* assigned to police the excitement and surprised but respectful nods from the Asian staff. They had already taken up their positions behind the trestle tables where the entrance interviews would be conducted. The Commissioner did not normally attend such routine events and whispered conversations broke out. Was an Important Person about to disembark?

Meg led the way onto the jetty. Walter had the binoculars and was able to get a view of the passengers as they clambered slowly down the swaying ladder. The first launch collected its permitted load and laboured clumsily away, noticeably lower in the water. Winnie was not in it.

Nor was she in the second launch and they had to wait while

the first two boatloads scrambled onto the jetty, stressed and excited by the awkwardness of the process. The first launch then returned for a second helping. It would probably be the final one, Walter realised, since the second launch's crew made no attempt to follow. Most of the passengers would be headed for Durban and Cape Town, and seasoned travellers on this route would know that a few hours spent in Dar-es-Salaam held very little of interest. A rubber of bridge in the saloon would take a higher priority.

The first launch edged up to the liner's platform and again the painter ropes secured it in position. An elderly man began a tortuous descent, shepherded by a seaman who preceded him down the ladder, one arm extended to catch the man should he lose his grip.

'Sisal wallah,' Meg said, having once again commandeered the binoculars. 'What's his name? Edgeworth?'

'Egerton, if it's who I think it is. Let the boy see his girl, darling.'

Meg took no notice. 'Sikh male, then another dark type, Greek at a guess, then a young lad – what's he doing, too young to be on his own? – and that's the lot, no girl.'

She handed Walter the glasses. 'Could be teasing you. Is she that sort?'

Yes, Walter thought but said nothing. He focussed on the ladder. He located the boy immediately and then, after a gap, he saw the brown-and-white brogues he knew so well.

'Winnie,' he said. 'Last off.'

'Likes to make an entrance, does she?' Meg said.

It was true, but stray remarks became inflated in this small world. He'd have to warn Winnie.

'No,' he said. 'Something must have delayed her.'

'And no topi,' Meg added. 'I like that. But I don't know that a cloche is a good idea in Dar.'

Winnie's cloche was pulled down over her curls, with just a few tendrils poking out. The effect was striking and fashion-conscious and, as Walter knew, deliberate. They watched as she stepped lightly from the platform of the ladder into the launch and immediately sank onto the kapok-stuffed seating alongside the steersman. A European officer had followed and now handed her a large raffia shoulderbag and they then began what Walter recognised as a pantomime of reluctant goodbyes. She'd made another conquest. He couldn't restrain a smile; there was pride rather than jealousy in him. This was, at least in the eyes of Dar-es-Salaam, his girl. The launch whistle shrilled and the man jumped back onto the platform from where he watched and waved to her. Winnie waved back briefly and then turned to face the jetty and the town.

Walter lowered the binoculars and as he did so his heart turned over. He put a hand on his chest and could feel the beat, irregular and fast. And the faster his heart beat, the more the launch seemed to slow. It crept across the glassy water, a snail traversing an enormous mirror. But edge forward it did and the *askaris* began to prepare a passageway. They wore khaki tunics and shorts, khaki puttees wound around their calves, broad leather belts with brass buckles and scarlet tasselled fezzes. Even their bare feet seemed to add to their elegance and efficiency, and as they maintained an easy control of the jetty Walter felt a growing pride in Dar. Forget that aberration, that woman, a man could be allowed the occasional passing insanity. No, the Empire functioned and he assisted it and his promise to Winnie of a wonderful life would be justified.

As if to welcome her it seemed to him that the dirty, oily industrial aromas of the port had given way to richer ones, the scents of the natural world, of copra and frangipani and acacia. He breathed in deeply and his heart settled back into its regular rhythm. The launch docked and one by one the newcomers clambered, jumped or were handed up onto the jetty. The elderly sisal grower exchanged a brief word with McLeod and finally, finally, the last arrival that day in Dar-es-Salaam took an *askari*'s hand and stepped up onto the jetty. There she paused and looked around her. The *askari* stepped back a pace and with the greatest courtesy, gestured her forward. Walter wanted to rush to her, embrace her, hold her to him, say *Look, look, what a prize*.

He didn't. He stood, rooted, waiting as she walked towards them, slow and deliberate, looking about her, aware of the interest she provoked. Then, some few yards from Walter, she halted and cocked her head, a tiny movement only, but enough. It was a summons. Walter stepped forward and took her hand. She lifted her face to him and he kissed her. With the scent of her face powder a mixture of nostalgia and desire swept over him and he swayed and clutched at her to steady himself. His heart leapt again: it was as if somewhere, at some long past time, it had withered and shrunk, had been reduced to half its capacity, and now without warning had begun its resuscitation. The tremor lasted barely a second and then he was able to release her, stand back and be himself, controlled and sensible. But a look had passed between them and her eyes widened in recognition of the moment.

'I love you,' he whispered.

He took her hands in his and, after a brief pause, led her a few paces across the jetty to her waiting hosts-to-be.

'Mr and Mrs McLeod, this is Winnie.'

Handshakes followed.

'My dear,' Meg said, 'welcome to Dar-es-Salaam. And congratulations on your engagement.'

'Thank you,' she said, and tucked an arm into Walter's, simply and artlessly falling into the role of the loving fiancée.

'It's easy to see that you're in love,' Meg said. 'What lucky young things you are.'

Winnie simpered. *Don't overdo it*, Walter thought. They strolled down the jetty towards the Customs sheds, where Catarina Fernandes was waiting with a bouquet of yellow hibiscus.

'From the staff,' she said. 'To welcome Mr Barnes's special lady.'

'How very thoughtful,' Winnie said. 'Thank you.'

'This is Miss Fernandes,' Walter said.

'Catarina, please, and on behalf of all of the staff I can say we're thrilled to meet you.'

She looked anything but thrilled.

'Can we get a move on?' McLeod said.

The entry formalities went through at speed; they'd been jumped to the head of the queue. Two men loaded Winnie's cabin trunk into the boot of the Singer. She sat beside McLeod in the front and Meg took the role of back-seat tourist guide, with corrections and addenda from her husband. Winnie responded with chirrups of interest but Walter said little throughout the journey. He was irritated by Meg. He had wanted to be the one to introduce Winnie to this new world, to assess her reactions and convince her that Dar offered the perfect combination of the exotic and the modern. As it was he could see very little of her: the cream cloche with its lilac trim almost sealed her off entirely and forced him to concentrate his attention on her nape and shoulders. She had no necklace on and he imagined rather than saw the light dusting of down that bloomed there.

'We'll dine at home this evening,' Meg announced as the little car negotiated the rutted driveway to their house. 'We want to get to know you before the rest of Dar does.'

Juma emerged from the house and stood on the steps to the veranda, framed by magenta bougainvillea. He bowed, if a marginal inclination of the head could be counted a bow, and opened the shuttered double doors to the hall.

'There's Juma,' Meg said. 'The guardian angel of the house.'

'God's sake, woman,' McLeod muttered, just loud enough for Walter to catch the words.

Meg cuffed him on the back, not quite playfully, and clambered out of the car.

'Juma,' she called, and waved. 'Our guest has arrived.'

But as she spoke her skirt caught on the interior door handle and held her back so that she missed her step, stumbled and fell forward. The skirt ripped. Juma ran down the steps and held out a hand but she shook her head and remained kneeling. It was instead McLeod who grabbed her by the shoulders and hauled her to her feet. She was flushed and angry and pushed him away before shaking the skirt to rid it of the debris it had collected. McLeod stepped back a few paces. He'd left the driver's door open and now he slammed it forcefully, too forcefully, too fast for the catch to do its work. The door sagged open again. McLeod ignored it. As Winnie and Walter hovered, uncertain, he headed for the house and leapt up the veranda steps. He stopped by Juma for a brief moment and pointed back at the car.

'In the boot,' he said, 'one trunk. You know where.' He disappeared into the house.

Meg looked up. 'The trunk to the guest bedroom, please, Juma,' she called, and then having abandoned any attempt to repair the skirt went round to the rear of the car and opened the boot. Juma glided across the drive to join her and they stood side by side inspecting the trunk, its green imitation leather held by a protective frame of three wooden ribs. Juma made no attempt to lift it. Walter tugged Winnie by the arm and steered her towards the house.

'Yes, yes, go on in,' Meg said and waved at them. Her attention stayed fixed on the trunk.

'It's too heavy for you,' they heard her say. 'The *shamba* boy can do it.'

Juma reached into the pocket of his *kanzu* and produced a silver whistle. He gave it a single blast and then stood, impassive, beside Meg.

'What a handsome man,' Winnie whispered once they were in the hall.

'Don't,' he said. 'Sore spot with the boss.'

He wanted to kiss her but McLeod had reappeared. He marched past them and out onto the veranda. Winnie raised her eyebrows. The moment passed.

'Meg,' they heard him shout, 'let's get tea under way.'

'I thought you called it tiffin,' Winnie said when he returned.

'Oh no, no, that's very old-fashioned. We're not the Raj here.'

'She's teasing,' Walter said.

'Ah.' McLeod inspected Winnie as if seeing her properly for the first time.

Aware of him, she pulled off her hat and ruffled her curls. 'I'm sure I have so much to learn. This is all so fascinating.'

She inspected the hall. A carved camphorwood chest with silver fittings sat beneath an ebony-framed mirror, flanked by hanging oriental carpets. Winnie ran a hand over the nap of one of them: the pattern used an octagonal base with a repeat motif of key-like figures, and she concentrated on it, her fingers tracing the repetitions, moving from left to right and then back again. The two men watched her as if hypnotised by the rhythms of her hand. *Bracelets*, Walter thought, *I'll buy her bracelets*. McLeod caught his eye, raised his eyebrows and nodded towards Winnie. Approval given. Walter forced a smile.

'It's Persian, my dear,' McLeod said. He smoothed the non-existent hairs on the top of his head. 'The symbols have meaning but I couldn't for the life of me tell you what. I bought the pair from a Parsi dealer for our fifteenth.'

Walter clasped his hands behind his back and turned away.

He could hardly bear to look at Winnie, hardly bear the thought that he might have let her slip from him.

'Tea's on its way,' Meg said as she came in. 'What on earth are you doing standing out here?'

She waved them into the drawing room. An occasional table was already laid with crockery for tea. Walter headed for the smaller sofa but Winnie didn't sit beside him, instead choosing the armchair in its matching chintz. She straightened the antimacassar and laid her head back onto it with a long and theatrical sigh.

'I can see the temptations of this life,' she said.

'There are drawbacks,' Meg said, and rang a small brass bell.

'I'm sure there are drawbacks,' Winnie said, and paused. 'Maybe drawbacks for some are attractions for others. Or perhaps I'm so thrilled to be here I can't yet imagine anything remotely deserving of the word.'

'There you are, Meg darling,' McLeod said. 'She's right, and we're in danger of becoming jaded, the gloss coming off.'

'It certainly has,' Meg said.

They lapsed into an uncomfortable silence. Juma appeared.

'Oh, Juma, tea, please, whenever you're ready.'

McLeod shifted in his chair. Juma surveyed the tea table and bent to adjust the cloth, tugging at one of its tasselled corners and running his long fingers along the lace fringe. He straightened up, checked and approved his handiwork and left.

'I wish you wouldn't,' McLeod said. 'He's arrogant enough without you fawning on him. "Whenever you're ready" indeed. He's a bloody servant.'

Meg ignored him, turning instead to Winnie. 'The house is the memsahib's territory, my dear. In the house the woman makes the decisions.'

'That's true,' McLeod said. 'But even so, servants should be ordered, not asked.'

'I'm not having this conversation, Johnny. I promised to show you the shells, my dear. Come, come over here.'

She unlocked the cabinet door and took out her cotton gloves.

'The shells the shells, the bells the bells,' McLeod chanted in a quavering tenor.

'Not funny, Johnny. Ignore him, my dear, difficult though it is.'

Winnie caught Walter's gaze and her eyes widened a fraction. She joined Meg at the cabinet, was handed a *Turbo marmoratus* and made a mew of appreciation.

'I'm beginning to hate those shells,' McLeod whispered to Walter. Meg's back stiffened. *She heard that*, Walter thought. *Did he mean her to?*

The shell ritual was halted by the arrival of tea. To Walter's relief, Winnie took control of the conversation, describing her journey, her cabin, her dinners at the captain's table – more than any other passenger, her steward assured her – the flying fishes she'd seen as they passed Socotra. Walter refused a second cup of tea and was pleased when Winnie did the same. They had the same priorities, it seemed.

Meg took them up to Winnie's room. Her skin showed blotches of deeper colour.

'Take your time,' she said. 'Dinner's at seven. Juma's very punctual, runs the place like clockwork, so seven it will be.'

She held out a hand. Winnie was about to shake it when Meg leaned forward and pulled her into a hug.

'So lovely to have a girl about the place. I always wanted a daughter but the Good Lord decided that I'd have sons, two great lubberly louts. They're at school in the UK and I see them once a year.' She held Winnie a moment longer, then released her and left the room without another word.

Walter relaxed. He held out a hand, inviting an embrace, but Winnie ignored him and walked over to the steel-framed picture window. She pushed back the netting, revealing a row of cowries on the sill. She picked one up and then put it down again, distracted, unseeing.

'Well,' she said, facing out towards the garden, 'well, here I am. Have we done the right thing, darling? Have we? God, the heat. Meg's needy, isn't she? I don't want to end up like that, or is it inevitable – just what happens to women in Africa?'

Walter joined her and they stood side by side. The garden, its lawn pockmarked by the patches of bare earth where McLeod had put down the ant poison, led down a shallow slope to the cliff edge, and white horses reared and broke where the ocean met the distant reef.

'Don't you like it?'

'I do. I like it very much.'

'It's not Bristol, is it?'

A small puff of breath broke from her, as if a laugh had been cancelled a fraction after it had begun. 'No. It's not Bristol. But, Walter…' She looked at him and took his hand and squeezed it. 'As we drove out here, past those shacks and those ragged children watching us, and she talked about botanical gardens and cathedrals and how we'd go shell-collecting, I thought…'

'Yes?'

'Have I walked into a trap?'

He looked away. 'Why would you think that?'

She said nothing. He took her by the shoulders but again she pulled away from him.

'Not yet,' she said, and moved across the room to sit on the only chair, a Victorian button-back in green velour. Alongside it, on a low table, sat her trunk. She perched on the chair edge, a primary school teacher waiting for her class to settle, and surveyed the room.

'Not my taste at all,' she said. 'A bit pompous, don't you

think? Frills everywhere. Look at that netting: what a devil to look after. I suppose it keeps the servants busy. What servants would we have?'

'Probably a houseboy and a cook.'

He'd forgotten so much about her – the pattern of pale freckles that bridged her nose; her short, square, sturdy hands; her habit of taking a strand of hair and pulling it across her mouth as though tasting it; her sensuality. He wanted to kiss her, taste her skin, more, to explore her body, make long, slow love, to confirm that marrying her was the right thing to do, and to dismiss his doubts.

He was about to speak when Winnie bounced to her feet.

'Come on,' she said, 'this won't do. I want the beach. I want to walk on the beach with my fiancé, my man Walter.'

She held out a hand. He took it, pulled her closer and wrapped his arms around her. She did the same. Walter searched her face, as if to acknowledge his uncertainty, and wondered whether for her, too, the charade of their engagement extended beyond the public pose to her own feelings. No acting, be honest, always honest.

'Yes,' she said. 'I'm going to possess you, I am, even if you are a… sssshhh…' She released him and put a finger to her lips.

'A what?'

'Sssshhh… A phoney, just like me, a pair of fake fyancees. This is a good game, isn't it? I like games and I'm going to like it here. We'll have such fun. And if I get bored I'll sail away back to England and I'll tell the world, sob sob sob, *I'm heartbroken*, I'll say. *I've been betrayed. A dark seductress has stolen my man's affections, so it's ta-ta, toodle-oo, goodbyeee!*'

'What do you mean, a dark seductress – why would you think that? It's a cliché. It doesn't happen. And why does it have to be me who does the betraying?'

'Because it has to be. That's one of the rules I've just invented.

You're heartless, I'll tell the world as I cry my way onto the boat, so croool, so croool, betrayed by my croooool lover.'

She laughed, delighted, and her smile broke out into its full dimpled glory. 'I'll accuse your Catarina, I think. She can be the dark-skinned temptress.'

'I think Catarina's hardly convincing as a dark-skinned temptress. Besides, I don't think anyone will believe in me as a cruel lover or as a betrayer. They're a bit extreme for me.'

'That's true. You're not an extreme person, are you? I am, or could be. In this place I could be very extreme. And what's more…' She did a little dance, spinning round so that her light cotton dress twisted about her, outlining her and then falling back as she slowed and stopped. '…I suspect that this is a place in which extreme things can happen very easily.'

She studied him. 'Tell me. Do they?'

He forced a laugh. 'No more than anywhere else,' he said.

'No? But do you know, you've changed. You seem… what am I trying to say? So much more in charge of yourself. Have you changed?'

'Perhaps. I'm certainly more definite about you. The longer I've been away from you the more I've realised, the more certain I've become that you – yes, you and only you – are the one…'

He couldn't elaborate further. *Love on its own is never enough*, the woman had said and he wasn't a natural liar. What he'd experienced on the jetty had slipped away from him, driven off by Winnie herself, by her controlling presence, her clear refusal to play the required role. *As far as our relationship is concerned*, he thought, *we could be back in Bristol.*

'No, it's not that,' she said after a pause. Her eyes narrowed and he was aware of the black flecks in the hazel of her irises. They seemed to show assessment, calculation and amusement all at the same time. She waited, expectant.

He blundered on. 'I want you so badly, Winnie.' That at least was true. 'And I do love you, I know that now, now I'm sure. Let's just do it, let's marry.'

She raised a hand, head-high, palm towards him, arm outstretched, a traffic constable's stop signal. 'Too soon, too soon.' She held the pose for a couple of seconds and then relaxed. A muscle in her cheek twitched and a shallow depression appeared. It was not quite a smile. 'Come on, come on, terrible man, *beach*!' She seized his hand and led him to the door. 'And this is because you're being so sweet. And you do love me, I can tell. And maybe, just maybe, I won't need to be betrayed.'

She kissed him, at first with delicacy, so that he could taste the layer of lipstick, and then with more urgency, pressing on him, her tongue finding its way past his parting lips, flickering against his teeth and then delving into his mouth. He began to respond but as he did so she pulled back.

'Don't wipe your mouth,' she commanded. 'There's a smudge of lipstick there, so leave it. It's just what they'll expect.'

She flung open the bedroom door, skipped down the stairs, along the hall and out of sight. He leaned against the door frame, and closed his eyes to combat the giddiness that threatened him. An image came to him, pulsating and shifting its shape, as if in some distorting mirror. She was in profile, seated at her counter, finger on a page of her book, dignified but needy. *Must get rid of her somehow, exorcise her. Time will do it, of course it will. She'll fade with time – time's the priest I need.*

He started down the stairs, clinging onto the banister. As he did so, he could hear raised voices from the drawing room, too faint to distinguish words but not the anger in them. The giddiness passed and with it the image of the woman.

Winnie had found a sandy path down the cliff and now stood on the beach below with shoes and socks in her hands. He watched from the cliff top as she stepped across the dry wrack that lined the foreshore. The dying breath of a wave rolled towards her and at first she backed away, but then allowed it to touch her right foot before it retreated. Growing bolder she walked further into the sea, allowing small waves to reach to ankle height.

Meg joined him; she had changed her skirt. 'I'll take her shopping tomorrow,' she said. 'Get her a decent hat to start with.'

Meg was wearing her broad-brimmed straw. Unnecessarily, Walter thought, since the sun was already low in the sky behind them, silhouetting Winnie as she paddled.

'I see what you've been doing,' Meg said, and wiped his mouth with a forefinger. She showed him the result. 'Naughty!'

CHAPTER 14

They waited at the entrance to the ward, held there by a nurse's upraised hand. She didn't look up but sat at her desk studying a set of typed notes. After a minute Winnie stepped forward and placed the flat of her hand on the desk. The nurse stared at the hand, then looked up at them. Her facial skin had a raw quality, as though scrubbed too hard and too frequently.

'Hello,' Winnie said in a voice brimful with false sincerity.

'Visiting hours are over.'

'Not what we were told, were we, Walter? Sunday morning until one o'clock.'

'That requires advance notice.' Her white cap, tied in an elaborate bow beneath her chin, undermined her severity and reduced it to mere rudeness.

'You're from Waterford, aren't you?' Walter said.

'You can tell?'

'I recognised the accent. We have friends back home in Bristol, sisters from Dungarvan – Kitty and Deirdre Brennan. They're nurses too, at Bristol General. It's a lovely accent, so soft and yet so rich.'

'You think so?' It was a dismissal. Soft soap no good. Next tack.

'We were hoping to see a friend, Robert Petrie.'

The nurse contemplated them.

'We're in rooms at the same mess,' Walter said. 'He's my best friend here.'

'And you are?'

'Walter Barnes.'

'Yes, I've heard him talk of you.' Her expression had changed. She stood up. 'Dear Robert,' she said. 'I'll make an exception for him. He needs to see friends.'

They followed her down the corridor to Petrie's room. It was dark, shutters closed to block out the heat and Petrie was asleep on the iron-framed cot, lying on his back with his mouth open. His pyjama jacket was unbuttoned and the gloom robbed his exposed chest of any colour.

'He's so pale,' Winnie whispered. 'I hadn't realised malaria could be so bad.'

'He'd been upcountry, you know that?' the nurse said.

'Yes,' Walter said.

'In rural areas.'

'Yes.'

'It's a pity we didn't see him sooner. He should have come straight here.'

'We brought him as soon as he got back to Dar.'

'I'm not blaming you. He should have come back to Dar immediately he fell ill. It's easy to confuse in its early days: the symptoms are much the same, fever and headaches.'

They stood in silence.

'Oh my God,' Walter said. He took Winnie's hand. They looked at the nurse.

'We still have to confirm it, of course,' she said. 'There's a lab in Nairobi and we've sent them a fluid sample.'

'What is it?' Winnie demanded.

'Oh my God,' Walter said again.

'Walter?' Winnie took his arm.

'Sleeping sickness?' he asked.

The nurse nodded. Petrie's breathing was erratic, short hauls of air followed by brief coughs as he exhaled. The nurse shifted him over onto his right side and his jacket bunched up beneath him. She tugged at it to free the cloth. His left arm tensed and his hand bunched into a fist. The nurse smoothed the sheets around him.

'It's serious?' Winnie asked.

Walter didn't reply. He sank down onto the only chair in the room and clasped his hands over his head.

'It's a question of how soon we've caught it,' the nurse said.

She began to feel Petrie's neck, her hands probing for the lymph nodes. 'Doctor Alexander has prescribed suramin as a precaution. We just have to hope that the parasite hasn't passed through the blood-brain barrier. If it's reached the neurological phase we won't be able to continue treating him here. He'll have to be taken to Nairobi. He seems such a sweet man.'

Walter's hands slid off his head to shade his eyes.

The nurse straightened up. 'I think we should let him sleep.'

Winnie had backed towards the door.

'Heavens to Betsy,' the nurse said. 'It's not catching. And it's the suramin that's making him sleep, not the sickness. It's horrid stuff and it knocks you out completely.'

A jug of water with a facecloth draped over it stood in a bowl on the small table beside the bed. The nurse took the cloth, poured water over it and wrung it out. She then began to wash Petrie's forehead and temple, moving the cloth in small circles as though he were newborn and unused to such intimacy. He stirred slightly and the tension left his fist. Winnie left the room.

'What brought you here from Waterford?' Walter asked.

'It's a way forward for an Irishwoman.'

She put the cloth back in its place on the jug. The severity had left her. *It's as if she loves him*, Walter thought, *and wouldn't anyone?* As they watched, Petrie tucked his legs up towards his chest. A fly landed on the pillow beside him and the nurse bent down to flick it away. She began again to smooth the sheets.

'This country,' she said. 'You'd better find your friend.'

He'd asked the taxi to return for them in half an hour. Winnie sat on a shaded bench in the hospital gardens, surrounded by oleander blossoms. She removed her cloche and shook out her curls, damp with sweat, running her fingers through them and teasing them free. She dropped the cloche onto the bench between them. He picked it up and turned it round and round in his hands.

'When are you going to buy a proper hat? Or is that Meg's line?'

She ignored him. Her feet began making circling movements in the dust. 'He looks like a ghost already,' she said.

'Don't say that.'

'No. But nevertheless he does. He was so pale.'

'Is pale, please, not was, and he's not a ghost.' He spoke sharply, unable to conceal his anger. Her feet came to a full stop, punctuating her unease.

She bent forward a little as though to inspect them. 'Why's it called sleeping sickness? Does it make you sleep?'

'Not sleep exactly, more lethargy, or so I gather. It's a fly that does it, a little devil of a thing which bites you and infects you with its wretched parasite. You don't fall into a coma, nothing like that, you just lose all energy and then your coordination goes, you become lethargic, confused, and then, then, you go mad.' He stared ahead, seeing nothing. 'And after that, the inevitable. It's so bloody unfair!' he cried. 'Petrie loves Africa and this is what he gets from it. No, it's not unfair, it's worse than that. It's malevolent, it's evil. The rewards go to the undeserving and all the good people get is a kicking. What is that but bloody perverse? Eh? Answer me that.'

He didn't expect an answer but was taken aback when she stood up and walked away from him, back towards the hospital entrance. She stopped to pull a bougainvillea flower towards her and plunge her face into it. She stayed, face obscured, for several seconds before releasing the flowers. They sprang back but still she didn't move.

'Winnie,' he called, lifting his voice. She didn't answer. 'You needn't worry, there's no tsetse fly at the coast. He'll be all right, too – he's tough, you know. I'm sure they've caught it early enough.'

She didn't respond but turned away from him and marched briskly back towards the hospital, where she scurried up the broad stone steps and disappeared inside. He didn't follow but hovered, holding the cloche, uncertain. The taxi arrived, its wheels scattering the raked gravel of the hospital drive. He spoke to the driver, asked him to wait, and went in search of Winnie. She was in the main hall, curled up at the end of a rattan couch. A porter was sweeping the tiled floor around the couch, and she lifted her feet and swivelled to lie lengthwise on her back, her feet hanging over the end arm.

'Taxi's here,' he said. She waved him away. He waited a few seconds but she didn't move. Her behaviour had begun to annoy him. He'd have to send the driver away and pay him for a wasted journey. The whole fiancée charade was costing him too much and he resented it. From a position of financial comfort as a single man, he now had to count the pennies. He walked back down the hall and as he reached the entrance doors he heard her heels clacking behind him.

They drove in silence until they reached the Bagamoyo Road. She put a hand on his knee. 'I'm such a bitch,' she said.

'No, no.'

'I'm so sorry. I know he's a good friend.'

***

Two days later he watched as Petrie was hoisted on board a packet heading up the coast to Mombasa, where it was scheduled to arrive next evening in time for the overnight train to Nairobi. A black nursing assistant went with him. The hospital insisted that she was competent and anyway there was no alternative care on offer. There was then an altercation about where she should sleep, the ship's mate at first insisting that she could not be allowed to stay in a first-class cabin overnight. The captain was summoned and after much quoting of company regulations agreed to override them and let her stay. She wasn't to use the second bed, however, but would have to sleep in a chair. The woman didn't seem to mind. Walter put a hand on Petrie's shoulder.

'They'll sort you out in Nairobi,' Walter said.

'I know they will.'

'You'll be fit as a flea, hopping all over the place.'

'I will.'

'And your report can wait.'

'I know it can. But…'

'But nothing.'

'They need to know, Walter, they need to know they're getting it wrong. I love Africa and they're getting it wrong.'

'It's no longer your problem.'

'It's not, is it?'

'No.'

Petrie tried a smile. It didn't succeed, defeated by worry. He raised a limp hand.

'Shake a paw,' he said.

***

Walter checked the Club noticeboard. There was no note so he presumed that Mallinson would show up as promised, neither too busy nor too engrossed in the charms of the Humber. He opened up the billiards room, confirmed the supply of chalk and selected a cue.

McLeod put his head around the door. 'There you are,' he said. 'Cab driver McLeod at your service. I've done as ordered. Now it's your turn: she needs signing in.'

'Winnie?'

'Who else? Another fine example of the species she-who-must-be-obeyed – you'd think I had enough of that from Meg. It's not as though I was intending to come in this evening.'

'I'm sorry. It's quite a way.'

'Yes, it is. Now and then fine, just don't want it to become a habit, don't want her presuming I'll drive her wherever, whenever.'

'I'll have a word.'

'You do that.'

They walked down the hall to the small visitors' lobby. Ferriggi, elegant as always in dinner jacket and bow tie, stood by the lectern holding the guestbook.

'Hello, darling,' Winnie said. 'Have you come to rescue me from this fiend?'

Ferriggi beamed, delighted. 'Women must be signed in, madam. It's the rule.' He settled the book on the lectern and handed Walter a fountain pen.

'I'll be off then,' McLeod said. 'You'll get a taxi back.'

It was a statement of fact, not a question and there was an edge to his voice.

'Thanks so much for bringing her in,' Walter said. 'Very much appreciated.'

Winnie smiled, modest, sincere. 'Johnny's a darling.'

McLeod thawed a little. 'Don't mention it,' he said, and left.

'Gosh, you look good,' Walter said.

Winnie wore a dress in a dark maroon crêpe, with bell sleeves and a matching bolero draped around her shoulders. She pirouetted, allowing the soft material to follow her movements and then to settle as she herself settled into a fashion-plate pose, her bare right hand by her face, forefinger extended. Her left hand was gloved in white kid, and in it she held its pair. Ferriggi applauded.

'It's a devil to put on, buttons all the way down the back. But worth the struggle, would you say?'

'Definitely.'

'I thought so.'

'You will explain the rules to madam?' Ferriggi asked. 'Ladies are only permitted in the dining room and the visitors' lounge.'

'But I want to watch the billiards,' Winnie said. Ferriggi spread his hands and shook his head.

'Alas, madam, in Italy you would be welcome everywhere, but you are not in Italy now.'

'You'll find the Gymkhana Club more welcoming. You can have your revenge there – girls only in the evenings.' Mallinson had appeared. 'Good place if you're a sporting gal. Otherwise, ho-hum. You must be Winnie, hello.'

'Hello,' Winnie said. 'And who and what are you?'

Mallinson grinned. 'Oh, I'm Charles Mallinson, the poor victim about to be slaughtered on the altar of the billiards table. There will be blood on the baize. You're better off in the visitors' room.'

'Oh, but I like blood. I was an Ancient Roman in a previous life.'

They walked on down the central corridor. The mock-grandeur of the studded mahogany door to the visitors' room gave way to a spectacular drabness.

'You'll enjoy yourself here,' Mallinson said with the wave of a hand. '*The East African Standard*, always a fascinating read – look, this one's only three days old. Chairs not bad, the occasional protruding spring, easily avoidable. Calendar for 1931: portraits of great men. That's Mr Baldwin, I do believe. You can learn so much from studying a politician's face. I do recommend half an hour in contemplation of him. No *Stag At Bay*, sadly.'

Winnie was silent. After a moment she walked over, seized an armchair and hauled it into the corner furthest from the door. A hand brushed the seat. She lowered herself into it and looked away from the men.

'Is it always so hot?' she said and fanned herself with her glove. A foot began to tap.

Walter recognised danger signals.

'Now, now,' he said, 'no arson.'

She looked back, and a small grin tweaked the corner of her mouth. 'Haven't brought my matches.'

'Thank God for that.'

'If it wasn't so funny, it might almost be thought to be insulting.' She waved the glove at the room. 'As it is, it's just dreadfully sad.'

'Isn't it?' Mallinson laughed. 'But the game will take, what, ten minutes? If Barnes plays up to his reputation.'

'Then I'll just have to wait, won't I?'

'After which we'll have dinner, yes? The three of us.'

'Thank you, that would be lovely.' She removed her remaining glove, placed it on the arm of the chair, laid her head back and closed her eyes. 'What fun it is to be a woman,' she said.

'We'd better get on,' Walter said. 'Hundred up?'

'Hundred up.'

The match was uneventful. Walter attempted nothing too stylish but played a quiet and methodical game and was soon well ahead. Mallinson spent his waiting time eulogising the Humber and as he listened to him, it came to Walter to wonder whether the billiards project, combined with Winnie's arrival, had not already succeeded. A step-up in the social order had been achieved: dinner with Mallinson, just possibly friendship with Mallinson. The thought was followed by an image: Winnie draped across the armchair, glove in gloved hand fanning furiously, a foot tapping, and Mallinson – oh yes, Mallinson – concentrated on her, assessing her and surely, surely, attracted by her?

Walter lined up what was the final stroke, a simple canon to take him past the hundred mark. The certainty that he would score was matched by a conviction that Mallinson was more than amused by Winnie. The step-up in the social order had a price.

'Fancy a snorter?' Mallinson asked as they pulled the canvas cover back over the table and racked the cues. 'G and T for her, I imagine?'

He didn't wait for an answer but headed straight for the bar, where he ordered two G and T's before glancing at Walter.

'And me,' Walter said, and regretted it immediately. It was an admission of weakness, the young male submitting to the pack leader's choice.

'Three, steward,' Mallinson said, 'and bring them through to the visitors' lounge. On my tab.'

'Who's the lady?' a voice rasped. Spencer leaned against the bar.

'Secret,' Mallinson said.

'Her name's Winnie and she's my fiancée.'

'Oh, you, Barnes. Fiancée? Rash move. This is no country for women, I can tell you.'

'And so we're all the more grateful when one turns up,' Mallinson said.

Spencer turned to Walter. 'Bit of skirt, you see, gets all the young bloods up and eager. My advice, Barnes, keep the key with you at all times. The one for her chastity belt. As for the women themselves, three years here and they go crazy. Seen it happen time and again. R.C. is she?'

'She is,' Walter said and turned to follow Mallinson.

'You'll be spending time in the confessional box, no doubt,' Spencer called after them.

'Some of these old-style District Officers,' Mallinson said, 'when it comes to women, stuck in the past – either that or they're eunuchs. In his case, both.'

'I think he heard you,' Walter said.

'Good.'

Winnie still sat in the same armchair in the furthest corner of the visitors' room. Mallinson flung himself onto a sofa and stretched out with his long legs resting on the end arm.

'Can't apologise enough for this place,' he said. 'Food's not bad though, if you like Eyetie stuff, and there's usually a decent roast on offer as well, complete with dead vegetables à la Buck House. Ate there once, terrible food, conversation worse, and yet you come away thinking you've been privileged. Odd. What are your plans now you're here?'

'We don't have any as yet,' Walter said. He remained standing.

'Revolution mightn't be a bad idea,' Winnie said.

Mallinson snorted and sat up the better to inspect her. 'Love the frock,' he said.

She'd already responded to the man, Walter could tell, and now she softened further, relaxing an arm and letting it fall to her side. 'Thank you,' she said, gravely.

The drinks arrived.

'I've been terribly rude,' Mallinson said. 'Ordered without asking what you wanted, just presumed on a G and T.'

'Bad boy. G and T is fine. No beer, Walter? I knew you'd changed.' She sipped her drink.

They ate roast pork with roast potatoes and a side-helping of stunted parsnips, followed by a small miracle conjured up by Ferriggi: vanilla ice cream. Winnie dominated the table, asking questions, grilling both men equally, all unembarrassed curiosity. Walter recognised the symptoms: Mallinson's capitulation to Winnie's charms would be, already was, inevitable. They stayed in the dining room for coffee, Winnie having refused to return to the visitors' lounge, and then strolled out onto the deserted veranda. The African night wrapped itself around them. Winnie silenced Mallinson's chatter with a single finger raised to her lips and then curled up in one of the basket-weave chairs. Walter stood behind her and laid a hand on her shoulder. She glanced up at him and touched his hand lightly. Mallinson produced a silver cigarette box.

'A fag to defeat the mozzies,' he said. 'Black Russians – how's that for affected?'

Winnie took one and inspected the black tube with its gold tip. 'Dreadful,' she said, 'impossible, intolerable. I herewith dismiss you from my sight.'

Mallinson laughed. She put the cigarette to her scarlet-stained lips and he crouched before her to flick his lighter. The cigarette glowed and once it was properly alight Winnie waved it in an arc so that it became a firefly dancing to her orders.

'I must admit though I've always liked Passing Clouds, those oval ones, scented too. So you see, I'm quite as pretentious as you.'

'What a pair we are,' Mallinson said. He offered the case to Walter, who shook his head.

'Walter now,' Winnie said, 'Walter isn't pretentious. He doesn't smoke at all, and if he did it would be Woodies. I keep hoping for signs of a little more style in you, darling.'

She reached up and again patted his hand. Mallinson lit his cigarette, inhaled and took up a position on the other side of Winnie's chair, so that she was now bracketed by the two standing men. They gazed out into the night. Walter felt his back muscles tighten. Mallinson, too, was still. The sounds of Dar at night took over. The insistent buzzes and clicks of the night insects surrounded them, while drumming from the direction of Kariakoo provided a steady if muffled bass line. Somewhere towards the sisal plantations to the north, a creature began a series of yelps which lengthened into an extended ululation before dying away, pausing, and beginning again.

'What's that?' Winnie asked.

'Bushbaby,' Walter said. 'You'll get used to it.'

Winnie finished her cigarette and held up the stub. 'Dispose of this, slave,' she said.

Mallinson took the stub and flicked it so that it sailed in an arc of sparks upwards, outwards and onwards before falling onto the gravel drive in front of them, where it expired.

'Better not stay out too long,' Walter said. 'I can hear a mozzie. I'll order a cab.'

'No need,' Mallinson said. 'I feel like a drive. Wait here, I'll get the beast.'

He brought the Humber round, leapt out leaving the engine running, and opened the front passenger door. Winnie climbed in and Mallinson waited while she arranged her skirt before he closed the door, not slamming it but pushing it shut. The catch took with an easy click. Walter sat in the back. Mallinson put the car in gear and eased off the clutch too soon. The engine stalled.

'Now there you have me,' he said to Winnie. 'Revealed as the thorough incompetent I am. Mind you, I do have an excuse, don't

I, Barnes? Haven't had her long, relationship still in its early days, still getting to know the lady. So what d'you think of my new love?'

'She's beautiful,' Winnie said.

'Isn't she just? And wait till you see her with her hood down – that's something to behold. What say one day we take her for a proper spin?'

'Mmmm, yes please,' Winnie said.

'Tell you what, next week I'm due a few days' leave – how would that suit you? What say we go upcountry, Morogoro perhaps. The three of us. Barnes can get time off, can't you?' he added.

Walter said nothing. He was probably, no, certainly, due a few days' leave, but spending it with Mallinson? He wanted Winnie to himself.

'Could try a hill station, Morningside, say? Bit of walking needed to get there, I'm told. You up for that?'

'Fit as a flea,' Winnie said.

'Attagirl. You on, Barnes? I'll fix it then.'

It was all happening too fast.

* * *

The McLeods had gone to bed by the time they reached Oyster Bay but there was a pale glimmer of light from the hall. Mallinson stayed in the car, allowing Walter to open Winnie's door. She swung both legs out together and held out a hand. He took it, pulled her to her feet and they walked hand in hand to the villa's steps, where she paused and lifted her face to him. The hall light did little more than outline her and her eyes were dark recesses. If it hadn't been for the still powerful aroma of Shalimar he might have wondered who she was. He wanted to hold her to him, to run his hands around her, to be a blind man making new discoveries. He kissed her.

'I want to make love,' he whispered.

'Not here,' she said. 'Not now.'

She broke the embrace, waved in the direction of the car and trotted up the steps onto the veranda. The door opened as she arrived and Walter caught a glimpse of Juma's white *kanzu*. Winnie went in without looking back. The Humber's engine was running. He climbed in and Mallinson let in the clutch.

'She's something different,' Mallinson said.

'Yes.'

'I like a feisty girl.'

He's fishing, Walter realised. He was determined not to respond.

'Mmmm.'

'I have a sense, though… There's something that tells me…' Mallinson left the sentence hanging.

Walter's resistance crumbled. 'Tells you what?'

'Oh, how to put it? That Dar's a small town and that she's a big-city girl.'

'What does that mean?'

Mallinson didn't reply. There was no moon that night and to see the road at all he had to rely on the thin yellow beam of the headlights. They swung into Ocean Road and the lights picked out the skeletons of palm trees as they flexed in the night breeze off the sea. The hospital was on the right. 'I heard it's bad news about your pal.'

'Yes. It's been confirmed, sleeping sickness. He's in Nairobi for treatment.'

'Nairobi? Why the hell did they send him there? He should have been packed off back to London.'

'The medics seem to know what they're doing.'

'The London School of Hygiene and Tropical Medicine, that's his best chance. Up to date in every way. My mother's a trustee.'

'He wants to stay in Africa.'

'In Africa? Why would anyone want to stay in Africa? Great place to visit, see the sights, collect a few anecdotes, make sure the project is going well, paying its way, then back to the proper world, theatre, concerts, society. He must be mad.'

'Yes, well, perhaps he is. Thanks to the sleeping sickness, actually going mad.'

'Ah. Foot in mouth, sorry.'

'Also, they wanted to get treatment underway fast.'

He didn't want to talk about Petrie. 'What do you mean, the project?'

'The project? Oh, the project. Us, here, Empire, bringing home the bacon, got to make sure it's operating properly, got to check on it from time to time, keep it delivering the goods.'

'Oh. Isn't that a bit—' He searched for the word. '—exploitative?'

'Exploitative? That's a harsh word but I suppose you could argue a case. After all, what's the point of Empire if the colonies don't feed the centre? Colonialism isn't charity, and why else are we in Africa?'

Walter said nothing. He didn't want to talk about Africa, still less argue about Empire. He didn't even want to think about it. Africa was changing him, unleashing traits he didn't know he had and some of which he didn't want to acknowledge. Making love to that woman. Still, over now.

'Why d'you think Winnie's a big-city girl?' he asked.

The Humber had reached the start of the track to the mess. It slowed to a halt.

'I don't much fancy taking the car down there, not in the dark. You can walk from here, can't you?'

'Of course. And anyway, what does it mean, a big-city girl?'

'Oh, nothing.'

The night was too dark for him to see Mallinson's face. Walter stayed in his seat, leaning back as if about to close his eyes and sleep. A distant shriek sounded followed by the response, a single scream of outrage, or so it seemed to him, and then another and another.

'Time for bed,' Mallinson said.

He gave up. Mallinson probably hadn't meant anything, it was just something said, and meaningless. He knew that people said things, did things for reasons obscure to them let alone to others. He opened the door.

'Ambition,' Mallinson said suddenly. 'A girl like that in a place like this, she'll have ambitions.'

'What are you saying?'

'She's not one for second best, is she? This is a small town in a small country, population no more than a few thousand whites. And my hunch is that the only way she'll tolerate it is if…'

His voice trailed off.

Walter decided to leave it at that, to refuse the bait. And as soon as he'd made the decision he reversed it, unable to resist.

'Go on. Is if?'

He wondered if Mallinson was smiling.

'Is if she's the queen. It'll be queen or nothing, queen or away, I could see it in her eyes. Got your work cut out, haven't you?'

Walter swung his legs out of the car and hauled himself upright. 'Goodnight,' he said as he slammed the door. The Humber snorted, coughed and headed off into the night. Walter trudged down the track.

I asked for that, he thought. The night seemed unnaturally dark and he could barely make out the track.

The shriek sounded again. This time it was much closer and had changed its note. It was deeper, less shrill. Hyrax, definitely hyrax, but in the obliterating dark the call seemed that of a larger creature, more physical, even threatening. A new call responded; a rapid clacking, *kek-kek-kek*, at first as of angry geese but then, as the shrieks fought back, it ratcheted up the power and mutated into the stutter of a machine gun. He could see nothing and began to feel afraid. *Irrational – no lions, no hyenas in Dar. Baboons, yes, but they stay well outside the urban limits.* Vervets were harmless, weren't they? But the atmosphere was charged, there was a prickle in the air as of static electricity about to break out and ignite a fire. The night spoke to him of violence. He groped forwards with arms outstretched but touch, too, had deserted him and he could feel nothing. The night sky which in Wiltshire folded itself around him like a blanket now gripped him in the embrace of a straitjacket. The dark pinioned his arms. The stars were useless, burning absences. He broke into a trot, aware of the folly of moving fast but seized by a panic that his rational mind could recognise but not defeat. Shapes began to emerge, flinging themselves at him before sliding silently away without contact. Bats, only bats, what else could they be? A creature slipped across the track ahead of him and as it did so the machine-gunners took aim once more and he ducked to avoid them, at the same time twisting his torso sideways and catching his left foot in a trap of root and brush which hurled him forwards onto baked earth.

He lay quite still, aware now of a new threat: silence. The machine-gunners had gone elsewhere but a shape circled him. He hoisted himself up into a kneeling position and as he did so became aware of a throbbing in his left temple. The pain was dull but it served a purpose: it drove out the panic. He settled back onto his haunches and as he did so the shape appeared again, recognisable now.

'Bella?' he whispered. The shape held its ground and his eyes, freed of the blindness of his panic, could now make out the characteristic droop of her tail.

'Were you looking for me?' he asked. *Or are you looking after me, a guardian angel in the disguise of a mangy pi-dog?*

'Thank you,' he said, and held out a hand. Bella edged away. Her shape lost focus and she faded into the dark. Not a guardian angel, just a hungry cur.

He got to his feet and felt his temple; the skin was broken but there was little blood. He tried to laugh, but although the absurd panic had evaporated the sense remained of a motiveless violence present somewhere. He was conscious of his heartbeat, telling him not to relax, to stay on guard, on guard against, against what? Ghosties and ghoulies and long-leggedy beasties?

That's the way to do it!

No, forget the ghosties and all that crew. You're the one to watch, Mr Punch.

* * *

He reached the sanctuary of the mess, fumbled his way down the feebly lit passage to his room, left his clothes on the floor, ignored his toothbrush, and was about to drop naked into his cot when he realised that his clothes lay not on rush matting but on an elegant Persian carpet. The mystery of its presence was too much to solve. He shut his eyes and fell back onto his mattress.

Despite his tiredness sleep would not come. The air was still, the heat stifling. He thought of Winnie in the Oyster Bay villa that faced the ocean, lapped by the sea breeze. He gazed up at the netting that surrounded and pressed down on him. The panic he'd felt seemed more and more justifiable. It was as if there were an actual presence in the place, here in Dar, unnameable but malevolent. Or rather, it was not itself directly malevolent, no; instead it acted to release the malevolence latent in others. There was a weight lying on his chest, and there was no way to relieve himself of it. It was not amenable to the laws of physics.

He began a rosary.

Our Father who art in heaven, hallowed be thy name.

His eyes closed and he now found himself seated in a comfortable armchair.

Hail Mary, full of Grace, he murmured. *The Lord is with thee.*

The armchair was saturated with a perfume.

Sandalwood.

Glory be to the Father and to the Son…

The armchair was the woman and he settled into its arms, her arms.

'I'm sorry,' he told her. 'But what can I do?'

He slept.

CHAPTER 15

McLeod brought a message from Winnie. She couldn't be at Choitram's before four and McLeod had no idea why not. He was in a foul mood, having been woken before six that morning by wailing and shouting. His *shamba* boy had been taken ill in the night with racking stomach cramps and convulsions, and the man's wife was determined to let the world know about it. In order to shut her up, McLeod had been forced to drive her and the *shamba* boy back to their village some ten miles further north and deliver him into the hands of a native herbalist.

'What's wrong with him?' Walter asked.

'God knows. At least he's off my hands. Bloody useless though he was I'm now stuck with finding a new gardener. As if I haven't better things to do.' He tapped his desk. 'Where's that bloody thing?'

'This?'

Walter held up a draft copy of the Interim Report. McLeod

took it, opened it, groaned, and dropped it back on his desk. 'Get Da Silva in here, will you? And I need a coffee.'

***

McLeod left the office shortly after midday, clutching the report and ignoring Walter. The office staff began their Saturday exodus at one o'clock.

To kill a little time before four Walter decided to try some detective work. He took out the office copy of a Royal Navy chart of the coastline north of Dar and now, by careful analysis and comparison with the Royal Engineers' road map, he began to check out the most likely creeks for smugglers to operate from. Intercepting smugglers was a police job but he thought he could probably make some useful suggestions. He'd been involved in an arrest a few weeks earlier. It was purely accidental and was thanks to the incompetence of a drunken skipper whose dhow had gone off course and drifted into one of the mangrove swamps to the south of the town. Walter had stumbled across the crew as they attempted to unload their cargo, staggering up to waist-deep through the fetid water with packages balanced on their heads, cradled in their arms, strapped to their backs. He'd only gone there out of curiosity. The Land Survey Department was constantly searching for better access road routes into the town and their latest suggestion involved developing a new area which, they suggested, could have useful facilities for the management of shipping.

'Quite idiotic,' McLeod had said, dismissing the idea. An hour later he'd backtracked a little. 'Better show willing,' he said. 'Pop along, Barnes, and see whether there might be a grain of sense in it.'

Two of the on-duty *askaris* insisted on accompanying him – they'd spotted a better way of passing the time than hanging about the docks. Stumbling across the dhow and its plight made the outing better again. The crew dropped their loads and fled in time but the skipper was not so lucky and received a severe beating from the police batons. Blood bubbled from both nose and mouth and his back was a pattern of purple weals by the time the *askaris* had finished with him. It was the first time that Walter had seen the police in action and it disturbed him. He had a word later on with Jackman, the Police Superintendent, who seemed puzzled as to what the problem might be.

'Criminal, caught in possession,' he said. 'It's what he'd expect. Anything less, think we'd gone soft. Only way to stop thieves, beat the message into them.'

He accepted that Jackman had a point but even so the cheerfully applied brutality seemed excessive.

He could hear the chatter from the outer office as the staff now began to leave. 'Catarina,' he called.

She hovered at his door, arranging her headscarf.

'Before you go there's something I wanted to ask you.'

'Yes, Mr Barnes?' she said, and looked at her watch.

'Someone's left me a Persian carpet,' he said. 'An anonymous gift. It was there in my room last night, no note with it, nothing.'

He'd cross-examined Joseph but he had little explanation to offer.

'Boy,' he kept saying. 'Boy for *Bwana* Barnes.'

'A boy brought it? What boy?'

Joseph didn't know. 'For *Bwana* Barnes,' he said again.

'Roll it up, take it away.'

Joseph was reluctant. '*Maridadi*,' he said.

'Yes, I know it's *maridadi*, very stylish. But I don't want it, so take it away, store it for now. Find a cupboard.'

He was in no mood for mystery. Carpets didn't arrive without reason. It was probably a bribe in waiting, a hostage to fortune, a debt to be called in at some future date. The most likely donor was Abu Saleh. He'd encountered the man earlier that morning at the launch of a new dhow, and no mention had been made of carpets but Abu Saleh's greeting had been suspiciously effusive. He could well be biding his time before pouncing, sucking Walter into his clutches. The carpet had to go.

Joseph rolled up the offending article, hoisted it over his shoulder and shuffled off.

'I presume it's the preamble to an attempt to bribe me.'

'Bribe you, Mr Barnes? Impossible! Everyone knows Mr Barnes.' Catarina raised her hands to frame her face, palms facing forwards. The action was flamboyant and over-insistent and had the effect of undermining her words. It was not a vote of confidence in his honesty.

'I was wondering though, why me? Have I been singled out? Or is it routine? Does everyone get tested in this way?'

She blinked.

'Mr Thornton, say, has he been offered gifts like this, valuable ones?'

'I wouldn't know, Mr Barnes. I know nothing about that sort of thing.'

He gave up. She was evidently not prepared to offer help of any sort. He waved her away and returned to his maps. After a further hour's study, and with a rough itinerary sketched out, he folded them away.

There was still time to kill and he needed to find some lunch. He left the building, walked past and nodded to the caretaker at his station by the building's entrance, whose name he'd forgotten, and stepped out into the street. He needed to adjust his bush hat, pulling the brim down the better to shade his eyes from the early afternoon glare.

A local was loitering in the semi-cover of a spindly acacia.

A boy stood beside him. As Walter walked past, the man called out. '*Bwana* Barnes, I can speak to you, *Bwana* Barnes?'

Walter stopped. Did he know this man? The man obviously knew him and now, concentrating, Walter realised that it was the crane driver. Divorced from his work the man had lost his individuality and melted back into the general mass of dockyard workers. *Must make more effort*, Walter thought, *get to know at least a few of them by sight.*

'Yes?' he said.

The crane driver clasped his hands. '*Bwana* Barnes, this is my son.'

Unlike his father who wore a calf-length *kanzu*, the boy wore an approximation of Western dress, trousers and a short-sleeved shirt pinned at the neck by a spotted bow tie. He also wore shoes. Borrowed ones, Walter suspected, because they were obviously too large for him. Had they been waiting specifically for him? And for how long?

'His name is Anthony. He is twelve, *Bwana* Barnes.'

Walter waited for an explanation.

'Very clever boy, *Bwana* Barnes. Teach himself to read.'

The boy muttered something and scuffed the gravel at the base of the acacia.

'Teach himself?' Walter said. 'He doesn't go to school?'

'No, sah, school in Dar cost much money, try teach himself.'

There was a silence. Anthony stared at his feet. The crane driver's hands knotted themselves tighter.

'Get to the point,' Walter said.

'*Bwana* Barnes, Anthony want good job, office job, not job like me.'

Another silence. Walter turned to Anthony. 'Your father has an excellent job,' Walter said, 'and does it very well. You should learn from him.'

'Want office job,' Anthony said, and stuck out his lower lip.

A surly child, Walter thought, and turned back to the crane driver. 'I'm not sure what you think I can do for your boy. Are you saying he can read?'

'He learn fast, work hard.'

'You mean he can't read.'

The crane driver said nothing.

'In which case I doubt we could employ him. Anyway, staff appointments are not my business. You have to talk to *Bwana* McLeod.'

Anthony had turned away from them and was watching the complicated unravelling of a seine net. Walter knew what McLeod's response would be, and also knew that the crane driver knew. And yet, after all, why not, why ever not? An office boy could prove useful, someone to fetch and carry. Reading wasn't strictly necessary and he could demonstrate his abilities if he had any. He could see advantages in introducing an African face into the sea of Asians, why not? Education was the way forward for any society and as far as the locals were concerned it was almost entirely lacking. Given a chance the boy's manners might also improve.

'Anthony!' he called. The boy turned back.

'Do you really want to work in an office? It can be very dull, you know. There's no point in it if you'd really rather be doing something practical, like your father.'

Anthony muttered something.

'I didn't hear you.'

'Want good job. Want to learn good job.'

'That's an admirable aspiration.'

'Want to be boss, office boss, big boss.'

'Big boss?' Walter couldn't help laughing. 'I don't think that's very likely. And while I approve of ambition it has to be realistic. If you can't read…'

The crane driver was tugging at the boy's shirt. 'No, no, that wrong, Anthony. *Bwana* Barnes, his English not good sometimes. He not mean that, only want office job, not mean boss job.'

'I suspect that his English is very good. And ambition is not always a bad thing.'

Anthony's lower lip protruded, defiant. He stared at Walter, almost as if challenging him. There was something unnerving about the boy, a muted hostility alongside the ambition, and just possibly a sharp mind behind the resentful façade. Wanted to be the boss? Absurd, of course – unimaginable. Where did he get that idea?

'Office job, small job,' his father said.

Walter's belly rumbled. He needed to find food. 'I'll think about it,' he said. 'See what I can do.' But even as he spoke he knew that he would do nothing.

The crane driver inclined his head but Anthony maintained his challenge. Walter nodded to them and walked on.

He bought a curry from one of the stalls that lined India Street and ate it standing up. Was there hostility to the colonial project? Among the kids, Anthony's generation? But no, more likely Anthony was just awkward, unschooled in the necessary arts of compromise. He'd soon learn those from his dad and settle down.

There was still time to kill before meeting Winnie. *What to do? Two turnings and I could be in Stanley Street. Funny that. Less than five minutes and I could be there. Hear her voice, recapture it, that'd defeat any remaining sourness. No denying it, despite the occasional outburst of temper she's a lovely woman, never met anyone like her*, and the lovemaking had been, well, special. There was something about her and whatever it was Winnie could do with a helping.

'*Bwana* want beer?' The stallholder held out a bottle of Tusker, poised to snap it open.

Walter stared at him and, very slowly, shook his head. *Off my trolley. Ridiculous thoughts, have to watch it. Focus on Winnie. Why this delay? What's she doing? She's only been here a couple of weeks and already she's changing things. Bloody woman, can't get a grip on her.*

He returned to his office and the charts.

***

Choitram's was crowded and an assistant with a nervous tic in his left eye was forced to leave them with the jewellery tray while he attempted to deal with an Asian matron with a long and carefully itemised list of kitchen requirements. The assistant went and came with item after item of cookware and suffered rejection after rejection. His tic worsened.

'Where've you been?' Walter asked.

'Lunch with Charles. And friends of his,' Winnie said. 'A married couple, the Buchans, Jim and Betty. He's in Admin, a Treasury wallah. I'm going to have a sundowner and supper with them tonight.'

'And am I invited?'

'I've no idea. If you've not heard by now I suppose not.'

'And Mallinson?'

'I think so. They've a house at Msimbazi, just before the bridge.'

She held up a silver band set with a cluster of three large rhinestones and tilted it in order to examine the inner surface. 'These are fairly awful, aren't they? And not even hallmarked. How on earth are we to know where it's from?'

'We don't. Most of this stuff comes in on dhows from Arabia. My guess would be that it was made in Damascus, shipped to Aden and then on to Zanzibar and finally here.'

'Very exotic. But could I wear something like this? As an

engagement ring? All the time? No. It's cheap, it screams cheap. Maybe I am cheap, but if I am I don't want to advertise the fact.'

He began to protest but she silenced him.

'It's funny, isn't it? If everyone knows you're rolling in it, then you can wear this sort of stuff. But not us church mice. We're trapped, we can't afford the good, so we do the sensible thing and buy what we can afford, and what then happens? Our little box gets a nice fat tick. Cheap people.'

'I could afford a diamond.'

'No, you couldn't. Or if you could we'd need a magnifying glass to see it.'

'All I have to do is go to the shipping agents and get a refund on your return ticket.'

She put the ring down. Her eyes met his in the tall mirror behind the counter. It advertised BSA Rifles: three guns leaning against each other like the inner scaffolding of a tepee. One of the barrels partly obscured the right side of her face but her eyes were in full view.

'That's a rather sideways proposal,' she said.

'It's not a proposal, it's a reminder. I've already proposed, in case you've forgotten.'

'Yes, I suppose you have. Very badly.' She broke eye contact.

Walter could hear raised voices: the assistant was starting to demand a decision from the Asian matron. He shifted slightly and his face in the mirror broke clear of its prison. A hand laid itself on his. 'Is something wrong?' he asked.

She ran her fingers up his arm, little dancing taps at first, then slowing down and finally ending with a forefinger resting on his shoulder. 'I don't think I need to wear a ring.'

The forefinger was no longer resting. It was, he thought, pointing, almost accusatory. 'Well, don't, it's not compulsory.'

A porter lurched past them with a sack of grain on his back, his sweaty odour trailing after him. The Asian matron also departed, abandoning her quest. Winnie closed her eyes, waved her hand across the tray and selected another ring. It was again silver but with a large yellow stone perched awkwardly on it. Choitram's assistant edged closer to them.

Winnie held the ring up to him. 'What is this stone?'

'It is citrine, madam, a very valuable stone, very beautiful.'

Winnie looked at the small tag tied to the ring. 'Very valuable and remarkably inexpensive.'

'A good buy, madam.'

Winnie snorted. She dropped the ring back into the tray and adjusted the scarf she wore wrapped turban-style around her head, pulling its stray ends tighter and then tucking them out of sight. She glanced at the mirror and, satisfied, picked up her handbag. 'Thank you,' she said, 'you've been most helpful.'

'Are you really not going to buy a hat?' Walter asked once they were back on Acacia Avenue.

'Don't you start. I've had enough from that woman – mornings looking at shells and afternoons getting costume advice. And all the time simpering and making goggle-eyes at the houseboy.'

Walter laughed. 'Come now.'

'I'm not imagining it. At least he has the sense not to take a blind bit of notice.'

'She's just being polite. I approve.'

'Stop being so nice. Johnny isn't nice, he gets fearfully ratty. There was a dead bushbaby on the veranda steps this morning; it fell off the roof which apparently they never do. Meg said Johnny'd poisoned it – he's put arsenic everywhere in the garden it seems. You know the *shamba* boy's been taken ill? Meg thinks that's down to the arsenic too. They had a splendid row, masses of effing and blinding. I learned several new words. Can't wait to get out of there.'

She slipped her arm inside his and they strolled on towards the harbour front. The sun was already low behind them and the calm water had turned from silver to a caramel yellow. What did it matter if she didn't wear a ring? Here they were, arm in arm – didn't that announce their status to the world? And there was Mohinder Singh, wheeling his bicycle away from the shuttered telegraph office. Leaving early, of course. He would have seen them, true lovers wrapped in an aura of mutual adoration, and would now pass on his observation to anyone and everyone. An engagement ring wasn't necessary. He'd save some cash, too.

They continued past the Customs outbuildings and on towards the beach where a few fishing boats, mostly canoes with outriggers, were being prepared for the evening activity, the nets checked and folded, the simple triangles of sail hoisted and tested. Walter stopped by the furthest shed. He detached himself from Winnie and crouched to look beneath the building.

'Bella!' he called. 'Here, girl.'

He clicked his fingers and whistled, then looked up at Winnie.

'She's in hiding. Bella is my secret woman. I've fed her a couple of times. She should know my voice by now. Here, Bella, come girl, come – biscuits for you, Bella.'

'Anyway, I've got a job,' Winnie said. 'I don't need the McLeods any more. I can afford a room at the Gymkhana Club. I might even be able to move in at the weekend.'

'Here, Bella,' he said. He stayed in his crouched position but swayed slightly forward, so that he had to put his hand on the dry earth to steady himself.

As he did so Bella peered around a corner of the shed, tail tucked between her legs.

'Bella! Good girl.' He felt in his jacket pocket. He'd bought shortbread from an itinerant hawker who'd called at the mess with goods he presumably thought of interest to the European palate.

'Well,' Winnie said, 'what do you think?'

Still crouched, he laid the shortbread on the baked earth.

'A job? How?' he asked.

'Do look at me. Why aren't you pleased? Is getting a job so awful?'

He scrambled to his feet. 'She still doesn't trust me. We'd better back off.'

'Charles fixed it – the job I mean. I'll be working in Government House. For Jim Buchan.'

'Who?'

'I just told you. He's very senior, in the Treasury.'

'Never heard of him. Come, Bella, biscuit for you.'

'That's why we had lunch, so Charles could introduce me. It was Betty who asked me to supper. I could hardly refuse, could I?'

'Good, a useful contact,' he said.

'You don't mind?'

'No,' he lied, 'why should I?'

'Well, then.'

Bella's tail had unfurled a little. He took a step backwards.

'Can't get too close to her, or she'll take off.'

'I knew you'd take it badly, and you have, haven't you?'

He took her hand and pulled her in the direction of the beach but his eyes remained fixed on the dog. When they reached the edge of the soft sand he halted. 'That's as far as we need go,' he said.

'Please, Walter, please react. I can't stand silence.'

He raised a finger to his lips and shook his head. Bella had inched forward and begun to smell the shortbread. Then, a momentous decision, she grabbed it and ran off, vanishing once more into the jumble of machinery and timber behind the sheds.

'Good girl, Bella, good girl!' Walter called.

'And another thing,' Winnie said, 'I can't stand moods. So you'd better learn that I do what I want to do, not what some bloke wants me to do.'

His anger erupted. 'Some bloke? I'm some bloke? You can't see it, can you? How it looks when you do things like this, where it leaves me? I'm not some bloke, some old pal you happen to be visiting, I'm your fiancé. You don't do things like this without reference to your fiancé. It's, it's...' He struggled to find the word. '...demeaning, it's demeaning. What do these people think when you ignore me? How irrelevant I am, how thoroughly unimportant, someone who can be brushed aside.'

Winnie stared at him, then turned and walked away along the beach, her shoes scuffing up the sand. He trailed after her.

'I suppose...' he began and stopped as she stopped too. She looked down at her shoes, white plimsolls laced with blue ribbon, dropped her raffia bag onto the sand and sank down beside it. She sat with her hands clasped around her knees and watched as a flock of pink-backed pelicans made a majestic progress across the harbour, their slow and methodical wing-beats interspersed with effortless glides. As they headed away from the watchers the early evening light transformed them. They became spectral creatures, giant bats escaped from some African fairy tale, and then as they reached the far shore their pale bodies merged into the luminescent boles of a coconut grove and they vanished.

Winnie brought her hands up to her forehead to shade her eyes, searching the distant trees for a final glimpse of the birds. When she spoke she didn't look at him. 'Walter,' she said, 'I haven't said it, have I? But thank you, thank you for bringing me here. But you have to accept me as I am. I won't change.'

'You will if you stay here. Look at me, haven't I changed?'

He crouched next to her and then shifted to a kneeling position. 'I'm glad you came,' he said. 'But I just wish you'd tell me things. The job, the room. Meetings with Mallinson. It's all happening so fast.'

'I have told you. You should be pleased. A room at the Gymkhana Club means we can be private, it means we can make love at last.'

'That's not the point, is it?'

She didn't answer. The smile had gone. She reached down and pulled off first one shoe and then the other, not bothering to untie the laces. Trickles of silver sand spilled from them and she leaned forward to shake them clean, then lay back to rest propped up on her elbows. Her heels dug into the sand. Walter was aware of curious onlookers, fishermen, a gaggle of ragged children, a passing cyclist. His fingers played in the soft sand.

'Nearly sundowner time,' she said.

'Not for me, it seems.'

She said nothing. He was aware of the steady drone of frogs in the culvert to their left. Then he too lay on his back and stared upwards. The darkening sky had already collected a smattering of dim stars. He thought: everything happens in the night in Africa. There was something that needed to be said. He couldn't hold it back any longer.

'It is going to work, isn't it?' he said, and as the words came out his throat constricted, as if to prevent him from saying more.

She turned her head to look at him, then sat up, took his face in her hands, and kissed him full on the lips.

'Of course it is. It'll work and it'll be brilliant,' she said. A second squadron of pelicans began their low undulating progress over the water.

'I want you to be sure. I know you want someone but is it me?'

''Course it is,' she said. After a moment she undid her scarf and ran her fingers through her thick curls. 'There's a decent hairdresser, Meg says, in Bagamoyo Street, somewhere past that mad

Barclays Bank building, the one that looks like a castle owned by a poverty-stricken knight.'

He felt certain that the phrase was Mallinson's.

Fine sand had found its way into every crease in his clothes. He scrambled to his feet to shake himself free but a few grains clung stubbornly to his sweaty skin.

'You'd best be off,' he said.

She looked up at him and smiled. 'And now you want to get rid of me. At least let me put my shoes on.'

He watched as she dusted her feet, poking her fingers between her toes to clean out every grain. 'Do you have to go to these people tonight?'

She didn't answer.

He had the excuse he needed, the justification. She did what she wanted. So could he.

CHAPTER 16

It was still early evening when he got there but it was busier than before. An overweight white sat perched on the edge of the bench. He'd opened his shirt collar and his regimental tie hung loose but he was sweating nonetheless. He pointedly avoided looking at Walter. The man in the leg brace was behind the bar and the supposed accountant leaned against it, propped on his elbows. He wore the same shabby safari suit. Walter joined him. Sitting alongside the other white was not an option.

'A Tusker for the gentleman,' the accountant called out, and straightened up the better to slap his hand on the bar and emphasise the order. Walter was annoyed by the presumption but felt obliged to nod a frosty acknowledgment. A Tusker appeared before him together with a glass, and having served the beer, the man in the callipers shuffled off towards the back door and stood there as if on sentry duty.

'I'm waiting for Margaret. She'll be free soon,' the accountant whispered. 'Very good – I recommend.'

'A beer is all I want,' Walter said.

'You should try, you might be surprised. She is… flexible, yes. You know, flexible, active, yes, my dear sir – an experience not to be missed!'

He wanted to move away but was aware of the unspoken protocol initiated by the presence of the other white. Chance eye contact was to be avoided at all costs. He was reduced to staring straight ahead. A small row of spirit bottles, brandy, gin, cherry and other liqueurs, stood on a shelf at the back of the bar. None were of a brand he recognised.

The back door gave a thin, high-pitched whine as it opened, but not far enough for Walter to see who stood there. The florid white man got to his feet and hurried over. The door whined shut behind him.

'Is Madame Rosa not here tonight?' Walter asked.

'Oh yes,' the accountant said and indicated the back room. 'Busy, busy lady. A fine woman. We admirers have good taste, a fine thing, good taste. I love poetry, you know, the beauty of the English language, romance!' He coughed and cleared his throat. '*I am half sick of shadows.*' He pounded his fist on the counter. '*The Lady of Shalott*! So beautiful! Yes, yes, the Lord Alfred Tennyson, a noble soul. I know it all, all by heart. I could recite it but I must not, no my friend no, it is too beautiful, too sad, it makes me cry. You love poetry, I can tell you do. We shall recite poetry together one day, yes?'

Walter took his beer over to the bench. He'd had enough of the accountant and his poetry and his insinuations. He refused to accept them. She couldn't be with that fat ugly sweaty man, she couldn't be, and that was that. The Tusker tasted sour.

He waited.

The accountant accepted his snubbing.

The man in the leg brace came and went through the back

door several times. Walter learned to ignore its siren scraping. He listened to the world outside, to the buzz of evening activity as it built slowly, in tune with the cooling street. He examined the room, ticking off the now familiar sights.

The girls peered over the wall.

Secrets, he thought. *They are about to uncover secrets.* He imagined Winnie climbing the ladder, Winnie uncovering secrets. He'd not had secrets before he came to Dar.

The fat man left.

The accountant left.

Another white face appeared, saw Walter and retreated.

Then, somehow, by some silent alchemy, she was in the room, behind the bar, a book in front of her, and there was no one else present.

'You're always reading,' he said. 'What is it now?'

'Some story,' she said.

She turned a page and then laid the book, still open, face down on the counter.

'I don't like stories. Why are you here?'

'To see you.'

'I'm busy. Go away.' She picked up her book.

'You won't get rid of me so easily.'

He came across to the bar. His beer glass was empty and he rapped it on the counter. 'Another Tusker, please.'

Without looking at him she reached under the counter, produced a bottle and pushed it over to him. A bottle opener followed. He ignored them and instead reached across and took the book from her.

'Page seventy-three,' he said and closed it. 'I came to say I'm sorry. We didn't part well. It was my fault.'

At last she looked at him. 'Yes,' she said, 'yes, it was your fault. You took but you did not give.'

'I offered to pay.'

She flung a hand upwards. 'Money, money, money! No, that is not what I meant. That is not the issue.'

He knew it wasn't. He picked up the Tusker bottle, gave it a quick shake and snapped it open. Foam erupted and spilled over his hand and onto the book, which he picked up and shook.

'Have you a cloth?' he asked.

She stared at him, making and holding eye contact, and then slowly and with deliberation took the book from him and dropped it onto the floor behind her. The action was a challenge, but to what? He returned to the bench.

The back door whined its warning. The lame man came in and took up his sentry duty.

He couldn't look at her. All he knew was that he wanted her, was possessed by desire for her. Did he want her wholly for himself or in part as punishment for Winnie? Some form of atonement was required, for his sake as much as for hers.

'I try to be a good man,' he said, 'but I'm out of my depth here. Tell me what I can do to make things better between us.'

'You have done it,' she said. 'The decent thing, isn't that what you whites call it, the decent thing? You said sorry. Now you can go away and feel pleased with yourself. Sahib has done the decent thing.'

She waved a contemptuous hand. 'Go,' she said.

The instruction had its effect. He knew instantly that he was not going to obey it. 'And if I prefer to stay?'

'Why? To hear me talk, is that why? You like to hear me talk, you say. You like many things – Tusker, yes – but most of all you like to hear me talk. About my life, yes? But I don't want to.'

'No, no, we don't have to talk about you. Other things will do, cabbages and kings, things that would be less interesting, but safe.'

'Cabbages? No, I do not believe you. You are like me – you too are a liar.'

'Yes. I'm a liar. Can I stay?'

She leaned down and picked up her book. Damp pages clung to each other. She walked past Walter and handed it to the sentry, who was evidently unhappy about something. There was a brief exchange of opinion in heightened voices after which she pulled open the inner door.

'Bring your beer,' she said and, releasing the door, went through into the inner area. Walter was forced to hurry, snatching the door before it closed completely.

He followed her, ignoring the waiting girls in the first room and continuing down a narrow, unpainted corridor into the room at the end. It was papered in a Georgian stripe and the only items of furniture other than the broad divan were a table on which sat a green and white basin and ewer and an upright chair with a coat hanger dangling from it. Rosa sat on the bed and looked up at him.

'Talk then,' she said.

Talk was not enough. What he wanted involved danger. He'd thought once of training as a harbour pilot, and while working at Avonmouth docks had taken a preliminary course, had learned of reefs and shallows that hint at the nearby presence of land, of safety, but which also concealed craters where the ocean floor fell away and riptides seized the unwary traveller. Safety and danger coexisted. This was a dangerous place. As if to confirm his diagnosis, a too-familiar caw punctured the silence.

'Talk,' she said again. 'Say what you want to say.'

He lowered himself onto the bed beside her, took her nearer hand in his, and closed his eyes. The bird screeched again. He was pursued by devils. Why? She was waiting.

'I don't know what you expect to hear. Mine's been a conventional life. I've never questioned it, always behaved as I was expected to behave, observed the correct social codes – yes, tried to do the decent thing. Until I came to Dar I was happy, content with my boring, unexciting, sensible life. But now… now, in this place, I've lost my balance. I've realised, I'm realising now, here, in this moment, that my life needs more, but more of what? I don't know. I'm being dragged into another world, and you're partly to blame. You've unbalanced me.'

He opened his eyes and looked at her. 'I want you.'

She shook her hand free of his. 'What stupidity is this,' she said.

A door in the passage slammed and heavy footsteps trailed away along the corridor. They sat in silence. He scanned the room.

'I hate this place,' he said eventually. 'Not because it's so…' He searched for the words. '…so desolate, so desperately sad. I hate it because you work here. You should not be here, should not be doing this.'

'I agree. So are you going to rescue me? Are you a prince from a fairy story?'

Yes, he thought, *that's what I'd like to do, become a prince and rescue you. A fantasy, of course. But I'm trapped in the limited mundanity of Dar's dullness, its stratified social orders. Our worlds have no points of contact, or rather none that can be put on display.* His collar had begun to chafe him, and he scratched at the back of his neck.

'I had a book of fairy stories,' she said. 'It had a picture on the cover: a princess in a high tower, with golden hair, so long it reached almost to the ground. I forget her name, but she was so sad. She was a prisoner, locked in her tower. You know this story?'

'Rapunzel,' he said.

'Was that her name? I don't remember. I remember the picture though. There was a picture of her, like so, waiting.' She held her hands up to her neck, nestling under her jawbone with her fingers enlaced. 'Waiting…'

He loosened his tie and undid his collar button, releasing the pressure, and then ran a finger round his neck, feeling the slight tenderness left by the starched collar.

'…and watching. For a prince to come riding, riding, a prince to rescue her, to ride away with her.' Her voice level had dropped to a whisper. 'To ride away.'

Did she really think he could be her prince? *She's changed*, he thought. *Her eyes are no longer the comforting deep brown I found at first. They've darkened, become not so much a colour as an absence of colour, a black – no, not even a black – rather an emptiness. I don't know her, I've never known her, never known for sure what she's thinking, about me or about anything. How can I feel such need for a woman I know nothing about? But I do. I want to be her prince, if only I knew how.*

She clapped her hands. 'Of course, the nuns took my book away. They said fairy stories gave girls stupid ideas, stupid dreams – they were right, do you not think? But I remember that picture, remember her waiting and watching.'

She edged away from him. Their bodies no longer touched. The bird screeched again. The silence extended. She spoke first. 'We are such liars, you and me and the whole world, liars.'

Was she telling him something? About herself? There was something here he needed to understand, to explore. As he searched for the words he needed, a series of male shouts erupted from the room next door. He looked up, startled, but she didn't react. This was it seemed a commonplace event, a hazard of brothels. It had however caused his chain of thought to slide away from him and he had to take a moment to locate it once more. He took her hands in his.

'The strange thing is, my girl, I feel that I understand her, I know her, but despite that I can't get close to her. Whereas you, I don't think I know you at all, not in the way I do her, yet it seems that with you—' He stumbled over the words. '—that with you…' He got no further.

She pushed him away from her and stood up. 'No, no, you are comparing me. I will not be compared: it is a form of judgment. Someone wins, someone loses.'

She began to pace up and down, agitated, her hands clasping and unclasping, her bracelets chattering angrily. 'Your life has nothing to do with me, nothing, nothing, but still you come here, you search for me. Why?'

He looked down, hands clasped, seeing nothing but the cracks in the mud floor. 'I don't know. I don't understand myself.'

Her restless pacing ceased and her breaths became shorter and deeper. He waited for her to speak but she didn't. Instead, a silence enveloped them and in that silence a thought arose, unbidden, and he began to test it, examine it, turn it over and over in his mind. It was as unlikely as lightning on a cloudless day and as dangerous.

Is this love?

He could talk of love with Winnie and the immediate truth of what they said didn't matter. The exchanges were exploratory, neither of them quite sure if what they were saying was what they meant. Half-truths, intimations of truth could be examined and discarded or on occasion used as stepping stones to a better understanding of what the word meant. There were many routes to the truth about love and with a girl like Winnie he could be confident that the cave systems of language would lead eventually to light, to understanding.

But with Rosa he sensed that such a process was impossible. The word would not, could not be used as a base for exploration. For her it would be absolute or it would be nothing. She had stopped her restless pacing and now stood still, within touching distance, embraceable. He held out a hand but she didn't respond.

'You must go,' she said.

Did he love her? Yes or no, the question was irrelevant. In this place, in this town, he knew that to say it would be ridiculous, to mean it disastrous. He thought of the Greeks who bore gifts. Love was also a wooden horse. Love was also a word that could unlock iron doors, could destroy cities. And here, in the Haven of Peace, in this confident world, in the Empire he so believed in, in 1932 he knew that such a love was unacceptable and if spoken could, no, would destroy them both.

He stumbled to his feet and tried to put his arms round her. She shook him off.

'Go,' she said again. 'Go to your girl and leave me alone.' She was of course right.

He lurched into the corridor and on into the bar, into the street, into the town, seeing nothing, aware only of the tumult within him. Somehow he arrived at the Club.

***

Ferriggi had a message for him.

Winnie was out at Oyster Bay, packing. The hoped-for room at the Gymkhana Club had come free. There were no taxis available so he was forced to hail the first cycle rickshaw he came across. It had no tyres and was running on the steel rims of its wheels. Twenty-plus minutes of lurching and jolting followed, which at least had the effect of part restoring his composure.

Winnie was upstairs organising herself and insisted on being left alone to do it. Meg was sorting out a number of newly acquired shells. She was in a bad mood and took the opportunity to explain to Walter exactly why. McLeod had been summoned to a meeting in Tanga, near the Kenyan border, where the Inspector-in-Charge, Fairweather, had been having problems, the border being the source. The planners at the 1884 Berlin Conference charged with drawing up the demarcation line between British Kenya and German *Ostafrika* had drawn a satisfyingly neat straight line from Lake Victoria to the coast, with a single kink around Mount Kilimanjaro. This detour was regarded as testimony to the flexibility of their thinking.

Annoyingly, however, Maasai tribesmen persisted in ignoring the demarcation line and continued to carry goods backwards and forwards between the two countries without informing the authorities and in defiance of Customs regulations. It seemed that they had no grasp of the concept of a border, nor indeed of the concept of a country, and expressed surprise when arrested. Crispin, the Kenyan Deputy Commissioner, had travelled down from Mombasa to Tanga and the three men were charged with producing a report and, ideally, a solution. This seemed unlikely, as McLeod happily acknowledged.

'They'll never get it,' he said of the Maasai, 'not in a month of Sundays.'

'Maybe they do get it,' Walter said, 'and choose to ignore it. After all, the border does cut through their traditional territory.'

'Well, things have changed, and the sooner they learn that simple fact and join the modern world the better for them.'

To Meg's annoyance, instead of using sea transport for the journey, picking up a lift on a local packet, he'd decided to drive.

'He won't risk a trip to the reef at Mbweni but he will tackle Tanga,' she said. 'Ten times as far, if not more. Not a decent road of any sort from Bagamoyo onwards unless you go fifty miles inland. I know why he's done it, of course.'

Walter didn't rise to the bait. He wanted nothing to do with the McLeods' domestic squabbles. He picked up a shell, a ghostly off-white mass of jagged projections, roughly triangular in shape and with a gaping mouth rimmed with pink as though it had been experimenting with lipstick, but unsuccessfully. He didn't like it. Winnie was taking her time.

'It means I can't have the car.'

'I didn't realise you could drive.'

'I can't. Juma can. But Johnny wouldn't have him in the car, would he? That's why he decided to drive: spite.'

Walter returned to the study of the shell. Unlike the spider conch the sexuality on display here seemed trivial and adolescent, too obvious. He turned it over in his hands.

'Now we'll have to take a taxi.'

He continued his examination of the shell. Meg was coming with them? He could barely contain his irritation.

At the Gymkhana Club a stick-thin Lebanese woman showed them Winnie's new accommodation. It was a wooden chalet, one of a group of three in the bougainvillea-dominated thicket behind the tennis courts, lit by oil lamps and hardly better furnished than Walter's room in the mess. It did, however, mean that Winnie was able to put on a convincing show of sadness at leaving Oyster Bay.

'I just have to be in Dar for the job,' she said to Meg, who patted her on the shoulder in commiseration. They stood, silent and awkward, as the Lebanese woman lit a coil of mosquito repellent and then supervised the delivery of the green trunk. She slipped away as the coil began to release its acrid fumes.

'Well now,' Winnie said, 'this is fun.'

She didn't move. A bonfire somewhere in the Club gardens made its contribution to the day's scents. Walter looked down at the linoleum-covered floor. It had a pattern of repeating squares in shades of orange and green. Someone actually chose this?

'You've been so helpful,' Winnie said, but still didn't move.

'I'll leave you to it then,' Meg said.

'Yes,' Winnie said.

'I'll go and hunt up some of the old witches who infest this place, pick up the scandal. That's something I wanted to say to you both. Watch yourselves, won't you? One false move and every mem in Dar will know about it. You may think you're worldly-wise but I know innocence when I see it.'

Walter felt a surge of appreciation for McLeod. Living with Meg would irritate anyone.

'Thank you,' Winnie said.

Meg took her hand. 'Oh my dear, I hope you like Dar better than I do.'

She pulled Winnie towards her, wrapped her arms around her shoulders and hugged her. Six inches the shorter of the two, Winnie's mop of curls pressed into Meg's collarbone. The two women began a rocking motion, Meg shifting her weight from foot to foot to initiate it. Her mouth had lost its severity, her lower lip protruding slightly and turning down. There was a glistening dampness in her eyes and Walter was forced to recognise that the emotion on display was genuine. Eventually Winnie began to push herself away and Meg released her. For a brief moment she scanned the room as if remembering something left behind and then with a flutter of her fingers towards Walter, she left. They could see her hurrying back along the path towards the main building.

Walter sat on the single bed and watched as Winnie began to unpack.

'Such a relief!' she said as she removed the maroon dress from the trunk and shook it to remove the creasing.

'She's needy.'

'I can see that. This room is pretty ghastly, isn't it? This lino! But at least it's my own. I wondered if she'd ever go.'

He said nothing, but ran his hand over the bed's thin cotton top sheet, then looked up to examine the mosquito netting. It hung down from a ceiling hook and had been gathered and bunched into the standard loose knot. He sat on the bed and tugged at it. The netting fell into place around him enmeshing his head and upper torso. Winnie hung the dress in the heavy mahogany wardrobe and adjusted it so that the bolero jacket sat square on its hanger. She stepped back to admire it.

'Winnie.'

She didn't respond.

'Winnie, please. Come and talk to me.'

She came across and sat on the end of the bed.

'We should talk,' he said.

'The funny thing is,' she said, 'she's telling us there's wickedness about, and I think she's right.'

'Why on earth d'you say that?'

'Because it's true. She means in us, the Europeans. We're the lords and masters here and that's dangerous. Charles knows it but doesn't care – he's wicked himself, so that's all right. But you don't see the wickedness, you're too good. As for me, I'm beginning to think…' She paused. '…perhaps I fit in very well.'

'You? Why?'

'Because I'm a woman, and I know myself.'

'I don't know what you're talking about.'

'No, that's what's so good about you.' She stared ahead, her chin cradled in her hands. 'Shall we make love?' she asked.

He didn't want to. 'Of course,' he said.

Afterwards they lay side by side, sweaty and dissatisfied, forced together by the narrowness of the bed. He tried to roll away from her to avoid the clamminess of contact but found his hip resting on the iron frame. He sat up. There was a small closet off the main room with a basin and ewer in it and Walter shut himself in. There was no facecloth, so instead he wiped himself down with a dampened towel and then inspected his reflection in the small mirror propped against the back of the washstand.

Winnie was asleep, or appeared to be.

He sat in the only chair and closed his eyes.

CHAPTER 17

Mallinson flung open the Humber's boot.

'It'll be quite a ride,' he said. 'Hundred plus miles, my bet is five hours, which means we won't be there before early afternoon, hence the emergency supplies. 'Fraid it doesn't leave much space for bags.'

There were two large jerrycans of petrol, a water barrel, a leather Gladstone bag and a rolled-up canvas toolkit in the car's boot. Winnie handed Mallinson the suitcase she'd borrowed from Meg and he squeezed it into the only remaining space. Walter proffered his satchel.

'Have to have that inside. You much of a mechanic, Barnes?'

'Never had a car.'

'Pity. I was relying on you to be a practical sort.'

Pigeonholed, as he might have expected. 'The toolkit has the basics?'

'God knows. Take a look?'

Walter pulled out the toolkit and unrolled it. There was a set of Armstrong wrenches, a choice of three screwdrivers, a small claw hammer, pliers, a roll of friction tape and a wire stripper. 'Not bad. The jack?'

'Tucked away behind the cans. It does look ominously well used.'

'And you've checked the spare tyre?'

'Ah.'

The spare tyre was in its housing, strapped to the bonnet passenger-side, just ahead of the running board. Walter undid the wing nuts holding it in place. It appeared to be properly inflated but testing by hand was pointless. What can go wrong, will.

'The Governor's squad of *fundis* checked it out for me,' Mallinson said.

'And you trust them?'

'Why wouldn't I?'

Walter shrugged and concentrated on levering the tyre off its spindle and bouncing it on the compacted clay at the side of the car. 'Seems fine.' He slapped the tyre, gave it one more bounce and began to replace it, taking his time. 'Any idea of the road conditions?'

'To Morogoro? The best road in the country, I'm told. And don't be modest. I can see you know your stuff – we're safe in your hands. I'll shove your bag on the back seat with the food hamper.' He took the satchel, opened the rear door and flung it in. 'I thought some extra rations might be a good idea. Champagne, caviare, that sort of thing.'

'I don't believe you,' Winnie said. 'Let me see.'

'All right, I lied about the caviare but I did liberate a bottle of Dom Perignon from the Governor's icebox.'

'Prove it!'

'See for yourself, oh doubting Thomasina.'

The food hamper sat on the back seat, driver's side, clamped shut by leather straps. Winnie knelt on the seat alongside it in order to prise the buckles open.

Walter rolled up the toolkit, replaced it and closed the boot. *Maybe I should offer to drive and put on a chauffeur's cap while I'm at it.*

'Look, Walter!' Winnie had backed out of the Humber and now stood beside it waving a squat bottle with a long neck.

'Dom Perignon, warm and shaken – just how it should be,' Mallinson said, and laughed. 'And the hood down, Win, what d'you say?'

'Oh, the hood down, no question.'

'That's a girl.'

'I certainly was the last time I looked.'

She leaned into the car to replace the champagne. Mallinson glanced at Walter, a slightly skewed smile arriving and vanishing. He began to unfasten the hood. *Win?* Walter had never called her that and the easy familiarity was yet more evidence of something going on. If so, this trip would sort it out for good and all. Winnie could either commit to him one hundred per cent, no doubts, no ifs and buts and maybes, or they'd finish it.

He settled the last strut into its folded-down position. Five to one they'd finish it. As for that other woman, he'd forgotten her already.

* * *

The first twenty or so miles were on a macadamised surface, and for stretches they were able to travel at over forty miles per hour but the tar had petered out by the time they reached Kibamba. The murram surface that replaced it meant that the Humber was reduced to a maximum twenty as Mallinson negotiated the ruts and potholes.

'Goddamn,' he kept saying. The Humber's chassis groaned as it lurched and crabbed sideways yet again. His passengers kept silent. The dry earth began to moisten as the road climbed and for a time the driving became easier. The thorny scrub with its acacias and isolated baobabs thinned out and gave way to scrawny yellow-woods. The tonal aspect of the countryside darkened too. Pale greens gave way to darker, richer notes, vegetation unfamiliar to coastal dwellers. The temperature had dropped and there was evidence of recent rain with small pools of water on the road. Mud was the problem now.

Mallinson pulled over. 'Hood up, I think.'

They had stopped up beside a plantation of tall grain. Dry brown seed heads almost a foot long topped tough stalks. Walter ran a hand through them.

'Kaffir corn,' he told Winnie. 'Joseph grows it in his *shamba*.'

'Do give a hand, Barnes,' Mallinson called. 'No time for agricultural instruction.'

Walter held up a warning hand. 'Someone's in there,' he said, inclining his head towards the plantation.

'Priorities, please, Barnes. This is the devil of a thing.'

And it was true, the hood was easy to take down but not to put back up. The material unfolded easily enough and getting the side struts into position was straightforward but the canopy refused to fit the fastenings.

'You've done this before, I take it,' Walter said. *As if he has.*

'Not me, heavens no, I rely on the *fundis*, hand it to them to deal with.'

'Bit risky taking it down, then.'

The tip of Mallinson's tongue was visible for a second as he contemplated Walter. 'Noooo…' he said, elongating the 'o' until the word itself seemed to lose meaning, to become simultaneously both agreement and rejection.

'Boys, boys,' Winnie said.

Walter tried once more, hauling the material's lead bar forward towards the windshield. It ended half an inch short. 'Take the other side,' he ordered. 'Can't do it by myself.'

'We're being watched,' Winnie said.

A crowd of women and naked children had emerged, silent, from the forest on the other side of the road. Mallinson glanced at them and then took hold of his side of the lead bar. As they began to pull, the corn stalks thrashed and crackled and a boy of perhaps eight hurled himself past them and raced across the road to bury his head in a *bibi*'s belly. A bundle of seed heads lay half-hidden, half-revealed by his violent passage through the stalks. Winnie picked it up and held it in both hands as if attempting to assess its weight. She took a step towards the watchers who retreated, several melting back into the vegetation as silently as they'd arrived. The mother alone remained steadfast, arms wrapped around her child. He was trembling and his eyes were shut tight.

'Muzungu,' she kept saying, 'muzungu, muzungu.'

Winnie held out the corn, offering it. The watchers didn't move. Winnie laid the bundle down on the edge of the road. 'What are they saying?'

'Means "white man",' Mallinson said.

'But why are they so worried?' Winnie asked.

'God knows. Dim creatures. Probably think we're ghosts. Or devils.'

'There must be a knack,' Walter said. 'We're doing things in the wrong order. D'you have any instructions, any at all?'

Mallinson didn't answer.

Walter released the bar. 'We'll try with the side fastenings first,' he said.

This was a better strategy. The sides clipped home without

excessive force, and the lead bar eventually mated with the windshield. Walter then took the struts one by one and forced the elbow joints past the 180-degree mark, locking them into place. The hood was secure. Winnie applauded.

'Let's get on,' Mallinson said.

Winnie looked back at the watchers, statuary at the side of the road, silent and immobile. 'They remind me of my dolls. I used to imagine them coming to life when I was asleep, living a life I knew nothing about. One night something woke me and I thought – it's them, I'll catch them at it. But when I switched the light on they were exactly where I'd left them, all in a row, my favourite Jemima, and Rosie and Baby, propped against the wall under the window, and I knew they were just dolls after all.' Mallinson punched the horn and let in the clutch. 'But I wished they weren't just dolls. I wanted them to have their own lives, even if I couldn't be a part of them.'

She twisted in her seat to look at Walter. 'Why wouldn't they take it? The corn, I mean. Do they think we've contaminated it?'

'Just being cautious, I suppose.'

Mallinson grunted. 'Let's get out of here.'

Walter closed his eyes. Mallinson hadn't thanked him.

* * *

A quarter of an hour later they had their first sight of the mist-clad Uluguru mountains, and Mallinson began to relax.

'What a bloody nightmare!' he said cheerfully, accelerated up to twenty-five miles per hour, and drove into a small puddle. The car dipped sideways, the chassis gave a loud crack, and the rear-wheel drive forced the back of the car sideways. It slewed round ninety degrees and stalled. No one spoke. Walter was the first out. They were some yards beyond the puddle, which was now no longer a puddle. Most of the water had been expelled by the impact and what was now revealed was a deep rut, its end capped by a lump of stone.

He peered under the car but couldn't get low enough to see anything without lying down. Winnie joined him, her plimsolls flecked with mud.

'What's the damage?' Mallinson called, unmoving, hands on the wheel.

Walter didn't answer. Instead he lay down on his back in the mud and edged beneath the chassis. *Luis Veiga should see me now.*

'Moment!' he shouted, and found to his surprise that his sour mood had lightened. The journey had improved, had become an adventure, had produced a challenge, if a very small one. Besides, the likely cause of the crack they'd heard was now apparent. He'd never driven a car, let alone owned one, but he could recognise a fractured pipe and the volatility of the fluid that leaked from it. The impact had forced the petrol feed out of position and that in turn had caused the fracture. Otherwise the car seemed to have survived remarkably well.

'Can you see anything?' Winnie asked.

'Moment.'

This was good. He liked it here, looking up at the complex machinery above him. *Should have become an engineer, something useful, not a tax-gatherer.* The smell of petrol was raw but pleasant, like ether, or was it chloroform? He inhaled, and then tapped the chassis with his fingernails to alert the listeners to his busyness, his practicality. He peeled off a few bits of trapped vegetation. A cricket's corpse was trapped as well but he decided to regard it as a talisman and to leave it in place.

'You are my guardian,' he told it in a whisper. 'My future is in your hands.'

But what now? He could see what was needed – a simple

binding to seal the fracture. The friction tape would probably do. Better get on with it. But he didn't move for a further twenty seconds. It was only when he felt a dampness between his shoulders, a sign that the water in the mud had separated out that he began to edge back out. Mallinson had forsaken the driver's seat and now stood beside the car, a foot tapping on the murram. Walter extended a hand to him and was hauled to his feet.

'Is it bad?'

Walter tugged at his shirt, twisting it around to inspect the mud stains on his back. 'Filthy, I'm afraid,' he said. 'A challenge for the dhobi. I've got a spare shirt though.'

'The car?'

'Oh, the car. Yes. I think I see the problem.' He mimed stroking a non-existent beard.

'Walter!' Winnie said. 'Stop playing the goat. Are we stuck?'

'The fuel pipe's fractured, I'll have a go at it but there's no guarantee I'll succeed. Now we know why the train's so popular.'

He gave them his best smile, opened the boot, unrolled the toolkit and selected the hammer and the wrench set and then, as if as an afterthought, the electrical tape. A man appeared from the direction of Morogoro, perched on a tyreless bicycle. He stopped some twenty yards away and dismounted. Two women, babies strapped to their hips, emerged from the bush.

Mallinson leaned back against the bonnet and flicked his collar up. 'They're everywhere,' he said, 'watching us. Place looks empty but it's stuffed with people. Extraordinary. And why did no one tell me it would be so cold?'

Walter disappeared beneath the Humber. The first thing he had to do was force the pipe back into its original position. A bit of leverage from the forearm and a good sideways shove was all that was required and he did it easily, the pipe grateful to settle back into its proper home. It was all too easy and he wanted to give the others a sense of a difficult task requiring skill and labour. He gave the chassis a tap with a hammer and liked the resonant result. He followed it up with a few more taps accompanied by grunts of faked effort, all quite unnecessary and oddly satisfying.

The tape's powerful adhesive was more of a problem. As Walter unpeeled it, lying prone, his head inches below the broken pipe, it attached itself to his fingers, to itself and to any protruding metal it could find. Winding it around the pipe was also tricky, the roll having to be slipped sideways through the narrow space between pipe and chassis. He worked it round and round and as he did so the bandage he'd created fattened and the gap narrowed and the roll had to be squeezed and forced through the reducing space. The result was crude, lumpy and inelegant but the leak had dried up. *Job done*, he told himself. Should hold as far as Morogoro where there'd surely be a competent mechanic. If not, it might even hold all the way back to Dar. He gripped the pipe again to test it. Yes, a good job, crude but good, effective. What now? He could hear both Mallinson's voice, querulous, and Winnie's quiet responses but couldn't distinguish words.

It came to him that this weekend would no longer be the one in which they might separate. There was no might about it. They would. He subjected himself to a cross-examination by the cricket.

Did he love her?

No.

Had he ever loved her?

This was more difficult and required time but the answer was the same. No.

Did he care if they broke up?

Yes.

Really?

Yes.

He refined the thought. It wasn't losing Winnie he cared about, was it? It was the circumstances of the defeat.

Hurt pride, is that it? Losing her to Mallinson?

He couldn't deny it. He ran his tongue into the gap in his lower jaw where years before he'd lost a molar, and as he did so realised that he'd forgotten to bring toothpaste and would have to borrow some. The voices from the car rose and fell and once or twice mutated into laughter. *Show some gratitude, please!* The voices needed interruption, punctuation, needed to understand the extent of the thanks they owed him. He groped for and found a wrench and at first looked for a convenient nut to tighten. There was none, so he gave the chassis another sharp rap. It rang with a sting of sound, a satisfying reverberation of metal on metal. He repeated the blow, more powerfully this time, and to his satisfaction the murmurs ceased. Winnie's blue-laced plimsolls moved into sight once more. He turned his head to contemplate them and then rapped again – another, softer tap.

'Walter?' she said. 'Is there anything we can do?'

That was more like it. They were aware of him, of his efforts, of their reliance on him.

'Moment!' he called, and touched the corpse of the cricket.

'Thank you,' he whispered to it.

He celebrated with a grand finale, a tattoo of raps and clunks and clangs and then, satisfied, inched slowly out into the open air. The cloud cover had thickened, unfamiliar trees hung over him and there was a prickle of rain in the air. He hauled himself to his feet. Winnie had returned to her seat and Mallinson stood on the far side of the Humber, his blond forelock hanging over his brow.

'Well?'

Walter shrugged. 'Fuel feed was fractured. But I've done my best, should hold.'

'Should? Should? Goddamn. Let's bloody hope you're right.'

Walter put the tools away and closed the boot. His mud-soaked shirt was unwearable and he stripped it off, aware as he did so of a ripple of comment from the watchers, the original three joined now by half a dozen others, men as well as women. They had drawn closer, plainly curious, and he reacted in turn by posing for them in his mock-Charles Atlas style, leaning forward with his right knee bent, right arm crooked, elbow on knee, fist to forehead. The giggles turned to laughter and Walter obliged by repeating the pose on his left side. The audience applauded.

He enjoyed the response. It was the first fun he'd had all day. Mallinson gave a blast on the horn and pressed the ignition switch. Walter raised his hands in the air, posed, and then flung himself sideways in a less-than-perfect cartwheel, his feet failing to find purchase as he completed the circle. He scrambled to his feet, laughing, dignity gone. The audience applauded vigorously. The horn sounded again.

'Come on, Barnes,' Mallinson shouted. 'Stop arsing about.'

'Hang on,' Walter called. The sweat he'd generated had evaporated and gooseflesh pimpled his arms; he needed a shirt. He opened the rear door, rummaged in his satchel and pulled out his reserve.

'No hurry, is there?' he said as he did up the buttons. Winnie twisted in her seat to look at him. He grinned at her but she shook her head. *A cartwheel too far?*

'Heaven's sake, Walter, we want to get on,' she said.

He bowed to the watchers, received further applause, and then settled himself regally on the Humber's rear seat, stretching his arms out along the leather backrest.

'Let's do it then,' he said. 'Morogoro, chauffeur.'

Mallinson said nothing but now he drove with greater care. They were delayed by another vehicle, an ox-cart laden with corrugated iron, which spent several minutes clinging obstinately to the road's best line, veering from side to side in an attempt to find it. Passing was impossible. Mallinson gave a single burst of the horn, and when that appeared to have no effect followed it with a longer note and then a series of short, angry blasts. A black hand waved an acknowledgment but the cart showed no sign of pulling over. Dust had begun to accumulate in a thick layer on the windscreen of the Humber and was seeping through the gaps in the hood before finally, finally the cart swerved away down a side track.

* * *

It was four o'clock by the time they reached the town and the wide sandy road which was evidently the hub of local life. Mallinson pulled to a halt beside what appeared to be a bar. The words WELCOME FRIENDS were hand-painted on a square of cardboard propped against a stool, and a torn poster advertised Tusker. A dog crouched under the stool. Mallinson turned off the ignition and wound his window down. An ominous odour of petrol became apparent. The dog stirred, got to its feet and sniffed, appreciative.

'Better not drive much further,' Walter said.

A man appeared from the depths of the shack. He was carrying a live chicken, holding it by its legs, head pointing down.

Mallinson beckoned to him. 'Boy! Garage, we need a garage.'

The man looked blank.

'Surely there's a garage in this benighted hole? *Fundi*, a *fundi*.'

This was a word the man recognised. He nodded vigorously and waved the chicken along the street. It didn't protest. Mallinson drove on.

The *fundi*'s workshop was no more than a few hundred yards away, an open space beneath a sheltering tamarind, alongside a hut of unshaped logs. A small pit had been dug into the sandy earth and a brazier burnt steadily alongside it. The space was shared with a tailor who sat at a treadle-operated sewing machine and clattered away at the hem of a length of white cotton. The *fundi* beckoned the Humber forward until it straddled the pit, and he then slid neatly underneath it.

'I'm not greatly impressed by Morogoro so far,' Mallinson commented as they waited for the mechanic's report. Winnie sat on a three-legged stool provided by a hugely pregnant woman wrapped in a bright green kanga, who then squatted on her haunches beside the pit and handed the *fundi* the tools as he called for them. The regulation crowd turned up to see what was going on.

'How much further is it?' Winnie asked.

'God knows,' Mallinson said. 'We're supposed to drive up the mountain to a way station where the porters should be waiting for us. I say *supposed* – this is Africa after all. There's a lock-up there for the car, and an *askari* guard. Then we have the trek, about an hour I'm told. Daylight's the problem.'

The *fundi* wriggled free, clutching a length of pipe festooned with shreds of peeling sticky tape.

'Oh my God, what's he done?' Mallinson said.

'*Hakuna matata*,' the *fundi* said, and beamed.

Mallinson groaned. 'How I've learned to dread that phrase,' he said. 'No problem. Invariably means disaster.'

It was clear that the car would not be ready before morning.

'I suppose there's somewhere to stay in Morogoro itself,' Winnie said. So far they'd seen a few shops and a shebeen or two but no sign of a pension or a guest house.

'Do we need to stay here?' Walter asked. 'All we need do is find a lift to the way station. There must be a vehicle of some sort that'll take us.'

There was. The request had been anticipated and a pick-up

truck with an awning covering its rear platform lumbered up to them. Winnie was hauled up into the cab alongside the driver while Walter and Mallinson scrambled onto the platform with its two parallel benches. The bags were handed up, the contents of the food hamper were removed and repacked in a satchel of khaki hemp, and twenty-five jolting minutes later they'd reached the way station where the road died and the path began.

The two porters were waiting for them, one resting on his staff by the side of the road, the other squatting on his haunches underneath a nearby acacia. The man with the staff raised it in a salute.

The path was broad, well used and patched with gravel wherever mud threatened to overwhelm it. For the first twenty or so minutes of the walk the rich vegetation closed in on them and they could see little beyond the track itself. But then it started to climb and as it did so it opened out into clearings of coarse grass and they could at last see the world that stretched out beneath them. They were on the eastern side of the Uluguru range and the setting sun had already begun to disappear behind the mountain. As it did so the dying light seemed to gain intensity: it outlined the world below them with a hallucinatory sharpness. Winnie took Walter's hand and pulled him to a stop. They said nothing but absorbed the precision of the images before them. Greens and golds fought each other for dominance, interspersed with blood-red daggers, stabs of light from the expiring sun.

'It's hard to believe it's real, isn't it?' Winnie said.

'It's not real,' Walter said. 'It's a painted world, an exaggeration, a fake.'

She took his hand and squeezed it. 'Don't be cynical, it doesn't suit you.'

'I'm not being cynical. I mean...' How to find the words?

'I mean… it's as if we're looking through a kaleidoscope. I mean it's better than real – it's a dream world, richer and stranger than ours.'

He pulled his hand away from hers and cupped his face, his hands shielding his vision from everything except the forest and the light directly ahead of him, as if to concentrate on them, to penetrate their meaning.

Her tongue flickered across her lips as she watched him. 'Dream worlds can be dangerous.'

He didn't reply, captivated by the impossibility of the evening. 'Yes,' he said, although he didn't know what he was agreeing with.

A creature in the forest howled and howled again.

'You're an old romantic,' she said.

'Am I?'

It was an odd thought and a new one. He knew how he was viewed, so practical, so thorough, so reliable, but perhaps that was just surface, characteristics imposed on him after Dad died and he became the head of the family.

'Don't linger!' Mallinson called from further up the track. 'Light's going.'

They walked on. The track was broader now and they were able to march side by side. Winnie's paces were smaller and the two-tone brogues she'd changed into lost step with his chukka boots, then briefly coincided, then lost step again in a rhythm of eight paces to his seven.

They were lagging well behind. Mallinson, some thirty yards ahead, stopped and looked back.

'God's sake,' he shouted, 'do keep up. How far is this bloody place?'

Walter grunted. 'What's he so fussed about?' he muttered. 'As if a few minutes make any difference.' A creeper had begun to snake its way across the path, the first hints of dew glistening on its leaves. 'We'd still be stuck on that miserable road if it wasn't for me. Did he thank me? Not a dickie bird.'

'Don't get in a mood now.'

'I'm not getting in a mood, just stating a fact. And don't think I don't know what this trip's about, what *he's* about.'

'Oh, and what is he about?'

'Don't pretend.'

She didn't answer but moved ahead of him, walking faster.

Ten minutes later they saw storm lanterns, fuelled by paraffin, pinned to stone pillars that straddled the track. The porters waited to let them move ahead onto a bricked path that curved around the hillside to present them with a frontal view of the villa. Morningside had been built by the Germans, a sturdy stone construction intended to last for centuries. The final vestiges of daylight picked up and deepened the colour of the roof tiles, taking them from brick-red to scarlet. A long veranda extended either side of the carved ebony doors and faced east, the perfect place from which to welcome the morning sun. A tall servant in an immaculate white *kanzu*, tasselled scarlet fez and embroidered waistcoat bowed deeply as they approached and ushered them inside. A hall bisected the building, with to the right a further branching corridor from which a woman erupted, heels clacking busily on the tiled floor.

'You are here! My dears, at last! What an hour… What kept you? Are you exhausted? You must be! Come, come – rest… Leave everything! You are in Morningside: no cares permitted, no cares at all. No, no, not in Morningside, no cares here, just welcome, *welcome*!' She flung her arms wide, as if about to hug the three of them in one smothering embrace. 'Lydia! I am Lydia – you know all about me, I am sure. Yes, yes, I am Lydia Christakos. I am your hostess. Whatever you wish for, come to Lydia and ask – you will ask, won't you?'

The torrent dried up and they were able to take her in. She was tiny, her figure shapeless under the flowered tent of her dress, her complexion lightened by powder, her nails pink, her hair bleached and piled in a bun. *Look at me*, she seemed to say. *Don't you dare not to take notice.* It was as though she had a flag centred slap-bang on top of her bun, Walter thought, waving and fluttering.

Mallinson extended a hand. 'Charles Mallinson.'

'Oh! That accent! So English – I love the English. Lord Byron is my hero. Lydia Christakos at your service, but of course you know. Everyone knows Lydia.' She took his hand and pumped it enthusiastically.

'My friends, Miss Winifred Docherty, Walter Barnes.'

'So pretty, so handsome! Come, come.' She led them into a vast living room to the left of the hall. Animal skins were draped over sofas and chairs positioned so that they focussed on the open fire that blazed away beneath a copper hood. 'Sit, sit, be comfortable! A drink, a warming drink, a whisky mac, I insist. You young people love your cocktails, I know you do. Don't try to deny it!' She scuttled away.

'Hardly my idea of a cocktail,' Mallinson said, scowling. 'Who recommended this place? Why weren't we warned about that woman?'

'Don't look at me,' Walter said. 'A trip upcountry, you said. I'd never heard of it.'

'Goddamn.'

'Who cares, I love a whisky mac,' Winnie said. She kicked off her brogues and sat in the corner of a sofa with her feet curled up beneath her. The men chose armchairs.

'My guess is she was a hat-check girl in a Piraeus music hall who married a syphilitic rat-catcher, and when he kicked the bucket she came out to *Deutsch-Ostafrika* as the mistress of a German card sharp.'

'Don't be so rude, Charles,' Winnie said, and laughed.

'All right. Anyone got a better history for her? Barnes?'

Walter ignored the question. A servant brought their whisky macs. The songs of the forest night hummed and broke around them. They drank for a time in silence, aware that the day was ending badly.

Walter closed his eyes. He decided that he would like Lydia. There was life to her, vigour. He'd always liked that in people.

A gong sounded in the hall and they went in to a supper of cold cuts accompanied by a bottle of tooth-rattling claret, the first wine Walter had tasted since coming to Dar. No one drank more than a few sips.

They returned to the drawing room for coffee. Mallinson hurled himself onto the central sofa, draping a long leg over an armrest. He loosened his cravat and called for a brandy 'Win, Win, sit by me,' he said, patting the fat cushions.

'Oh, Sir!' she said, and gave him a simpering pout. 'Are your intentions honourable?'

'Absolutely not.'

'Oh goody!'

Walter pulled back a curtain and looked out into the Uluguru night. Clouds had crept up during the evening, and the only light came from a single dim lantern on the path. There was nothing to see but he stayed there, staring into the absence, unwilling to turn round.

Mallinson ordered a second brandy and when it came commandeered the bottle. It was remarkably good, he said.

Lydia came with crème de menthe for herself and Winnie and chattered about the minor royalty who'd honoured Morningside with a visit. 'I have a guestbook, private, very private, no one is allowed to see it, lock and key, yes! But oh, what they write. My favourite was my dear, dear Otto, the Crown Prince, you know, of the Empire. Not the British, of course, the Austro-Hungarian. Such an honour, the most charming young man – what he writes, glowing, glowing!'

'How absolutely fascinating,' Mallinson said. Winnie held back a giggle.

Lydia prattled on oblivious to the teasing. Winnie leaned her head on Mallinson's shoulder. Walter began to explore the room, picking up and pretending to examine ebony trinkets and ivory knick-knacks, all the time trying to keep a cap on his anger. What did Winnie think she was up to? And so blatantly?

He found a copy of *The Man-Eaters of Tsavo* behind a carved fruit bowl and flicked it open. It was the story of the attacks by lions on workers building the Mombasa to Uganda railway and he'd read it before; every literate adult in East Africa had. There had been a heated debate as to how many railway workers the lions had killed, and Colonel Patterson's introduction was appropriately equivocal: '*Between them the lions killed no less than twenty-eight Indian coolies, in addition to scores of unfortunate African natives of whom no official record was kept.*'

No official record. Lives thought not worth recording. He shut the book and put it back behind the fruit bowl. He did not want his to be an unrecorded life.

He returned to the window. The cloud cover remained and as he watched, the lantern on the path went out. He looked back into the room. Winnie had kicked her shoes off and sat with her stockinged feet curled up beneath her. Mallinson's eyes were closed. Their easiness together was unmistakable.

They could be lovers already, Walter thought. 'I'm for bed,' he announced.

There was general agreement. They headed for their separate bedrooms.

Winnie stood in her doorway and offered the men a cheek to

kiss. Mallinson glanced at Walter as if for approval before stooping to brush her lightly with his lips.

'D'you know,' he said, 'I think I could come to like this place, notwithstanding the mad hostess.'

Winnie laughed. 'For that you deserve a proper kiss,' she said. She stood on tiptoe with her face lifted towards him. This time he didn't look at Walter but bent down and their lips met. Winnie's arms moved forward as if about to wrap themselves around him, but then she pulled away and clasped her hands behind her back. 'That's quite enough. Go to bed now.'

Walter waited for Mallinson to shut his door. Winnie offered her cheek again but he didn't kiss her. Instead he took her hands in his and raised them so that they obscured her face, and held them there. He didn't know why.

'Who are you?' he whispered. She tried to pull away from him. He released her, pushed past her into the room, sat on her bed. She stayed by the door.

'Tomorrow,' she said.

He didn't move.

'But only if I feel like it.'

Eventually he stood and walked back to her. Taking her by the wrist he pulled her into the room and tried to kick the door shut. The catch didn't take and the door hung an inch or so open. She tried to prize her hand free but his grip was too powerful and as she struggled he took her other wrist and forced her arms backwards and then outwards. For twenty seconds or so they grappled with each other, both trying to remain as silent as possible, until his strength overwhelmed her and she collapsed backwards onto the bed. The momentum of her fall transferred itself to him and he stumbled forward on top of her.

They lay there, panting, immobile, as if both were obeying a temporary truce, wrestlers retired to their corners to gather strength. Then she turned abruptly onto her side, the move breaking his grip on one wrist, and allowing her to slide off the bed onto the floor. As she did so her other, pinioned arm twisted in his grip and she cried out in pain. He immediately released it and she was able to fold herself into a tight bundle, knees drawn up to her chest, her face turned away from him, pressed down into the rectangle of Persian carpet beneath her. He scrambled off the bed and stood over her before bending to put his arms around the bundle's waist and attempting to haul it to its feet.

'Boy, boy!'

Lydia's voice and the clattering of her heels in the corridor returned him to Morningside and the external world. He let go of Winnie and she lurched forward onto the bed where she lay on her back looking up at him. Very slowly, inch by inch, she pulled up her skirt and exposed her knickers, green silk with a lace trim. He shook his head.

'That's not what I want,' he said.

He knew what or rather who he wanted, and although it was impossible, even absurd to contemplate, the desire for her still burned inside him.

He sank onto the bed beside Winnie.

'Isn't it? What do you want?' she said, sitting up and adjusting her skirt as she did so.

He didn't reply. They sat side by side, both with their mouths slightly open, out of breath. She turned to look at him but he avoided her. She placed a hand on his chin and forced his head around towards her. As she did so she could feel his late evening's growth of stubble, and she stroked her hand against its grain.

'What's happened to you?' she said. 'Do you know what you're doing?'

He searched for the right phrase.

'I just want you to behave.'

'Ah. And if I don't behave, by which I presume you mean behave as you want me to behave, that entitles you to do what you want?'

He didn't answer. She again felt his stubble, this time running the back of her hand against it. A door slammed in the distance. She stood and crossed the room to look out into the corridor. She carefully closed the bedroom door, made sure that the catch held, and returned to him. Now it was her turn to stand over him.

'Do that again and our relationship is at an end.'

He nodded, and in that instant knew that this was confirmation that it already was.

'You know I flirt but you should know it doesn't mean anything. It's just me.'

He contemplated the rug-covered floor. He wouldn't say it, not now, this was not a good moment.

'You haven't even the excuse of being drunk, like Charles. Now go. I want my sleep.'

***

He lay on his back for ten minutes or so beneath a sheet and two unexpectedly heavy blankets, his eyes shut but unable to sleep, the chaos in his mind denying him rest. Abandoning the attempt he looked around for something to read. The only candidate was the Gideon Bible in the drawer of his bedside cabinet. He took it out, propped himself on an elbow, opened it at random and began to read Psalm 119, reading slowly, whispering the words to himself, taking his time.

> *Righteous art thou, O Lord, and upright are thy judgments.*
> *Thy testimonies that thou hast commanded are righteous*
> *and very faithful.*

My zeal hath consumed me, because mine enemies have forgotten thy words.
Thy word is very pure: therefore thy servant loveth it.
I am small and despised: yet I do not forget thy precepts.
Thy righteousness is an everlasting righteousness, and thy law is the truth.
Trouble and anguish have taken hold on me: yet thy commandments are my delights.
The righteousness of thy testimonies is everlasting: give me understanding, and I shall live.

He replaced the book and closed his eyes and as he did so a shiver ran through him. The mountain air was chill, no longer merely fresh, the room had turned cold and he was grateful for the blankets under which he could bury himself.

Give me understanding and I shall live.

CHAPTER 18

Walter woke early and dressed, shivering in the morning chill and grateful for the pullover he'd thrown into his bag at the last minute. The veranda was already in the sun, however, and a silent servant was laying out a breakfast table. He pulled a chair forward to get a better view of the forest, still with its dawn coat of mist. A bushbaby hung upside down from the roof beam, inspecting the preparations. The servant ignored it and the bushbaby ignored the servant. It was evidently a regular, with an accepted role as part of the visitors' entertainment. Walter dozed, a lizard waiting for the day's heat to invade his limbs and impel him into movement. When he woke Mallinson sat beside him, elegant in a cream shirt with a casually knotted cravat of pale rose silk.

'Morning,' he said. 'Where's the lady?'

'Here I am.' She leaned out of a window further down the veranda.

'And ravishing as always. Come spear a kidney with your admirers.'

'Hate kidneys.'

'Is bacon acceptable?'

She laughed. 'Bacon is acceptable.'

She joined them and they helped themselves. The hot dishes, bacon, kidneys, kedgeree, scrambled egg, lay in trays warmed by stubby candles. Toast was wrapped in warm towels. There were bowls of fruit, pawpaw, mango and guava and a tall silver coffee pot stood behind them, supervisor to the proceedings.

'I am definitely getting used to life in Tanganyika Territory,' Winnie said.

'It can get monotonous,' Mallinson said as he poured the coffee. 'My tour's got a year to go, and I can't say I'll be sorry to leave.'

'Where will they send you?'

'It's entirely down to London. But after a spell in purgatory the practice is to give you a treat. I've hinted at Berlin, which could mean a transfer to the Foreign Office, but I'll just have to wait and see if they take up the notion. Buzzy place, Berlin. We may have thrashed the Hun but now he's bouncing back.'

'I'd like to stay here,' Walter said. 'Just look.' He gestured at the immense sheet of mottled green that lay before and below them. 'Think about the lives being lived there, the strangeness of them, below that canopy – lives that have nothing to do with us. Mysterious lives: animals and insects and birds and people too.'

'Primitive lives, dull lives, monotonous lives,' Mallinson said. 'Come on, Barnes, admit it – primitive lives are of limited interest. Will you find Cervantes or da Vinci here? Or Dante? Wagner? 'Course not. Europe wins by a knockout in the first round.'

'Nevertheless it's beautiful,' Winnie said.

Mallinson handed round the coffee. 'No question. But beauty

palls, you know. Got to have more than beauty. You must agree, Barnes. In fact, I know you do. Beauty and spark, eh?'

He grinned. 'Ain't she the bee's knees?'

Winnie laughed. They sat in a row, cups in hand, gazing over the immense green ocean before them.

A young black man toiled up the path towards them. He didn't climb the veranda steps but stood below them, his head at the level of their feet, his expression blank. He reached into his shirt and produced a yellow envelope which he held up, offering it to no one in particular. Mallinson leaned down, held out an arm and snapped his fingers. The youth handed the envelope over and Mallinson ripped it open and removed the contents, a flimsy scrap of paper. He read it, puzzled over it and only then looked at the addressee name.

'Ah,' he said. 'Thought it was a report on the Humber. It's for you.' He passed the scrap to Walter. 'Trouble, eh?' Mallinson said.

Walter read, and read again. 'It would seem so.' He turned to Winnie. 'I'm summoned back to Dar. Immediately.' He handed her the telegram.

'Who's Thornton?' she asked.

'Johnny's Deputy. That's what's odd: why's it not from Johnny himself?'

'Sounds bad,' Mallinson said. 'Death and destruction, d'you think?'

'God knows. Something must have happened. Johnny taken bad perhaps? Damn and blast, whatever the problem is why can't Thornton manage. Why does he need me?'

'You'd better check if there's a train,' Mallinson said. 'Winifred, sweet one, I hope you're not going to abandon me too? I don't relish two whole days in Morningside solo.'

She looked at Walter.

'Stay,' he said. 'Of course you must stay.'

She walked with him as far as the stone pillars. The messenger waited further down the path.

'It's over, isn't it?' he said.

'Oh, Walter.'

She looked away. He waited, uncertain. Was she crying? When she looked back he could see droplets blurring the corners of her eyes.

'Stupid,' she said, and tried to smile.

'I'm right, aren't I?'

She took his hand but didn't look at him.

'No, no,' she whispered and took his hand.

'*Bwana*!' the messenger called.

They kissed. Walter flickered his tongue inside her mouth, and as he tasted her he knew that although love had retreated desire remained.

* * *

There was only the one train to Dar, which left at eleven and took six and a half hours to complete the hundred-and-twenty-mile route. Walter and the messenger walked fast and with purpose and arrived at Morogoro station with five minutes in hand. Walter tipped the guide and then hauled himself up the narrow step into the single first-class carriage. A White Father sat by himself in the first compartment. He glanced up as Walter passed and then immediately looked away. Walter hesitated. He'd recognised the man, a Father Sebastian – a German who'd come to the territory donkey's years ago when it was still ruled by the Kaiser, and who he'd seen officiate at a couple of Masses in St Joseph's. A courtesy greeting might have been in order but Father Sebastian evidently wanted privacy. Walter moved on to the next compartment, which was blessedly empty.

The train wheezed and clattered out of the station, lurching across the points and spewing soot in its wake. He hauled on the leather strap that pulled his window shut. A food vendor rapped on his door and held her produce up for him to see: roasted corn cobs and bananas. He ignored her at first but then saw that the priest had emerged from his compartment and was talking to the old woman. He joined them.

'Excuse me, Father. I wonder if you know whether the train will have a dining car?'

'A dining car?' The priest laughed. 'And perhaps silver service too? No, my friend, no, there is no dining car. There will be vendors at other stations but *Bibi* Angela is one of the best. Aren't you, my dear? Let's see what you've got.'

She followed the priest into his compartment. Walter leaned forward against the window. *An arrogant man*, he thought. Smuts from the groaning engine drifted past. Scrub had begun to replace forest as the train descended towards the coast. When *Bibi* Angela appeared again he bought a corn cob and two small bananas and tossed them onto the compartment seat.

'Monarch of all you survey?'

The priest stood by him, white-robed, ascetic, even cadaverous. His accent was guttural. He was a Bavarian, Walter recalled, and regarded with some suspicion by the British authorities. He had a reputation as a potential troublemaker and there had even been some talk of having him deported. Walter's first instinct was to ignore him but there was a long journey ahead and time had to be passed.

They introduced themselves.

'Oh, Customs and Excise, yes, I see,' Sebastian said. 'Part of the apparatus.'

'The apparatus?'

'The administration. Not a very glamorous part though.'

'I don't know about that. There's a lot of paperwork but we do chase smugglers.'

'So you do. Poor men, mostly. Foolish, too, yes? They cannot see the advantages to be had from paying duties to swell the wealth of the British Empire.'

The train whistle sounded its lamentation and they passed a collection of lean-to shacks made of concrete and corrugated iron. Two small naked boys with grossly bloated bellies watched them and waved, but slowly, as if the very act was painful. Walter waved back and it was only as they vanished from sight that he realised what they reminded him of: fairground automata, mechanical figures, their expressions fixed in rictus grins, slow-motion parodies of the human condition.

'You don't approve of us?'

Sebastian's gaunt cheeks puckered into a smile. 'Individually, certainly. I know many good men, servants of the Empire, honest men. But as for the enterprise as a whole, no, I cannot. You do approve, I take it?'

The train slowed to trundle across an embankment of raw earth, signs that the track had recently been shored up, the damage a regular feature caused by the monsoon rains. The priest was waiting for an answer.

'Kipling,' Walter said. 'Kipling represents my feelings best. I approve of Kipling, of his concept of Empire: Empire means the Law. We bring the Law.'

'That would indeed be good, the Law. If it was adhered to.'

'Which it is.'

'You think so? How long have you been in Tanganyika, Mr Barnes? Months? Weeks? Days?'

Walter didn't answer.

'Look,' the priest said. 'Look.'

He waved a hand at the view. The deep green indentations

of the foothills had been left behind, overtaken by drier scrub. Stunted trees and parched earth now dominated the landscape.

'What do you see? Tell me, what do you see. I'm interested.'

'Not much,' Walter said.

'No, tell me.'

He was aware that the man was manipulating him but he couldn't tell to what purpose. Nor was he in the mood to find out. He took a few steps back towards his compartment but the priest put out a hand, gripped his shoulder and pulled him back into the corridor. Walter was too startled to resist. A bony hand pressed his head towards the window.

'I will tell you what you see. Bush. You see bush.'

This was more than physical contact. It was offensive, a breach of social etiquette.

'Is that not how the apparatus sees it? Bush, empty land. Or so it tells itself – the cover story, is it not? The excuse to annex yet more territory.'

Walter jerked himself free.

The priest raised his hands. 'You should know what you are doing,' he said, 'and you do not.'

The incident was trivial but the physical contact made it unacceptable. He could not let it pass.

'I intend to report this,' Walter said. 'I regard it as an assault.'

The priest stared at him, blinked, and then burst into laughter.

Walter stumbled into his compartment. Still laughing, the priest attempted to follow but Walter forced him back, hauled the door shut and then realised that the only means of keeping it locked, a bolt, had no sleeve to retain it. The lurches of the train as it crossed the regular rail junctions ensured that it instantly worked its way open and stayed that way.

The priest stood in the open doorway but made no attempt to enter further. His laughter died away.

'Bush,' he said. 'Yes, bush, empty land, waiting for great empires to possess it, to create legal documents of ownership, to buy it, sell it, profit from it. But it is not empty land, it is owned, not with the formality of written contracts, but owned by centuries of evolved practice, owned in common.'

There was a grinding from beneath them and the train came to a slow, juddering halt. The priest stepped back to see what the cause was and Walter took the opportunity to slide the door shut. The train remained at rest and the door did so, too. Sebastian peered at him through one of the inset glass panels and then walked away down the corridor.

After a minute or so there was a jerk, a rattle of creaking machinery and the train groaned itself into motion. The door opened in response to the train's gathering speed but the air that entered was hot and fetid. Walter hauled off his sweater, ate his meagre meal and lay back on the seemingly inevitable sweat-inducing leather upholstery. The worries he'd been trying to suppress would not be ignored.

Was he himself the problem? Had he done something, unwittingly? That carpet business? Or had they found out about her? There was written law, yes, but there were unwritten codes, too, and he'd transgressed them. Not by having sex, no, but by his desire for her. That was what was unforgivable. But who could know his secret thoughts, who could read his heart? And as for what he'd done, she had wanted him, hadn't she? That was what justified it. He closed his eyes and tried to sleep. The problem must lie elsewhere.

His belly rumbled and he wondered if the food vendor would reappear. The train had already made two stops and she could well have stepped off. He should have bought more from her. He wondered what a Morningside lunch would be like. Game probably, perhaps eland steak? Winnie and Mallinson eating together, doing what else together?

It was late afternoon by the time the train reached Dar. He knew he should hurry but couldn't resist the lure of the food stall outside the station, where he stopped to eat curried okra wrapped in a flatbread. Sebastian emerged from the terminus building, carrying a suitcase. He saw Walter and stopped, hesitated and then joined him, dropping his suitcase to the ground as he did so.

'I apologise for lecturing you but I have seen things and I need to speak out about them. I have been in villages where I saw young men with their backs raw from beatings, crying with the pain. What had they done? What crime had they committed? They had left their tribal homelands and travelled to the city in search of work. That is a crime in this new country. As for their old country, it no longer exists. But then it never did, did it? It was never anything, was it? Empty land, bush.'

Walter ignored him. The priest's ascetic expression gave way to a wan smile.

'Goodbye, Mister Customs,' he said, hoisted his suitcase onto his shoulder and walked away. 'I look forward to my summons for assault,' he called, and laughed.

There was a rickshaw waiting and Walter took it for the brief hop to the office. It was shut. Barely ten to five, where was everyone? There wasn't even a message for him. Wasn't there a panic on? At least the rickshaw was still available. He decided to try the Club.

Ferriggi stood in the hallway, welcoming the evening arrivals, shaking hands and remembering names. It was said that he knew everyone in Dar. *And a fat lot of good that does him*, Walter thought. *He remains what Mallinson called him, an Eyetie.* Walter mounted the veranda steps. Ferriggi's expression changed. Gravity took over.

'Mr Barnes, I'm so pleased to see you. Mr Thornton is in the Committee Room.'

'He's expecting me?'

'Oh yes.'

Walter hurried past.

Superintendent Jackman was in the corridor. 'I'll probably need to talk to you, Barnes.'

'I have to see Thornton, I'm afraid. What about?'

'Tomorrow will do. Police HQ in the p.m., I'll let you know when.'

Police involved? But at least Jackman hadn't sounded over-anxious to see him; he was evidently a peripheral player in whatever drama was being played out and could begin to relax.

He paused outside the Committee Room door, and for a moment wondered if he should knock. Damn that. He pushed the door open.

Thornton sat with his eyes shut at the end of the square teak table around which the Club's business was commonly transacted. His rimless glasses didn't help the lack of definition in his face, nor did the moustache he'd trimmed back to a small sandy ridge. Walter recognised the folder on the table: the draft Interim Report on the East African Customs Union, the most boring document he'd ever worked on. He shut the door carefully but the click as the catch bit had its effect: Thornton's eyes snapped open.

'Thank God,' he said. 'You took your time.'

'What's going on?'

'You haven't heard? I'd have thought everyone in the whole bloody country would know by now.'

'I've been on that awful train.'

He had to get over the first hurdle. 'So tell me, please, this kerfuffle, what's it all about, am I involved in some way?'

'You?'

'Something I've done?'

'You didn't get my message?'

'You just said I had to come back immediately – urgent you said.'

'Ah. No. Nothing to do with you. Well, indirectly, of course.'

'So what's this about? And where's Johnny?'

Thornton didn't answer. Instead he took his glasses off and squinted at them from short range.

Walter's temper surfaced. 'For God's sake,' he shouted, 'will you please tell me what the hell's going on? What's so urgent? Why does Jackman want to see me?'

'No need to yell,' Thornton said. He put his glasses down on the table. 'I think I need a new prescription.'

Walter grabbed a chair, placed it opposite Thornton and sat with his elbows on the table, his hands clasped. 'Tell me,' he said.

'It's Johnny. Or rather, Meg.'

'Meg?'

'You've not heard then? She's dead.'

A steward pushed himself backwards through the door. He carried a tea tray which he placed carefully in front of Thornton.

'You want a cup?' Thornton asked.

'Dead?'

'Another cup, steward.'

'Dead? What do you mean? How did she die?' Walter asked.

'It's all in Jackman's hands. He's dealing with it.'

'I've gathered that. But why's he involved?'

Thornton stirred the contents of the pot and carefully replaced the lid. 'It's a nasty business.'

'So tell me.'

Thornton looked up and his pale eyes flickered away and back. 'One thing at a time, please, Barnes. The immediate problem for us is, it's affected Johnny. Badly, very badly. A total nervous collapse. Not surprising really, given the shock. He's in the Ocean Road Hospital; they've had to sedate him.' He tapped the file. 'That's why I need you. Admin still expect us to deliver this on Monday and as the Deputy it's up to me to sign off on it. There are sections I'm unsure about and you'll have to take me through them.'

'But what happened? How did she die?'

'Can we concentrate, please?'

Walter flung his hands in the air and rocked back on his seat. The ceiling fan was working well and a brief draught of fresh air fanned across his upturned face. *All things come to he who waits.*

'Go on then,' he said, not looking at Thornton.

'Above all else, I was a little puzzled by your remarks on mineral ores.'

Another pocket of fresh air came and went. What would send Johnny into shock? Something spectacular, a particularly gruesome accident? Johnny's such a lousy driver. On one of the tracks to the southern reefs she was always pestering him about?

'Barnes? Minerals?' Thornton leaned forward, unable to conceal his anxiety.

'Oh, minerals. Afraid I'm not of much use there. The minerals stuff was written by Johnny. He wanted to anticipate possible future developments, beef up the Tanganyika position. I know nothing about it. The rest is mine though.'

'Damn, that's no good, the rest of the stuff is less of a problem. No, it's the mineral stuff they'll come back at me about – anything with the whiff of minerals gets them excited. And if I've signed off on it then I have to be able to back up the argument with bags of evidence. Look at it, will you? I've marked the areas I need more background on.'

Might as well get it over with. 'Tell you what, I'll take a look. And if I can help I will.'

Thornton pushed the file over to him. 'Good. We'll go through it in detail tomorrow.'

Walter took the file. The steward returned with a second cup and saucer.

Thornton poured the tea. 'Help yourself to milk and sugar.'

Walter riffled through the document to the section on minerals. A paragraph heading caught his attention: *Likely Future Developments*. Thornton had underlined several words: mica, asbestos, magnetite, graphite, cassiterite.

'Trouble is, I really know very little about any of this. You probably know more.'

Thornton blinked. 'You must know something – you collaborated on it.'

'I told you, not on this section. The argument's clear enough but as for the detail, I mean I've no idea – give you an example, cassiterite. What's cassiterite?'

'Don't look at me, why would I know? Can't you do some research?'

No, not having this, that's asking too much. Not being dumped on.

'Me do some research? Why don't you do some research?' The moustache twitched. Walter closed the file and pushed it back across the table.

Thornton sipped his tea. 'There isn't time anyway,' he said. 'Not to get it typed up all over again. Buggeration. Can't you suggest anything?'

Walter folded his arms across his chest.

Thornton ran a finger down the page. 'What about gold? Why hasn't Johnny mentioned gold? Isn't there supposed to be gold? At Moshi, I heard. They'll want to know about that – the Territory could become the next Rand. Why no mention of gold?'

'Perhaps because there isn't any? Perhaps because the Moshi strike was just a rumour?'

'Yes, but still, gold…' Thornton picked up his glasses, breathed on the lenses, wiped them with a handkerchief, inspected the results and put the glasses back on the table. 'Tell you what,' he said after a pause, 'I'll sign for the rest of the document, you sign for the mineral section. Feather in your cap, your signature seen by Admin.'

'You mean, you sign for what I've written and I sign for what Johnny's written?'

'Yes. As I say…'

'A feather in my cap.'

'Exactly.'

'No.'

'I'm instructing you.'

'No.'

Thornton flushed and his freckles darkened. 'Are you disobeying me?'

Walter stood. 'Johnny's in Ocean Road? I ought to go and see him.'

'No point. I told you he's being kept sedated.'

'Then will you please do me the courtesy of telling me what happened to poor Meg. Get your priorities right. Why are the police involved?'

'Sit down, please, Barnes. The Interim Report…'

'To hell with the bloody Interim Report. What happened to Meg?'

'The Report is important. Admin wants…'

Walter leaned down and took Thornton's shirt in his fist, jerking him forward. His teacup rattled in its saucer but didn't overbalance. Walter held on to the shirt and Thornton's torso remained bent forward over the cup. He craned his neck backwards to look up.

'All right, all right. Case of murder.'

What? Murder? Walter's grip slackened. He couldn't think

coherently. His brain had stopped functioning, had seized up. Meg murdered? The thought was unreal, the act beyond unreal.

Thornton straightened his shirt where it had bunched. 'I'll remember this, Barnes. I could report you, get you sacked, you know.'

'Murder?'

'Violence will get you nowhere,' Thornton added.

Walter leaned against the table. It croaked in protest.

He's wrong though, isn't he? And you know it.

Walter brandished the file. 'Fuck you, Thornton. Report me then. And you know where you can put this.' He dropped the file back on the table and left without waiting for an answer.

'Come on, Barnes,' Thornton called after him. 'Help me.'

Another one to Mr Punch, violence validated yet again.

Walter went into the bar. Spencer was perched on a stool cradling a pink gin, his bony features grimmer than ever.

'Spencer, thank God, someone sensible. What's happened? Meg McLeod murdered?'

'You don't know? Awful business – brutal assault it seems. Beaten to death. World's in a state of shock. You too, by the look of you. Get you something?'

'A Scotch would be good.'

'That's the ticket. Johnny Walker!' Spencer shouted.

'What happened?'

'That poor woman, that poor woman.'

Spencer was genuinely affected. 'I liked her, she took an interest in things. Too many don't, yet it's a fascinating country when you get to know it. She wrote a very decent monograph, *Shells of the Tanganyika Seashore*, got a copy somewhere. In fact, 'twixt you and I, bit obsessed, always dragging poor old Johnny off to some wretched reef somewhere. Chin chin.'

'Cheers.'

They drank.

'But what exactly happened? I can't get anything sensible out of Thornton.'

'I heard Jackman's done his stuff, got the whole thing sewn up already: arrested the houseboy.'

'Juma?'

'That his name? Arrogant swine, Jackman says. Doesn't seem to care at all. He will when they string him up. He took a hammer to her, a hammer, mark you, and beat her head in. Unrecognisable, not a feature left intact. Raped too, I'd lay odds. Sex at the root of everything – she was still an attractive woman. Anyway, poor old Johnny, they found him in the bedroom curled up like a baby, sobbing like one too. Couldn't move, couldn't stand, muscles stopped functioning. They knocked him out – morphine or some such.'

He raised a finger to alert the bar steward and tapped his glass. 'Thought you were upcountry with the lady friend and young Mallinson?'

'Thornton hauled me back. There's a report to deliver.'

'Panicking as usual, is he? The lady friend come back with you?'

'No.'

'Ah.'

'She liked Morningside, wanted to explore a bit.'

'Nice place, Morningside. Used to go there with my *bibi* before she decided that looking after her old ma in St Leonards was more her thing.'

Spencer held up his refreshed glass and inspected it. 'Shouldn't have let her stay though. Tongues will wag.'

'I'm sure they will.'

Something seemed to disrupt Spencer's features: a cheek muscle twitched and a section of upper lip detached itself from its lower partner. His version of a smile, Walter realised.

'Approve of you, Barnes. I'll keep mum.'

They drank in companionable silence.

Thornton appeared. 'Just see what you can do, will you? It would be a great help.' He held out the file. 'Please?'

Walter took it. 'You want help with this? Okey-dokey. I'll do some effing research and if needs be I'll ask Catarina to do overtime if she will, but I won't sign off on something that isn't mine.'

Thornton edged backwards a few paces. 'Just Johnny's stuff, yes? The rest is fine, very good – in fact, you did an excellent job. Then convene in the morning perhaps? Johnny's office?' Thornton continued to hover.

Spencer turned his back on him. 'Fancy another?' he asked Walter.

'Why not?'

Thornton left.

Something puzzled Walter. 'Wondered what triggered it, the attack I mean. I'd not have thought Juma the type to lose his temper. Jackman say anything else?'

'Well now, interesting. Her shell cabinet, yes? Smashed to bits, hardly a shell intact. What Jackman thinks, suppose he was cleaning and broke one, a prize specimen, say.'

'A *Turbo marmoratus* perhaps.'

'Eh? And then she would have ticked him off, a thorough dressing-down, her prize item down the Swanee, well – suppose she gave the boy a fair old tongue-lashing? And that type, all bottled up, couldn't take it, could he? Lashed out, then couldn't stop, grabbed the hammer: a bloody savage after all.'

Spencer gazed into his gin, swirled it in the glass, but didn't drink.

There was a hammer at hand? In the drawing room? The story was gaining embellishments. Walter could see why: playing detective diverted attention from the horror of the event itself.

He forced himself to conjure up images, the rich Persian carpet beneath the bloodied body, the debris of broken shells scattered around it, the wind from the ocean entering ghost-like to ruffle the skirt, to welcome the liberated spirit. A hand stretched out towards the disc of an operculum, the door behind which the shell creatures found safety, the door she couldn't reach, and the face, the face – no, no, his mind balked, refused to go further, retreated into routine piety.

'How incredibly sad,' he said. 'A tragedy. I liked Meg, liked her a lot. And poor Johnny, what will he do now?'

'Fine folk,' Spencer said.

They held a minute's silence.

'I need a pee,' Walter said.

CHAPTER 19

He wanted to see the scene of the crime for himself, and summoned a cab to take him to Oyster Bay. Why was there a hammer in the drawing room? The Juma-out-of-control story was gaining authoritative status: his Sikh taxi driver regarded it as established fact. But surely the presence of the hammer implied a certain measure of planned intention? Brought into the drawing room with the intention of servicing an assault on the shells? Else why would it be there? There was something not quite right about the story.

An elderly *askari* stood at the entrance to the McLeod's drive and held out an arm to halt the cab.

'Superintendent Jackman here?'

The *askari* went in search of him. Walter dismissed the cab and walked through the garden towards the cliff. There were patches of fresh grass where the soil had begun to recover from McLeod's onslaught on the ants. A waxing moon illuminated a vast bougainvillea exploding with blossom that overhung the path. It had no fragrance that he could detect. The ocean rolled before him, a long silver curl billowing and dying. He thought, not of Meg, but of Petrie lying in his bed in the Nairobi hospital, suffering the necessary pain of treatment, necessary but not guaranteed to cure. He began to recite, aloud:

'The sea, the sea, the open sea,
The blue, the fresh, the ever-free…'

Petrie's favourite poem. Petrie so full of optimism. What a bugger life can be.

He'd brought the Interim Report file with him and riffled through it trying to summon up some enthusiasm for further research. He couldn't. The file fell onto the coarse grass and a gust of wind flicked at a page.

The *askari* coughed. 'Jackman sahib gone back to Dar, sah.'

Good.

Walter walked back towards the house, followed by the *askari*. He continued up the veranda steps and went inside. The *askari* made no attempt to stop him. He went into the drawing room. It had been cleared of the worst damage but flies had begun to gather on the deep crimson stains on the carpet, and the broken doors of the cabinet sagged open. A cardboard box held fragments of shell, and he began to search through it, looking for nothing in particular but sensing a need to rescue some token of Meg's life. He found a small ivory cowrie and placed it carefully on the padded arm of the sofa. The box was deep, however, and not wanting to tip out the contents he pushed his hand through the top layers of shell rubble until his fingers located a smooth, unbroken surface. He worked his hand through the debris until he could grasp his prize and withdraw it.

It was a small but richly coloured *Turbo marmoratus*, a palette of deepening greens and creams. He turned it over and over and could find no flaw. It lacked its operculum so the inner sanctuary was revealed, defenceless, a mother-of-pearl wound. He leaned back against the wall, eyes shut, fingers running over and over the shell, testing the contrast between the tough carapace and the iridescent velvet of the interior. Still with closed eyes, as though he could not bear to be a spectator of his own crime, he slipped it into his pocket. Meg dead, who else would love the shells? Hadn't Juma loved them? Not according to the story, or why destroy them?

The cab had long gone and the light was already dying but he didn't mind. What was there to do, anyway? The wretched Interim Report. Better get it.

He walked once more through Meg's garden to the cliff edge. Poison-proof ants had begun to explore the possibilities offered by the file. He picked it up, shook it, then dropped it again. There were more important things. The snowy crests of rollers were still visible as they shattered themselves on the reef, their self-destruction softened by silver highlights, reflections of the waxing moon. The wind had picked up; there'd be no mozzies tonight.

The *askari* approached him, grave and soft of voice. He was wheeling a bicycle. 'Would sah like something?'

'No thank you.'

'A bad business, sah, a good lady.'

'As you say, a good lady.'

'I have to go now, sah.'

'That's all right, you can leave me. Is the house locked?'

'Yes, sah.'

The *askari* held up a bunch of keys.

'I need to go back inside.'

The *askari* hesitated.

'You go, I'll take the keys.' He held out his hand.

The *askari* still hesitated.

'Don't worry, I'll make sure the Superintendent gets them first thing in the morning.'

The keys were handed over. The *askari* slipped quietly away.

Walter turned back to face the ocean. He could hear the soft crunch of gravel as the *askari* cycled down the drive. When he was quite sure the man had gone, he picked up the file, returned to the house, let himself in, found and ate a banana in the kitchen and then went upstairs to what had been Winnie's room. The curtains were undrawn and the moonlight meant that there was no need to turn lights on. The mosquito netting around the bed had been removed but that didn't worry him. Oyster Bay's sea breezes kept it largely free of mozzies. He lay down and read until the tensions of the day slipped away from him, the file slipped from his hand and he was asleep.

* * *

He woke in the small hours, disorientated, and for a moment imagined he was back in Morningside. But he then became aware of the distant roar of surf and remembered. He was in Winnie's room in Oyster Bay.

Winnie was in Morningside, with Mallinson.

Bodies linked, twined about each other.

Why should I care? Only jealousy, nothing more.

He was free from obligations to Winnie, that was what mattered.

He closed his eyes. Sleep hovered. There was a noise from downstairs, a cough, a human cough, and he was wide awake again. *Oh God*, he thought, *I forgot to lock the front door.* He sat up to hear better. A distant door creaked open. There was no doubt about it, someone else was in the house, someone moving about, someone careless of keeping silent.

Thieves?

Somewhere on the ground floor a light was turned on. Hardly thieves, he told himself; thieves wouldn't risk drawing attention to themselves. Had the police returned? Why would they? It was a few minutes past three in the morning. And if it was an *askari*, how to justify what he was doing, still here? He decided to lie low, and hoped that with any luck there'd be no need to explain. He slid quietly off the bed and lay half-beneath it, half-beside it, concealed from anyone who might glance into the room.

He tried to identify specific noises. The intruder or intruders had no concerns about keeping quiet. A door banged and there was a clattering of metal from a further room, followed by a shout of anger. The door slammed again and there was silence.

This is *absurd*, he told himself. *Get up, deal with it.* He didn't move. There were soft footsteps on the stairs and he edged further beneath the bed. As he did so he thought: *Where's the wretched file? I've dropped it somewhere, haven't I? On the floor? In full view?*

The intruder had reached the landing. The bedroom's central light snapped on. Someone entered the room. The light snapped off, then on again. He closed his eyes. *Go away, please go away.* Steps, soft, hesitant. A foot tapped him in the ribs. One eye squinted open. McLeod.

'Johnny,' he said, and scrambled to his feet.

McLeod stared at him. 'I came back,' he said.

He was wearing a long cotton shift and his feet were bare, encrusted with dirt and flecked with blood. 'They didn't want me to leave, I should stay for my own good, they said. Do you have any idea, any idea at all, how bad that road is? Look at me.' He lifted up a foot and placed it on the bed. 'See that, that's blood. Kicked a stone, no, more like a bloody boulder, gave it a right hammering. Good of you to visit, Barnes. Times like this, learn who your friends are.'

The moonlight drained his face of colour. His eyes disappeared into the shadows caused by his brow, and he appeared reduced, shrunken. He raised a hand, then dropped it again.

'You all right, Johnny?'

McLeod tapped Walter on the chest. 'Tell you what, I'm for a cuppa – you?'

They went downstairs and along the corridor to the kitchen.

'Staff all buggered off, I imagine,' McLeod said. 'God, my feet. Tea, tea, tea, where's the bloody tea?'

'Is that a caddy?' Walter said, pointing.

'Good man. Really glad to see you.'

'You're probably wondering what I'm doing...' Walter began, but McLeod wasn't listening.

'Times like this, soon find out who's on your side.'

'Everyone's on your side, Johnny. Everyone's so, so sorry, she was such a lovely lady, what a beastly thing...'

He stopped. Words were inadequate and anyway McLeod seemed incapable of taking them in. They stood in silence as the tea brewed.

McLeod hunted for cups. 'Don't need saucers, do we?'

Walter took his cup and followed McLeod back to the hall and into the drawing room. McLeod fell into an armchair, slopping his tea as he did so. A brown stain spread across the flank of his nightshirt. He took no notice. Walter remained standing in the doorway.

'I don't think we should be in here,' he said.

'Why ever not?'

McLeod's hand began to shake. The cup spilt more and more tea until finally he dropped it entirely, the tea merging with the crimson dye that was Meg's blood.

'Oh bloody hell, Walter, what a mess, what a mess.'

Walter put his cup down on a pewter coaster. 'Come on, Johnny, let's put you to bed. You shouldn't be up, you know.'

He held out a hand. McLeod ignored it. His hands covered his eyes.

'Need a friend, old boy, need a pal,' he mumbled.

'I'm a pal.'

'I know you are – you are, aren't you? You'll understand.' He looked up at Walter.

'I couldn't stay there, not in that place. They wouldn't listen to me, gave me injections. I had to leave – you see that, don't you?'

'You walked from Ocean Road?'

'How else to get here?'

'It must have taken hours.'

McLeod shrugged. 'I didn't notice. Only my feet do hurt.'

'They'll be looking for you by now. They'll be worried. Best place for you is bed. Come on.'

McLeod looked up. 'Thanks for coming,' he said. 'Appreciated. Touched.'

He took Walter's hand and allowed himself to be led out into the hall and up the stairs, along the balconied walkway and into his bedroom. Walter pulled back the netting around the divan and then the thin blanket and sheet. McLeod sat on the edge of the bed.

'I'll be back,' Walter said.

He walked further along the upstairs corridor to the bathroom where he found a jug and ewer, filled the jug with tepid water, collected a flannel and a towel and returned to the bedroom. McLeod hadn't moved. Walter knelt down and began to clean his feet.

'They are sore,' he said.

'I didn't mean it,' McLeod said.

Walter laughed. 'To kick that boulder? I don't suppose you did.'

'She'd been annoying me for weeks, months – no, years. Those bloody shells, on and on she went, nag nag nag, I only meant the shells, that's all – you see that, don't you? Only the shells.'

Walter squeezed out the flannel. Grey water ran into the ewer. He took the second foot in his hand but didn't bathe it.

'Just lost my rag. Anyone could do that, couldn't they?'

'I don't think you should say any more,' Walter said. He began to wipe the flannel around the heel and then, raising the foot slightly, the sole.

'Don't say that! That's what that clown Jackman kept saying, trying to shut me up.' McLeod laughed. 'That's why they stuck a needle in me, to shut me up. Didn't work though, did it? Go careful there, that hurts.'

'Sorry.'

Walter dropped the flannel into the ewer and took the towel.

'You see, Walter, what no one will understand is, I loved her. How could I do that if I loved her?' McLeod's face crumpled. It was as if he wanted to cry but had forgotten how to. 'But I did love her, I did, I did. I'm so sorry, Meg, so very, very sorry, my darling girl, my love.'

Walter sat on the bed beside him. 'Of course you did.'

'What will they do to me, Walter – will they hang me? I deserve to be punished, I do, I do. I want to be punished, only you see Meg, Meg wouldn't want that, not hanging. She's forgiven me already, I know she has.'

'They won't hang you.'

'They will though, they will.'

'No they won't. That's why they don't want you to talk. Go to sleep now and we'll make plans in the morning.'

McLeod seized his hand. Walter released the towel and, rocking him as he did so, lowered him back onto the bed. McLeod closed his eyes. Walter prised his hand free and stood up to arrange the nets. McLeod mumbled something but his eyes remained shut.

Walter stood in the doorway and looked back. McLeod's

breathing was deepening. He mumbled again, and a hand waved in the air, beckoning. Walter took a step closer.

'This lousy country,' McLeod said, still half asleep, the words barely audible. 'Should never have come here, that's what she said when we first arrived. But then she got to like it, bad mistake. First impressions, always trust a first impression. Trusted you, Walter – knew a good man when I saw one.'

His eyes fluttered open. 'It's this place that's to blame, you see. Hang Dar, I say, string it up and throttle it.'

'Go to sleep, Johnny.'

The instruction wasn't needed.

* * *

Walter dozed on and off through the rest of the night, stretched out on top of the coverlet on the guest-room bed. He got up a little after six, found some fruit in the kitchen, made himself a cup of tea and sat in the garden to watch the sun rise over the ocean.

Jackman arrived with a truckload of *askaris* shortly before eight.

Walter intercepted him before he could go into the house. 'He's in there,' he said. 'Still asleep, I think.'

'Has he said anything to you?'

'No, not a thing. Should he have? I was about to leave when he came lurching out of the dark. Apparently he walked all the way from the hospital. I saw him into bed and thought I'd better hang around. He's obviously very distressed by Meg's death.'

'Yes, he is. It got to him.'

'Hardly surprising. It would get to anyone.'

'Exactly so. Things like that can upset the balance, the world goes out of kilter, the imagination takes over. You're sure he didn't say anything?'

'Say anything? What would he say?'
'Anything odd.'
'Not a dickie.'
'Good. You'd better push off then.'
'I will. Any chance of a lift?'
'The *askari* truck's going back.'
'That would be perfect.'
Jackman turned to go.
'Spencer told me you've arrested Juma. Is that true?'
Jackman stiffened. He didn't look at Walter. 'We're holding him.'
'You would have to be very sure…' Walter began.
'Police business, Barnes. Nose out if you please.'
Jackman trotted up the steps into the house. Walter watched him go.

CHAPTER 20

The truck dropped him off at the lane to the mess. He put the *Turbo marmoratus* on top of the chest of drawers, its pearly wound exposed, and yelled for Joseph. He didn't expect an answer and didn't get one, so shaved in cold water, fighting the stiff stubble on the edges of his jaw, then hunted for a clean shirt and headed for the Customs offices.

Thornton hadn't arrived and the staff watched in subdued silence as Walter unlocked his office but didn't go in. He beckoned to Miss Fernandes.

'This is a bad business, Catarina.'

'Oh, Mr Barnes, it's so dreadful. Everyone is talking about it – the poor, poor lady…'

Walter held up a traffic policeman's hand. 'I know. But life goes on and there's work to do. Please see that I'm not disturbed for the rest of the morning.'

He closed the door on her. Gossip was having a field day, no doubt, but he expected nothing else. It was inevitable.

He opened the Interim Report and groaned. What a slab of congealed boredom. Minerals. Who knew about minerals? No one that he knew. There were a few geologists hired to map the underlying structure of the country and, with any luck, to map its riches as well but he'd had no contact with any of them. All he understood was that control of mineral production was what made the Interim Report of particular significance: there was potential for considerable profit to be made. He groaned again and began to read but his thoughts kept finding diversions.

Who had Johnny talked to? Jackman, evidently. But knowing that Johnny was guilty he surely wouldn't have arrested Juma, would he? Juma, always so careful with the shells. And the scale of the destruction! The shell cabinet broken, the shells smashed as if they were no stronger than eggs. Fragments of mother-of-pearl, of cowries and murex, of trapeziums and turbos and filamentosas, all reduced to shards and slivers, to mere memories of their former beauty.

His reverie was interrupted by Thornton tapping on his door and peering through the inset glass window. Walter gestured him in.

'What d'you make of it?' asked Thornton in some anxiety.

'I think it's fudged – I suspect deliberately fudged. No one really knows the extent of the deposits. They know they're there, but are they exploitable? So what I suspect Johnny has done is to take up a defensive position. His basic argument seems to be that decisions should be avoided for the time being, and that the Customs Union, if it's to happen at all, should defer any reference to mineral ores.'

'He doesn't actually say that.'

'No, he's being cagey.'

'We were specifically briefed to deal with minerals, to make concrete proposals, not to avoid them.'

'Well, he's ducked it and it's your call now.'

'Oh God.'

'Yes, you could always try prayer.'

'Not funny, Barnes.'

'No. But then it's not a very funny day, is it?'

Thornton pulled up a chair and sat down. 'What we must do...' he said, and stopped.

Ha! Like the we. 'Go on. What we must do?'

'Oh God.'

'What I'd do...'

Thornton brightened. 'Yes?'

'Make no changes. Sign it per pro and let the Admin men decide whether or not to include anything on minerals. Could well be that Tanganyika proves to be the best-endowed territory of the three so I think they'll take the hint and demand the exclusion of all references. But if they don't like it you can blame Johnny, let him carry the can.'

He handed the file to Thornton.

'Fresh air,' he said and took his jacket.

* * *

He left the building without a further word. *Walk, just walk, to walk is to heal. Dad, see him now, stiff-backed, fighting arthritis, forcing himself up onto Roundway Down on a long summer Sunday, saying as he grimaced against the pain in each stride, what was it? Only ideas won by walking have any value. Some famous man said that, but who he didn't know. Yes, to walk is to be in touch with the Earth, with the physical, with the unavoidable things with which life surrounds you, through them to discover what is real and what is the stuff of dreams.*

He struck out eastwards, passing first through the tangles

of discarded cables that marked the still adolescent electricity station, but his brain seemed unable to deliver coherent instructions to his limbs and his attempt to produce a marching stride failed. He lurched crab-like towards an upturned barrel from which an oily fluid still leaked and careless of his shorts leaned back against it, breathing deeply for a minute or so before resuming his walk, thinking of Juma, thinking of Rosa, the two coupled in his brain, *but why?*, stumbling onwards towards the lighter-age quay from where he could survey the harbour. There were no large vessels either on the move or at anchor other than a Liberian-registered tanker in need of repair which had crept in empty one night over a week ago. Dust eddies blew up around him, miniature sandstorms carrying with them the fierce odours of the nearby welding workshop.

A voice broke through the confusion in his head.

'*Jambo*, *Bwana* Barnes! *Jambo!*'

The crane driver hailed him, perched on a stack of bald tyres, a red bandana tied around his head. Walter waved him away but the man had already leapt from his seat and come running across to intercept him.

'*Bwana* Barnes, my boy, my boy Anthony.'

Walter ignored him. He'd forgotten all about Anthony, done nothing about him and knew with absolute certainty that there was nothing he was going to do. He swung away from the harbour and on towards Kichwele Street. He had no idea where he was going.

The crane driver kept pace with him. 'My boy, he is reading now, *Bwana* Barnes. He read great book, *Kings and Queens of England*. He tell me stories – King Alfred, he love the great King Alfred.'

Walter halted. 'Where did he get this book?'

'From the Mission, *Bwana* Barnes, Baptist Mission. I take

him. He must read, *Bwana*. To get office job he must read, must go to school. No school for poor boys, only missionary school.'

'And the missionaries will teach him, although he's Muslim?'

'Teach Christian boys. My boy Anthony now Christian boy. Christian boy learn to read, get office job.'

'Is that really the only way? To learn to read he has to convert?'

The crane driver removed his bandana and with it his exuberance drained away. 'He must learn, *Bwana*, must learn.'

The man's determination was evident.

'I don't know what I can do,' Walter said.

The crane driver didn't move.

These people should be treated better, Walter thought. *Not as social equals – no, of course not, that would be absurd – but legitimate ambition, limited ambition, should be recognised and applauded. The crane driver's efforts on behalf of his son should receive at least some form of positive response.*

The bandana twisted in the man's hands.

'If you like, I'll listen to him read.'

The crane driver's hands relaxed. He bowed his head. 'Thank you, *Bwana*, thank you.'

He reminded Walter of the girls in the brothel. Submissive, dependent, grateful. And at the same time, repellent. He could think of nothing more to say and so nodded, aware of the patrician nature of the gesture, and walked on, penetrating further into the Commercial Zone, trying to blank his mind to further thought, allowing his senses to take over, to absorb the aromas, the clamour, the hucksterish vitality of the lives around him. After a few hundred yards he arrived at a crossroads he recognised and stopped to take his bearings. The Hindu temple was just visible at the end of the street to his left and it was still morning. Would she be there? And if she was, what then? What words could he find?

The temple was packed with worshippers and he had to force his way in. There was no sign of her.

An elderly man, stooped over his walking stick, plucked at his sleeve. 'Help,' he asked, 'you need help?'

Walter ignored him. He didn't need help; he knew what he was doing. Next stop, her bungalow.

He found it with relative ease. As always (and why?) the man in the leg brace was there, now busily attacking the door with a paintbrush.

'No, no,' he said, waving his hands to block Walter. Droplets of distemper flew in every direction. 'Not good – no, no.'

'I was unaware,' Walter said, 'that you run her life.'

He took the man by his shoulders, feeling his frailty, and moved him out of the way. The door was propped open and he pushed it wider with a foot. The man followed him in, still carrying the paintbrush and talking rapidly and anxiously in Hindi. Walter crossed the empty front room and rapped on the back door. As he did so it opened, creaking slightly, and she came in, drying her hands on a towel.

'What are you doing here?' she demanded.

'I have something to say to you but it must be said in private.'

'No, no talk, nothing, go, go.' The lame man took him by the arm and tried to pull him towards the door.

Walter shook him off with ease. A drop of paint settled on his shirt. 'Send him away,' he said.

She shook her head. 'He cares for me,' she said. 'And you do not.'

'I do care, that is what I came to say.'

'Liar,' she said and opened the back door. She went into the back room.

He could hear the key turn and the door lock spring into place. He couldn't let her go so easily. He had to attract her attention. He pressed his head against the door.

'A bad thing happened,' he said. 'A killing.'

There was no response. The handyman pulled at his arm, this time strongly enough to cause Walter to take a step backwards and collide with the broken armchair. A foot shot from under him and he fell to the floor, pulling down a stack of fabric as he went. He shouted at the man, a wordless roar of anger, and scrambled to his feet, brushing scraps of material from himself as he did so. He heard rather than saw the door opening.

'Leave it,' she snapped and began to collect the fallen fabric, picking it up piece by piece, carefully folding each one and piling them on top of each other.

'A killing,' he repeated.

'We know about the bad thing. Everyone knows about it,' she said. 'Now go.'

'But do you know who did it?'

She threw her hands in the air. 'What is this to do with me? Nothing, nothing.'

'It wasn't the servant. My boss, my boss did it, the Commissioner himself – he told me he did, he confessed.'

She stared at him, then put her hands over her ears. Her bracelets fell back, jostling each other as they slid towards her elbows. 'Gossip,' she said. 'I do not hear you. Go away, go, go.'

The lame man had opened the door to the street. Walter shook himself free of a final swatch of mirror-encrusted cloth and seized Rosa's hands, pulling them down, away from her face. She didn't resist and he knew he had her attention. The words tumbled out.

'McLeod did it, the Commissioner himself did it – he told me. He beat his wife to death and there's going to be a hush-up and the police want a scapegoat. They've already taken the houseboy into custody. Suppose they charge him? Do I ignore it even though I know, I know, absolutely, that he's innocent?'

'What is this to do with me?' she asked and pointed at the open door.

And then it happened, unintended, the words escaping from him without the benefit of conscious thought.

'I love you,' he said.

A paralysed silence followed. It was broken by the lame man. An animal sound, not English, not Hindi, escaped him and he slumped to the floor, his face in his hands. She knelt beside him and spoke to him gently. He seized one of her hands and, his voice low, choked with emotion, stumbled out a question. Walter was struck by the man's evident dependence on her, by his reluctance to release her. They spoke for some time and after a little he calmed down and his questions acquired a practical tone. She looked up at Walter.

'He understands a little English,' she said. 'Now he wants to know more about this killing.'

'You heard what I said?'

'Of course, but I pay no attention to stupidity. Tell me about this killing and I will tell him. Speak slowly and tell everything.'

They sat on the divan side by side. He tried to take her hand but she pulled it away. Had he even said the word? Or done no more than imagined saying it? She had begun to ask questions about the McLeod killing and as he answered them she translated. The lame man threw in questions, holding up a hand from time to time to indicate a need for more detail.

'So there it is,' Walter said, aware of how thin his unsupported assertion must sound. 'Now I have to decide what to do about it.'

The lame man heaved himself to his feet. Rosa helped him, brushing the dust from his clothes as she did so, and then shaking her sari vigorously. The material billowed and settled. She smoothed her face, rubbed both hands down from her forehead, across her closed eyes, paused to conceal her mouth and then breathed in, a deep and audible intake of the day's stifling air. The lame man opened the door. The odours and aromas of Dar invaded the room.

'Go,' she said, 'you have no more to say, go.'

Walter didn't move. Yes, he could go. Perhaps he should go. She was waiting for him. But he had said the word and she had acknowledged it. He looked at her and then surveyed the room. As he did so it began to shed its former cheap, poverty-proclaiming tawdriness and in its place revealed a new, essential substructure, pristine and vibrant. In this rediscovered reality she was a queen and he her subject and they were figures in a painting, a hyperreal painting of such precise detail, of such intensity that each element was both separate and yet contained the whole. The painting's subject was the depiction of a moment of particular significance for the people in it. Even the observer, the man at the door, was somehow involved. A decision was being made, or was about to be made, or had been made. The drama was within him because he was inside the painting but it was also outside him, allowing him to observe it, to be able to see it with a bystander's objectivity and so to be aware of the profound relevance the moment played in the lives of the figures in the room. Change was imminent.

'I'm not going,' he said, 'not until we've talked. I understand things better now. But first, send him away.'

There was no response. No one spoke. No one moved. They were statues in a tableau. The man at the door broke the silence, his voice low, appropriate, asking a brief question of the woman. She waved an awkward hand and with that gesture, slowly, creakily, the static figures grew into movement. The lame man took a crudely carved walking stick from beside the door and propped himself upright with it. The woman opened the door into the back room. There was a brief exchange between them before the man hobbled off into the street beyond, kicking the door shut as he went.

They were alone together, alone and silent.

'What do you want?' she asked after an eternity that lasted perhaps half a minute.

'When we were last together…' he began.

'Stop this, stop this nonsense!' she cried and went into the back room. The door began to close behind her and Walter heard the scraping sound of the key in the lock. He snapped into action, forced the door open before she had time to turn the key, and followed her into the back room. She stood there, still, her eyes fixed on him. On impulse, he locked the door, sealing them into the small space, together. Her lips had parted and he could hear her breathing. He thought: *It's almost as if she's afraid of me.* He smiled, amused by what he took to be her docility, and took a step backwards, away from her. Her shoulders relaxed and she stood straighter.

'I don't want you here,' she said. 'Please go.'

'You don't mean that,' he said. He sensed that the power balance had shifted. She was no longer the queen. He was the king now, and she one of his possessions. He still held the door key. To confirm that she was now his prize he slipped it into a pocket.

'And I have something else to tell you. I've broken up with my girl. I didn't love her, and you taught me that. I realised that you, you are…'

'If you do not stop this,' she said, 'you will destroy me.'

'How would I do that?' he asked and smiled again.

She began to march up and down in the small room, four steps in one direction, then back and back again. He reached out to stop her but she waved him away, the bracelets giving emphasis to the gesture. After twenty or so reversals she came to a halt in front of him. She was breathing heavily, hauling in air, a diver surfacing. Then without warning she raised a hand and slapped him across the cheeks, once with her palm, the second time with the back of her hand as it swung back across his face.

His response was immediate. He put his arms around her hips, pulled her close to him and pressed his face into her taut belly, so that he couldn't breathe. He held her for as long as he could before he pulled back and gasped for air. As he released her she fell back onto the bed and lay there with her face turned away from him, staring into the wall. He tucked himself in behind her, his body following her contours, his right arm trailed across her, and their right hands clasped. He began to rock her in small, slow movements, taking pleasure in the harmony of the joint motion, the duet they played. After a little she shifted her hips away from him and released his hand. He brushed her hair away from his face and levered himself up on his left elbow. Her eyes were closed. There was, he saw, a smear of rusty red on the wall above the bed. He ran a finger across it but couldn't tell what its source was, paint presumably.

'If we were in another country…' he began but stopped. His voice was hoarse. He didn't recognise it. He had mutated into someone else, a stranger whose ways he still had to discover.

'In another time,' he went on, 'there would be things I could offer you…' and again he stopped. A silver comb had come loose and he pushed it back into place, letting his fingers play with the rich density of her hair as he adjusted it.

'Things I would promise you…' he said and for a third time couldn't complete the thought.

Her eyes flickered open, then closed again.

'Promises are thieves,' she whispered. And then, so quietly he could barely hear her, 'Every promise that has ever been made to me has robbed me. The nuns promised to protect me but they did not, no, they stole my youth. My husband promised to look after me and he did not, he stole my good name.'

She turned to him and reached up, clasping her hands about his neck. 'Mister Walter, what will you steal from me?'

He looked down at her but said nothing. Instead he placed his hands on her shoulders and pressed them down onto the thin mattress, forcing her hands apart so that they fell back onto the bed.

He wanted her and the world he lived in refused him permission. It was intolerable. It was unacceptable. Desire possessed him, and anger too – an anger with Dar, with the stupidity of life devised by men, anger with the whole bloody world and everyone in it; and it combined with his longing for her, with his desire to possess her now, here, why couldn't he have her, no reason, no reason at all, to demand release. His fingers began to fumble with the buttons on his fly.

'No,' she said, 'no,' and struggled to push him away.

He ignored her. He knew what she wanted. He gripped her shoulders ever more tightly and pinned her to the bed. She tried to struggle upwards but he was far too strong.

'Please, Mister Walter, no,' she said, her voice trembling so much that he could hardly hear her. 'This is not right, not right, not right.'

He was aware of her protests but they were of no relevance, mere convention. The decision had been made and rights and wrongs had no place in his consciousness any more. He loved her, he'd said so. His grip tightened.

'Not right,' she said once more and then her voice trailed off, her eyes closed and he could feel that her resistance was over. He entered her in one single movement, grunting as did so, luxuriating in power, lost in sensuality. He was hardly conscious of her as a separate entity, hardly aware that her cries were not like his, of passion.

When it was over they lay together in silence and slowly, very slowly, he returned to being Walter.

There was a sickness in him. He couldn't look at her.

The silence was oppressive.

'I must go,' he said.

He struggled to his feet and as he did so her lips moved. He had to bend down to hear her.

'Thief,' she whispered. 'Thief, thief, thief. What more will you steal from me?'

It occurred to him that the streak of red was blood, not paint.

A distant klaxon sounded, harsh, insistent. He pulled her black locks across her face, as if trying to obliterate it. The madness was over. Good.

Why reproach myself?

The klaxon sounded again. He placed a hand on the arch of her hip and rocked her. She turned and buried her face in the pillow. She was crying, he realised.

No reason at all.

He unlocked the door and left the room, left the bungalow. Stanley Street was filling with evening activity. The discus-thrower was at his post and stepped forward to prepare his missile launch. Walter ignored him.

If anything I've saved her, from herself, from the folly of dependence. If there was anything I could do for her, I'd do it. But what was there?

Nothing.

Nothing.

Welcome to my army, what kept you?

The voice was unmistakable.

I'm not in your army.

Oh yes you are. All rapists are automatically enrolled.

Rapist? He lurched, almost fell, thrust out a hand, felt the solidity of iron, one of the few lamp-posts in the street, and clung to it.

Say after me:
That's the way to do it!

He remained there, paralysed. That wasn't rape, never. The lamp-post's feeble glow focussed attention on him. Passers-by glanced at him, curious. He had to leave this place. He tested his stability, staggering a few steps before rediscovering his balance and walking on, mindless now, incapable of thought, incapable of dealing with the label Mr Punch had stuck on him.

He lay on his bed in the mess. He could hear Joseph singing as he mopped the central corridor.

Please accept my heartfelt congratulations.

Somehow he slept.

CHAPTER 21

An onshore wind had picked up and he had to pedal hard against it, battling down Ocean Road towards the hospital. He was grateful for the hard physical work. Yesterday's events remained vivid. He searched for excuses, no, explanations. The verbal protests she'd made were no more than mere convention. Had she really meant them she could have been much more forceful. Indeed, he could hardly remember what they were, what she'd actually said. As for physical resistance, well, had she not wanted to make love she could have done so many things, stabbed him with her nails for a start. He hadn't prevented her. No, his only mistake was that he'd used the word that mattered and shouldn't have. Love. That was what had unsettled her. She knew that love between them was impossible, unacceptable, and his use of the word had thrown her. That was where he was at fault, nowhere else.

That's the way to say it!

What d'you mean?

The script! The script all my enlisted men use. You've got the script off to perfection.

Fuck off, fuck off, bloody fuck off.

* * *

He found McLeod in his room, sitting in a Lloyd Loom chair facing the French windows, looking out over a scrubby lawn and a surprisingly fine display of roses.

'Ah, young Barnes,' he said. 'Interim Report duly delivered, eh? I heard that Thornton got in a bit of a pickle over it. He's a good deputy, very good, thorough, just not up to the top job, the responsibility.'

'How are you, Johnny?'

McLeod turned away. The skin on his neck was loose and shook like a turkey's wattle as his head jerked. 'Bad, Walter, bad.'

'I'm sorry to hear it. Do you know what they're going to do with you?'

The wattle shook again. McLeod's mouth opened, then shut. He glanced at Walter and then his eyes flicked away. A low hissing sound escaped him.

'Johnny?'

'Eh?'

'What will they do with you?'

A hand waved. 'Water, old boy, in the jug.'

He sipped, staring into the glass Walter had given him. His hand began to shake and the water began to slop out of the glass. Walter took the glass back and put it on a side table. McLeod reached up and took hold of Walter's shirt, tugging him closer.

'Seems I went a bit screwy – shock, y'know. Shock. Chaps in trenches had it, it's recognised now: bad things happen, result, chap goes off the rails. I did. You saw that, eh? You saw me, you'll agree. I was in shock.'

Walter said nothing.

'I imagined things – easy to do when you're in shock. You could see that, couldn't you?'

Walter straightened up. McLeod's limp hold didn't resist. His hand fell back.

'All in the mind, y'know. Astonishing thing, the mind, the imagination. Told Jackman I'd been gabbling nonsense. He understood – shock, he said, doesn't mean a dickie. You saw it, didn't you – you saw I was non compos?'

Walter could hear the wind as it howled around the building. Rose petals broke away and flung themselves into the air like migrating butterflies. The cloud of leaves and petals at first obscured a man and then, as he came closer, pulled him into focus. Jackman, appearing as though summoned by the mere mention of his name. He approached the French windows, saw Walter and rapped on the glass before beginning to wrestle with the lock. It remained firm. He gave up and headed for the main entrance.

'Good man, Jackman. Got the bastard. Don't have a fag on you? No, don't smoke, do you? 'Course not. Trouble with you, Barnes, too much of a goody-goody, no vices. Man's got to loosen up from time to time, for heaven's sake, not be such a tight-arse – too tight, tight, that's you. Tight! Tight!' McLeod began to shout. He struggled out of his chair, his face drained of colour, a fist punching upwards.

Jackman came in. 'What the hell!' he shouted, and pushed McLeod back down.

'Sit,' he ordered, as if speaking to a puppy. 'Sit, Johnny, sit.'

The brief vigour that had possessed McLeod vanished. He crumpled like an empty sack and the chair groaned and tottered as he slumped into it. Jackman pressed him down, gripping him by the shoulders, although there was no need. McLeod's eyes closed and his head slumped forward. A staff nurse, alerted by the noise, looked in.

'Get out,' Jackman barked. The nurse hesitated, then chose the wiser part. McLeod was breathing heavily.

'Don't we need the nurse?' Walter asked.

'He's fine. And less of the we, thank you, Barnes. I want you out of here – this is not your business. *Imshi!* Go on, buzz off, you heard me.'

Walter didn't move.

'Oh ho, like that, is it? Heard you could be an awkward sod. Heard other things, too. Heard you like the dusky maidens. A regular at the Taj, aren't you? Needn't look so surprised – I know what goes on in this town. And rogering the madame, too. Like the meat well hung, do you? Why is that? Can't get it up with the pretty ones – droopy cock problem? Need Mummy to get you standing? Very sad, brothels and limp dicks. Don't quite match up, do they? Still, full marks for trying. I'm curious though, how d'you get on with your young lady? Or does she think you're saving yourself for the honeymoon?'

Jackman knew? How?

Walter stared at the man, who smiled. A replacement metal canine caught the sun. Walter looked away. What would Mr Punch say?

Find a hammer and give him one. Or two. Or more. Go on, pulp him.

He could, too.

Miniature dust devils pirouetted in the garden. Attack is the best form of defence.

'You know that, or think you do. And I know who killed Meg. Johnny confessed to me.'

'He told you damn all, and don't you say otherwise.'

McLeod had begun to snore. Walter felt his jowl, finding a patch of bristle on his jawline. He should have changed his razor blade. He thought of the crane driver, of the power he held over the man; of the power that Jackman doubtless held over so many; of the power granted to so many thanks to their caste mark, their skin. Of the power he'd enjoyed over her. A peace offering was required.

'I don't mind you putting Johnny in the clear.'

'Good of you.'

'But you can't charge the servant.'

'I can do what I bloody well like. We're in Dar.'

Walter pressed his face against the window, flattening his nose and spreading his lips, enjoying the cool pressure it provided. He was in the playground at his village school and the voices around him went through their well-used objections. *Not fair, not fair, I'll tell my Dad on you.* He pulled back from the glass and faced Jackman. He had to reclaim at least some of the high ground. 'Course you can do what you bloody well like. So can I.'

Jackman inspected McLeod. He picked up an arm and then rested it back against McLeod's chest. He didn't stir. Jackman glanced at Walter and gave a brief sideways flick of the head. 'Come,' he said.

They walked back through the corridors and out into the hospital gardens. The wind greeted them with a buffeting warmth. Walter held his breath for a few seconds; he imagined that the wind carried more than heat and smells and dust. It whistled in an unknown language but its message was nonetheless clear: *Careful*, it said, *careful now*.

'How's your pal Petrie doing?' Jackman asked.

'I had a letter from him. Still in Nairobi, still in hospital, but says they've beaten it. Handwriting ever so shaky though – he may just be looking on the bright side. Ever the optimist.'

'Nice man.'

'Very. I miss him.'

Jackman stopped by a rose bush and began to snap off dead heads. 'Damask,' he said. 'Amazing. Hospital must have a competent *shamba* boy. Why hasn't he been snaffled by the top brass, I wonder?' He tossed a handful of dead roses onto the parched earth of the bed then took hold of the sleeve of Walter's jacket and jerked it once, then again. 'You don't get it, do you? No comprenez?'

'I think I do.' Walter tugged his jacket free.

A narrow crease appeared at the side of Jackman's mouth. 'Look,' he said, 'this is a major crime – you've seen the local press. We've got to produce a culprit. It can't be Johnny, just can't allow that. Too much blood, too much violence. That's not us.'

'The mask slipping?'

'What?'

'You know, the mask.'

'No, I don't know.'

'The noble mask, the British mask, the superior beings mask. The not-like-ordinary-folk mask – Huns or dagos or Eyeties or coolies or blacks. That mask.'

Jackman dusted the rose detritus from his hands. 'One way of putting it, I suppose,' he said, and walked on.

Walter hesitated, then followed. He was on sloping ground and the temptation was there, to keep on, to keep on downwards. 'So you'll hang him?' he said, softly. 'You'll hang Juma?'

'Up to the judiciary, that. He'll get his chance. We'll get him a brief, he can plead provocation, insanity, whatever, and there's a chance they'll just sling him in the can. After a bit might even deport the poor sod. After all, he's not a local – Somali or Eritrean at a guess. Job done, the mask, as you have it, kept in place, no one hurt too much.'

'Only a black and they don't matter, do they?'

Jackman paused to snap off another dead bloom. 'Damn,' he said. 'Thorn.' He paused, looking upwards at the sky.

Walter waited.

'Okey-doke,' Jackman said and transferred his gaze to the ground. A movement in the coarse grass had attracted his attention. He bent down, picked something off the ground and placed it in his open palm. He held his hand out for Walter to see it: a beetle, black and solid, with small horns. 'Dung beetle,' he said. 'Shit-lover. Found the right country, eh, Barnes?' He propelled the beetle into the air and caught by the wind it sailed off towards a thicket of oleander.

'McLeod's a sad old sod,' he said. 'What it is, this shithole has done for him. He'll take early retirement, head back to Blighty. I give him a year before he tops himself. You want to watch it, you know – get things wrong, Dar could do for you too.'

Jackman examined his right hand. A drop of blood welled up on the index finger. Jackman sucked at it. 'You need to be careful,' he said. 'For starters, careful who you fuck, and where.'

'I go to the Taj, yes, I like it there but I don't go for sex, I know that's hard to understand, but I don't.'

'So what do you go for?' The unanswerable question. 'I'm curious. Respectable chap like you. Don't go for sex, that's not what I heard, no. My source says ficky-ficky with madame, you and the old biddy herself.' Jackman leered at him.

Walter's hands curled into fists. He raised himself slightly and pushed his weight forward onto his toes. His heels lifted. Jackman's eyes glittered and he tilted his head back, offering his chin, inviting the blow, primed for a bare knuckle barney, more, itching for one.

Walter read the signals. Hit Jackman and his career was over. He relaxed.

Jackman was waiting for an answer.

Walter turned aside to calm himself before he spoke. 'You may not understand this,' he said, 'but I feel comfortable there, more than anywhere else in this town. I have a beer, I chat to Madame Rosa, have another beer, chat some more. I don't expect you to believe me, but it's true.'

Jackman edged closer. His expression changed, his eyes narrowing and his lips tightening. 'Chat? About what? What have you told her?'

Walter read the danger signals and backed off. 'About this business? Nothing.'

Lie and keep on lying.

'Good. Keep it that way.'

'I will. As long as there's a chance things sort out. In the right way, of course.'

'The right way? Which is? As if I care.'

'Oh, oh, oh! You care, I can see you do. So I'll give you my pennyworth. We, the powers that be, we could get away with letting Johnny off. Mercy is acceptable, even admirable. But charging Juma, no, no, that won't play well at all. It's wrong and people will know it is, people will object.'

'Will they now? What people? No one knows Johnny did it.'

Top of the slope.

'I know.'

Jackman examined him, thoughtful. 'Oh, and you represent the people, do you? Do tell, just who d'you think gives a monkey's about a jumped-up toerag like you?'

Walter shrugged. 'No one, probably.'

'Exactly so.' Jackman placed an index finger on the tip of Walter's nose and pressed down. 'From now on, not a fucking peep. Button it or I do damage. Affair with a brothel-keeper? In two ticks I could have you out of here, stamp in your passport, undesirable, end of career, *finita la commedia*. Get my drift?'

They faced each other. Jackman removed his finger, turned, and marched off towards the hospital entrance. Walter scratched at a recurrent itch on his left arm.

Never been threatened before. Good. Taking me seriously.

* * *

At sundown he joined Miller on the Club veranda and was treated to the standard series of laments on the inadequacy of the servants, the pettiness of Club rules and the difficulties involved in the siting of pumping stations. Boring, small-minded, harmless Miller. *Good man, Miller.*

Their conversation was interrupted by a pair of yellow headlights flickering across them. A limousine crunched across the gravel, a small Union Jack fluttering from its bonnet. The Club burst into life. Stewards lined up either side of the double doors to the hall, adjusting their fezzes and shaking straight their *kanzus*. Several members emerged onto the veranda, and Walter and Miller found themselves shuffled sideways, away from the entrance. A uniformed chauffeur opened the back door of the limousine and the Governor emerged followed by two middle-aged men. Walter recognised one of them as a legal wallah of some sort. The other was Dom Wellesley. They strode up the steps, ignored the smiles and offers of hands to grasp and disappeared into the Club. The members melted back in after them.

'That's odd,' Miller said. 'Doesn't often descend from the heights, does he?'

'Going for a walk,' Walter said.

He stepped out, away from the Club's lights, and into the night. The wind had died as suddenly as it had arrived and there was an unseasonal chill in the air. He shivered; he could have done with the pullover he'd taken to Morogoro. He walked away from the town, down the lane, past Joseph's *shamba*, past the mess and on through the coconut palms to the beach. The rising moon competed with the dying sun, turning the sands from red and gold to a bleached-out silver. The sea was still, hardly moving, a gentle tide that pushed up the sand and then relaxed and sank back, as if abandoning any attempt to hold onto its territory.

The night shrieks and ululations began in the distance from the direction of the sisal plantations at Msasani. There was no hostility in them, and he smiled to himself at the memory of his one-time panic. He hadn't known where the real threat came from, not then, but he knew it now. He strolled down to the edge of the ocean, removed his shoes and his knee-length socks and walked out into the warm water. It crept up over his knees and he stepped further out so that it reached his thighs and lapped against his shorts. He wanted to drop down into it, to bury himself in water, to curl up and float, to listen to the soft pulse of the ocean. It came to him that Dar was the most beautiful place he'd ever known.

A dugout poled its way towards him, its stability dependent on flimsy outriggers. A man stood up in the bows and with a series of casual flicks began to lay his net. Walter retreated to the beach. Shoes and socks in hand he walked around the headland at Magagoni, past the ferry station and on towards Azania Front, where he paused to put them back on. Once in the town he stopped at a curry stall and then, his meal wrapped in a pandanus leaf, he sat on the steps of the closed Customs building. He ate native-fashion, using his right hand, but didn't finish the meal.

'Bella!' he called, and put the leaf on the ground. He then retreated a few yards and waited. When she emerged he saw that she was carrying her left hind leg. A rusty-red stain clung to it. The curry was mild and Bella devoured it. He let her eat and when she'd finished held out a hand. She backed away and he knew she'd never learn to trust him. The wound might kill her but there was nothing he could do about it.

He sat a little longer, at a loss as to what to do or where to go. He could try the Gymkhana Club in case Winnie was back from Morogoro. But why? He no longer had a reason to see her. She wasn't his girl. He had no girl.

I'll see her, I have to see her, make sure she understands, but not for a day or two. Need to think about things, let them calm down.

'Home, James,' he said aloud.

CHAPTER 22

There was a message for him from Winnie pinned to the information board in the mess. She was back and suggested that they meet next afternoon in the Botanical Gardens. He scribbled a brief reply and gave it to Joseph's lad to take over to the Gymkhana Club.

There had been one overnight arrival at anchor in the harbour, a freighter down from Port Sudan with a cargo of agricultural equipment. He took the Customs launch out to it and was impressed by what he found. The skipper was Egyptian, young and practical, altogether a pleasure to deal with. On his return to the office he found Abu Saleh waiting for him, an unsipped mug of tea on the floor beside him. He rose as Walter came in, clasped both hands around one of Walter's and pumped it up and down. Miss Fernandes hovered.

'My dear friend,' he said, 'my dear Mr Barnes.'

Walter was immediately on his guard. Abu Saleh was up to something. Why else would he come here?

'May we be private?' Abu Saleh asked.

They moved through into Walter's office.

'Your tea?' Walter said.

'Indian tea,' Abu Saleh said and dismissed the subject with a flick of his hand. The untasted tea stayed where it was.

The purpose of the visit remained obscure. Abu Saleh was more than usually effusive in his praise for Walter and hinted at some information which he had obtained but the validity of which he could not yet confirm. He just wanted Walter to know, he said, that in a week or so he would be in a better position, would have facts at his fingertips, and would be able to brief Walter better. He then rose to go.

'Terrible affair,' he said, 'but I understand that the man has been arrested.'

'I believe so.'

'Good, good, that at least is some comfort for the poor fellow.'

'Mr McLeod, d'you mean?'

'He will take an early retirement, perhaps? And there will be promotions as a result? Mr Thornton? Or new young fresh blood? We know where our hopes lie.' He opened the door into the outer office. 'My dear Mr Barnes, a pleasure as always. You have our support.'

Before he would leave Walter had to accept another hand-pumping routine, if anything even more protracted than before. The staff watched with interest.

Miss Fernandes followed Walter back into his office. They could see Abu Saleh as he walked with regal assurance towards his waiting car, an ancient Daimler, picking his way past the tangles of rusty wire, the broken pallets, the general detritus of the harbour front.

'He gave me this for you,' Miss Fernandes said.

It was a small ebony box, intricately carved with birds and

houris. Walter prised it open. Inside, on a velvet cushion, sat a ball of carved ivory. Not a ball, he realised, but a ball within a ball within a ball, each one visible through the latticed framework of the next larger one. It was a miracle of detailed craftsmanship.

'He said you'd asked him for it, and he was honoured to present it to you.'

Walter snapped the lid shut. 'You realise he's lying?'

'Of course. What shall I do with it?'

'I don't know. I just want it clear that it is not mine, I did not ask for it, and I am not now accepting it.'

'Shall I put it in the office safe?'

'For now, yes.'

He remembered the carpet. That still needed to be dealt with. Joseph had stuffed it in a cupboard somewhere, but so long as it remained in the mess it was exploitable. He was sure he was being set up, but he didn't know why.

'And this came while you were with that man.'

She handed him an envelope with Government House printed on it. He ripped it open. Headed embossed notepaper instructed him to attend a meeting at 5.00 p.m. that afternoon at Government House. It was signed in elegant italics by Dominic Wellesley. A PS told him that Superintendent Jackman would be in attendance.

'And he was rude about the tea I made him.'

Catarina returned to her station in the general office. Walter shut his door and leaned back against it, eyes closed. A tremor ran through him, a flicker of, what was it? *Yes, can't deny it, excitement, I'm excited. A chance at last, never before seen as likely, but that's what it is, a chance to impress the top brass. They're having to take notice of me.*

***

They lingered at the Garden gates, uncertain in each other's company, but reluctant to cut short their farewells. An elderly *shamba* boy was whistling in the azalea shrubbery behind them.

'Winnie,' he said. He didn't look at her when he spoke. 'It really is over, isn't it?'

Winnie's hand took his, raised it to her lips and kissed it.

'Yes,' he heard her say, 'yes, it is.'

Now he could lift his eyes, could look at her. She was smiling. And as he studied her the smile grew broader and ended in an easy laugh.

'What a relief!' she said. 'I was worried that you might have changed your mind and I'd have to tell you. But you've realised anyway. Maybe you're not such a fantasist after all.'

He had something else to ask her. 'Charles,' he began but she interrupted him.

'Oh, Charles! We had such fun, Charles and I – he's such a fool. We let the *fundi* drive while we sat in the back and drank warm champagne and laughed and laughed. You see, I'm quite wrong for you, Walter. I'm a trivial creature and I'll never change.'

'No, you're not trivial.'

'Oh yes I am. I want Dom Perignon and glamorous dresses and parties and I'd have made you miserable with my gadabout ways and very probably my affairs. And now it's over I feel like dancing, whirling about and giggling and being silly, released into frivolity. But, darling Walter, thank you so much. You've been wonderful – you brought me here and you set me free.'

She kissed his hand again and they were silent for a moment.

'Such a relief!' she cried, the words bursting out from her.

He began to smile. 'Isn't it? Liberation.'

'Yes. Best we found out.'

Now he was free. Now he had no more personal obligations.

Now he could begin to think clearly. A loose end remained, however, a nagging thought he needed to have resolved.

'Did you?'

'Did I what?'

The *shamba* boy came towards them wheeling a barrowload of garden detritus. He was still whistling his tuneless song, but broke off when he saw them.

'*Salaam, Bwana; salaam, Memsahib.*'

Winnie acknowledged him with a regal hand. The *shamba* boy reached in a pocket of his Gardens-issue waistcoat and produced an insect impaled on a pin.

'Bug,' he said, holding his palm out for Winnie to see the insect.

The bug was the length of Walter's thumbnail. It was etched in an iridescent rainbow of colours, blue spots and stripes against a background of a livid emerald green, with orange highlights and a vermilion belly. Despite the pin it wasn't yet dead. Its legs waved feebly and its antennae still flickered. Winnie gasped and the *shamba* boy beamed, delighted by her reaction. He stuffed the insect back in his pocket, picked up the arms of the barrow and wheeled it off, whistling.

'So cruel,' Winnie said.

Walter would not be diverted. 'With Mallinson,' he said, 'did you?'

'Did I what?'

'Did you?' he asked again, more insistent this time.

Her eyes opened wide in mock puzzlement and then she laughed and clapped her hands. 'What fun! I do like my lovers to be jealous, it's soooo flattering. Not that it's any of your business who I sleep with, not any longer.' She wagged a scolding finger at him and her dimple appeared, always a sign of a good mood.

'Walter, dear Walter, aren't we clever, isn't it wonderful? We'd have made each other miserable, we'd have rowed all the time, and we'd have hated, hated, hated each other. And as for Charles, of course not. I knew straight away, the first time I met him. A lot of fun, but not one for the ladies. I suppose women are better tuned to know such things.'

'What things?' he asked, baffled.

'Oh, Walter! Think!'

He stared at her. 'What do you mean?'

'You know.' She spread her arms and her eyes opened wide. 'He's Not As Other Men,' she said, with emphasis. 'His interests are not fixed in the more usual direction.'

It took a moment to sink in.

'What? Mallinson? Nonsense,' he said. 'He's famous as a lady's man.'

'Camouflage. He'll marry, of course he will, some droopy-drawers from the shires who prefers horses to sex and who'll be perfectly satisfied with once every three months for the purpose of getting sprogs. While Charles goes up to London to prowl St James's Park for guardsmen.'

'You can't know that.'

'Not for sure, no,' she admitted. 'But I'll lay good money on it.'

He shook his head. Incomprehensible.

She tugged at his hand. 'Come on,' she said. 'It'll soon be time to hear your fate. No more fantasies, remember. You nod and you agree, job done.'

The bird's harsh cry sounded again. It was nearer now and as it called again and again it seemed to him to mutate, phrase by phrase, into laughter.

CHAPTER 23

He'd never been inside Government House before. He'd admired it at first, impressed by its castellated exterior, but that was from a distance. Now he thought it absurd. The concrete latticework surrounding the two stories of verandas gave it a self-consciously exotic exterior, but it was Arabic rather than African-inspired. Now, inside the building, he wondered if this was not due to a failure of the colonial imagination. There were indeed significant Arabic cultural influences affecting in particular the coastal regions, and it was good that they were recognised, but were there really no African equivalents? *Bush*, he thought, *empty land*.

A waistcoated servant led him down a marble-floored corridor past game trophies, antelope skins and snarling lions' heads, into an anteroom where photographs of African scenes took over. They were disappointing, however, very much what might be expected – warriors in tribal dress, thatched huts, *bibis* with sacks of grain perched on their heads. Clichés, sufficiently familiar not to be worth a second glance.

A leather sofa beckoned but he felt too much on edge to sit. Not that there'd be a problem, he told himself. He knew what he'd say. First he'd assure Wellesley of his desire to stay onside, his commitment to them, to Empire. His sterling qualities established he'd present his case, simple, undeniable, that Juma had to be released. Jackman would offer his nonsense and Wellesley would dismiss it. The Law would be upheld. There'd be handshakes all round. The room was eleven paces long. There was no clock and he wasn't wearing his watch.

The servant reappeared and led him to a corner office where Dom Wellesley stood silhouetted in the open sash window.

'Barnes,' he said. 'Excellent. It's late for tea but I ordered it anyway – too early for anything stronger, don't you agree? Do take a seat.'

He pointed to a hard-backed chair positioned at a slight angle in front of a leather-topped partners' desk, bare of all furniture save for an inkstand, a paperweight and a blotter on which the tea tray rested. A carver with a cushioned seat was pushed back a few feet behind the desk. The walls were papered in a pale green and white stripe. Spy caricatures, flags of Empire and portraits in oil of explorers and administrators clogged the walls. Stanley greeted Livingstone at Ujiji, their handshake observed by the Territory's first two governors, Horace Bratt and Donald Cameron.

Walter sat.

'You know Superintendent Jackman, I think?'

Jackman sat to the left of the desk, perched on a high-backed chair the wrong way round, his belly pressed against the back of the chair, his chin resting on the chair's topmost strut. An empty teacup sat on the inevitable Persian carpet beneath him.

'And Charles Mallinson asked to be present. You have no objection?'

'None.'

Mallinson lounged in one of three armchairs surrounding a low table at the back of the room, his expression blank.

'Barnes,' he said.

There was a brief silence. Wellesley beamed. Walter shifted his view away from the man. Apart from the vast desk there was little sign that this was a place of work.

Wellesley crossed to the desk. 'They've given us Darjeeling,' he said. 'To be frank, not my favourite – too consciously fragrant, don't you agree? Don't much care for Spode, either. Too consciously decorative. Where is restraint these days? How d'you take it? Milk, yes? Sugar?'

'Two lumps,' Walter said. 'Thank you.'

He didn't want tea. His guts had begun to churn. He wanted them to get on with it.

'Good, good.'

Wellesley poured the tea and handed the cup to Walter, who took a sip and looked for somewhere to put it. The desk was too neat, too organised, to be violated even by Spode and the tray was out of reach unless he stood. The solution was provided by Jackman's example. He leaned down and rested the cup on the Persian carpet.

'And we can take our time, can't we? No need to hurry,' Wellesley said. 'This is an entirely informal meeting, off the record and no notes will be taken. It is being held purely for the sake of clearing the air.'

He crossed back to the window and banged it shut. The distant noises of early evening vanished. Walter wondered if the meeting's late start was deliberate. Wellesley unbuttoned his cream jacket to reveal a belly that overhung his trousers. As if on a second thought he removed the jacket completely and flung it onto a chaise longue. It slipped to the floor. Wellesley ignored it. He remained facing outwards, a landowner inspecting his estate. A hand shaded his eyes from the descending sun.

'Now, Barnes, let's clear this up. The Superintendent seems to be under the impression, which I'm confident is entirely false, that you are not fully satisfied with the outcome of his investigation into this unfortunate affair. Would you care to reassure me? Barnes?'

This wasn't what he'd expected. They were testing him and he wasn't sure how to respond.

'Barnes?'

He thought of the old joke, of the priest who advised his congregation to be careful, to be sure to walk the straight and narrow path between right and wrong. Tricky, tricky.

'I quite understand,' he began, and paused. 'I quite understand that putting Johnny McLeod on trial for an act as brutal as this could be seen to be politically unwise.'

Wellesley returned to his desk but didn't sit. He picked up the glass paperweight and began to rotate it in his fingers.

'Murano,' he said. 'Marvellous, quite marvellous. How is it done? But? I sense a but.'

He held the paperweight up so that it caught the late afternoon sunlight. Reflections danced on the wall behind him. 'Do go on, Barnes. But?'

'But I'd simply like to be reassured that the servant will not be charged.'

'That is a police matter.'

'But I know, you know, we all know Johnny did it.'

Jackman snorted.

'So you say. But the Superintendent has his doubts,' Wellesley said. 'And I repeat, it is a police matter. If the police decide that the servant is guilty, then he will be charged.'

Walter looked to Mallinson. They couldn't mean this, could they? Mallinson looked away. He turned back to Wellesley and clasped his hands. The words came tumbling out. 'Look, you're in a jam. I see that, you need an alternative explanation. But forget Juma, instead just make up a story, robbery gone wrong, say, unknown assailants, Juma innocent, simple. Everyone accepts it, or if they don't too bad, matter officially closed. Simple.'

There was no reaction. Walter spread his hands.

Wellesley smiled, affable. 'Tempting, very tempting,' he said at last. 'Simple, yes. Alas, if only it were so easy. Superintendent?'

'Won't wash. Murder of white woman, can't let it go. Example must be made, order maintained. Guilty man found, charged, punished, end of matter.'

Walter could feel a dampness in his armpits. The atmosphere in the room was stifling. He took a deep breath. 'But…'

But what? The words declined to come.

'Yes?' Wellesley said.

Walter tried again. 'But it's not right.' He groaned inwardly, appalled by the feeble nature of his response. He might as well be back in the schoolyard saying, whining, *Miss, miss, please miss, it's not fair, miss.* Wellesley shook his head.

'Not right? Explain, do.'

He felt uneducated, simple-minded, reduced to banalities. Sophisticated arguments were called for if these sophisticated men were to be won over. He had none. He only had the obvious. 'To charge a man you know to be innocent is, surely, or at least it could be argued, couldn't it, morally, argued morally, to be unacceptable.'

The paperweight rotated once more and was then lowered to the desk where its position alongside the blotter was carefully adjusted and readjusted.

Wellesley looked up. 'Unacceptable? Strong language. And I

agree, I agree. Were it the case that the man is innocent. But my dear Barnes, the Superintendent says not; the Superintendent says that the man is guilty, and we must listen to the Superintendent. He is after all the investigating officer.' Another beam with this time a glint of white behind the full lips. 'Barnes?'

'I don't understand. The man isn't guilty and Jackman knows it, and he knows I do too. What's the point of pretending otherwise?'

'Told you,' Jackman said, 'won't listen. Troublemaker.'

The lips tightened. Wellesley cupped a hand across his mouth and turned away to look towards the window. After a moment the hand dropped to his side and he turned back and leaned forward with both hands on his desk. 'I hope you're not suggesting that the Superintendent is acting on politically motivated instructions?'

Walter stared at the floor. 'I've never thought that,' he mumbled.

'I'm pleased to hear it. You used the phrase "politically unwise" just now. It might be thought by some to be politically unwise for a junior official in the executive branch to involve himself in said politics.'

'I'm sure it is.'

'Good. And yet the implications of your position would seem to indicate that you persist in your suggestion that the Superintendent is not acting on purely police grounds.'

Walter looked up. He needed to backtrack, backtrack now. He stuttered the beginning of a reply, paused and then, as if some demented idiot had commandeered his tongue the words came rattling out.

'No, no, the fact is,' the idiot said, 'the fact is I don't want anything to do with any of this. I don't want to be here, I don't want to be involved. It's a bloody stupid thing to do, to get involved. It's stupid, stupid, stupid.'

Wellesley's eyebrows rose in pantomimed surprise. He

straightened up. 'Well, that's good to hear. Sense at last. Mallinson assured me that you were a reliable man. I'm delighted that his assessment may after all prove correct. You are happy to retract any doubts? To support the Superintendent's account of this unhappy affair? We may close the meeting?'

The idiot in his brain agreed. 'Yes, yes.'

There, he thought, *I've given in. After all my pretensions to moral superiority I've proved myself to be just another third-rater, a blaggard, backslider, coward and all-round parasitic cheapjack.*

Wellesley was saying something. 'Are you listening, Barnes? Excellent. On the presumption that you would indeed demonstrate sense I took the liberty of preparing a document.'

Wellesley pulled open a drawer.

A document? A vestige of clarity pushed its way through the burbling chaos of his mind.

'It's just that… I just…'

The eyebrows rose again.

'I just need to know what will happen to Juma.'

The drawer slammed shut. Wellesley raised his hands in mock exasperation. 'Barnes, Barnes, for Heaven's sake. I have no idea what will happen to him, none of us have.' The hands descended. Wellesley leaned forward.

'Barnes, you seem unable to understand that that is a matter for the police and subsequently for the judiciary. Both are independent branches of the administration and neither I nor anyone else can influence them in any way. There will no doubt be a trial and the result of the trial may of course be that the man is found not guilty.'

'Mind you,' Jackman said, 'If he is let off, he'll be one lucky bastard, ta very much, bloody pernickety lawyers. He's guilty as hell.'

'Thank you, Superintendent,' Wellesley said. He contemplated Walter. 'What shall we do with you, Barnes? First you agree and then you quibble over details. Can we please stick to the essence of the matter? Yes?' He didn't wait for an answer. The drawer slid open.

'Now, in order to close this meeting I need to receive your formal assurance that you accept the position that has been outlined and that you are satisfied to leave the matter in the Superintendent's hands. You will kindly sign this document to that effect. The corollary, of course, is that you will remain silent about any, what shall we say, any alternative opinion. Barnes?'

Wellesley's lips extended themselves. His teeth gleamed and at the sight of them the idiot fled. Leave it to Jackman? Walter knew what that meant. He stood up and crossed the room to the window. To the left he could see the gates to the drive and the *askari* in his red fez standing beside his booth. As he watched, the man hefted his rifle from left to right as though weighing it in his hand. The Law, he thought, that was what it was about, the proper rule of the Law. This man, Wellesley, was failing to meet Kipling's standards. They were all failing to meet Kipling's standards. Walter had come to Africa believing in the Law and in the Empire as the upholder of the Law. He could not abandon his beliefs so casually, as these men seemed prepared to do. Expected to sign his acceptance of a lie? Was he satisfied? Like hell he was. He held the ace. It was time to play it. He knew the truth and they knew he knew.

He turned and looked at them, three men waiting on his words. They were all watching him and as he looked from one to the next, from Mallinson to Jackman to Wellesley, he knew he was in charge.

'No. No, I'm not satisfied. I will not let you do this.'

'See?' Jackman said. 'Troublemaker.'

Wellesley breathed in and held his breath for a few seconds before exhaling with an audible grunt. 'I'm beginning to suspect that the Superintendent has a point.'

Walter leaned back against the wall. He folded his arms. Their eyes remained fixed on him, and he felt again the pleasure of power. *Running the show*, he told himself, *I'm running the show*. He couldn't hold back a smile. The moment extended. When at last he spoke he released his full Wiltshire burr, letting its soft richness distance himself further from his audience. 'Understand this. I'm the one who received Johnny's confession. I'd much rather he'd confessed to someone else, but he didn't, he confessed to me. I know what happened, and I'm stuck with the knowledge. Juma's innocent, so it's quite simple: Juma must be released.' He laughed, a brief snort of satisfaction.

Wellesley pulled his chair forward and settled himself into it. He gestured to the chair in front of him. 'Please sit, Barnes.'

Why not? Walter strolled back to his chair and sat, arranging himself carefully, crossing one leg over the other and tucking his damp shirt into position. The chair was too upright for comfort, and he wished he hadn't agreed to take it. By doing so a little power had leaked away. He avoided looking at Wellesley, but instead stared at the wall behind him, focussing on a wallpaper join which had begun to sag open. The silence stretched on.

Wellesley began to tap his desk. 'Very well,' he said at last. 'This so-called confession concerns you, I can understand that. But perhaps the Superintendent may like to comment.'

'Certainly would,' Jackman said. He sat up straighter, but remained straddling the chair. 'Man's an ignorant, amateur meddler, no understanding of psychology. McLeod feels guilty, 'course he does, knows he should have sacked the houseboy months ago, never trusted him but didn't act on it. Result, feels he's responsible for his wife's death, just as if he'd actually done the deed himself. Psychology, you see. Funny thing the mind, plays dirty tricks.'

Walter continued to look straight ahead.

'Barnes?' Wellesley said.

'That's nonsense, and he knows it and you know it,' Walter said.

Jackman stood, spinning the chair round as he did so. He came over and stood behind Walter, putting his hands on Walter's shoulders. 'Nonsense? I think not. Opinion of outside authority. I had the quack in, Doctor Goetze – trained in Vienna, knows all there is to know about the mind. Had two sessions with poor old McLeod, that's the conclusion he came to. Hundred per cent certain, he said, deluded. Never laid a finger on his wife.'

'Goetze is a vet,' Walter said.

'Among other qualifications.'

'He's a vet. I've seen his notice in the *Standard*– that's what he does, full stop, nothing else. What would a vet know about psychology?'

Jackman removed his hands from Walter's shoulders, but the intensity of his presence remained. It was enough to confirm his decision. He would not give in. He licked dry lips. 'No,' he whispered.

'What was that?' Wellesley asked.

'I said no. Johnny did it.'

'The Superintendent…' Wellesley began.

'The Superintendent is a lying bastard.'

Jackman laughed.

'Kipling,' Walter added, 'Kipling.'

Wellesley leaned forward.

'You lose me. Kipling? The relevance?'

Walter breathed in, an audible signal of his determination. This man, Wellesley, this senior administrator, didn't understand the relevance? Walter spoke slowly, allowing his thoughts to gather before each sentence. 'The Rule of Law. Isn't that it? Isn't that what justifies our presence here, what justifies Empire? That is the other reason why you cannot make Juma carry the can. It would be an action that betrays the Empire, its reason for existence.'

There was a silence. Wellesley leaned back and glanced at Jackman. 'Ah,' he said. 'The man's a philosopher. He believes he understands the concept of Empire.'

'He's more like a plain awkward sod,' Jackman said. 'Only one way to deal with awkward sods. Liar, am I?'

He pushed Walter forward on his chair, bunched his fist and gave him a quick, powerful short-arm jab in the back, below the rib cage. Pain flooded through him. Walter grunted and fell sideways. A foot collided with the teacup and the contents flooded across the carpet.

'Goddamn,' Jackman said. He picked up the cup and saucer. 'Sorry about that. Not broken, anyway.'

Mallinson had scrambled to his feet. 'Come on, come on,' he said, hauling Walter back onto his chair. 'Say something, Dom. We can't have this.'

Walter slumped forward. His forehead made contact with the lip of Wellesley's desk and rested there. He was aware of the pressure of his skull's weight against the beading, but of nothing else, the pain replaced by a near-paralytic numbness.

Jackman returned the cup and saucer to their home on the tea tray, retired to his chair and blew out his cheeks.

'Carpet's done for,' he said.

Mallinson stayed standing, shifting his weight from foot to foot. 'Treat the man decently, can't we?' he said.

Wellesley raised a hand, an authoritative stop sign. 'Thank you, Charles, point taken. Enough of that, Jackman. Barnes, Barnes, Barnes. You have a version of events, the Superintendent has a version of events. They conflict. What are we to do?' He paused to sip at his tea. 'I had hoped it wouldn't come to this. I really had hoped. But failing your voluntary agreement I have prepared an alternative proposition for you, Barnes, and a very generous one it is too. Barnes?'

Walter blinked and straightened up. He was unable to speak. The unexpected nature of Jackman's kidney punch, and its accuracy, had not only forced all the oxygen from his lungs but had for a moment rendered them incapable of re-inflation. He opened his mouth, sucking greedily at the warm air, and bit by bit, cubic inch by cubic inch, began to feel his chest responding. As it did he became aware of the pain's return. It radiated outwards, up his spine and around his chest, a hot compress squeezing him with an anaconda grip.

Wellesley ignored Walter's distress. 'I have a different document for you to sign,' he continued. 'It contains an offer for which you must thank Charles and his powers of persuasion. As the first document does, it asserts your initial misunderstanding of the situation and your retraction of any comments you have made about it.'

Walter clambered to his feet.

'Hear me out,' Wellesley said. 'It is to your advantage to do so.'

'Sit down, Walter,' Mallinson said.

Mallinson had never before called him by his first name. He sat again, encouraged.

'There is then an additional paragraph. It would clearly be safest for the continuing good order of the Territory if you were no longer to remain resident here.'

Walter opened his mouth, but even had he been capable of speech he could think of nothing to say. He closed it again.

'Merely a precautionary measure. We do not wish contradictory stories to circulate. Anticipating this possibility I have accordingly already been in touch with London, with Sanctuary Buildings, and they are prepared to terminate your contract with immediate effect. Passage to Southampton will be booked for you on the *Llangibby Castle* which leaves, I understand, in three days' time. You will return to your previous employment. That too has been provisionally arranged.'

'And, as well…' Mallinson said. He was still hovering at Wellesley's side.

'Thank you, Charles. Yes, and if you deem all to be satisfactory, we will as well put in a recommendation that once back in the UK you be promoted to the rank of, I believe the title is Chief Preventive Officer – Chief, eh, that always has a ring to it, brings a sense of pride, yes? With immediate effect. Barnes?'

His head had cleared and he could focus at last. Wellesley's florid complexion offered an encouraging smile. One thing was clear. Now he could speak.

'A bribe,' he said.

Wellesley took an audible breath and shook his head, a pantomime gesture of disapproval. He sipped his tea, frowned, pushed the cup away, pulled open his drawer, rummaged in it and removed a cardboard file, tied in the corner with green string. He untied the knot, removed a single sheet of paper and pushed it across his desk. 'Here's a pen,' he said.

Walter read. The document was short. In addition to agreeing to the withdrawal of his earlier assertions a second paragraph stated that he accepted the terms and conditions of his termination of contract. It did not specify them.

'Pretty vague,' he said.

'You will in the course of the next day receive a further letter which goes into more detail. It will not contain any specific references to the events surrounding the death of Mrs McLeod.'

'And in return for this Juma will be released?'

'Oh dear,' Wellesley said. 'Barnes, you persist in failing to grasp the point. I cannot negotiate with the police, I must support them. Kipling, I suggest, would agree. Mind you, he's a sentimentalist, as most writers are.'

Walter shook his head. His guts seemed to have settled down, and the pain in his back had lost its edge, but the sense of outrage remained with him. 'Then I won't sign.'

'Time to put the boot in,' Jackman said.

'Thank you, Superintendent,' Wellesley said. 'May I remind you that I am in charge here? Very well, very well.' He picked up the paperweight, balancing it in his hand as though testing its efficiency as a weapon.

'Then show him who the boss is,' Jackman said.

Wellesley turned to contemplate him. He threw the paperweight from one hand to the other, as if now pondering a choice of victim.

Jackman grinned. 'Bugger's winding you up,' he said.

Wellesley replaced the paperweight.

'Barnes,' he said. 'Barnes, you are making my life very difficult. Kipling, eh? Delusions, delusions. But what to do, what to do? I have been patient with you, but it would seem to no avail.'

Mallinson coughed.

Wellesley raised an eyebrow. 'Charles?'

'Do we have to charge the man?'

'What?'

'Couldn't we hold him in custody pending a full police investigation, and then deport him to his country of origin? He's Somali, I believe, so let the Italian authorities deal with him as they see fit. We could suggest a few years inside, but whatever, it becomes their problem, not ours.'

'No go, crime was committed here,' Jackman said.

'So we say we couldn't find conclusive evidence, had to let him go, but remain convinced he did it.'

'Pathetic,' Jackman said.

'It might be a way out though. What d'you think, Dom?'

'Not sure. It's possible.'

Jackman groaned and stood up. He pointed at Walter. 'Stop pussying about and tell this little fucker what's what. If he doesn't like it, stuff him. You know we can.'

Wellesley slapped the flat of a hand on his desk. 'I've told you already, Jackman, I make the decisions. Deportation, eh? Jackman?'

'I'll have a think.'

'No, you won't bloody have a think, you'll agree now.'

Jackman shrugged. His lower lip protruded. 'Okey-dokey, I've thought. I agree. Dunno what to though.'

'To my decision. We deport the man.'

'Oh, right. Decision made, eh? Goody gumdrops, let the Eyeties have him. Come to think of it, not a bad move. I've seen that jug in Mogadishu, that's not the place to spend a night. A few years in there and our man will be begging for the rope.'

'Good. Barnes?'

'Still better if we string him up,' Jackman said.

Wellesley's hand slammed down on his desk. 'Good God, man, will you try, just for once, to be a little helpful? Just once? Barnes, no objections I trust?'

Wellesley's florid complexion had darkened, and patches of purple highlighted his cheeks. *Stay out of range*, Walter told himself and edged his chair back a few inches.

'Letting the Italians do the dirty work?' he said.

Wellesley levered himself up on his desk, chin thrust forward, lips barely visible. 'All right, all right, all right!' he shouted. 'I'll make one last final absolutely. This is it, Barnes, and you will accept it, hear me, accept it? I'll brief Moretti at the Legation here and make sure they won't give the wretched man more than a couple of years in the jug.'

Jackman raised a cautious hand.

Wellesley swivelled towards him and stabbed a finger. 'Goes

for you too, Jackman. Not another bloody peep. Matter finished.' He slumped back into his chair and folded his arms. 'Barnes?'

Wellesley on the defensive. Give him a push. 'You're sure the Italians will agree? How can you know that?'

'I can, and you will just have to accept my word that I can. We have our arrangements.'

'You scratch mine I scratch yours?'

'If Dom says it,' Mallinson chipped in, 'you can bank on it.'

Walter re-read the letter. 'And my employment on return to the UK?'

'You will also before you leave receive a letter re-appointing you to your former position and recommending your promotion.'

Walter picked up the pen, then put it down again. 'And who will sign that?'

'I will.'

'You have the clout?'

'I do.'

'To appoint me to a job in the home Customs and Excise service?'

'Yes.'

Walter leaned back in his chair and stared upwards. 'It won't wash,' he said. The room's cornices were of a traditional leaf pattern that Walter recognised. He couldn't remember the pattern's name and felt irritated. There was, he now saw, mould in one corner. 'Head Office in London make appointments.'

'Indeed they do. Knowing this, I anticipated your rather tedious reluctance to cooperate and have therefore already initiated a preliminary exchange of telegrams. The appointment is agreed.'

'I would like to see the telegrams.'

'No.'

'Why not?'

Wellesley bellowed with rage. 'Because I bloody well say so.'

'All right. But I want a signed document on headed notepaper guaranteeing the Italians' position.'

Wellesley's complexion darkened further. He inhaled, then spoke slowly, emphasising each word with a stab of a forefinger. 'Not in a million fucking years.'

Walter stood. 'Then I won't sign.'

'You think not? You will.'

'Tell him the alternative,' Jackman growled.

Wellesley yelled with fury. 'Good grief, does no one listen to what I say? Just shut up, Jackman, just for once shut up, will you?'

'Can we calm down?' Mallinson said.

Wellesley turned on him. 'And that goes for you too, Charles. Stay out of it. You're here on sufferance.'

Mallinson retreated to the door.

'All right, Barnes, all right. Enough is enough. Get this. Just in case you still refuse to sign or indeed having signed were to use the next three days to adverse effect, for example, by asserting to anyone whatsoever your opinion that a fix has been struck, just in case, I should warn you that your passage to the UK will be switched to a deportation order, your future employment with the Customs and Excise service will be cancelled, and we will issue a press release testifying to the fact that you have been medically examined and have been found to suffer from paranoid delusions. Your regular visits to a brothel and your inappropriate relationship with the madame will also be made public. I may say, that is a thing I personally find quite, quite bizarre – almost old enough to be your mother, I'm told, and black. What an odd creature you are, a thoroughly bad appointment, and the sooner we're rid of you the better.'

Wellesley clambered to his feet, his face purple, shining with sweat. 'Final offer!' he shouted.

Walter glanced towards Jackman. A crooked smile greeted him. He looked back at Wellesley, back again at Jackman, then Wellesley again, and Jackman again and as he did so both men appeared to change, mutating feature by feature, their skin crackling as it did so, no longer the upright servants of Empire but now with skin and bone replaced by papier mâché, painted, varnished and moulded into gurning parodies of their respectable alter egos, exposed for what they really were, not the pious images of God proclaimed in the biblical texts but more truthfully, officers in Mr Punch's army, in the Empire, in the benevolent disguise that hid the essential powering force of violence. At least he was only a poor bloody infantryman, cannon fodder, no more than that.

The Jackman puppet was clearly the source of Wellesley's information, of the version of Rosa they'd all accepted without question. A black whore. *How can I defend her, defend myself?* To clear his head he looked up again. There was another stain, this one on the edge of the ceiling rose, creeping out from under a plaster leaf, and as he did so he remembered the name of the pattern. Acanthus! Acanthus leaf, that was it.

'Takes bribes too,' Jackman said.

Wellesley groaned and sank back into his chair. 'I give up,' he said.

Slowly, ever so slowly, Walter lowered his gaze and swung round to look at Jackman. 'That's another lie and you know it,' he said.

'I have my witnesses.'

'Abu Saleh?'

'Witness names confidential.'

'God, you're a shit.'

Jackman laughed. 'And a bloody effective one.'

'Final offer, Barnes,' Wellesley said. He leaned back and stared at the ceiling.

'Sign, Walter,' Mallinson said from the back of the room. 'You have no choice. You can trust Dom, believe me. If he says he's got the clout then he has. The Italians will cooperate if he asks them to. And he will, won't you, Dom?'

'If he bloody signs.'

'Sign, Walter,' Mallinson said. 'Just sign and you've saved the houseboy from a hanging.'

The pain had eased. *A kidney punch, what a bastard thing to do. Banned in boxing, but then boxing has rules.*

'Promotion too?'

'I will recommend it,' Wellesley said.

'Scout's honour, I presume? Dib dib dib.'

'Walter,' Mallinson said, and shook his head.

Energy drained from him. He couldn't hope to defeat them. And after all, what would be the point? He'd done all he could. Why punish himself as well as Juma? At least there was a chance now that the man wouldn't hang, that Wellesley would deliver on his promises. The brief hint of power he'd thought he possessed had been a delusion. He leaned down, picked up the pen, unscrewed its cap, inspected the nib, a slight italic cross-cut, and signed.

Rosa, Rosa, he thought as he handed the document to Wellesley, *what a rotten world we make for ourselves.*

* * *

Mallinson offered to drive him to the Gymkhana Club, but he refused. He wanted to be on his own. He needed time to think. Winnie could wait.

'I'll make sure they deliver,' Mallinson said as they stood beside the Humber. 'On the promotion, I mean. The rest is copper-bottomed.'

'Never thought I could be bribed.'

'It's not a bribe, it's a reward for seeing sense. Sure I can't give you a lift?'

Walter shook his head. 'You know we've bust up, Winnie and me?'

'She told me.'

Mallinson opened the driver's door but then paused, his head bowed, his blond forelock hanging down. A grunt escaped him, and he climbed into the Humber where he sat, leaning forward with his hands on the steering wheel. He stayed frozen for some twenty seconds before slapping the wheel several times with his palms. 'What on earth have you been playing at?' he cried. 'I took you for a solid fellow, reliable, and then, then…' He paused and the forelock fell forward, obscuring his eyes. 'This relationship, this woman, are you insane? She's, she's… for God's sake, she's a black whore.'

Not the salt of the earth any more.

Mallinson ran a hand through his hair. 'And Winnie? Does Winnie know?' he asked.

'I don't think so. Unless you told her.'

'As if I would. That's something anyway. And you'd better lie low from here on. Just keep out of the way, just go, *go* – get out of here, get back to bloody Bristol!' He slammed the door shut.

'You'll look out for Winnie, won't you?' Walter said.

'Of course.'

They said nothing further. Walter watched as the Humber crunched away across the gravel.

CHAPTER 24

He lay on his cot. The gecko had claimed its place, its rightful place. It belonged here, on this wall, in this room, in Dar, in Africa. His mind raced, febrile, jumping tracks in its confusion. *What now what now what now? Must block it all out, obliterate it, move on.* He closed his eyes and, without intending to, fell asleep.

When he woke it was late evening and his mind had cleared itself of all unnecessary detritus. He had done what he could for Juma, but more was needed if he was to leave Dar knowing that he had made a difference. He would not leave Africa without having achieved something, without having had a positive impact on a human life, her life.

He would show her that princes came for Asian girls as well.

Rapunzel would let down her black hair.

And then…

Would they ride away together?

Do I love her?

I don't know. I don't know!

What I do know is that I care for her and caring is the gate at the start of the long path that ends in love.

He had to convince her, but once she realised the strength of his commitment it would all work out. He'd tell her about Bristol, make plans about their future, hear her views. There would be problems for her as a dark-skinned woman, but they could be solved, she could pass as say Italian, or Spanish, issues of race could be solved. He'd need to raise cash for her fare but that too could be solved. He wasn't sure how but he'd find a way. Everything was possible – he'd have a Tusker, relax in her comforting presence and together they'd discuss their future. Together. Yes, together. He let the word linger in his mind and after a few minutes 'together' had changed from a simple connective to an essential piece in the jigsaw puzzle. Love remained a complex mystery but 'together' was the key to its solution. *Doing things together.* And all he had to do was offer it to her.

* * *

In the evening light Dar was as beautiful as ever and he took his time. The moon was still full, poised above the outline of the distant uplands, and the harbour's oily water shimmered with a muted rainbow of silver and grey. The charcoal fires glowed in the braziers where the vendors roasted their groundnuts, and the ice-cream aromas of vanilla and chocolate and clove infiltrated the evening air. Distant shouts transmuted into song as Kariakoo partied. He felt for the place where Jackman's bunched fist had driven into him. *That'll be a fine colour in a few days' time.*

There was a light on in the Taj but when he pushed at the door it stayed shut. He hammered on it, paused and hammered again. The curtains moved slightly: someone was checking visitors.

Why? A bolt was pulled back and the door opened. Walter stepped in. The only person in the room was the accountant.

'Closed,' he said as he let Walter in and bolted the door once more. 'There's beer though.'

'Where's Rosa?'

'Have one.'

A crate stood in the middle of the floor. It held several empty Tusker bottles and a dozen or so full ones. The accountant produced a bottle opener and snapped the top off one of them. The beer erupted in a cascade of foam and he mopped at the bottle with his handkerchief before handing it to Walter and wiping his hands on his safari suit.

'Bottoms up,' he said.

The beer was warm. Walter sank onto the bench.

'Where's Rosa?' he asked again. 'Has something happened?'

'Things come to an end. Taj is gone, gone for ever,' the accountant said, and sighed. He began to recite, his beer bottle clutched to his chest.

'*We can make our lives sublime*
And, departing, leave behind us
Footprints in the sands of time.'

He took a long swig of beer. 'Beautiful. Longfellow. So sad, everything is so sad. I have been crying, you know, yes, me. Me, crying.'

He waved his hands at the ceiling. Drops of beer flew upwards. 'I feel so sad,' he added cheerfully.

'What do you mean, gone?'

'*When even lovers find their peace at last,*
And Earth is but a star that once had shone.'

He drained his beer and dropped the empty bottle back in the crate.

'Fletcher, great poet, yes? No? *Tales, marvellous tales.*'

'I think you'll find his name is Flecker, not Fletcher. Will you please tell me what is going on?'

'Flecker? I don't know Flecker. I'm not drunk, y'know. Well, yes, I am. Beer must be finished, you see. She would like that, her special friends. We deserve beer.'

He pulled the crate over to the bench, opened another bottle, dealt with the overspill and then sat beside Walter and patted his knee.

'She liked you. She wanted to say goodbye. Yes, yes, I'm sure she did, to stay a little longer, say goodbye to everyone. But these men, these blacks, they must be obeyed.'

'Men, what men? What are you talking about?'

'*Askaris*, all above board and tickety-boo, paperwork in order, I insisted on looking, but no, no giving, ten minutes is all, no more, ten minutes. Could give a little stretch, I said, but no, no stretching – laws must be obeyed: deported.'

He waved a hand to demonstrate. Beer spattered the floor, the walls.

'Ten minutes!' he cried, and drank.

'Deported?'

'Poor Rosa. One hour ago, two hours, I don't know how long. I am winding up her affairs.'

This is nonsense, must be. Man can have no idea what he's talking about.

'You think she's been deported? Rosa? Why d'you think that? On what grounds? These men, *askaris* you say, were they in uniform? Were they official?'

'Yes, yes, all correct, I check everything, all things. Taj closed, she taken to home to collect things, marched away like criminal. Husband cry so much, poor fellow.'

He stared at the man, bewildered. This was obviously some other woman, must be. 'Who are you talking about?'

The accountant raised his bottle. 'Rosa, Madame Rosa, our friend – so sad, so sad. Drink up: we must raise our glasses to Madame Rosa, raise our bottles, bottoms up to Madame Rosa. So sad, so sad.'

None of this was making sense.

'Husband?' He could barely say the word. 'Don't be ridiculous. Who are you talking about? Rosa has no husband – her husband's dead.'

'No, no, other husband dead. This husband not dead, this husband, poor man, yes, but not dead.'

Walter dropped his half-full bottle back into the crate. *All rot*, he tried to tell himself, *a drunk's ramblings, quite worthless*. Nevertheless they had something almost convincing about them.

'I know Rosa very well and she has no husband. If he existed I would know about him – more than that, I would know him.'

The accountant laughed and slapped Walter on the back, lurched as he did so and sent a splash of beer down Walter's jacket.

'You do know him! Everyone come here know him. Poor man, crippled, but generous. Taj boss – give her job in exchange marriage. He love her so much, do anything, everything for her but jealous, very jealous man. Very jealous of *you*. Said you bad man.'

His index finger prodded Walter in the ribs, slightly too forcefully and with such deliberation that it became a distant echo of Jackman's assault.

'Bad man!' he said, and laughed again. 'Yes, you are bad man! He was not jealous of me because she made me pay, but you, no, no, he did not like that at all. Very angry, swearing – we do not swear, you know, it is not approved of in our community, but he swore about you. I swore too, I too very jealous. Bad man!'

This was information impossible to digest. Rosa married to that man? He rejected the thought. She'd have told him, of course she would. He had to find someone sensible, someone sober, someone who knew the facts.

'Nonsense,' he said.

The accountant's laughter erupted again but now there was a new quality to it. It no longer mocked him and the angry undertone had calmed. Walter attempted to stand but as he did so his knees buckled and he had to clutch the accountant's shoulder to prevent himself falling. He sat again. The accountant patted his knee again.

'Yes, yes,' he said, as if to a child, and took and held one of Walter's hands. 'You did not know. Why should you know, why should she tell you?'

Walter inclined his head and watched as the accountant began to stroke the back of his hand. It was true, of course it was. Why hadn't she told him? To protect him, to allow him to dream, why else? Perhaps because she loved him, yes, loved him despite what he'd done to her, that was the reason, had to be. The thought lingered and deepened and then he closed his eyes and the accountant's hand became her hand, her hand stroking his. A minute passed before a more urgent thought took prime position and demanded action.

'Deported, you say – you're sure of that? What else d'you know? Where to? When? And the girls, have they been deported?'

His voice was a hoarse croak.

'No, no, girls can stay, only she deported. Husband stay here too, useful man. The British like husband.'

He released Walter's hand and put a finger to his lips.

'Information,' he whispered. 'Who come here, what they say, he tell them. Taj a very good place for hearing secrets. He know everything, only tell them some things, what he choose to tell, a very clever man. Foolish, too. He told the policeman, the Jack man.'

The room had become a prison cell and Walter had to escape. He forced himself to his feet and stumbled the few paces towards the door.

'Stay, stay,' the accountant cried. 'We must finish the beer. She would want us to finish the beer.'

Walter reached for the bolt. 'What did he tell Jackman?'

'That you tell her things. Things bad for her to know.' He no longer appeared drunk. There was an authority in his voice. 'They could trust him, but not her, no, no, a woman – how can you trust a woman? She would talk, tell what you told her. Gossip, yes? You were foolish and so was he. He thought they would thank him, reward him, all would be the same, they trust him. But not her, no, they couldn't trust her, he didn't see that. Foolish, both of you, foolish. Poor foolish men.'

Walter gripped the door bolt with both hands and pulled it back. 'The *askaris* took her home to pack? And then where? The Fort?'

The old Portuguese-built jail contained holding cells, he knew, where the petty hoodlums of the town would be kept pending trial. It was the obvious choice.

'Home, pack, that is all I know.' The accountant waved his hands. 'She is gone and we can do nothing, my friend, my dear friend. Stay, stay and talk and recite, yes, Longfellow, Tennyson, beautiful poetry, what we must do. We must weep together, my friend, we must weep and drink and recite. What else can we do? Nothing, nothing. *I am half sick of shadows.*'

Walter stepped out into the dark street. He began to walk, faster and faster and then breaking into a trot. He lost his way twice but at last came to the row of small concrete bungalows. They were indistinguishable in the dark. A local loomed up before him, rolling a lorry tyre and Walter had to step aside to avoid colliding with it.

A man appeared at the door of the third bungalow, his shape outlined by the glow of an oil lamp inside the house, his iron-encased limb visible. He propped the door open and hobbled back inside, to emerge immediately hauling a tea chest. The lamp light was sufficient for Walter to read the words stencilled on it: Dunlop Rubber. He stepped forward. The tea chest was filled with material, scraps of cloth, samples, strips of braid.

'Where is she?' he demanded. 'Is she here?'

The man ignored him but dragged himself back into the bungalow, attempting to shut the door as he went. Walter blocked it open with a foot. There was a brief contest but Walter was much the stronger. The man gave up and retreated further inside. Walter followed him. The sewing machine stood isolated in a sea of packing materials. He pushed the man aside and continued on into the back room. As far as he could see in the dim light nothing in it had been touched, but he had the sense that this was a place abandoned by its inhabitants, a ghost room. He opened the back door and breathed in the still hot and fetid air.

He could hear the scraping sound of the other man's callipers. He turned and found himself confronted by a small kitchen knife clutched in the supposed husband's hands. The man's face was contorted with emotion. He aimed the blade's point at Walter's chest, his hand trembling as he attempted to thrust it forward. Walter took a step back.

'Don't be silly,' he said and reached out and took hold of the man's forearm. He forced the thin wrist backwards and upwards and one by one prised the slender fingers from the knife.

'We're each as guilty as the other,' he said.

He threw the knife into the yard. The man was crying. Walter took him by the arm and propelled him back into the front room and sat him down. The man's leg stuck straight out, rigid. Head bowed, he laid both hands on its iron cage. Walter lifted his head. He found a crumpled handkerchief in the hip pocket of his shorts and wiped the man's face, but the tears kept coming.

'Where is she? Where have they taken her? Where? You understand me, I know you do. Where? The Fort?'

The man struggled to speak, his voice choked with emotion.

'No Fort, Zan, Zan, Zanzi—'

He was unable to complete the word.

'Zanzibar?' Walter said.

'—zibar.'

It was a shout of rage, of bafflement, of hopelessness. Walter pushed the handkerchief into the man's hand, and left. As he went he heard a dull sound from behind him. He looked round. The man lay on the floor, his body curled into the foetal position but with his leg stretched out at an awkward angle. He began to wail, a series of long-drawn-out cries interspersed with gulps of indrawn breath and sobs. Walter left him to his misery. His mind raced.

Zanzibar? Zanzibar meant that getting her out of Dar was the priority. Forget the Fort, they wanted her out of the Territory. She'd be taken to Zanzibar and held there before being moved on to Aden where she'd no doubt be picked up by a British India heading for Bombay. And the quickest way of getting her to Zanzibar would be by putting her on a mailboat. There was a regular service of small packets that served the coastal towns from Lindi in the south up northwards to Tanga and then Mombasa, diverting to Zanzibar and occasionally to Pemba. Walter knew them well. The scheduled departure time was every night at eight-thirty and it was already some minutes past the half-hour, but delays were frequent, even routine. It could well still be there. All he had to do was get to the harbour, commandeer a launch and go out to it. As for what happened then, he had no idea. Something would emerge, it didn't matter what, just something.

He started to run, careless of dignity. The evening crowds were on the streets and he had to shout to clear his way. A child froze in panic in front of him. He sidestepped to avoid it and ran into the outstretched arms of a turbanned Sikh. A basket went spinning and sweet potatoes spewed across the road. A food stall's kerosene lamp teetered. He hurdled a *pombe* seller's jerrycan, but tripped on landing and sprawled forward onto his knees. He ran on, aware only of his heaving chest and the unfolding map in his head. Bagamoyo Street, past the market, across Sultan, a left-and-right into Selous, thank God, the edge of the European Zone where the crowds abruptly thinned, over India Street and now at last he could see the lights of Main and the harbour beyond. He summoned up more energy and stepped up his pace, eyes scanning, scanning, scanning the few vessels as one by one they came into view. Where was the mailboat?

He heard the truck before he saw it. There was a squeal of worn-out brake pads, a shout, and a rattle of untuned metal as it lumbered out of a dark side street. It had no lights and he could do nothing to avoid it but instead thudded into its nearside wing, bouncing back from the collision as if pulled by an elastic rope. He lay half stunned as a crowd gathered, and for a moment lost all understanding of what it was he'd been running towards, or running from. His right shoulder had taken the force of the impact and he was dimly aware of pain but even so he knew he had to stand, if not why. With a hand on the truck's bonnet he hauled himself to his feet. Murmurs of concern filtered through to him. A shoeless local was thrust forward to stand in front of him, bowing and clutching a skullcap which he alternately crunched into a ball and then attempted to return to its proper shape. He seemed paralysed by fear. Walter brushed him aside and staggered forward. A pathway cleared. As it did so he saw the harbour, moonlit with a silver swell, and remembered what his mission was.

The mailboat was still there.

It stood at its anchorage some hundred yards out. The silver moonlight created a path that led towards it but didn't reach it, breaking up as the incoming tide disturbed the waters. He crouched and rested his hands on his knees while he recovered his breath. He could see the Customs launch as it bobbed gently in its regulation berth and having forced himself to stand he stumbled his way along the jetty towards it, then clambered awkwardly over a rail and jumped down into the well of the boat.

But where was the crew? The launch required a helmsman and two assistants, drawn from a larger pool of workers. Had they all gone for the night? He'd call for them but couldn't think of any of their names. A few spectators lingered on the jetty and he scanned their faces. They all seemed oddly similar. There was no one he recognised. The launch's outboard motor was tilted, its blades out of the water, shining with reflections from the lapping tide. He could start it, he felt sure, but could he handle the launch on his own? A scratchy, grinding, metallic and far too familiar sound caused him to look up. At first he could see nothing but then the waters by the mailboat's bow foamed and its anchor broke the surface.

'*Bwana*?'

A young native male in a ragged *kanzu* emerged sleepy-eyed from the small cabin.

'*Bwana*?' he said again, tentative, uncertain of his welcome.

Walter couldn't remember having seen him before.

'Are you crew?' he asked. The youth stared blankly at him.

'Crew, are you crew?' Walter shouted. The youth looked back into the cabin. A blanket twitched and from under it a second man emerged, rubbing his eyes and scratching his left thigh. He was older than the first and despite his bare feet and equally tattered *kanzu* he had a vague air of authority. He was surely crew, even if unfamiliar.

'Thank God,' Walter said. 'The mailboat, I must catch the mailboat you understand?' He clapped his hands and pointed at it. The anchor had been stowed and the vessel had swung round showing its stern lights.

'The mailboat,' Walter said again, pointing. 'Come on, move, let's go, *imshi*.'

The man nodded. He issued a brief order and the youth scrambled onto the jetty. The older man waved a hand in the direction of the mailboat, nodded several more times as if to confirm his understanding of what was required, then put both hands together, bowed to Walter, and then began to haul himself up onto the jetty.

'Where are you going? Start the outboard!' Walter shouted. But with only the briefest of backward glances the pair had gone, melted into the gathering crowd, their temporary bedroom abandoned. He heard a distant cough and a change of engine note and knew that the mailboat was getting under way and that he was on his own.

The outboard was heavier than he'd anticipated and to shift it he had to bend his knees and lift from the shoulders, his biceps taking some of the load off his damaged ribs, but he hardly noticed the pain. With the blades in the water and the motor settled into position he took hold of the starter rope and pulled. The motor responded with a feeble cough, spluttered briefly, and died. He tried again, increasing his power, and then again, faster than before and with a stutter and a groan the engine fired. A small wave caused the launch to bump against the fenders of the jetty. It was still roped fore and aft to the stanchions.

Black faces looked down at him.

'Release the ropes!' he cried. 'Come on, come on, someone, help me.'

He gave a demonstration tug on the aft painter. The onlookers showed no sign of willingness to help or even of understanding what he wanted. He gripped the painter in both hands and attempted to free it by looping it and hurling the slack rope over the stanchion. It fell back, having missed its target by several feet.

He tried again but could barely lift the rope. His reserves were drained. The launch rocked briefly at its moorings, the painter tautened then slackened, the motor groaned, and they remained tied fast. The spectators waited, reluctant to become actors in the entertainment.

'Help me,' he said. 'Please help me.'

No one moved. Walter's throat constricted and he began to choke, his chest heaving as he gasped for air. His body shook, spasms running through it, forcing him to fling his arms back in an effort to expand his chest and let the cooling evening air do its healing work. His knees gave way and he collapsed onto the padded seat. It took time but gradually he began to breathe more easily. The port was unusually quiet. He looked out across the gently lapping waters and thought how well it deserved its name: Dar-es-Salaam, the Haven of Peace. There was some low-key activity in the dhow harbour on his right but otherwise only one thing disturbed the placid night, the only vessel no longer at anchor.

He watched as the mailboat made its steady progress towards the harbour entrance and the ocean beyond. The stern lights grew faint, obscured by a low mist. They blinked as the vessel turned into the passage beyond Magagoni, rocked slightly as the mailboat met the ocean rollers and then vanished entirely, out of his sight and out of his life. He turned off the outboard, closed his eyes and lay back, his torso curled into the foetal position.

He pictured her in the packet's small brig with its platform that served as a bed, the one porthole too high to see out of. She was in profile, her hair pulled back and fastened with silver combs. A hand lifted to tuck an escaped strand back into position and her bracelets fell and rose with the movement. As they came to rest she turned to look at him full face. He could read nothing into her expression, neither demands nor accusations.

A distant boom from a vessel yet to enter the harbour dislodged the image and brought him back into the present. He shook his head, stood, placed his hands on the jetty and attempted to climb up onto it but the pain in his ribs was too much for him and he collapsed backwards into the well of the boat. The shock of the fall cleared his mind of everything bar the dull, purely physical sensations in his back and chest. He closed his eyes and after a few blank seconds a new emotion invaded the vacuum. He tried to resist it but it demanded to be recognised.

Relief.

He tried to deny it but could not. He'd been liberated, rescued from his own folly, his sentimental pretence that he could do something for her. Love was a two-way transaction and he didn't know her, had never known her. How could that be love? And what in turn did she think of him? What evidence did he have that she wanted him or cared for him? And even if she had loved him, fleetingly, uncertainly, how could it survive his assault? Assault! Yes, that was what it was and lying here, his eyes shut, his thoughts turned inwards, he could at last acknowledge it. He had assaulted her; she had not consented. He still baulked at Mr Punch's label.

Another small wave caused the launch to rock slightly. His eyes flicked open and a million pinpricks of light glittered and danced above him in a ballet of mockery and scorn. And had she wanted him, forgiven him, loved him, what then? His mind whirled, *thank God, thank God, thank God*, and his body shook as he tried to digest the consequences. Rosa's story would certainly have followed him to Bristol in a garbled and exaggerated form. He'd have to have left the Service, left the city, gone where? He had escaped a potentially disastrous future, rescued by accident and by his own incompetence. So many problems had vanished with the mailboat, had vanished with her.

A second emotion followed the first.

Shame.

Shame that he could feel like this, that he could abandon even a façade of love so easily. Shame that his love had been so feeble. Shame that its origins lay in power derived from lies, from violence, the Empire's violence as well as his own. Shame that he had, as she prophesied, destroyed her.

He lay still and silent in the well of the boat. A chill bit into him, though the night remained warm, and he shivered. The sky now appeared to him as a ragged blanket and he wanted to pull it down and wrap himself in it, disappearing from the world of humankind. A hand appeared in front of him, palm uppermost.

'*Nikusaidie, Bwana.*'

He'd learned the word by now: an offer of help. He reached out and took the hand, gripped it tightly and used its leverage to haul himself slowly, painfully, awkwardly up onto the jetty.

The spectators parted before him, silent, watchful. Walking with no conscious compass he found his way back along the ill-lit streets and down the dark path towards the mess.

In his room he collapsed onto his cot and lay still. Shame still gripped him. He no longer wanted to be Walter Barnes. He wanted to do no more than exist, to be a spider conch, no, something less grand, a small cowrie tucked away under a branch of coral on a distant reef, without the curse of hope.

That's the way to do it!

The familiar nasal screech still haunted him. It was intolerable. He had to exorcise it. There was a necessary starting point: confession.

Total honesty would be required. He wasn't sure that he was capable of it, of the searing simplicity of truth. Furthermore, proper confessions had to be spoken aloud, that was the point of them, they had to be put into the world to be tested, to see if they were viable. He needed a witness, a priest, a listener who heard his admission of guilt and acknowledged it.

The gecko was in its customary position on the wall.

There was no other candidate.

He breathed in, collected his thoughts, and began.

'I confess,' he said to the gecko, and took a pause before continuing. 'I took her against her will. I raped her, and having done that I destroyed her. I told myself I was good by coming here and instead I caused harm. I am indeed a true servant of the British Empire. I am a private soldier in Mr Punch's army, and I am a rapist.'

Was that enough?

He looked to the gecko for a sign.

The gecko offered nothing.

Mr Punch, too, kept silent.

He lay down and waited for sleep that did not come.

He listened to the distant whispers of the ocean rollers as they died on the soft pearl-grey sand.

There was a moistness in his eyes. He was crying, but not for Rosa, nor for himself.

He was crying for Dar, for the Haven of Peace, whose beauty would not last.

CHAPTER 25

The *Llangibby Castle* docked at Southampton. Walter made his way to Bristol, changing trains first at Bournemouth Central and then at Bath Green Park. The English countryside in the late autumn was soft and muted, lacking the vibrant colours he'd become accustomed to.

Mrs Amos had a room ready for him. He'd sent his letters airmail and they'd beaten him back to England by ten days.

'Lovely to have you home, dear,' she said. 'See sense, did you? I wouldn't want to live in Africa, all those insects and animals.'

There was also a brief note from Adamson confirming his re-appointment. There was no mention of promotion. He wasn't surprised.

He opened his suitcase and searched it for the other mementoes of his time in Dar, the spider conch and the *Turbo marmoratus*. He'd wrapped them in a vest but it wasn't enough. A finger had broken off the conch and at first he thought of glueing it back on, but instead dropped it into the wastepaper basket. The shell itself was otherwise intact and he turned it over, feeling the rough back and the smooth underside, stroking the glowing, pearly iridescence of the aperture. But he'd had enough of broken shells – they needed to be forgotten, as Meg was being forgotten. The shell followed its finger into the basket. The turbo was intact, so he stuffed it into his jacket pocket: something to show the Brennan sisters in the pub that evening.

He waited for Reg outside the Town Hall. They bought fish and chips wrapped in the *Western Daily Press* and ate them walking down to the old docks, now nothing more than the silted-up home of a few rotting hulks. Turnstones congregated on the blackened timbers. *Heralds of winter*, he thought, *a proper season on its way*.

'Good to have you back, mate,' Reg said. He finished his last chip, screwed up the fat-sodden *Daily Press* and flung it into the oily water.

'Got some tales to tell, eh?'

'Not really,' Walter said.

'Liar.'

'Yes.'

Reg laughed and Walter forced a smile.

They made their way through back streets to the Prince Consort. In the evening light and under low cloud Bristol was a grey city, echoing its countryside, its colours and scents leached out. A chill wind blew up from the Bristol Channel and funnelled along the Avon Gorge. The pub sign, a splash of yellow and blue, creaked as it swung sluggishly in response. Walter buttoned up his jacket.

He bought two pints of Ushers.

'Best beer in town,' Reg said. 'Lovely stuff. Bet you missed it.'

'Yes,' Walter said, but in truth he found the ale too bitter to enjoy. It would take him time to get used to it.

'There was a good beer in Dar-es-Salaam: Tusker,' he said. 'I liked Tusker. There was a bar I went to.'

'Tusker, eh?' Reg said.

They drank in silence.

'Come on then,' Reg said. 'Tell me about it.'

Walter looked into his pint but said nothing.

'Look, mate,' Reg said. 'I'll tell you what. She was never right for you, you're well out of it. Ball-crusher. I spotted her a mile off. You wouldn't want that.'

The potman, glasses in his huge red hands, stopped beside them. 'I know you, don't I?' he said to Walter. 'Used to be a regular, didn't you?'

'And will be again,' Reg said.

The potman raised an empty glass. 'Cheers, lad,' he said, and moved off.

'What you want in a woman,' Reg added, 'is good sex, good cooking and no bloody squawking. One out of three? Not enough. I could see it from the start – she just didn't fit in, not properly. Not in my book anyway. You've got to fit in, haven't you, become one of the pals.'

Walter pushed his glass away from him and scrambled to his feet.

'Fresh air,' he said.

He stood beneath the creaking pub sign. The only sounds of the night were of traffic, mechanical sounds, and he missed the animal cries of a Dar evening. His hands were cold and he plunged them into his jacket pockets. His fingers touched something, the turbo shell. He took it out and examined it. In the evening light it lacked pigment. He angled it to catch the dim glow of a street lamp but could no longer tell that it was green. It was as if it had died, he thought, and then corrected himself. The creature whose home this had been was long dead, boiled alive, killed for its beauty. The shell was nothing other than its external skeleton. Possession of it repelled him. He threw it up into the air and caught it, then flicked it up a second time and as it fell back punted it down the street. It bounced once, twice and then came to rest lodged against the grill of a drain.

A shiver reminded him of how cold England could be, at night, in October. He walked away from the pub, ignored the shell as he passed it, and headed on into the wind, turning right into an unfamiliar street, then into another and another and another.

GLOSSARY OF SWAHILI TERMS

askari – local soldier serving the British
bibi – wife, grandmother, mature woman
bwana – Sir
coolie – unskilled labourer
dhow – local boat used for fishing and to carry cargo
fundi – artisan, craftsman, worker
gonjwa sana – very sick
hakuna matata – no worries
imshi – get lost!
iroko – large species of tropical hardwood tree (*Milicia excelsa*)
jambo – hello!
kanzu – traditional long, light-coloured robe or tunic similar to a kaftan
kitenge – sarong-style cloth worn by women

Maasai – an ethnic group of northern Tanganyika and southern Kenya
maridadi – stylish
matata, *mingi matata* – troubles, many troubles
memsahib (**mem**) – madam, mistress
muzungu – white person, European
nikusaidie – can I help you?
panga – large machete-style knife
piccaninny – native child
pombe – millet beer
sahib – sir
salaam – greetings!
shamba – smallholding
shamba **boy** – male farmer of a *shamba*
wahuni – layabouts, hooligans, crooks
wallah – person with a particular trade (laundry wallah)

ACKNOWLEDGEMENTS

I owe heartfelt thanks to Jacqui Hazell for her advice and encouragement. Amanda Schiff was an unfailing support throughout the process, and through Monica Byles, my excellent editor, I discovered the real meaning of the word 'rigorous'.

Two resources stand out from the research for this book:
Andrew Burton's *African Underclass: Urbanisation, Crime and Colonial Order in Dar Es Salaam, 1919–61* (James Currey, in association with The British Institute in Eastern Africa; Ohio University Press, USA; Fountain Publishers, Uganda; East African Educational Publishers, Kenya; 2005)
The South and East African Year Book and Guide for 1929 (Sampson Low, Marston & Co., Ltd, 1929)